GET OUT!

by Brian Meiser

PublishAmerica
Baltimore

© 2004 by Brian Meiser.

All rights reserved. No part of this book may be reproduced, stored in a retrieval system or transmitted in any form or by any means without the prior written permission of the publishers, except by a reviewer who may quote brief passages in a review to be printed in a newspaper, magazine or journal.

First printing

ISBN: 1-4137-2969-X
PUBLISHED BY PUBLISHAMERICA, LLLP
www.publishamerica.com
Baltimore

Printed in the United States of America

This book is dedicated to my mother, Ida Meiser, who passed away in August of 1993. She was an inspiration to me throughout my life and a wonderful storyteller. Also, I would like to thank my wife, Donna, and my children, Vanessa and Jesse, who were quite patient with me as I spent endless hours in front of my computer writing my first novel.

Acknowledgements

Many of the local towns and cities in my novel are factual and were part of my childhood. There also actually was a General Phil Sheridan who supposedly made the quote I included on page four referencing Texas. My father, Bill Meiser, found the quote somewhere on the Internet, and I thought it would lend credence to how much Elijah hated the military and where he was stationed in Texas. Fort Bliss is also an actual military base in Texas. My father was instrumental in finding information for me on the Internet concerning televisions and other products of that particular era in American history.

The storyline has some basis from my departed mother, Ida, who would tell my brothers, sister, and I ghost stories as children. She would swear the stories were true. I took quite a bit of liberty with one such story, modified it and fashioned it into a novel, changing names and adding many more fictional characters. The storyline itself is fictional, and therefore, any names which might be associated with anyone in my community is entirely coincidental. I also want to thank my daughter, Vanessa, who helped with the final grammatical editing of the book.

Lastly, I want to thank Publish America and my editor, Adrianne Brigido, for their professionalism in making my first novel a reality.

The cell was dark, dusty, and smelled of stale cigarette smoke. It had rained for two days straight, making the air muggy and hot.

Curled up on his threadbare cot in the corner of the cell, inmate Elijah Stone began to perspire heavily. A hint of light filtered through the cell window while the sun sank in the evening sky. Shadows danced around the room as military police officers walked back and forth in the adjoining room. It was early July in Texas, and due to the smoldering heat, it was almost unbearable in the tiny cell with no fan to circulate the air.

Private Elijah Stone stood at six feet two inches tall. He was a slender, good-looking young man in his early twenties. His dark black hair and compassionate blue eyes had always seemed to attract the opposite sex. Growing up, he'd had more than his fair share of women. Men, on the other hand, had always seemed to resent him for his rugged good looks. Elijah was filled with a new anxiety as his fear of this fateful day — growing in the back of his mind from the start — was finally being fulfilled. Dressed smartly in his military uniform, he was taken from the tiny holding cell in handcuffs and led to his military trial. Perspiration was evident on him, soaking his uniform, as his captors pushed him toward the door.

While walking Elijah to the building where his trial would take place, the military police officers joked with each other and shoved Elijah to keep him moving. Finally, arriving at the courtroom, they shoved him into the main aisle and grunted for him to keep moving. The courtroom was a brightly lit, large, open room located right on the base. As Elijah walked toward the front of the room he felt uneasy, as if all eyes were upon him. The two military police officers, each grabbing one of Elijah's arms, led him to his seat and removed his handcuffs. Forcing him into a chair, they turned and walked to the back of the courtroom. Once there, they stood at either side of the exit door as if fearing he might make a break for it. Elijah nervously shuffled back and forth in his seat, glancing quickly at his defense attorney who was seated directly to his right. He was quite a young officer, fresh from the academy. Elijah had only met with him twice before, both times in his holding cell. The man had introduced himself as Lieutenant Tom Bowman, Elijah's court-appointed defense attorney in his upcoming trial.

Sitting in the courtroom, Elijah's mind drifted back to the first time he had met Tom Bowman in his cell. He remembered wondering why he had been assigned someone with no courtroom experience. *The establishment is out to get me,* he had thought to himself when the whole ordeal began. Carefully he had explained to Lieutenant Bowman why he had gone AWOL (absent without leave).

"I had been granted a two-day leave when I made the decision not to return to the base. There was no way in hell I was going back to the abuse from my commanding officer and the men I was forced to bunk with in those God-forsaken barracks. It seemed as if everyone hated me from my first day in the barracks. I had been AWOL for a week before they found me hiding in a hotel room thirty miles from the base," Elijah had explained. "I didn't put up a fight when they came to my hotel room door. They shoved me to the ground, handcuffed me, and brought me back to a holding cell, and now here I am."

After roughly twenty minutes, Tom had risen from his seat and told Elijah, "I'll do what I can, but you'll probably be spending some time in a military prison."

Elijah had thanked him as he left. Now, looking across the room, Elijah noticed the prosecuting officer. He was a short, balding, heavyset man. He looked to be a no-nonsense sort of person as he glared at Elijah from across the room. Minutes later, three high-ranking senior officers marched into the courtroom. Everyone in the room, including Elijah, stood at attention. All three walked to a large oak table at the front of the room and sat down. The highest-ranking officer was the presiding judge, and he was seated between the two other officers. "Sit down," he barked to everyone in the room. He was a dark-haired, tall, slender man in his late fifties, with thick, bushy eyebrows. His face was rough and creviced with lines, giving him a gruff, angry appearance before he even spoke.

Taking his seat, Elijah again began to perspire. A definite hatred toward the military was brewing within him and had become literally uncontrollable. He had to keep himself from jumping out of his seat and telling them all just what he thought of them, including his defense attorney. They had ruined his life. Why was he forced to enlist? The government had no right choosing his destiny. They had abused him from day one in basic training, and he hated where he was stationed now, Fort Bliss, Texas. Fort Bliss sat atop a high mesa overlooking El Paso, Texas. It was stifling hot and dusty in the summer, unlike back home. In fact, Elijah had heard it said that when General Phil Sheridan, military governor of Texas after the Civil War, had visited Fort Bliss, he had brushed the desert dust from his uniform and declared, "If I owned both hell and Texas, I would rent out Texas and live in hell." Well, if that were true, Elijah felt the same way. Fort Bliss was established in 1848 at the end of the Mexican War. There were few amenities available for the soldiers, and the living conditions left much to be desired. Now it was 1959, and conditions were not much better.

Everyone hates me, he thought to himself, *including the men I was forced to stay with in the barracks.* They knew he didn't want to be there, and that made it all the worse for him. He could never seem to make a friend. Even in basic training he had kept to himself, never socializing. He simply didn't want to be there. It had all climaxed with him going off the base without leave. He couldn't take it anymore. Having lived his entire life in a small community in western Pennsylvania, he was taught the following morals: love your country, obey the laws of the land, and do your duty. How could he return home a traitor in his parents' eyes as well as the community's? They would never understand just how much he hated the military.

Now he sat before those he loathed. The military judge would pass sentence on him, but Elijah no longer cared. They could do with him as they pleased. He stirred as the presiding judge told the prosecutor to present his case.

"The case is simple," the prosecutor shouted for effect as he spoke. "The defendant knowingly and willingly refused to return from leave. He had been AWOL for a week before he was located in a hotel thirty miles from the base. This court needs to make an example, showing that this type of unlawful behavior will not be tolerated! There are no extenuating circumstances in this case; therefore, I ask that you give him the maximum sentence under military law guidelines." The prosecutor was red in the face from shouting.

Elijah's mind was in a whirl as the prosecutor returned to his seat and sat down. The presiding judge directed his attention to the opposite table and asked if the defense had anything to say on behalf of the defendant.

Standing to his feet, Officer Bowman walked to the front of the courtroom. "Sir, my client does not deny the charges. He is currently in a mental state of depression brought on by military life. He has stated that he no longer wished to serve his country; therefore, he made a conscious and willful decision to leave. We ask that you be lenient when you pass sentence on him because of his mental state." Tom returned to his seat and sat down.

Elijah was in a state of limbo while the presiding judge caucused with the other two officers in a back room. Returning fifteen minutes later, the presiding officer asked the defendant to stand as he passed sentence on him. Elijah rose to his feet. "I sentence you to ninety days in Leavenworth Disciplinary Barracks, after which you will be dishonorably discharged for your conduct," stated the judge gruffly.

Officer Tom Bowman stood and reached to shake Elijah's hand. "To hell with you," Elijah said as he turned away. Two military police officers approached Elijah once again and roughly forced him into handcuffs. Pushing him forward, they led him back to his cramped holding cell.

The next morning, he was cuffed once again and taken from the tiny holding cell. Pushed outside into the blinding sunlight, his eyes focused on a dirty white prison van with security wire on the passenger windows. Forced inside the van, his captors unlocked one hand from the handcuffs and relocked it to a bar mounted solidly inside the van. After closing the door, the two guards climbed into the front seat of the van and began to transport Elijah to Leavenworth Disciplinary Barracks located in Kansas. Due to the intense heat outside, it turned into what seemed like a never-ending drive. Everyone was soaked with sweat. Dealing with the heat was one thing, but when the guards made it a point to not allow him to relieve himself, Elijah thought his bladder would burst. When they did stop, it was for gas, cigarettes, and sodas for themselves. Elijah received nothing during the thirteen-hour drive. Finally, the van came to a stop in front of a large, well-kept, old brick building. The building had a certain presence about it, adorned with bars on every window. The entire outer perimeter of the building was wrapped with a ten-foot-tall fence. At the very top of the fence was razor-sharp barbed wire. It was obvious that when you came to this place, you weren't going to leave until they let you.

They removed Elijah from the van, handcuffed him once again, and pushed him toward the building's entrance. Once inside, he was forced into the arrival area for new prisoners. Removing Elijah's cuffs, the guards signed some paperwork and left.

Elijah stood quivering in front of a new set of guards, who seemed to thoroughly love their jobs, and an overweight prison warden. The warden, wearing a disheveled brown uniform, reeked of sweat. Elijah's bladder ached with pain, but he thought it best to keep his mouth shut while the warden began to speak in a loud, controlling voice. He explained what was expected of Elijah for the next ninety days, beginning with, "Your stay in Leavenworth will be very structured and disciplined. Do not expect it to be easy, or you will be sadly disappointed. Do as you're told, and your stay will be bearable. Break the rules, and you will be punished severely. Try to escape, and expect to have at least five years added on to your sentence."

After the warden had finished explaining the rules of the prison to him, Elijah nodded, acknowledging that he understood. He had not spoken a word to anyone since he was sentenced — he had nothing to say. *To hell with them all,* he thought as he was led to a prison cell that was much larger than his holding cell.

The guard pushed Elijah inside the cell and closed it. "Get used to it. It'll be your home for the next ninety days," he yelled.

Elijah ran to the foul-smelling toilet and began to urinate, relief overcoming his weak, drained body. The cell was small and restrictive; there was just enough room for a single bed, sink, and toilet. The toilet was out in the open where guards could watch a prisoner at all times.

Leavenworth was a harsh, demeaning place. The days seemed like an eternity, and the nights even longer. It felt as if he would never be rid of that horrific prison. The guards made sure that each passing day was a personal hell for each and every prisoner. Elijah did as he was told and kept to himself. This seemed to infuriate the guards even more as they tried to get him to slip up. Beatings became frequent as days passed into weeks for Elijah. Still, he feared each passing day because it meant he was one day closer to returning home to his parents, friends, and neighbors. One day closer to never-ending shame. Sometimes Elijah felt it would be easier to take his own life in the cell rather than face his parents. All he'd have to do would be to slip his belt through the bars and fashion a noose. He continued to push the thought out of his mind.

Weeks turned into months, until the day of his release finally arrived.

Walking through the guarded gate to his taxi, he felt a sense of relief. It was over. Once inside the vehicle, Elijah asked the driver to take him to the nearest bus station. Before he knew it, he was on a bus heading home. The hours passed slowly on the hot, cramped bus; however, this did not deter Elijah because he realized that, for the first time, he was at peace with himself. He was finally rid of the military and the God-forsaken state of

Texas. *Soon I'll be home in my own bed, sleeping and not having someone tell me when I have to turn out my lights or eat or drink or even go to the bathroom,* he thought gratefully to himself. For the first time in a year and a half, he finally felt like he had something to look forward to.

As the bus pulled into the terminal in Altoona, Pennsylvania, Elijah realized that he had not written or talked to his parents in over a year and a half. He yearned for the small, close-knit town where he was raised. Claysburg, Pennsylvania was a small town where everyone knew each other's business. The extremely picturesque area was surrounded by overwhelming mountains. The community had always rallied round those in need. Now, as he dialed the phone to have his father pick him up at the bus station, Elijah was nervous.

His father answered the phone and was surprised to hear his son's voice. Of course he would drive the twenty miles to pick Elijah up, but he was now curious. Why was his son on leave? Why had Elijah not written to tell them he was on leave in the first place? These were all questions that would be answered soon enough.

Francis Stone, at six feet three inches tall was a rugged, hard-working man in his late fifties. Working almost thirty years in a brickyard had made him tough. He sported a graying beard and was quite a presence with his 275-pound frame. He had lived his entire life in Claysburg, raising one son whom he had never seemed to understand. Growing up, Francis had not disciplined Elijah any more harshly than any other parent in town did their child. In fact, he often worried that because of his large stature, he might hurt the child if he spanked him too hard. He was, however, extremely proud when Elijah was drafted to serve his country. One of the few times he had ever actually hugged his child was when he had received his draft notice. Even when Elijah had revealed that he didn't want to go, Francis had consoled him, explaining that it was his duty as a citizen of this great country.

Now, pulling into the bus station, he would finally see his only child. It had been over a year with no letter or phone call. There stood Elijah in his civilian clothes. Elijah got into the car without saying a word and averted his eyes downward. As his father headed toward home, the silence was finally broken when Francis asked why he was in civilian clothes. As Elijah explained what had happened, his father's face reddened.

Harsh, angry thoughts raced through Francis's head at this unexpected news. His son was a traitor. Was there no way to undo the damage? What would his neighbors think of them? His only son had disgraced him. Nothing more was said as they finished the drive home.

GET OUT!

Pulling into the driveway, Elijah realized that the house was just the same as he remembered it. It was a small, two-story home with peeling white paint. The garage out back was badly in need of repair. Missing shingles and broken wood siding revealed years of neglect.

As it was currently the autumn of the year, there was a chill in the air as Elijah stepped out of the car and realized just how beautiful the yard was with the changing color of the leaves.

As Elijah walked into the house, he said nothing to his mother, instead he went straight upstairs to his room. After dealing with his father, he didn't think he could stand another confrontation tonight. His room was just as he had left it. He collapsed onto his bed and buried his face in his pillow. What had he done? How could he face his father again? Before drifting to sleep, he heard his parents shouting at each other downstairs in the kitchen, their voices echoing off the thin walls.

Waking, he looked at the clock. It was three in the morning. The house was silent. The day's events raced through his head once more. He would feel better in the morning. Finally, at five o'clock, he slowly drifted back to sleep.

The sun was shining through his bedroom window as Elijah woke to the sound of pots banging in the kitchen. Climbing out of bed, he dreaded going downstairs to greet his parents. The smell of coffee brewing and his mother's voice, which he had not heard in over a year, finally gave him the courage to go down the stairs. There she stood in the kitchen, cooking breakfast and softly singing a hymn. Maddie Stone was a short, plump woman, barely five feet tall. At fifty years of age, her graying hair made her appear older than she really was. She had always looked odd standing between her tall husband and son. Elijah walked over to her and kissed her cheek as if he had never been gone. She turned away from his kiss and proclaimed, "I never dreamed I would raise a traitor as a son. How could you betray us and, even worse, your country?"

Elijah's face flushed red as he screamed, "You have no idea of the misery I was in. Can't you just accept me for who I am and what I've done?"

"Elijah, as far as your father and I are concerned, you are dead to us. You need to leave this house and town before you disgrace us any further."

Elijah raced back to his room, locking the door behind him. He fell into bed and began loudly sobbing into his pillow. He would make them all pay. The military, his parents, the community, they would all pay somehow, someway. Elijah slowly rose from his bed and walked to his desk. Picking up a pencil, he began to write a suicide note.

Mom and Dad,

    As you have seen fit not to allow me to continue my life in the community I have grown up in, you leave me no choice but to take my own life. I am sorry I could not be the perfect soldier you had hoped for. I'm also sorry you feel I've disgraced you with my dishonorable discharge. Please try to forgive me for the grief I've caused you. I wish I could have made you proud. The army ruined my life and is now taking it from me. Heed my warning: Do not give me a military funeral or bury me in my military uniform. I hate the military and everyone associated with it. My soul will not rest peacefully if you do not honor my last wishes. I love you both.

                              Your son,
                              Elijah

    With tears streaming down his face, Elijah folded the letter and placed it on his bed. Silently, he walked down the stairs and past his mother, who was still in the kitchen. Opening the front door, Elijah walked into the chilly autumn air. The wind was blowing the leaves in swirls as he walked around the house to the garage directly behind their home. Pushing the rotted door open, he smelled that familiar, musty smell he had enjoyed as a child. The garage was dark and lonely. Looking around, he found a piece of rope and tossed it over the rafter. After he tied a noose on one end, Elijah climbed an old, weathered ladder and secured the other end to the rafter. Sitting on top of the ladder, he slipped the noose over his neck. *I'm not what they want! They don't want a son,* he thought angrily.

    He jumped off the ladder. It wasn't what he had expected. His neck did not break; instead, he struggled as he gasped for air. He suddenly realized he did not want to die after all. He pulled at the rope, trying to lift his body up to grab the rafter, but as he struggled, the rope tightened. Slowly, the light faded from his eyes.

    Elijah's father returned from work at five-thirty. Opening the door, he had his mind made up. He was going to tell Elijah to leave his house that night. His heart was broken that his only son had mortified him. Entering the kitchen, Francis demanded to know where Elijah was. His wife motioned upstairs. As he climbed the stairs, his anger seemed to grow. Tramping up the carpeted stairs to Elijah's room, he felt a sense of relief. He would force his son to leave the town before anyone heard about his dishonorable discharge. His honor in the community would not be compromised.

GET OUT!

He opened the door without knocking. No one was in the room. Francis yelled down to his wife; she quickly climbed the stairs to his room. Where had Elijah gone? They searched the room for clues to his whereabouts. Finding the folded note on his bed, Maddie opened it and began reading. She started to scream as Francis pulled the note from her hands. After Francis read the note, he sat on Elijah's bed and began crying. What had he done? Racing down the steps, Maddie ran outside, hollering for her son. It was now dark outside, and with no lights in the backyard, she realized she needed a flashlight. Racing back into the house, she rummaged through the junk drawer and located a small flashlight. Francis was now beside her as she went back out into the yard and began searching for her son. Shining the lights into the trees in the backyard revealed nothing. Walking slowly toward the garage, a sense of fear came over them. Pulling the door open and shining the light in, Francis felt overwhelming grief as he saw, through the dim glow of the flashlight, the lifeless body of his only son hanging from the rafters. Elijah's face was pale, and his lips were blue. His eyes were wide open and seemed to bulge from their sockets. It was a gruesome sight. They hugged and cried, slumping to the damp garage floor as they realized they were to blame for their son's death. Why hadn't they supported him? Why had they not realized he was in as much pain as they were? What would the community think of their son committing suicide? It was too much to handle.

Walking back to the house, they felt lonely and isolated. As Francis called the police, he carefully planned what he would say. Police Chief Robinson answered the phone. In a community as small as Claysburg, there were only two full-time and three part-time officers, all of which Francis had known for many years. Chief Robinson was a short, slender, balding man, about the same age as Francis. He absolutely couldn't believe what Francis was telling him. "I'll be right there," he yelled to Francis through the phone, slamming the receiver down upon finishing his last words.

John Robinson had watched Elijah grow into a young adult. Elijah had always been so well-liked in their tiny, cohesive community. John, as well as the rest of the town, had attended a dinner in Elijah's honor before he had left for basic training. Now this fine young man was hanging limply in front of him. The paramedics and John slowly lifted Elijah's cold, dead body up into the air and cut the rope that had choked the life from him. Carrying his body to the stretcher, they covered the lifeless form with a sheet. The paramedics would deliver the body to the hospital where they would perform an autopsy and determine the exact cause of death.

John walked to the kitchen where the smell of fresh-brewed coffee hung in the air. As he pulled a chair up to the kitchen table, Maddie slid him a cup of coffee. He struggled for words to comfort his friends of over thirty years. Soon, he began unintentionally interrogating the Stones. "When did Elijah come home? Was he distraught? Did you have a clue he was contemplating suicide? Did he leave a note?" John spit all four questions out, one after another.

Francis did most of the talking as they explained what had happened. It was necessary, Francis felt, to lie about most of the facts. After all, he wanted to preserve Elijah's good name in the community. He told John, "Elijah had arrived yesterday on leave from the military to visit us. We had joked and talked about his experiences from the past year in the service, and we had enjoyed a nice supper before Elijah went upstairs to bed. Honestly, John, we had no clue he was planning to commit suicide. He left no note, and his mother said she had no idea he had left the house during the day as she was doing her cleaning chores. It wasn't until I came home from work and went to his room to see him that I realized he wasn't in the house. Shortly after we started searching for him, I found him in the garage."

Rising from the kitchen table, John finished his coffee and gave his condolences to Maddie and Francis once more. As Francis walked John to the door, tears streamed down his face. Before leaving, Francis reached to shake John's hand, but John brushed his hand aside and hugged him as Francis sobbed uncontrollably. John decided then and there that he would write up the report exactly as it was told to him by Francis and the case would be, without question, closed.

Returning to the kitchen, Francis and Maddie were totally exhausted. He explained that no one must ever know the truth about their son. They would never speak of it again. Maddie was to go directly to bed, and he would take care of the note and Elijah's personal things. Maddie went to the bathroom to get ready for bed, and Francis returned to Elijah's room.

The room seemed lonely as he searched for a small box in which to put the suicide note. On the top shelf of the closet, he found a small wooden box. Opening it, Francis found treasures from Elijah's childhood. Baseball cards, a gold chain, childhood pictures, and a small black book of witchcraft no larger than the palm of his hand. Removing the book, he could not believe his son would read such material. He had been brought up in the Brethren church and had attended Sunday school his whole life. Not wanting to think about it anymore, he shoved it all back in the box, including the suicide note and pictures taken of Elijah in his military uniform. He looked so handsome in those snapshots, Francis reflected miserably.

Placing the lid on the box, he went out into the hallway, retrieved a stepladder, and pushed open the hatch to the attic. Retrieving the flashlight from his pocket, he shone it around the dark attic. He had not been in the attic for over ten years. He pulled himself up into the dark dusty room and felt a chill run down his spine. There were old boxes of clothing that Maddie had stuck up there years ago. As he crawled along the floor to the far corner of the attic, he realized just how badly he wanted to get this whole ordeal over with. Prying up a loose floorboard, he slid the box between the floor joists and pushed the floorboard back into place. All evidence of the day's events were now hidden forever as far as Francis was concerned. He crawled back to the attic opening, lowered himself down to the stepladder, and closed the hatch. Putting the small ladder away, he went to get ready for bed. As he fell into bed, the grief overwhelmed him, and he wondered how his wife could be asleep already. Slowly, Francis sobbed himself to sleep.

Both the Stones were early risers, and that Friday morning was no exception. At five in the morning, Maddie was already cooking breakfast. Soon Francis joined her at the kitchen table. Cold cereal and eggs, the same breakfast he had eaten every morning for the past twenty years. It wouldn't be long before the news traveled through the community, and phone calls were sure to come. By seven in the morning, the neighbors were calling, wanting to know what all the commotion was about the night before. As Maddie explained what had happened to her long-time friend and neighbor, Delores, the phone fell silent. After all, how does one respond to such news? Delores, shocked, dropped the phone and ran next door to Maddie, hugging her as tears streamed down her face. Her son, Roger, had grown up with Elijah, and he was overseas in the military that very day. *Why had Elijah done such a thing?* she wondered.

Committing suicide, both Delores and Maddie had been taught, was an unpardonable sin. His soul would surely be damned. They didn't dare vocalize the thought, but both knew what each other was thinking. Now the phone was ringing again. Francis took it off the hook, for he could not deal with having to tell his friends and family what had happened over and over again.

Soon his older sister Lois was pulling into the driveway. She was a big, tall woman with a loud, booming voice. Folks in town knew that she always had the latest gossip before anyone else. She had talked to John Robinson early that morning; thus, she already knew the entire story. After hugging her older brother, she told him she was there for support, to answer the phone, and to help plan the funeral. As much as he could barely tolerate his sister, he was glad she was there.

Lois fielded over fifty phone calls that day and told the same story over and over just as it was told to her by John Robinson. In between calls, she called the funeral home and made plans for a full military funeral. Francis sat by idly as she planned the entire thing. Going into Elijah's room, she retrieved the uniform that he had worn while in the military. Strangely enough, he had only one dress uniform in his closet. Her nephew had always looked so handsome dressed in it, she thought ruefully. After telling Francis she had promised Tom Latchkey of Latchkey's Funeral Home that she would drop the uniform off on her way home, Lois hugged both Maddie and Francis and left without having shed a single tear the entire day.

As she was backing her car out of the driveway, Francis ran from the house, motioning for Lois to stop. She rolled down the window in time to hear Francis yelling to her that he would drop the uniform off himself. Apparently he needed to see his son one last time before the funeral tomorrow. Lois scowled as she handed him the uniform. "Haven't you been through enough?"

Francis grew irritated with his sister. "Just give me the suit, and I'll see you at the funeral tomorrow."

Francis yelled to Maddie that he would be back in an hour and got into his car. Latchkey's was only ten miles from his home, but the drive seemed to last for an eternity. Pulling into Latchkey's parking lot, Francis felt extremely overwhelmed. He had to tell his son how sorry he was for not supporting him. He no longer possessed the boiling anger of yesterday. He would gladly allow his son to stay in their home now if he had it all to do over again. If only he had not been so concerned of what others in his community thought. It was too late now.

As he opened his car door, he realized he was the only person in the parking lot. The driveway at Latchkey's was dimly lit, almost haunting in a way. Walking to the side door with uniform in hand, he knocked. Tom Latchkey, wearing a black suit with a colorless plastic apron over it, answered the door rather quickly. "Francis, I thought your sister was dropping the suit off."

"Tom, I have to see my son one last time before tomorrow," Francis replied solemnly.

GET OUT!

"Francis, I'm sorry for your loss, but Elijah's body is on the marble slab downstairs, and I'm preparing his body for burial."

"I don't care; I want to see him alone with no one around."

"Follow me," Tom consented reluctantly.

Handing Tom the uniform, Francis walked down the steps to the basement. Walking into a brightly-lit room where his son's body lie unclothed and rigid, he gazed upon Elijah's stiff corpse. Immediately, Francis's eyes were drawn to the deep rope burn on his son's neck. The body was pale white, and his lips were purple in color. Tom explained to Francis that he had drained Elijah's blood and was about to start the embalming process.

"Are you sure you want to see him this way?" Tom gently inquired of Francis.

Solemnly nodding yes, Francis asked Tom to leave.

"I'll give you as much time as you need with your son." Leaving the room, Tom closed the door behind him.

Walking to his son, the finality of Elijah's death hit Francis hard. Tears streamed down his face as he hugged the cold, stiff corpse, spilling his tears upon Elijah's face. "Elijah, please forgive me!" he sobbed. "I never meant for you to do this, son. Why did you have to bring this heartache upon your mother and me? How can I live with myself?"

He kissed his son on the forehead one last time and left the room. Finding Tom upstairs, he thanked him. As he was getting ready to leave, Tom asked Francis if he would like to pick a casket while he was there.

"Didn't my sister ask you to bury him in the cheapest casket you have?"

Tom nodded as Francis forcefully retorted, "Well, that's what I want. I'll see you at the cemetery tomorrow." Briskly leaving the building, Francis returned home.

It was now eight o'clock in the evening and, thanks to Francis's sister, the funeral, in its entirety, had been planned. The funeral would take place the next day in Upper Claar Cemetery, not more than five miles from the Stones' home. They would have an open casket at graveside for one hour prior to the burial, allowing the viewing and burial to take place all in the same day. Following the funeral, they would go to the Brethren Church for a supper.

The Stones just wanted it over and done with so they could grieve in peace. Maddie voiced her reservations about burying Elijah in his military uniform. After all, he had explicitly forbidden it in his suicide note. He wanted nothing to do with the military, and Francis knew this as well as her.

Francis, however, was adamant that he be buried in the uniform, ensuring that no one would find out about his dishonorable discharge. After all, he was dead now; why did it matter what clothing he was buried in?

They ate supper that night and went straight to bed. Tomorrow would come soon enough and promised to be another trying day for both of them.

Waking early Saturday morning, Maddie looked out the window to see a mist of rain falling. She put on her Sunday clothes and went downstairs to make breakfast. Francis was a little slower than usual getting out of his bed. Today he would bury his only son, something he never dreamed would happen. *Your children are supposed to bury you,* he thought to himself. Sobbing, he put on his one and only suit. It was a snug-fitting, black suit he had purchased seven years ago. It was obvious that it was too small for him. The sleeves on the coat and the pant legs were several inches too short. Sitting down to put on his faded, weathered, black shoes, he could not control himself as tears dropped and glistened down his shoes. This tragedy would not have occurred, had he only been more sympathetic toward Elijah. If only he could change it all. If only he had it to do over again. *It's my entire fault,* he cursed to himself. Rising from the chair, he wiped the tears away and walked down the steps to have breakfast with his wife. It was eight o'clock in the morning, and they were getting a late start. Usually both of them would have been up hours ago, but because they were so extremely exhausted from yesterday's events, they could not seem to move any faster. Eating quickly, Francis stated that the viewing at graveside was to take place at ten sharp, so they needed to be there no later than nine to ensure that they were there to greet any early arrivals. Throwing the dirty dishes in the sink, they left the house and stepped out into the cool autumn air. There was a mist of rain falling, chilling them to the bone. It made Francis wish that he owned an overcoat. No matter; it would all be over soon enough. They got into the car and were on their way to the cemetery.

As they arrived at Upper Claar Cemetery, Maddie realized that the last time she was here was fifteen years prior, when they buried her father. The cemetery sat on a hill, and it was quite a hard climb to the gravesites. At the bottom of the hill sat a small Baptist church.

They were now parked in the church parking lot. Elijah was to be buried halfway down the hill. Leaving the car, Francis was grateful that the rain had stopped, but it was still quite overcast and gloomy. *How fitting,* he surmised. It was a perfect day for a funeral. Climbing the hill to the gravesite, they had to stop repeatedly to catch their breath due to the steep climb. Finally, walking to Elijah's final resting place, they sat under a makeshift pavilion housing the casket. Maddie could not bring herself to walk over to it and view her son. They were the only people there. It was eight forty-five in the morning, and even Tom Latchkey was nowhere to be found. Mustering all of his courage, Francis edged toward the casket. It was a cheap wooden model made of what appeared to be pine. Gazing down at his son, he found it hard to believe that this was the same body he had viewed last night. With the aid of makeup, Elijah's face now appeared to have some color. He looked extremely handsome in his military uniform. Motioning for Maddie to come over, she finally summoned the courage to approach the casket. There lay her only son. He seemed so peaceful. "I hope he found in death what he could not find in life, Francis," Maddie tearfully exclaimed.

By now Tom Latchkey was walking up the hill beside Lois and her husband Bob. Their son, Andy, was lingering a few steps behind. Shaking hands with Tom and Bob, Francis seemed in a daze. Maddie began to cry on Lois's shoulder. Everyone thanked Tom for doing a wonderful job in preparing the body for burial. It looked almost as if he were alive. In fact, Francis could have sworn there were times that his chest was rising and falling as though he was taking breaths. This made it all the harder for him to stand by the casket.

It was now nine forty-five, and friends, coworkers, and family were filing past the casket. It was a small town, but it seemed as if everyone had heard about Elijah's untimely death and decided to turn out to pay their respects. Then again, knowing how some of the townspeople were, they probably just came out of curiosity, to see the boy who had hung himself. By ten forty-five, Francis motioned to the pastor to start the service early. He couldn't stand it any longer. They were torturing him, gawking at his son. Delivering the eulogy, the pastor talked of how well-liked Elijah had been, how he was a young man who had served his country without hesitation when he was drafted. Everyone was so proud of the considerate young man he had turned into. The words stung Francis as the pastor finished by quoting scripture from the Bible. Finally, it was over. Maddie had been hugged so many times that she was physically numb. As Francis turned to leave, Tom Latchkey asked him to stay while they closed the casket and lowered it into the ground. Francis gruffly told Tom to finish it without him; he simply could not take any more.

Walking back to the car beside Maddie, no words were exchanged between them. Even as they drove to the Brethren church's social hall, he could not bring himself to look at his wife. He knew he was more to blame for Elijah's death than his wife. The night he brought Elijah home, he had screamed at her as if it was her fault. Because of the way he had treated her that night, her anger had exploded on poor Elijah that fateful morning. Wishing it was all over so they could try to get on with their lives, Francis pulled into the church parking lot. It was now pouring down rain with lightning and thunder cracking in the background. It seemed very unusual to have lightning and thunder this late into autumn, given how chilly it was outside. Because of the rain, he dropped Maddie off at the front entrance and parked the car himself. Why did he have to go to this dinner? It made no sense. Whoever came up with the notion that it was necessary to eat after you bury a loved one must have been an idiot. How could he eat and socialize? He had just buried his only son. Rage grew within him as he pulled out of the parking lot and headed home. *Maddie can socialize with them if she wants to; I'm going home, damn it,* Francis stubbornly thought. *Lois can bring her home. After all, Lois loves to socialize and rub elbows, even if it is at my son's expense,* thought Francis heatedly.

Arriving home, Francis hurried into the house and collapsed on the couch. He had not been home more than five minutes when the phone rang. It was Maddie, wanting to know why he had left her there alone. He argued on the phone for ten minutes, explaining why he could not eat or talk about his son any longer. "I just want to be left alone. Can't you understand that, Maddie? Just leave me the hell alone! If you want to entertain everyone at the church, that's your decision. Go right ahead. Lois will bring you home." Just as he was finishing his sentence, Maddie hung up on him. Francis didn't care. "Let her be mad," he grumbled to no one in particular. He preferred to grieve alone anyway. To hell with all of them. Rising from the couch, he went to his bedroom and collapsed onto his bed, falling into a deep sleep.

At four in the afternoon, Francis was awakened by a car door slamming. It was Lois dropping Maddie off. She threw open the front door as she entered the home. Francis met her at the top of the stairs, but before he could say a word, she began screaming at him. "How could you embarrass me like that? Everyone was asking where you were!"

"Maddie, I am going to say this once and once only. Never bring up this day to me again. I want it over with. Do you hear me?"

Not saying another word, Maddie went into her bedroom and slammed the door behind her. She pulled herself out of her black dress, put on her nightgown, and fell into bed. She was sure everyone had noticed that she had hardly cried during the entire service. It was her way, after all. She tried never to show her emotions in public. Burying her face into her pillow, she now sobbed uncontrollably for her son. As Maddie cried herself into a deep, restful sleep, Francis went downstairs and turned on the television.

Francis loved his new television set, manufactured by RCA. It was a state-of-the-art Fliptop model in 1959. He had been one of the first in the area to purchase a television and was very proud of it. He had saved for over a year to buy it and had even put off painting the house to ensure he would have enough money. Maddie thought he was crazy for wanting a television so badly. After all, they had a perfectly good radio they had listened to and enjoyed for years. "Women just don't understand," he had told her the day he brought it home.

By nine in the evening, Francis had fallen asleep on the couch, the television still droning on in the background. That is where he stayed the entire night.

Sunday morning was a bright, sunny day. It was a harsh contrast to the day before when they had buried their son. Rising from the sofa, Francis felt stiff and sore from the night spent there. Maddie was already in the kitchen making breakfast when Francis crept up behind her and kissed her neck. "Let's skip church today, Maddie." Nothing was said about the prior day. It was as if it never happened. They ate the usual cold cereal and eggs, did yesterday's dishes, and went into the living room to watch television and read the morning paper. They spent the rest of the morning and afternoon raking and burning leaves.

No one expected Francis to be at work on Monday morning, but there he was, as if he had not lost a son three days prior. His co-workers acted as if it were any other day, joking and making small talk. Francis was glad, for he wanted it all behind him. Finishing his normal workday, he drove home and pulled into his driveway like clockwork at five-thirty. As he opened the front door, he felt a chill go down his back. "Maddie, is the furnace broken?"

"I don't think so," she replied. "There's been a chill in here all day, though."

It was just starting to get dark as Francis went down the basement steps to check the furnace. Using a flashlight, he checked the old oil burner for problems. Just as he drew closer, the furnace turned on, and the burner fired perfectly. Shaking his head, he went back upstairs for supper.

As he slid his chair up to the kitchen table, Francis tried to make small talk. He felt hollow inside as he went through the motions of pretending to care. "How was your day, Maddie?"

"The same as every other day," she replied wearily. "I cleaned the entire house today. This house never seems to be clean enough for me. Oh, Francis, there has to be something wrong with the furnace. I couldn't seem to get warm today. This place was unusually cold. The temperature outside was even in the sixties today."

Without answering, Francis finished his pot roast, pushed his plate to the side, and stood up. Giving Maddie a look of disgust, he turned and went into the living room. Before sitting down on the sofa, he turned on the television. He could hear Maddie clanging the dishes as she slipped them into the sink to be cleaned. Just as the news was ending, Maddie screamed. Running to the kitchen, Francis found Maddie sitting on the floor shaking uncontrollably.

"What the hell is wrong now?"

"There's a man in our backyard looking through the window. I saw him as I was washing the dishes!"

"Maddie, it's pitch black outside. How on earth could you have seen a man?"

"I'm telling you, I saw something."

Grabbing the flashlight, Francis went into the backyard. He was unnerved as he shone the light around the back kitchen window. It was pitch black outside; even the moon was hidden by the clouds. The air was breezy as he walked around the house, searching for the intruder. The garage where Elijah had taken his own life was just twenty feet from the kitchen window. For some reason, Francis could not seem to bring himself to check inside the garage. Instead, walking quickly, he returned to the house to find Maddie standing at the front door. He assured her that no one was out there. Maddie, nevertheless, begged Francis to help her finish the dishes.

"Woman, I work my ass off all day long, and you expect me to do housework? I told you nothing was out there. Now get your ass into the kitchen and finish the damn dishes!"

Giving Francis a cold stare, she returned to the kitchen and continued washing the dishes. Finishing the dishes, she walked to the kitchen table and wiped it clean. Sitting down at the table, Maddie began to sob. *I can't take it anymore,* she thought, rubbing her eyes. Suddenly she became angry. *He has no right swearing at me because he feels guilty!*

Standing up, she turned off the kitchen light and went to the living room to confront Francis. He had already gone upstairs without saying a word. The climb up the stairs seemed endless. Looking into the bedroom, she found Francis in bed, reading the newspaper.

Biting her lip, she exclaimed contentiously, "I don't think you need to curse at me, Francis."

Lowering the paper and looking out over the top, Francis yelled back, "I'll do whatever I damn well please, Maddie!"

He picked the paper back up and resumed his reading. Disgusted, Maddie opened the closet door and pulled the winter comforter out.

"If the house is going to stay this cold, I'm just going to have to buy more covers."

"Do whatever you please," he mumbled back. However, Francis wasn't about to complain; he was freezing as well. The comforter helped, but the chill seemed to be all around them as they drifted to sleep. At three in the morning, they were awakened by a door slamming somewhere upstairs. It startled them out of a deep sleep. Francis jumped out of bed and grabbed the gun he kept in his closet. It was a double-barrel shotgun with a worn stock. His father had given it to him when he was a boy. It was the only gun he had ever owned. He had killed many a squirrel with that gun. Now, as he fumbled for the shotgun shells, he noticed that the chill in the air was worse than before they had gone to bed. *Who could be in the house?* he wondered nervously. Loading the gun, he slowly opened the bedroom door and switched the hallway light on, yelling that he had a gun and was not afraid to use it. There was dead silence in reply. Feeling braver, he ventured into the hallway. First, he opened the hallway closet door. It was empty. Then, opening Elijah's bedroom door, he felt a rush of cold air. Turning the light on, he noticed that the window was wide open. Why had Maddie left the window open? It's no wonder there was a chill in the house. The wind rushing in must have slammed his door shut.

Returning to the bedroom, Maddie was sitting up in bed. "What was it? Is someone in the house?"

Returning his gun to the closet, Francis exclaimed, "Well, Maddie, I know why the house is freezing. You left Elijah's window open while you were cleaning, and the wind must have slammed his door shut. That's what woke us."

"Francis, I did not open his window today while I was cleaning. I think I would know to close a window."

"Well, it was open, so I closed it."

Thinking no more of it, they drifted to sleep.

It was five o'clock in the morning when the alarm went off. Maddie and Francis climbed out of bed to a bone-chilling cold. "Francis, I thought you said the furnace was working and it wouldn't be chilly anymore."

"I don't know," he said in a grumpy tone. "Call a repairman today and have him come take a look at it."

Maddie nodded her head and put on her robe. Heading downstairs, she could be heard starting breakfast. Maddie was not in the kitchen for more than a few minutes when, for some reason, a strange feeling came over her. Shaking her head in a confused state, she climbed the steps and turned the hall light on. Staring at Elijah's bedroom door, something drew her to it. Opening it slowly, she felt a rush of cold air. "Francis," she screamed, "come here! I'm in Elijah's bedroom!"

Running out of his bedroom, he saw Maddie standing in the doorway of Elijah's room. Walking over to her, he could not believe his eyes. Staring blankly at the window, he saw with his own two eyes that it was wide open again.

"I thought you said you closed it last night, Francis!"

"I did! I'm absolutely positive that I closed and locked it." Pulling it shut once more, he locked it. "It just doesn't make sense, Maddie. That's the damnedest thing I've ever seen. When I come home from work, I'll check out the window and nail it shut if need be."

Walking down the steps to breakfast, both had puzzled looks on their faces. The morning breakfast ritual was as always, cold cereal and eggs. Together they laughed at how scared they had been the night before when the door had slammed shut from the wind. It was first time either had laughed in almost a week. Kissing Maddie on the cheek, Francis left the house and drove to work. As was Maddie's daily routine, she drank her morning coffee and read the newspaper. Finishing the paper, it was time to clean the breakfast dishes. In the past, she had always enjoyed her time when Francis went to work. However, during the past two days, she didn't want him to leave. Of course, she would never tell him that. She always kept her emotions in check.

Noticing the chill again, she went to the phone and called the local heating company. They informed her that a repairman would be coming around lunchtime. The dishes done, she sat down to watch television. She just did not feel like cleaning today. She drifted to sleep while watching television. Around eleven-thirty, she awoke to a knock at the door. Strangely enough, the television was now off, and the house was even colder than this morning. Maybe the power went out, she surmised. As she answered the door, she realized it was the repairman. He was a tall, slender, handsome young man.

"Hi, my name is Todd," he exclaimed with a boyish grin. He reminded Maddie immediately of her dead son. "What seems to be the problem, ma'am?"

She explained that the house would not seem to get warm. He also noticed the chill. "I'll check it out." Walking to the thermostat, he noticed it was set at seventy degrees. *Well, I know it's not seventy in here,* he thought to himself. Maddie directed him to the basement and told him to watch his step as she went to the kitchen to fix herself lunch. Heating up leftovers from last night's supper, she was startled as Todd came up the steps and informed her that the furnace was fine. He cleaned the electrodes just to be sure. "Should work fine though," he said as he handed her a bill and walked toward the door.

"Thank you for coming over right away, young man," Maddie said warmly.

"No problem, ma'am. If you have anymore trouble with it, just give us a call." With that said, he was gone.

Maddie started supper at four-thirty, racing between the kitchen and television as she watched her favorite soap opera. Hearing Francis pulling into the driveway, she glanced at the clock. It was five-thirty already. Just like clockwork, he was always home at the same time. He would never dream of going to the bar like so many of his buddies after work. Opening the door, Francis yelled, "What's for supper?"

"Beef stew," Maddie replied.

"Damn, this house is still cold, woman. Didn't you call a repairman?"

"Yes, I did. He was here around noon, looked it over, and said it was working fine. A nice young man. He reminded me of Elijah."

"I asked you not to talk about Elijah again," Francis yelled.

Maddie dropped the subject.

Sitting down to supper, neither spoke of her slip of the tongue. After eating, Francis got up, grunted, "It was good," and went in to read the paper. As was her daily routine, Maddie cleared the table and did the dishes. It was almost seven already. Where had the day gone? Sitting down to watch television before bed, both were startled by a loud thud upstairs. Jumping up, Francis ran upstairs and, as if drawn by some unknown force, ran straight to Elijah's room. There it was again. "That window seems to be possessed, Maddie. It opened itself again." He went downstairs to the basement, got his hammer and nails, and returned to Elijah's room, nailing the window shut. "Now let's see the damn thing open," he cursed as he went back downstairs to watch television.

When Francis crawled into bed that night, he moaned once again at how freezing the room was. He pulled Maddie close to him, something he rarely did. Turning the light, out they drifted to sleep. They were not asleep more than an hour when they heard a loud slamming noise in the hallway. Francis rose from his bed, cursing. "This house is driving me crazy lately, Maddie."

"Francis, come back to bed. The noises will go away."

Crawling back under the covers, he placed a pillow over his head to drown out the noises. The sun peeked through the window at five, waking Maddie before the alarm went off. She mumbled, "Francis, get up and get ready for work." Grumbling, he crawled out from under the covers, yawning.

"No more noises last night," he said with relief in his voice.

"How would you know? You slept the entire night with a pillow over your head," Maddie retorted.

"Well, it worked, didn't it? I slept better last night than I have in days."

Going to the bathroom, he was once again complaining about the temperature of the house. "We need a new furnace, Maddie." She didn't hear him. She was on her way downstairs to make breakfast.

The days came and went. The chill never left, and loud noises continued every night from the attic, hallway, and Elijah's bedroom. Francis and Maddie slept with pillows over their head to drown out the noises. This continued until one night when Francis heard what sounded like Elijah's voice in the hallway. Even with a pillow over his ears, it woke him. It was a whispering sound that made the hair on the back of his neck stand up. Maddie was still sleeping, so he rose from his bed and opened the bedroom door slowly. The noise was coming from Elijah's room. He cracked open the door to Elijah's room. It was dark, but he noticed a silhouette adorned in a military uniform sitting at Elijah's desk. It turned to him, displaying an anguished face, clearly in pain. "You betrayed me!" The apparition spoke and then quickly disappeared. Francis was shaking from head to toe. Was it his son's spirit who was in torment? Was Elijah's spirit not at peace? *I must be going crazy,* he thought from the guilt of what he had done, forcing his son to take his own life. Lately, it seemed as if his whole life was a lie. *I must be going crazy. There's no such thing as spirits walking the earth,* Francis tried to reassure himself.

Walking back to his bedroom, Francis crawled under the blankets and stared at the ceiling. Glancing at the clock, he noticed it was three. He remained in bed, staring at the ceiling, until five. The alarm sounded, waking Maddie. "Get up and get ready for work, Francis," she said, as usual. She did not know he was up half the night, and he thought it best not to tell her. Going down to breakfast, he heard Maddie singing in the kitchen. As far as she was concerned, things were back to normal except for the constant chill in the air.

Francis gulped down his breakfast and went to the living room. Attempting to read the morning paper, he could not concentrate. At six-thirty, he left the house and got into his car without having said a single word to Maddie the entire morning. When Maddie noticed he was gone, she wondered what was wrong with him. He seemed too quiet this morning; something must be on his mind.

That day at work Francis was solemn. He ate his lunch alone and spoke to no one. Everyone at the plant tried to avoid him anyway. No one knew quite what to say to him. He seemed to withdraw into himself more and more each day. Punching out on the time clock at five, Francis drove home and pulled in the driveway. He stepped out of the car and strode to the front door before he realized he had not closed his car door. *My mind is really slipping. I can't take this anymore. I have to confide in someone what I have done,* he realized. The guilty feeling would never leave him, and he could do nothing more than just keep pushing it aside in his mind.

As he opened the front door Maddie yelled "Hi, Francis!" from the kitchen. "How was your day?"

"Fine," he said halfheartedly.

"We're having steak for supper. Get cleaned up because it'll be ready in a few minutes."

When Francis sat down at the kitchen table, he would not start a conversation. No matter; Maddie made up for it by not shutting up. As usual, Francis finished his supper, rose from the table, and went in to finish reading the paper he had started in the morning. Maddie did the dishes, cleaned the table, and went into the living room. She turned on the television and sat down beside Francis. No sooner had she sat down than the power went off in the house. "Great," Francis said. "A perfect ending to a perfect day. Get me a flashlight, Maddie."

She felt her way to the kitchen, opened the junk drawer, and pulled out the same flashlight with which they had found Elijah's body. Turning it on, she noticed that the batteries were weak. *It'll work well enough to find the fuse box,* she thought. She went back to the living room, sat down on the couch, and handed the light to Francis.

Cursing once again, he rose went to the basement door, opened it, and walked down the steps. Shining the light over to the corner where the fuse box was located, Francis felt a chill deep down in his bones. Someone was in the room with him. He just knew it. Shining the light around the room revealed nothing. He roughly opened the fuse box, pulled out the main fuse, and replaced it with a new one. The lights came on upstairs. He closed the box and hurried back up the stairs. The television was playing, and Maddie was still sitting on the couch. She had a smile on her face. "Scared, Francis?" she joked. He scowled and joined her on the couch. They stayed up until ten watching television, a late night for the Stones.

Rising from the couch together, Francis asked Maddie to lock the front door as he was heading up the steps to bed. She walked to the door, locked it, and headed up the stairs as well. Francis looked as though he had not slept in a week. He collapsed into bed. Maddie went to the bathroom, put her nightgown on, and walked to the bed. Francis was out cold. *He must have been tired,* she thought. He didn't even have the pillow over his head, as had been the custom for both of them the past two weeks. Maddie slid under the covers and drifted off to sleep with a pillow covering her ears.

At three, Francis and Maddie were jarred awake by the sound of the front door slamming. "Didn't you lock the front door, Maddie?"

"Yes, I did, Francis!"

Francis ran to the closet and grabbed his gun, which he now kept loaded at all times. Running out into the hallway, Francis turned the hall light on and rapidly made his way to the top of the stairs. Just before he reached the stairs, it was if someone tripped him. He tumbled head first down the stairs. As he continued rolling down the steps, his neck snapped, killing him instantly.

Maddie, hearing the crashing noise, ran to the top of the stairs.

When she saw Francis lying at the bottom of the steps, she lost control of her emotions and starting screaming and crying. "Francis, are you all right? Get up, Francis." He did not move. Running down the stairs, Maddie stooped down and cradled Francis's head in her arms. Tears were streaming down her face. "Francis, please don't leave me." She knew he was gone. Gently laying his head back down, Maddie walked to the phone and called the ambulance. She told the person answering the phone that her husband had fallen, and she thought he was dead.

"What is your name, Ma'am?"

"Maddie Stone," she replied.

"Stay on the line with me, Maddie. I'm dispatching an ambulance. Where do you live?"

Still in shock, Maddie gave the dispatcher her address. She then let the phone drop and slumped to the floor. She heard voices on the phone but chose not to answer.

Within ten minutes, paramedics were knocking at the door. She could not move. "Open the door!" the voices screamed. No one answered. Trying to

GET OUT!

open the door, they found it was locked and dead-bolted. Nevertheless, they continued pounding. One of the paramedics ran around the back of the house. The kitchen light was on. Peering through the window, he saw Maddie slumped to the floor. Tapping on the window, he screamed, "Ma'am, open the door!" Looking up, she came to her senses and walked to the front door, opening it weakly. *Strange,* she thought, *because she and Francis had heard the door slam. That was why Francis was running down the steps in the first place.* Maddie continued to stare off into space.

The paramedics were working on Francis. They could not find a pulse. They tried to revive him for thirty minutes with CPR, but it was to no avail. Looking at each other helplessly, they lifted his lifeless frame onto the stretcher. They covered his body and face with a sheet. Turning their attention to Maddie, they realized she was in shock. They forced her to lay flat on the floor, covered her with a blanket and elevated her legs. One of the paramedics returned to the ambulance and brought out a second stretcher. Gently, they lifted her quivering body onto the stretcher. They rolled the stretcher to the ambulance and placed her inside. By now, the neighbors' lights were on. It was four in the morning. Delores walked over to the paramedics, inquiring as to what had happened.

They explained that Francis had fallen and was dead. Maddie was in shock, and they were taking her to the hospital as well. Delores agreed to lock the door of their home and watch the house until Maddie was released from the hospital. She also said she would call Francis's sister, Lois.

The paramedics loaded Francis's lifeless body into the ambulance beside Maddie and sped away.

Maddie Stone awoke in the hospital. It was morning, and the sun was shining in her window. Lois was beside her, holding her hand. "Maddie, what happened?" asked Lois.

"Oh, Lois, he's dead isn't he?"

Tears filled Lois's eyes as she replied, "Yes, he is. His neck was broken."

"He fell down the steps. We heard someone slamming the front door in the middle of the night, and he ran to see who was breaking in. The strange thing is the door was locked when I went downstairs. We must have been hearing things. That house is evil, Lois."

"Maddie, you're talking crazy. The doctors have you on nerve medicine. Go to sleep. We'll talk about it later."

Waking at two in the afternoon, Maddie's mind was clear. She was in Spring Cove Hospital and had just lost her husband. Rising from the hospital bed, she walked to the nurse's station. "I want out of here now," she yelled forcefully. The nurse informed her she could not be released without the doctor's consent. "Well, get him now, or I'm leaving anyway."

She went back to her room as the nurse paged the doctor over the intercom. Minutes later, her family doctor of twenty years, Fred Stoltz, appeared in the doorway. "Maddie, are you sure you don't want to spend one more day here?"

"No, I want to leave now."

"All right, I'll sign your release papers, but it's against my better judgment. I still want you to take these pills when you feel anxiety coming on. They will calm your nerves."

"Fine, I will. Now get me out of here, Fred." Fred left, and Maddie called Lois to come pick her up. An hour later, she was being driven to her home by Lois.

"How do you feel, Maddie?"

"Well, considering I have lost both my son and husband within the past month, I guess I'm holding up."

"Maddie, I hope you don't mind, but I have already started making the funeral arrangements with Latchkeys."

"Thank you, Lois. I honestly don't know what I would do without you."

"You know, Maddie, it is a shame you don't have a driver's license. You need to be able to get around."

"I guess I always assumed Francis would be here to take care of me. I'll worry about that later. Right now I need to concern myself with burying my husband."

"Maddie, when you were in the hospital, you said your house was evil. You really don't believe that, do you?"

"No, I was out of my head when I said that. It's just that Francis and I had been hearing and seeing odd things lately in the house since Elijah passed away."

"Why didn't either of you ever mention it?"

"Well, we've just been so consumed with grief and assumed it was from that."

"You're probably right, Maddie. Grief can play tricks on the mind. It will be even worse for you now as you cope with both deaths. Call me any time of the day or night if you feel these panic attacks coming on. Promise me you will."

"I will, Lois. I promise."

"How are your finances, Maddie?" Lois gently asked.

"Well, I mean, now that Francis is gone, things will be tough without his income. I'll be all right for a while. I mean, we have a small savings built up, and Francis had enough insurance to bury himself. But really, the last thing on my mind right now is finances."

Pulling into the driveway of her dead brother's home hit Lois hard, and she began to cry. These were the first real tears she had actually shed for her brother. She put the car into park and leaned over to hug Maddie. They both had a good cry. Finally, opening her car door, Maddie thanked Lois once again and stepped out gingerly.

Rolling her window down, Lois yelled to Maddie not to worry about any of the funeral arrangements; she would take care of everything with Tom Latchkey later that day.

"Thank you, Lois. I love you." With that, Lois pulled out of the driveway.

Unlocking the front door, Maddie heard the phone ringing. Rushing to answer it, she was greeted by the voice of her neighbor Delores. "How are you, Maddie?"

"I'm doing the best I can, Delores."

"I just called to tell you if you need anything I'm right next door."

Maddie thanked Delores graciously but said that right now she just wanted to lay down.

"Okay, Maddie. Well, call me later, and take care of yourself."

Thanking Delores, Maddie hung up the phone and then took it off the hook. She didn't want to talk to anyone else that day. It was now five o'clock, and she was absolutely exhausted. Those pills made her so tired. She went upstairs, put on her nightgown, and lay down in her bed. The house was so chilly that she had to get back up and add another blanket to the pile of covers on the bed. Lying back down, she fell into a fitful sleep. She woke at three in the morning to noises in the hallway. *I wish Francis was here,* she couldn't help but think. Reaching over to the nightstand, she swallowed another pill and placed a pillow on top her head. Within minutes, she was asleep again.

The sun was bright in her bedroom window when she awoke. Looking at the clock, she saw that it was seven in the morning, and she felt refreshed. Crawling out from under the covers, she could see her breath in the room. *The furnace must be off again,* she deduced. She walked downstairs to the thermostat. It had been turned back the whole way. *Who would have done that?* She turned it up to seventy degrees and went back upstairs to take a bath. After bathing, she dressed and went downstairs. She could now hear the furnace running, but there was still that awful chill in the air. She put the phone back on the hook, and within minutes it was ringing. Answering the phone, she heard Lois's familiar voice. "Maddie, I'm coming over to get a suit to bury Francis in."

"Okay, Lois, I'll have it ready. Thank you."

Maddie quickly ate some cereal. She was starving, as she had not eaten anything yesterday. As she was putting her dishes away, there was a knock at the door. Answering it, she was greeted by Lois.

"That was quick. Wait, I'll run upstairs and get the suit." She climbed the stairs and went into their bedroom. Opening the closet door, she retrieved Francis's one and only suit, the same suit he wore on the day they buried Elijah. She grabbed the old black shoes he had also worn to Elijah's funeral and headed downstairs. Handing them to Lois, she inquired about the arrangements Lois had made.

"Maddie, I decided we will view Francis tonight between seven and nine at Latchkey's Funeral Home. He will be buried beside Elijah in Upper Claar Cemetary, tomorrow morning at ten. Tom Latchkey said not to worry about paying him until you get the insurance money. He said if you need help calling the insurance company, he'll do it for you."

"No, Lois, I'll call my insurance agent when you leave, and he can handle it."

"Okay. I'll pick you up at six tonight to go to the viewing. Bye."

Maddie closed the door behind Lois and went to the phone. She dialed her agent Thomas Philmore's phone number. The Stones had been with him for the last thirty years. Answering the phone, Maddie explained to Tom what had happened, to which he replied, "Maddie, I'll take care of everything. The policy is for two thousand dollars. That should be enough to bury Francis. They should send you a check within a month."

"Thank you, Tom." Maddie hung up the phone and went to the living room and plopped down on the couch. It was already ten in the morning, and the house was a mess. She got up and cleaned furiously. *I know people will be dropping by constantly,* she thought to herself. The people never came.

Francis's death spread through the community like a wildfire. People were constantly talking about the run of bad luck the Stones seemed to be having.

Six o'clock came quickly, and Lois was pulling into the driveway just as Maddie was buttoning her black dress. She slipped her shoes on quickly and ran downstairs. Lois had been knocking at the door for some time when Maddie answered. "Are you ready, Maddie? We'll be late."

"Yes, I suppose I'm ready."

As they walked to the car, Maddie noticed that Lois's husband Bob was driving. Her son, Andy, was in the backseat. Maddie opened the door and slid in beside Andy. Nothing was said as they drove to Latchkey's. Everyone was very solemn. They arrived at the funeral home at six-thirty. No other cars were in the parking lot yet. Getting out of the car, they walked slowly to the front door of the funeral home, almost dreading going in.

Tom greeted them at the door. "Come on in," he exclaimed. He walked the family to the casket. It was a nice-looking casket, much nicer than the one Elijah was buried in. *Must be expensive,* Maddie thought to herself. Looking down at her husband, she began to cry. "Oh Francis, what have you done?" *Now I'm alone,* she thought to herself. His body was stiff and gray in color. It didn't even look like Francis. Maddie and Lois hugged in front of the dead body of their husband and brother, tears filling both their eyes. They were interrupted by mourners who started filing past the casket. Maddie had forgotten her nerve medicine, and it was showing as she stared out into space. Lois had always held up like a true Stone, so to speak. The emotion had now left her face, and she was shaking hands and hugging people she barely knew. Maddie sat down and greeted no one. Everyone seemed to understand that she was distraught. Everyone, that is, but Lois. She was angry at how Maddie was behaving. The two hours of the viewing seemed like an eternity to Maddie. Finally, it was over, and Lois retrieved the guest book. Over three hundred people had viewed her brother. "I guess Francis was an extremely well-liked man," Lois said to her husband Bob. Only seventy-five people had turned out to view and bury Elijah.

Lois handed the book to Maddie. She tucked it under her arm and asked Lois to please drive her home so she could take some nerve medicine. They left the funeral home at ten-thirty that night. The house was dark as they pulled into the driveway. Not a word was spoken on the way home or as Maddie got out of the car and walked up to her driveway. In fact, Lois made Bob back out of the driveway before Maddie was even in her home. *Strange,* she thought as she opened the door. *I know I left the kitchen light on.*

She reached to turn on a lamp in the living room, but it did not light. She began to cry. The main fuse down in the basement must have blown again. Feeling her way to the kitchen, she found the junk drawer and pulled out the flashlight, the same flashlight she and Francis had found their son's body with, the flashlight Francis had used the night he died. She was sobbing uncontrollably as she walked to the basement door. The batteries were now so weak that only a glimmer of light radiated from the flashlight. She had always been a tough old woman, she thought. She tried never to show emotion. But now she could not help herself as she sobbed, walking down the cellar steps. She shone the dull light over to the fuse box. It was so cold she felt her breath crystallize as soon as it hit the air. Someone was here with her; she felt it in her bones. Shining the light around the room revealed nothing. Suddenly the silhouette of a man in a uniform appeared and vanished quickly. She began to shake uncontrollably. "Is someone here?" she screamed. *I must be hallucinating,* she thought.

Quickly, she opened the fuse box, found the main fuse, and pulled it out. Looking around, she could not find a replacement. Francis had used the last new fuse and did not buy replacements. She shone the light around once more. No one was there. Maddie ran back up the steps quickly, tripping on each step as she went. Going back into the kitchen, she found a box of candles. She lit several and placed each in its own candleholder. Leaving one in the kitchen, she took the remaining two candles to the living room. Placing one on a coffee table, she climbed the stairs to her bedroom where she placed the last remaining candle. *At least I can see now,* she thought to herself. The hallucination from the basement still troubled her as she went back downstairs and locked the front door. She thought of calling Lois. No, she didn't want everyone to think she was helpless. *I'll get through the night and pick some fuses up after the funeral,* she thought. It was now eleven-thirty, so she picked the candle up from the coffee table and went to the kitchen to blow out the candle she had left there. She scooped it up in case she needed it in the middle of the night. Turning, she left the kitchen and walked back upstairs. At the top of the steps she could swear she heard noises coming from Elijah's room. Scared, she darted into her own bedroom and locked it. She had never locked her bedroom door before, not when Francis was alive, at least. *I must be going crazy,* she concluded. Walking to her nightstand, she swallowed three nerve pills instead of the prescribed one at a time. The house was freezing since the furnace could not run without power. She couldn't even wash her face because the well pump needed power to run.

She collapsed into bed, rolling the covers around her. Leaving both candles burning, she fell into a deep sleep. At nine o'clock the following morning, she woke with the sun shining in her eyes through the bedroom window. The candles had burned out in the middle of the night with the wax running out over the candle holder and down to her nightstand. Looking at her watch, she realized she had less than an hour to get ready for the funeral. She went to the bathroom to wash and realized her power was still off. She really needed a bath. Reaching over out of desperation, she went through the motion of turning the faucet on. The water gushed out. That made no sense at all she thought. She walked over and turned the light switch on. The lights came on. *I must be going crazy,* she thought. She quickly bathed and put on her black dress for the funeral. It was now nine-thirty. She unlocked the bedroom door and walked downstairs. Strange, the light was on in the living room. She went into the kitchen and fixed breakfast. It was a bowl of cold cereal, as usual. Putting the dish in the sink, she heard a horn blowing. Looking out the window, she saw that Lois was waving for her to hurry. Opening the door, Lois yelled, "Come on, we're going to be late if you don't hurry up!" It was nine forty-five, and the funeral was going to start at ten.

She got into the backseat with Andy, and Bob sped away. "Thank goodness the cemetery is only ten minutes away," stated Lois. They arrived at the cemetery at five till ten. Parking in the lot at the Baptist church, they quickly walked up the hill to where Francis's burial place was located. There was a crowd of approximately one hundred people gathered around the grave site when Maddie and Lois sat down in the seats provided for them in the front. Lois nodded for the pastor to begin. Maddie seemed to still be a little groggy from the nerve pills.

The pastor delivered a beautiful eulogy about a loving father and husband. "A wonderful man who was always ready to lend a hand to those in need, Francis was a fellow Christian who attended church regularly." Maddie gazed around and noticed that no one was crying. Most eyes were turned toward the ground with solemn expressions on their faces. She wondered whether they were here out of friendship, love, or just plain duty. Maddie was all cried out. She made up her mind this morning that she would shed no more tears, so there she sat stoically, no expression on her face. Finishing up, the pastor informed the crowd there would be no reception after the service. This was a decision made by Francis's sister, Lois. He said a final prayer, and it was over. The crowd slowly walked down the hill to their cars, leaving Maddie and Lois alone on the hill with Tom Latchkey. "You ladies can go. I'll finish up here," Tom said.

Turning without saying a word to Tom, they walked to the car together. "Maddie, if you need driven somewhere this week for groceries or whatever, call me," Lois reminded her.

"Okay, I will, but I'm fine. Thank you."

They got into the car, and Bob drove Maddie home. Upon pulling into the driveway, Maddie thanked Bob and Lois for everything they had done.

"Good-bye, Andy." She opened the car door and went to the front porch. Waving as they pulled away, Maddie sat on the front stoop of her porch. She didn't feel like going into the house. It was a bright, sunny day so she just sat there and daydreamed. Finally, after what seemed like an eternity, she got up, unlocked the door, and went inside. She tried the lights. They worked fine. Shaking her head, she turned the television on and sat down on the couch. She was lonely. It seemed so strange with no one to talk to. She did not move from the couch all day. At five-thirty, she fixed herself supper. *I better get used to eating alone,* she thought. A canned bowl of soup was all she could manage to eat. Putting the dishes into the sink, she returned to the couch and lay down. Chills ran down her back. It was so cold. *Winter is just around the corner,* she thought. Her mind kept racing from one thing to the next. Glancing at the clock, she noticed it was nine o'clock. Where had the day gone? She did not feel like going upstairs yet. *Maybe I'll sleep on the couch.* Just then, there was a crashing sound upstairs. Without thinking, she raced up the stairs.

Elijah's bedroom door was hanging wide open. As she reached to close it, the door slammed shut by itself. Maddie did not believe in spirits, and she was not about to start that night. She must have closed the door herself, she thought. Her mind seemed so confused. She turned, stumbled downstairs, locked the front door, and went back upstairs to bed. Walking to the nightstand, she picked up and swallowed another nerve pill. With her dress still on, she collapsed into bed and kicked her shoes to the floor. She was dizzy, and the room was spinning. *I must be having a panic attack,* she thought. Tears streamed down her face. She had no energy. Maddie drifted to sleep.

At three in the morning, she awoke and began choking. Someone seemed to be strangling her. Opening her eyes, there was no one in the room. She struggled free, went to the bathroom, and turned the light on. There were reddish-purple bruises on her neck. *The covers must have wrapped around my neck,* she thought foolishly. She flicked the light off and returned to bed. Lying on the bed, Maddie reached over, grabbed another nerve pill, and gulped it down. Within minutes, she was sound asleep. She did not wake up until ten-thirty the next day. She never got out of bed. The phone rang and rang all day. She never moved. Every few hours, she would take another nerve pill. The house seemed cold and damp. She didn't care; she stayed under the covers. For three days she lay in bed not moving, not eating, only drinking water and gulping down nerve pills. Doors and windows slammed throughout the night as she stayed locked in her bedroom, falling deeper and deeper into depression.

Finally, on the fourth day of Maddie not answering her phone, Lois drove to her house and knocked on the door. It was nine o'clock in the morning. "Maddie, let me in."

She continued to knock until Maddie rose from bed for the first time in days, tottered down the steps, and walked to the front door, cracking it open.

"Maddie, are you all right?"

"Yes, I'm fine," she replied.

"Well, just let me in," Lois pleaded.

"No. I'm fine. Just let me alone," Maddie replied in a harsh voice.

Lois turned to leave. "Are you sure you don't need anything?"

"I said to leave me alone, Lois." Maddie slammed the door in her face. Locking it, she went back to bed.

Slouched on her bed, Maddie made the decision to end her life that night. Everything she had ever cared about was gone, and neither her son nor her husband was coming back. She gulped down the four remaining nerve pills and began drawing a hot bath. She staggered to the medicine cabinet, opened it, and pulled out Francis's straight razor. Walking back to the bathtub, she noticed stream rising from the hot water. Maddie removed her clothing and slid into the scalding water, which was so searing she could barely stand it. The water was filled almost to the top of the tub when she shut it off. Maddie opened the razor as if in a trance, then held her left wrist under the water and slit it wide open. Funny, she couldn't even feel it. She repeated the process with her right wrist. The water immediately turned a deep crimson red. Looking up, dazed, she saw a silhouette of Elijah in his uniform, watching the cherry blood drain from her body. He seemed to be smiling. She reached out toward him, but as quickly as it had appeared, the figure vanished. Slowly, she lost consciousness, and her head slid delicately under the water. Maddie was dead. The house was silent.

Maddie's body lay in the tub decaying for three days. Her skin began to wrinkle and turn a pale white. Amazingly, the house was so cold that it had preserved her body quite well; nevertheless, rigor mortis had begun to set in. Every ounce of her blood seemed to have drained into the tub. The water was still colored scarlet.

There was a knock at the door on that very overcast Friday morning. No one answered, and the knocking became louder. It was the next-door neighbor, Delores. She had not seen or heard from Maddie since the funeral. *Something must be wrong,* she thought. She ran to her home to get a spare key Francis and Maddie had given her years ago. Delores lived alone. Her husband had been killed in an accident ten years prior, and she had never remarried. Now, as she searched for the spare key, she became frantic. She had deliberately avoided Francis and Maddie since Elijah died. She did not want to relive the pain of death again. She was sure Maddie would forgive her for not going to the funeral of Elijah and now Francis. Finally, she located the key in a kitchen drawer. It was labeled Stone, so she knew it was the right one.

Running back to the house, Delores opened the front door. "Maddie, are you home?" The house was so cold she could barely stand it. There was also a foul stench about the home. "Maddie, where are you?" Delores screamed. She was so nervous she began shaking. Looking in the kitchen, she found no one. The living room yielded the same result. Fear engulfed her as she climbed the stairs. "Maddie, are you up here?" There were noises in a bedroom. It was Elijah's room. Opening the door, she found nothing. *Am I hearing things,* she wondered. She went to the other bedroom door and opened it. No one there either. The bathroom was accessible through Maddie's bedroom as well as an outside door in the hallway. Not knowing this, Delores closed the bedroom door and opened the last door upstairs. It was the bathroom door.

Seeing Maddie in the tub full of blood, Delores passed out. Minutes later, she came to her senses and began screaming. She ran down the steps, out the front door, and to her house. She was in such a hurry she had left the front door wide open at Maddie's house. Calling the police station, Officer Nick Singles, a young man in his thirties, answered the phone. He had just moved to Claysburg and had become the youngest police officer on their force. Delores was crying hysterically as she explained the scene at Maddie's home. Nick tried to calm her down. "Can you go to the house and stay there until I arrive with the paramedics?"

"No!" was the answer he sternly received. "I am staying right here in my home," replied Delores.

"All right, I'll be right over."

It seemed like an eternity until Delores could see the police lights flashing in Maddie's driveway. She would not go over. She wasn't about to look at Maddie's body one more time. She picked up the phone to call Lois, who answered on the first ring. "Lois, this is Delores, Maddie's neighbor. There has been an accident of some sort. Maddie is dead. Can you come right over?"

Before Delores could say good-bye, Lois had dropped the phone and was screaming for Bob to take her to Maddie's house.

"What's wrong?" Bob asked.

"It's Maddie. She's dead."

"What happened?" Bob yelled, surprised by the news.

"I don't know. We need to get right over there. The police are there now."

Nick Singles arrived there before the paramedics. The door was wide open, so he entered the house and ran up the steps. The bathroom door was open, and what he saw made him gag. Maddie's naked body was wrinkled and bloated. The decaying corpse was lying in a tub full of blood, with only the top of her head rising from the water. A putrid stench emanated from the bathroom. Making his way closer, Nick turned pale. The smell was so bad that he ran down the steps and outside. After vomiting, he began to gasp for fresh air. In all his life, he had never seen anything like this. He hadn't been prepared for such a gruesome sight.

Finally, the paramedics arrived. After receiving Nick's explanation of the situation, they removed a black vinyl body bag from the ambulance. Placing it atop a wooden stretcher, they climbed the stairs. Minutes later, both paramedics ran down the steps and out into the fresh air. Asking Nick to help them lift the body from the tub, they got the reply, "There is no way in hell I'm going back up those steps." Both paramedics returned to the ambulance; donning white medical masks, they walked back toward the house once again.

"You don't really think that will help," Nick said sarcastically.

"No," they replied in unison, "but it's better than nothing."

As the paramedics were making their way up the steps, Bob and Lois pulled into the driveway. Before Nick could spit out a word, Lois said, "That's my sister-in-law. What happened?"

"I'm sorry," was his reply. "Your sister-in-law has passed away."

"How?" screamed Lois.

"I'm not sure. We'll have to let the medical examiner determine that."

"I want to go see her," Lois pleaded with Nick.

"Ma'am, trust me, you do not want to see her this way. She has been dead for several days in a bathtub. Just wait here. The paramedics are going to bring the body down soon."

It took the two paramedics forty-five minutes to drain the tub and place Maddie's body into the body bag. They then lifted her bloated, foul-smelling body onto the stretcher and carried her downstairs to the ambulance. Both were pale as they closed the ambulance door and turned to Nick. "We'll talk to you later, Nick. I'll have the medical examiner call Chief Robinson."

"Thanks, guys," Nick replied.

"No, thank you," they said jokingly as they left.

"Lois, will you and your husband lock up here?" asked Nick.

"Yes," she replied. "Will you call us as soon as you know anything?"

"I will," Nick promised.

Lois and Bob went into the house after Officer Singles drove away. "Bob, I need to find Maddie's house keys so we can get back in the house from time to time to check on it. I'll look in the kitchen, and you check the living room."

"Lois," Bob yelled from the living room, "check to see if Maddie and Francis have any important papers in the kitchen drawer."

Lois appeared in the living room hallway. "What kind of important papers, Bob?"

"Well, while we're here we should see if they had a will."

"Bob, that's morbid. Maddie's not even buried, and already you want to know if we'll benefit from her death!"

"Lois, I didn't mean it that way. We'll need to make funeral arrangements for her. Latchkey's hasn't even received payment for Francis yet. Do you want to pay for Maddie's funeral with our savings?"

"All right, you have a point, Bob. I'll look around in the kitchen." She rummaged through drawer after drawer, finding nothing. "Bob, nothing is in here." She returned to the living room to find Bob watching television. "What is wrong with you, Bob? Help me find the damn keys so we can get out of this house. It gives me the creeps in here. So much death has come from this house in such a short time. Don't you think it is a little odd?"

"Lois, don't get superstitious on me. The Stones were responsible for their own deaths, not the house. After all, they had lived here most of their lives with no problem until Elijah committed suicide."

"Yeah, I guess you're right, Bob. Come on, let's find the keys."
He got up to turn the television off but not without first admiring how nice the black and white picture was. "I think we should take this television home, Lois. It's so much nicer than ours. Francis must have paid a fortune for it. It's RCA's newest console model. Would you take a look at this, Lois? Lois?"

"Bob, if you don't get off your ass and help me find these keys, we are going to have a major argument!"

"All right, Lois, I'll look for the stupid keys." Bob started searching for the keys on top of the coffee table and under the couch cushions, finding nothing. "They must be upstairs in her bedroom, Lois."

Looking toward the steps, Lois hesitated. "You go first, Bob."

"Get out of the way." Bob quickly climbed the steps with Lois right behind him. Rounding the corner, he saw that the bathroom door was wide open. The floor was wet from where they had placed Maddie's body after lifting her from the tub which was now bloodstained. He closed the door before Lois could see anything. Walking past the closed door, Bob opened Maddie's bedroom door. There on her nightstand, he saw a set of keys and an empty pill bottle. Retrieving the keys, he handed them to Lois. "Here are the keys you wanted so badly." Bob opened the bedroom closet doors.

"What are you doing now, Bob?"

"I'm looking for a will, checkbooks, or any other important papers they might have tucked away."

"Why would they be in a closet, Bob? Use your head."

"I don't know. I'm just looking, Lois, for heaven's sake."

Lois walked to a small desk in the far corner of the bedroom. Opening the center drawer, she found a checkbook and a savings book. "Here it is, Bob." Lois opened them and exclaimed, "What a shame! You work your entire life and all you have to show for it is one thousand three hundred and fifty dollars? That's checking and savings combined. Maddie would never have been able to survive on her own."

Bob pulled open the bottom drawer of the desk and exclaimed, "There it is, the last will and testament of Francis and Maddie Stone."

"Read it quick!" Lois exclaimed excitedly. No sooner had Lois spoken than a door slammed somewhere in the house.

Running to the top of the steps, Bob yelled, "Who's down there?" No one answered. He walked down the steps with Lois in tow, holding the checkbook and will pressed tightly against her body. "Anyone here?" he yelled again. Still no answer. Looking up, both noticed that the front door was wide open. "Didn't you shut the door, Lois?" She insisted that she had.

"Well I guess that's our cue to leave," Bob said jokingly.

"Real funny," Lois snorted.

"You must not have closed the door tight, and the wind blew it open," Bob chuckled. "Lois, let's get out of here anyway. I'm tired and hungry." That said, Bob locked the door and pulled it shut. Looking up, he noticed that Lois was already in the car, and she had begun reading the will. Jogging to the car, he opened the door and, poking his head inside, said, "Well, what's the verdict?"

"They left everything to Elijah, and in the event of his death, the entire estate is to go to Francis's only sister, me. Bob, do you hear? They left everything to me."

"Lois, didn't Maddie have any family?"

"No, just some distant relatives she'd never met. It says that I am also to serve as executor of the estate. Well, I know they had no debts, and the house was paid for years ago, so I guess we made out all right."

"What do you mean we? They left everything to you."

"Stop clowning around, Bob. Let's go home and I'll make supper." Bob pulled from the driveway and headed home.

Arriving home, Lois prepared a meal of leftovers from the preceding day for Bob and Andy.

"Lois, I'd like to say it was a great supper, but I'd be lying," Bob joked as he left the kitchen and went to the living room. "If you need me I'll be reading the paper," he yelled from the living room.

Lois did not bother to answer him. Funny, she felt no remorse for Maddie's death. She kept telling herself Maddie could never have survived without Francis. She would have been a burden to her and Bob anyway. Her death was for the best. Picking up the phone in the kitchen, she called the hospital. Nurse Betty Wysong answered. Lois knew her from playing bingo together. "Betty, did you hear about Maddie Stone?"

"Yes, I did, Lois. They delivered her body here for an autopsy hours ago. I'm so sorry for your loss. Your family has sure had more than its fair share of grief the past two months."

"Betty, will you call me when they're done with the autopsy?"

"I sure will, but they probably won't do it until later tonight. The medical examiner said he would be over after supper, so he should be here any time now."

"Thanks a million. Call me or have the medical examiner call me with the results. Do you have my phone number?"

"Yes, I have it somewhere in my purse. I'll talk to you in a little while."

Lois hung up the phone and went to the living room to talk to Bob. Sitting down beside him on the sofa, she sighed.

"What now?" Bob asked

"Do you think I should call Tom Latchkey? He'll think I'm nuts. Three funerals in a month and a half from the same family."

"Call him and get it over with," Bob grunted at her.

She went back to the kitchen and dialed the number. By now she had it memorized. "Tom, hi, yes, it's Lois Wyandt. You'll never believe me when I tell you this."

"Yes, I will," he countered grimly. "I've already heard the news about Maddie. Lois, in a small town like this, you know there are no secrets."

"Oh, yes. Of course. Well anyway, it falls on my shoulders to bury Maddie. She had no insurance on herself, so Bob and I will have to shoulder the expense of burying her."

"I'm sorry to hear that," Tom said halfheartedly.

"After they paid for Elijah's funeral, it really hurt their savings, so they basically had no money left to bury Maddie. When the insurance check comes for Francis, I'll endorse it over to you."

"How can you do that?"

"I'm the executor of the estate now."

"That will be fine then. When will they transport Maddie's body here?"

"Sometime tomorrow, I guess. They're doing the autopsy tonight."

"What type of funeral do you want to have for Maddie?"

"Well, since I'm paying, I want to keep it simple. Bury her beside Francis, in the cheapest casket you have. Bob and I have decided that there will be no viewing or funeral services. Keep the expenses down, Tom. After she is buried, I will take her pastor up to say some words over her grave."

"Well, if that's the way you want it, Lois. I'll do it."

"Tom, one last thing. Can you give me a ballpark figure of how much it will cost us?"

There was a pause on the other end of the line. In a disturbed voice, Tom answered, "No more than seven hundred and fifty dollars."

"That's fine, Tom. Thank you so much." Lois hung up the phone. Returning to the living room, she once again sat down beside Bob.

Looking at her, Bob asked, "What's the verdict?"

"Well, Tom won't bury her for less than seven hundred and fifty dollars. I told him we wanted no viewing and no funeral services at graveside to keep the expenses down."

"Lois," Bob replied, "you are one cold woman."

"No. Do you realize that after we bury her there will only be six hundred dollars left in cash from her estate?"

"Is that all you can think about, the money? You just lost your sister-in-law."

"Bob, I don't want to talk about it anymore. It's done, okay."

Bob stood up and told her he was going to bed. She got up without speaking, turned on the television, and sat down on the sofa once again. She watched television for two hours before the phone rang. It was the medical examiner. "Lois, this is Robert Simons. Betty asked me to give you a call. I'm sorry to tell you this, but Maddie Stone took her own life. She slit her wrists and bled to death. I'll be writing this up as a suicide."

"Thank you for calling me, Robert." There was no emotion in her voice.
"You're quite welcome, Lois."
"Oh, and could you tell everyone that Tom Latchkey's Funeral Home will pick the body up tomorrow for burial?"
"I'll do that for you. Good night."
Lois hung up the phone, locked her front door, and went upstairs to bed. Bob was already fast asleep as she crawled under the covers and turned out the light.
Morning came early in the Wyandt household. Bob was up and out the door by five in the morning. The alarm usually was set for four. He was a logger and usually worked from five-thirty in the morning until three in the afternoon. He tried never to wake Lois that early in the morning, but somehow, he managed to make just enough noise to stir her from a sound sleep every day. Lying in bed, staring at him through half-closed eyes, she often wondered how, day in, day out, he could get up and work that job. It demanded so much energy, and the pay wasn't all that good. She had wanted him for years to try to get in the brickyard. He would not hear of it. He liked the outdoors. After getting dressed, Bob went downstairs and made his own breakfast. By five, Lois could hear the front door closing. She quickly drifted back to sleep.
Waking at six-thirty, she yelled for Andy to get ready for school. He was in eighth grade and was slow to get out of bed every day. He had to be out the door by seven to catch the bus. Andy only needed half an hour to get ready for school. He never ate breakfast. Lois dressed and went downstairs to make herself some coffee. Sitting down at the kitchen table, she heard Andy yell, "Bye, mom!" as he slammed the front door and ran to catch the bus.
It would be a busy day for Lois. She planned on driving to Maddie's house to clean up the place and bring home the items she wanted to keep for herself. She would stop at a lawyer's office to validate the will and have him do what was necessary to transfer the house and estate into her name.
Finishing the dishes, she left the house at eight-thirty. First she drove to the law office of Matthew Brinks. She had used him to prepare her and Bob's last will and testament. Lois never made appointments. She marched into the law office and asked the secretary to announce her to Matthew Brinks.
"Wouldn't you rather make an appointment?" the secretary asked politely.
"No, I would not. I have pressing matters that need taken care of right away." Her voice was louder than it should have been, considering the circumstances.

GET OUT!

Matthew poked his head out of his office and asked her to come back before there was a scene in his front office. "What can I help you with, Lois? I see you've met my new secretary."

"Matthew, she is very rude, and I think you should rethink hiring her."

"She does a fine job. It's her duty to make appointments. She was just doing her job."

"Well, I'm sorry for being so loud. I've been under a lot of stress lately. My sister-in-law just passed away, and now I'm the executer of her estate."

"I take it you're referring to the Stone estate, Lois."

"Yes, how did you know?"

"Lois, we live in a community where you can't sneeze without your neighbor finding out. What do you need from me?"

"I want to be able to write checks from Francis and Maddie's accounts to settle their bills. I also want the house transferred into my name."

"Do you have the last will and testament of the Stones?"

"Yes, here it is." She handed Matthew the paper.

Reading it quickly, he looked up and said, "This is all I need. Everything is to go to you, I see. You're within your legal right to do with it as you please. I'll take care of everything and send you a bill."

"Thank you so much, Matthew." She shook his hand and walked out the door.

Getting back into her car, she drove to Maddie's house. Pulling into Maddie's driveway she began looking over the exterior of the house. *It really needs a fresh coat of paint,* she thought to herself. After she parked the car, she began walking around the house. Looking over, she noticed Delores staring out her living room window. Lois motioned for her to come out. Coming to the front door of her house, Delores yelled for Lois to come over. Lois walked across Delores's yard and said, "How are you doing, Delores?"

"Well, I've been better. I can't believe what happened to Maddie. It's a tragedy, Lois. Did she leave a suicide note?"

"No, she didn't, Delores. She was so upset after Francis died, I guess, that she just didn't want to live anymore."

"I truly believe that house is cursed, Lois. Maddie told me she heard noises all the time. Ever since Elijah died, Maddie and Francis acted very strange. Lois, I will never go into that house again. It gives me the creeps. I don't like living next door, to be honest with you."

"Delores, you're overreacting," Lois almost laughed as she spit the words out. "The house is old, so you're going to hear noises. It's probably settling or something."

"Well, Lois, you can believe what you want, but you'll see when you go inside. It's like an ice box in there. Maddie told me they could never seem to get the place to warm up. Francis even had Maddie get a repairman to check the furnace out. It supposedly is working fine. Finding Maddie dead in that tub was the last straw for me. I want nothing to do with that house. Here is the spare set of house keys Maddie gave me. Do with them as you please. What will become of the house now that the entire family is dead, Lois?"

"She left the entire estate to me, Delores. I intend to fix the house up and rent it."

"Well, good luck, but trust me, be careful when you're in that house."

Lois was shaking her head as she turned and walked away from Delores. Walking back to the house, Lois continued to look the exterior up and down, trying to decide what would need to be done to rent it. Glancing up into the upstairs window, she thought she saw a figure pass by the window in Elijah's old room. She became nervous. "That damn Delores is just trying to spook me," she said out loud to herself. Looking to her left, she surveyed the garage in the back. *What an eyesore,* she thought. Most of the siding had either fallen off or was ready to fall off. *That's the last thing we'll put money into,* she decided. She went back to the front door of the house and fumbled through her pockets for the keys to the front door. She twisted the doorknob before putting the key in the lock. The door swung open. *How is that possible? I watched Bob lock the door yesterday before we left. I bet Delores was in the house last night. There had better be nothing missing,* she thought to herself.

Entering the house, she noticed the chill Delores had talked about. She walked to the thermostat on the wall. It was set at seventy degrees. There was no way it was seventy in there. She turned it up to eighty and immediately heard the furnace kick on downstairs. Walking to a floor vent, she felt warm air flowing. *Now it will warm up,* Lois thought with satisfaction.

She went to the kitchen and started opening drawers. In the corner of the kitchen, Maddie had a stack of cardboard boxes. Lois grabbed the stack and put them in the center of the room. She began clearing everything from the drawers and placing them into the boxes. Knives, forks, spoons, the toaster, everything went into the boxes. After she filled a box, she took it to her car, continuing the process over and over. Soon the entire kitchen was bare. *What I don't want to keep, I'll sell at a yard sale,* she decided. Next she went to the living room. Knickknacks, pictures, and lamps all went into cardboard boxes. Lois' car trunk was so full she had to tie it shut with a piece of rope. She went back in, gathered more items and began carrying them to the backseat of her car. By three o'clock, her entire backseat and passenger seat were full.

Going back into the house, she noticed it was so cold she could see her breath. *This is crazy,* she thought. The furnace had not stopped running yet, and the house was still like an icebox. She went to the kitchen, picked up the phone, and called her house. Bob picked up the phone. "Bob, this is Lois. Bring your pickup truck over; I'm cleaning out Francis's house. I want to get it ready to rent."

"Lois, you never said anything to me about renting the house."

"I didn't know I had to tell you. It will be a nice second income for us. Just get over here. You can load up this television you wanted so badly."

Hesitatingly, Bob replied, "I'll be right over."

After hanging up, Lois went back to the living room. She began to take an inventory of what else she wanted and what could stay. *The couch, end tables, and coffee table can stay. The more I leave in the house, the more rent I should be able to get for it if it's furnished,* she decided. *I'll leave the stove and refrigerator also.*

She was still deep in thought when she heard what sounded like someone walking around upstairs. It terrified her so much that she ran out the front door and was greeted by Bob. He had just pulled into the driveway in his beat-up pickup truck, the same truck he had driven to work in the past twelve years. "What the hell is wrong, Lois? You act like you've seen a ghost," he said jokingly.

"Bob, someone or something has to be upstairs. I was in the living room and heard someone walking around up there."

"You mean to tell me you have been downstairs all day and didn't hear someone until now? You're hearing things, woman." He went into the house, walked straight up the steps, and looked in every room upstairs. He yelled down the steps to Lois, "The coast is clear; you can come on up."

"Stop being sarcastic, Bob. I know what I heard."

"Well, I'm telling you, Lois, there is no one up here."

Lois went up the steps slowly and stood beside Bob, who said matter-of-factly, "There, see what I mean."

She just stood there and shook her head. "Delores from next door tried telling me this house is evil. I guess she just had me on edge."

"That woman is crazy, Lois. I told you that years ago. She stares out her window for hours on end and rarely comes out of her house. Why were you talking to her anyway?"

"I was just trying to be friendly."

"Well, next time don't, and maybe you'll stop overreacting."

"I suppose. While we're up here, haul down all of Francis's and Maddie's clothing, and put it in the back of your pickup. I also want the desk and lamps in Maddie's bedroom. I don't want to leave anything here today except for the furnishings I am including when I rent the house. Take all the sheets and covers off of the beds. Leave the beds in every room, as well as the night tables. You can also leave that old desk in Elijah's room. You don't want it, do you, Bob?"

"No, we have enough desks at home. I don't know why you want the desk in Maddie's room."

"You're right. Just leave it. Clear everything else out while I go to the bathroom and empty the medicine cabinet and get the towels and linens in there."

"Well, if you're going to the bathroom, you'd better clean it up in there. There are bloodstains on the floor and in the tub."

"Bob, that gives me the creeps!"

"Well, if you want to rent this place out, you can't very well show it off with bloodstains in the bathroom!"

"Okay, I guess you're right. You just start hauling stuff to the truck."

Lois went into the bathroom and gasped immediately at the sight of the blood on the linoleum floor were they had laid Maddie's body after lifting it from the tub. Looking down into the white porcelain tub, she noticed more stains and a straight razor lying in the tub. "Poor Maddie must have been extremely depressed to kill herself in such a horrible way," Lois said out loud. She opened the linen closet and threw all but one of the washcloths and towels out into the hallway for Bob to carry downstairs to his truck. She found some cleaning supplies under the sink and began scrubbing the blood from the floor. She then cleaned the tub and toilet. When she was done, the bathroom gleamed. She could hear Bob huffing and puffing as he was making numerous trips up and down the steps. She lifted the straight razor from the tub and then opened the medicine cabinet. It was a small cabinet with a mirror on the front. All that was left to do was clean out the cabinet. Lois scooped all the toiletries into a small hat box she had retrieved from Maddie's bedroom. It was dark outside now. She had been there all day and was tired. Closing the medicine cabinet, she screamed.

Bob ran from the bedroom next door. "What the hell are you screaming about now?"

"Bob, there was a man's face in the mirror of the medicine cabinet. I swear to God!"

Looking into the mirror, Bob began to laugh. "Well, the man in the mirror isn't there now. Look, Lois, it's a plain old mirror. The only thing weird about this house is the chill in it. Why didn't you turn the heat up when you came in this morning?"

"That's another thing. I did turn the thermostat up to eighty degrees, and it's still ice cold in here."

"Well, the thermostat must be broken then. Simple, we just need to fix it."

"Well, if you're so smart, why has the furnace been running all day long and blowing warm air, mind you, but the house is still cold?"

"Lois, I have no idea, but I do know you are stressed out and tired. Can't we finish this tomorrow?"

"No. I don't want to come back here any more than I need to."

"I have to make two more trips and then I'm done up here, okay?"

"Fine, I'll finish up downstairs in the living room." Before going downstairs, Lois looked into Maddie's room. The closets were empty in Maddie's bedroom, and the sleeping area was cleared out except for the furniture they had agreed to leave.

Bob was in Elijah's bedroom clearing out his closet when the door slammed behind him, locking him in the closet. He thought Lois was playing a practical joke until he sensed someone else in the closet with him. He felt hands around his throat. He began screaming hysterically.

Lois ran to the bedroom and opened the closet door. "What's wrong, Bob? Are you trying to scare me?"

Bob ran from the closet. "Damn it, Lois, did you lock me in there?"

"You know I'd never do that! Besides, the door wasn't locked."

"The hell it wasn't! It wouldn't open for me, and I'll tell you another thing, it felt like something was choking me in there. If you want to clear out Elijah's closet, be my guest. Those clothes can stay in there for eternity, as far as I'm concerned. Why didn't Maddie and Francis get rid of his clothes anyway?"

"Bob, just leave them. Maybe whoever rents the house can use them. Either that or they can throw them out themselves."

"Well, I'll tell you what, Lois. I pity the poor bastards that rent this house. You couldn't pay me to spend the night here. Let's get the hell out of here."

With that, they went downstairs together. The only thing left to carry out of the house was the television. Bob lifted the heavy set and stumbled to the pickup truck, stopping every couple steps to catch his balance. Heaving it into the back of the truck, he looked at Lois. "Can we leave now?"

"Yes, I have everything I want from the house. Do you want to go through it one more time to see if we missed anything? You know, we didn't even check the basement or garage."

"Woman, as far as I'm concerned, there could be a pot of gold in that basement and I wouldn't go down there to get it. Just rent the damn house out the way it is. Tell whoever rents this place that they can have any thing they want from the basement or garage. If they don't want it, they can throw it out. Now can we go home?"

"Fine. Turn out the living room light, lock the front door, and then we can go."

Bob went into the house to turn the lights off; before he could flick the switch, he heard a door slam upstairs. He pulled the switch down and ran out of the house, closing the front door behind him. Running to his pickup, he saw that Lois had already left. *Nice of her to wait for me,* he thought scornfully. Backing out of the driveway, he noticed he had left a bedroom light on. *Damn, I could have sworn we turned all the lights off upstairs,* he wondered to himself. *The hell with it. It'll keep burglars away. I'm not going back in that house tonight alone. I pity someone if they try to break into that house,* he thought, chuckling to himself. Bob headed toward his house, thinking about how he would hook that nice big television set up after supper.

Lois was cooking supper when Bob pulled into the driveway. He got out of the truck and started hauling all the items he had taken from the Stone home into his garage. Everything, that is, but the television set. He hauled that up to his front porch. After finishing about twenty trips to the garage, he propped open his front door and hauled the television in to his living room. He unhooked his small DuMont table model 180 set and carried it to his bedroom upstairs. It was practically an antique compared to Francis's RCA Fliptop model. Coming back down the steps, he yelled in to Lois, "Do you realize we will be the only people in the neighborhood to have two televisions?"

"Why on earth are you so damn happy about that television, Bob?"

"Because I happen to like watching it, that's why."

"Well, come in here and eat your supper before it gets cold. You can play with it after you eat."

Bob washed his hands in the kitchen sink and sat down beside Andy at the kitchen table. Andy hadn't said a word since Bob had been home. "So, Andy, did you see the size of that set I just carried in?"

"Yes, I did, but it seems sort of weird taking Aunt Maddie's television when she's not even buried yet."

"Well, she can't very well use it now, can she?"

GET OUT!

Andy looked away in disgust at his father. *Poor Aunt Maddie,* he thought to himself in silence.

Just then Bob realized what food had been placed in front of him — cold lunch meat sandwiches and soup from a can. "You have been making some great meals lately, Lois. How do you do it?"

"Listen, Bob, I'm tired too. Take it or leave it; this is all you're getting."

He shook his head and began to gulp down his food. After supper, Andy and Bob went in to the living room. Lois stayed in the kitchen, doing dishes and clearing the table. Andy sat down on the couch while his dad went straight to the television set. Hooking up the antenna, he grinned at Andy. "Wait till you see this picture, Andy."

"Dad, don't you think you're a little obsessed with that television?"

"Well, then don't watch it if you feel that way." Upon Bob turning on the television, the local station came on. Bob walked to the couch and told Andy to get out of his spot. "You know that's where I sit." Andy shook his head and slid over on the couch so his dad could sit down. Watching the television, Bob yelled to Lois to come look at its big screen and great picture. "Now that is a perfect black and white picture. Look at the clarity."

Lois stayed in the kitchen, yelling back, "I'm glad you like it so much, Bob." Finishing the dishes, Lois came into the living room and smiled. Bob was watching the news with Andy. She sat beside Andy on the sofa.

An hour passed before Bob started yawning. "Well, I have to get up at four. I better hit the sack." That said, Bob stood up and went upstairs to get ready for bed.

"Andy, I think it's time for you to go to bed, too," Lois said slowly.

"Mom, I'm not tired, and I'm not a kid. I think I know when it's time for bed."

"Andy, don't backtalk me. Get your butt up to bed now."

Not saying another word, Andy jogged up the steps and slammed his bedroom door. It was nine o'clock in the evening. Suddenly the phone rang. It startled Lois so much that she jumped off the couch and ran to the kitchen to answer the phone. It was Tom Latchkey. "Sorry to call you so late, Lois, but I thought you would like to know I'm burying Maddie's body tomorrow."

"That's fine, Tom."

"I'll be doing it around ten in the morning if you would like to come up with your family."

"Well, I'll drive up, but Andy has school tomorrow, and Bob's going to work. Thanks for calling, Tom. I'll see you tomorrow at ten in Upper Claar Cemetery." Hanging up the phone, Lois decided she had better call the pastor.

Looking up his phone number, she felt bad for calling him so late. Pastor Thompson answered on the third ring. "Sorry to disturb you, Pastor. This is Lois Wyandt. I was calling to see if you would meet me tomorrow in Upper Claar Cemetery at ten o'clock tomorrow. Maddie is going to be buried at that time."

"Well, yes, Lois, I can say a few words. Poor Maddie just did not take Francis's death very well. She was in severe depression."

"How did you know that?" asked Lois.

"Well, I talked to Doctor Stoltz, and he told me he had to prescribe nerve medicine for her. I tried calling Maddie, but she wouldn't answer the phone. Did she seem stressed when you visited her, Lois?"

"Yes, she did. She as good as slammed the door in my face the day she took her own life."

"Such a tragedy," Pastor Thompson whispered, his voice quivering as he spoke. "Lois, will there be many people attending the service?"

"No, pastor, I'm keeping it small. In fact, just you, Tom Latchkey, and I will be present. I just felt a preacher should say a few words over her grave since she committed suicide. I fear for her immortal soul."

"Lois, don't worry about Maddie; she was a saved Christian. Her soul is fine. I haven't seen you or Bob in church for some time. Is something wrong?"

"No, we've just been so busy. We'll make an effort to get there more often, I promise."

"Sounds good, Lois. See you tomorrow."

That done, Lois locked the front door, and walked up the stairs to bed. Crawling into bed, she heard Bob snoring extremely loudly. He didn't stop as she had hoped he would, thus the reason she couldn't sleep. Elbowing him in the ribs, he snorted and turned on his side. The snoring stopped, and Lois drifted to sleep. As usual, Bob was up at four getting ready for work. It was still pitch dark outside. He woke Lois when he banged his shin into the bedpost, and let out a loud curse. Lois was so tired from carrying things from Maddie's house yesterday that she went right back to sleep. She didn't even hear Bob leave for work. It was fifteen till nine when she awoke. The alarm didn't go off.

Running to Andy's room she opened the door. There he was, sound asleep. "Andy, get up. You missed the bus."

Andy jumped from his bed. "Why didn't you wake me up, Mom?"

"I overslept, Andy. I'm sorry. Get ready quick, and I'll drop you off at school on my way to bury Maddie."

"Mom, can't I just skip today?"

"No, get dressed now." Lois returned to her bedroom and put on a black dress quickly. She didn't have time to bathe. Slipping into her shoes, she yelled for Andy.

He was already downstairs waiting at the front door. "I'm going to wait for you in the car, Mom."

"Okay, Andy. I'll be out in a minute." She ran down the steps and out the front door to the car. Realizing she forgot her purse, she ran back into the house and grabbed it. Opening the purse, she took her car keys out and glanced at the clock. It was nine fifteen. She ran back out the door and got into the car. Starting it, she backed out the driveway and started speeding to the school.

"Mom, don't you want me to go with you to Aunt Maddie's funeral?"

"No, Andy, you don't need to go."

"Mom, I want to."

Lois pulled off the road and looked at Andy. "Are you sure?"

"Yes, I'm sure."

She turned around and headed to Upper Claar Cemetery. They arrived in the cemetery parking lot at fifteen till ten. The pastor was waiting for Lois as she parked her car beside his. "Hi, Lois. I see you brought Andy along," the pastor said in a friendly way.

"Yes. He insisted on coming."

The three walked up the hill together. Tom Latchkey greeted them with the two men who had just dug the grave. The closed casket was over top of the freshly dug hole, ready to be lowered in. It was a very cheap model, much like Elijah's.

"You might as well start, Pastor Thompson," Lois instructed.

The pastor spoke of what a fine Christian woman Maddie was. "She was saved as a child," he said with a sad voice, "and I expect to see her in heaven." He ended his eulogy with a long prayer, and the service was over. The three of them watched as the casket was lowered into the ground.

"Thank you so much," Lois said, handing him an envelope with thirty dollars in it. "This is for you taking time from your busy day to perform the service."

"Thank you for the love offering, Lois. I do appreciate it."

They walked down the hill together. No one spoke; after all, what else could be said? Andy and Lois got into their car and drove away as Tom was speaking to the Pastor.

"Well, Andy, you got to skip a day of school. Happy? I need to stop at the funeral home and pay Tom Latchkey for his services, and then we'll go home and have lunch, okay?"

"Sounds good to me, Mom," Andy replied.

Pulling into Latchkey's Funeral Home, Lois parked the car. "Wait here. I'll be right out." Lois went to the side office door and knocked.

Tom's wife, Ann, answered and opened the door. "Hi, Lois, come in."

"Ann, I came to pay you for Maddie's burial."

"Sit down, and I'll get the bill." Ann came back with a bill for six hundred and ninety-five dollars.

Lois was surprised since it was cheaper than what Tom had quoted her on the phone. "Is a check all right?"

"Yes, that's fine.

Lois wrote out a check for the amount from her and Bob's personal account. She thanked Ann and walked out the door. It was a cold, bright, sunny day. She felt unusually happy today. Getting into the car, she looked at Andy and said, "Let's eat lunch at the diner."

"That sounds great, Mom."

Lois drove to Pat's Diner and pulled into the parking lot. Before going into the diner, Lois noticed there were quite a few people from town eating lunch. They went in and sat down. When the waitress came, Lois ordered hamburgers, fries, and Cokes for the two of them. After the waitress left, Lois looked at Andy and asked, "Will you miss Aunt Maddie and Uncle Francis?"

"Mom, you know I will. We never went to visit them much. Now I wish that we had."

Lois noticed that several people at the other tables kept looking at her and Andy. They whispered and stared like they didn't know her. Most of them she had known for ten years or more. No one spoke to her; it was like they were trying to avoid her. *I wonder what they are saying,* she thought to herself.

The food arrived, and Andy ate so fast that she had to tell him to slow down. "You act like you never ate in a restaurant before, Andy!"

"The food is great, Mom, and I'm hungry."

After they finished eating, Lois paid the bill and started walking out of the restaurant with Andy in tow. She felt like everyone in the restaurant was watching them leave. *What has gotten into these people?* she wondered, confused.

Lois and Andy got into their car and began the short drive home. Pulling into her driveway and parking the car, Lois was glad it was all over. Maddie

GET OUT!

was buried, so Lois, Andy, and Bob could get on with their lives. Andy opened the car door, jumped out, and ran into the house. He turned on the television and flopped down on the couch. Even though they could only get one station, it was the centerpiece of their home. A soap opera was on. Lois went into the house and sat down beside him. They watched television until Bob was heard pulling into the driveway. Lois got up and ran out of the house to greet Bob before he could get out of his truck. "Bob, do me a favor," she yelled as he rolled down the window.

"What do you need?"

"Go to the hardware store and get a For Rent sign. Get a wooden stake also. Then run over to Maddie's house and put it in the yard. Make sure you write our phone number on it with a permanent marker."

"Do I have to? I'm tired."

"Just do it, Bob. When you get back, I'll have a nice home-cooked meal ready for you."

"As long as I don't have to go inside, I'll do it."

"What's the matter? I thought you said there was nothing wrong with the house."

"Lois, I was just kidding. I'm not afraid of that house. Everything that happened last night in that house has a logical explanation. I'm sure of it," Bob replied confidently.

"I'm tired of talking about it, Bob. Just get the sign in place and come home for supper." Lois turned to go back inside as Bob pulled out and drove away. She opened and closed the front door and went directly to the kitchen. She took a roast from the refrigerator and placed it in a pan. She would make a meal fit for a king tonight. *I'm tired of Bob complaining about my meals,* she thought to herself. *If he complains about this, he needs his head examined.*

Lois was in the kitchen an hour and a half when she heard Bob come through the front door. "Is supper ready?" he yelled.

"Bob, get Andy, and go wash up. It will be ready in five minutes."

Both Andy and Bob rushed to the kitchen sink, turned the water on, and lathered their hands up with soap.

"You two must be starved," laughed Lois.

"I could eat a cow, Lois," Bob joked.

"Well, that's funny, because we are having cow. How does roast beef, mashed potatoes, corn, and gravy sound?"

"Now that's a meal." The food smelled great as Bob, Lois, and Andy sat down to eat.

"Well, Lois, how was your day?"

"Andy stayed home today and went to the grave with me to bury Maddie."

"Why didn't you tell me you were burying her today? I would have stayed home from work."

"That's why I didn't tell you. There was no need for you to miss a day of work. I had the preacher come up and say words over her before we buried her. It was a nice service with just Andy, the pastor, and me. After the service, we ate lunch at Pat's Diner. It was weird, Bob. It seemed as all the people were staring at us while we ate."

"Lois, there goes that imagination of yours."

Andy said nothing as they ate. He was too busy wolfing down his food.

"Okay, enough talking. Let's eat this delicious meal," Bob declared.

After finishing his meal, Bob rose from the table. "Lois, you outdid yourself with that meal."

"Yeah, Mom, it was awesome," Andy chimed in.

Both raced into the living room to watch television. As usual, Lois was stuck cleaning the table and doing the dishes. When she was done, she joined them in the living room and inquired, "Bob, did you get the sign up at Maddie's?"

"Yes I did, Lois, but don't expect the phone to be ringing off the hook for people to rent it."

"Well, we'll see what happens over the next couple of weeks. If it doesn't rent, I'll put it up for sale. Okay, Bob?"

"Sounds good to me. Now can we watch the television?"

"All right, watch your precious television. I'm going upstairs to read a book. I'm so tired from running nonstop the past few days."

"Goodnight, Lois. I love you."

"Night, Bob."

After telling Andy goodnight, Lois went up the steps to her room, changed into her bedclothes, and crawled into bed. Lifting the Bible from her nightstand, she began to read from the book of Daniel. A half an hour later, she was asleep. It was only seven-thirty in the evening.

Bob and Andy watched television until nine-thirty before going to bed. That was a late night for both of them. Unlike Lois, Bob hardly ever locked the door before going to bed. He always seemed to forget. After following Andy up the steps, he went straight to bed, and within minutes was snoring.

Waking up at four in the morning for work, Bob was startled by a noise from downstairs. *Don't tell me I'm going to start hearing noises in this house,* he thought to himself. Walking down the steps slowly, he realized he forgot to lock the door the night before. He ran back up the steps quietly and picked up a ball bat he had stashed in a hall closet. Walking back down the steps with the bat raised above his head, Bob was nervous. "Damn, how could I forget to lock that door again?" he exclaimed nervously out loud. At the bottom of the steps, he peered around the corner into the kitchen to see where the noise was coming from. It was Lois. "Lois, what the heck are you doing?"

"I got up to fix you eggs before work. Did I scare you?"

"Yes, you did! I thought someone had broken in. I forgot to lock the door again last night."

"Bob, how hard is it to remember to lock the door?"

"You usually lock it! I guess I just take it for granted that it's locked."

"How many eggs do you want?"

"Four would be nice, with toast. Thanks for getting up. You never cease to amaze me."

"Well, when you go to bed at seven-thirty, it's pretty easy to get up early."

Bob went back upstairs and put his work clothes on. He was wide awake when he sat down at the kitchen table to have eggs with Lois. "This is really nice, Lois. You haven't gotten up with me in over ten years. What's really going on?"

"I don't know, Bob. I guess with all this death lately, it made me realize how much I appreciate you and Andy."

Bob winked at her. "Keep it up, Sweetie. I just might get used to it."

Lois smiled at Bob, then leaned over and kissed him on the cheek. "Get to work, Bob, before you're late."

"Now that's the lady I married," Bob said jokingly. He blew her a kiss as he left the kitchen and went out the front door. She could hear him pulling out of the driveway as she went back to bed. Hours later she was awake again, getting Andy up for school. Things were back to normal. Andy was on time for the bus, and she was in the kitchen, drinking her morning coffee.

It was six-thirty in the morning when Mark Jessup pulled into the brickyard parking lot in Claysburg. The plant employed over five hundred workers and was the lifeblood of the community. It was by no means modernized. Most of the buildings were painted a dull brown or black to hide the ungodly amount of dust that was generated in a day's work. Because of the company's recent growth, buildings were added year after year with what seemed like little thought as to where they should be placed. Since most jobs at the plant were still done by hand, Mark's employment required that he be able to handle a physically demanding job. Mark had just been hired a week ago to the very day. He was a handsome young man with dark black hair. At nearly six feet tall and one hundred eighty pounds, he considered himself average height and weight. It was his boyish looks though that made people think he was much younger than he was. In fact, when he came to work a week ago and filled out his employment papers, the personnel director thought he was no older than eighteen, when actually he was twenty-seven. He had relatives in Altoona, Pennsylvania, about thirty miles from the Claysburg Brickyard. In fact, it was they who had told him the brickyard was hiring in the first place. That's how he got the job. He called from Ohio and was hired over the phone. They were experiencing tremendous growth there and were hiring over fifty people because the housing market was flourishing. It was his good fortune to be one of them. There was a downside though; he had to leave his family there and stay with his relatives in Altoona until he found a place to rent. He was looking for something fairly close to the plant. He and his wife Andrea had only one car, so if he found something close by, his wife could drive him to work and pick him up if she needed the car on any particular day.

    He had lived most of his life in Youngstown, Ohio. That is where his immediate family had relocated to when he was a child. His mother and father were both retired and still lived there. They now called the Youngstown area home and planned to be buried there. They were very upset when Mark told them he was relocating back to Pennsylvania. His parents were both originally from the Altoona area and insisted they never wanted to go back. He, on the other hand, wanted to make his own way. This would be a fresh start for them. It would be harder for Andrea to leave the area. She was born and raised in Youngstown. All of her childhood friends were still living and working there, so he understood why she was not thrilled when he told her of his new job opportunity in Pennsylvania. She understood, though, all things considered. He had lost his steady job that he had had since graduating from high school and was finding it difficult to locate another well-paying job. They had been living with her parents for over half a year, and it was just not working out. That's really what made him decide that a change of scenery would be for the best. Her parents looked at him like he was a deadbeat. *I'll show them,* he thought to himself. *I'll just take your daughter and granddaughter and move to another state.*

    Andrea had been his high school sweetheart. They married immediately after graduating from high school. That was almost ten years ago, and he still

GET OUT!

loved her as much as the day he married her. He thought about how much he missed Andrea and their daughter Amber. He just had to find a place to rent this week that was fairly cheap. After all, they would be living paycheck to paycheck.

His daughter Amber was the pride and joy of his life. There was a lump in his throat as he thought of his precious daughter. She was his life and the very reason for him to get up in the morning. He wanted to make his family proud. Glancing at his watch, he realized it was ten till seven. He jumped out of his car and ran into the plant to punch in his timecard. After punching in, Mark went to find his supervisor to find out what needed done that morning. He was a low man on the totem pole so he usually got the grunt jobs. He didn't care; it was honest hard work, and he enjoyed it.

Finding his supervisor, he walked over to him. "Good morning, Jake."

"Good morning to you, Mark." The supervisor was a jolly old fellow who liked to joke around with everyone. He had quite a bit of authority at the plant. He had worked at the plant for over thirty years and knew it inside-out. If there was a problem, they always seemed to call Jake.

"What do you need me to do today, Jake?"

"Tell you what, Mark, you worked so hard yesterday that I'm just going to give you the day off and pay you for it. How does that sound?"

"Are you serious, Jake?"

"No, I'm not serious, get your ass over and load those bricks onto that truck. Tell the driver to see me after its loaded, okay?"

Mark looked at Jake and smiled. "You got me good. I thought I was going to be able to coast today."

"Mark, you're a heck of a worker. Don't slack off on me now."

"Don't worry, I won't let you down." Turning, Mark jogged over to the flatbed truck and began loading bricks onto it.

It was lunchtime when Mark was finally able to sit down, sweaty and tired from all the physical work done that morning. He had made quite a few friends at the plant already, but today he felt like eating alone. He was lonely for his wife and daughter. Opening his lunch bucket, he opened a bottle of soda and guzzled it. Taking a bite out of his sandwich, he was interrupted by Jake, who sat down beside him.

"Aren't you going to eat with the other guys today, Mark?"

"Nah, thought I'd eat by myself today."

"Is something wrong, kid?"

"No, just trying to figure out how soon I can relocate my wife and daughter here from Youngstown."

"Well, what's the holdup?"

"I'm staying with relatives until I find a place to rent that's fairly cheap. I need something close to work so my wife can drive me here."

"Mark, you're not going to believe this. On the way to work today, I saw a 'For Rent' sign on the old house that Francis Stone used to live in. I don't know how much they want a month for it, but it can't be too steep. The house needs a lot of work."

"Who's Francis Stone?"

"He was about my age and worked here at the plant almost as long as me."

"Did he move?"

"No, he died. It was an accident at the house. He slipped going down the steps and broke his neck. It was a real tragedy. He was a nice fellow who kept to himself a good bit. His wife just died a few days ago too. It must be Francis's sister Lois who is renting the house out."

"How do you get to this house?"

"Tell you what, Mark. After work, follow me home. I go right past it every day."

"Thanks a lot; I really appreciate it."

"No problem, kid. Let's get back to work." Jake winked at Mark and walked away.

The rest of the day went fast. Mark was excited to go see the house. Maybe this would be his lucky day. At five o'clock, the whistle blew, and Mark punched out on the time clock. Walking to the parking lot, he waited for Jake. It seemed like an eternity until he saw Jake walking to his car. He yelled over to Mark, "Are you ready, kid?"

"I sure am, Jake."

"Follow me in your car."

Mark got into his car, started it, and pulled behind Jake. Jake drove toward his house slowly, with Mark following closely behind. They must have driven only ten miles from the plant before Jake pulled into the driveway of Francis's and Maddie's old homestead. Mark quickly pulled in behind him and stepped out of the car with a smile on his face. Looking at the house, Mark realized that it was exactly what he had been looking for.

"Jake, do you know anything about the house?" Mark asked.

"Well, as you can see the exterior is in pretty sad shape. Francis wasn't one for keeping his property in good shape, but the interior, as I remember it, looks pretty nice. His wife, Maddie, was a pretty good housekeeper. I'm sure it only has two bedrooms because they only had one child and never needed a big place."

"Where is their kid now?"

"Well, I'm sorry to say he also died recently. His name was Elijah."

"How did he die, Jake?"

"He committed suicide about two months ago. It was really hard on the family.

"You mean to tell me, Jake that the entire family died in the past two months?"

"That's what I'm telling you," Jake confirmed, shaking his head.

Both men walked to the front of the house.

"You can see it needs a new coat of paint."

"I'm not so worried about the outside, Jake. It's the inside I'm concerned about. As long as the furnace, wiring, and well-water are good, I can live with the exterior being in bad shape. It does have a nice yard that my daughter could play in."

They continued walking around the house. Seeing the garage out back, Mark walked over to it. As he pulled the door open, he felt a chill of cold air come from the garage. *That's strange,* he thought. It was now late fall and it is cold to begin with. *How could it be colder inside of the garage than outside of the garage?*

Jake walked up behind him and said, "That's the garage Elijah committed suicide in."

"How did he kill himself, Jake?"

"He hung himself from those rafters right there. All I can tell you is that it shocked the hell out of the whole community. In fact, he was on leave from the military when he killed himself. Francis told me at the plant that he never saw it coming. He had just brought Elijah home from the bus station the day before, and he seemed happy to be home. After his death, it seemed like this family just had a run of bad luck. At any rate, I doubt you would want to use this rickety old garage anyway."

"Yeah, you're probably right."

They walked back toward the car, stopping first to read the phone number on the 'For Rent' sign.

"Jake, you don't know how much I appreciate this. I'm so anxious to bring my family here from Youngstown."

"Well, kid, I hope it works out for you." Jake got into his car and drove away.

Looking back at the house, Mark smiled. *This just might work,* he thought to himself. He got back into his car, pulled out of the driveway, and headed back to Altoona. Arriving at his uncle's house, he went in, greeted his uncle, and exclaimed, "I think I found the perfect house to rent in Claysburg!"

"That's great, Mark!" exclaimed Uncle Ted.

"If you don't mind, I'm going to use your phone and call the number of the person renting it," Mark said.

Dialing the number, the phone rang five times before Lois picked up. "Hello, my name is Mark Jessup. I've just moved to the area and I'm working at the brickyard in Claysburg. I see you're renting a house about ten miles from it. Could I ask how much you want a month?"

"Hi, Mark. My name's Lois, and the house you're talking about used to belong to my brother, Francis and his wife, Maddie. Since they've passed away, I've decided to rent it out. My husband, Bob and I were thinking we would want around a hundred and fifty dollars a month."

"Well, that's within my budget, Lois. When can I make an appointment?"

"Um, how about tomorrow morning?"

"That would be fine, Lois, since tomorrow is Saturday, and I'm off work."

"Okay, we'll see you at the house tomorrow morning at nine. Thank you, Mark."

"Goodnight, Lois, and thanks a lot." Mark hung up the phone. Turning, he said excitedly, "Well, Uncle Ted, with any luck, I'll be in my own home by the end of next week."

"I hope it works out for you, Mark."

Lois was excited after she hung up the phone. "Bob," she yelled into the living room, "someone is interested in renting the house already! What do you think of that?"

"How much did you tell them per month, Lois?"

"I said we were thinking of one hundred and fifty per month. Do you think that's fair, Bob?"

"I think it's great. We can really use that money."

"He wants to see the house tomorrow at nine in the morning."

"That's good. I would rather show it in the daytime," Bob said, smiling. Lois smirked at him and went back to the kitchen.

Mark was excited when he pulled into the driveway at eight forty-five the next morning. He brought his uncle Ted along to look the house over. Getting out of the car, Mark said, "What do you think, Uncle Ted?"

"I like it, Mark. It needs some work, but a little hard work never hurt anybody, did it?"

Mark smiled at his uncle in reply. Just then, Lois and Bob pulled into the driveway in their pickup truck. Mark walked to their truck and reached out to shake Bob's hand as he stepped from his truck. "Hi, my name is Mark Jessup. This is my uncle, Ted Jessup."

Shaking both their hands, Bob said, "Nice to meet you, gentlemen."

"You have quite a strong handshake, Bob," Ted commented.

Bob smiled, saying, "I've been a logger most of my life. I guess that's why. Anyway, this is my wife, Lois."

Lois nodded to both men. "So you're interested in renting the house from us, Mark?"

"Well, I would like to see inside first, but yes I am."

Bob looked up and noticed that the bedroom light that he had left on the other day when he and Lois had emptied the house was now off. Maybe the bulb burned out, he thought to himself. "Well, gentlemen, let's go inside."

The door was locked when Bob tried to open the door. "Lois, did you remember to bring the keys?" Bob inquired.

"Yes, I did, Bob. Here they are." Bob unlocked the door and went inside. The house was not chilly anymore. It was actually quite warm.

Ted looked around the living room and said, "Well, at the least the furnace works well, Mark. It's nice and warm in here."

Lois looked at Bob and shrugged her shoulders. Looking at Lois, Mark asked if any furniture and appliances would be included in the rent.

"Everything that's in here now stays," she replied firmly.

Mark couldn't believe his ears. The house had everything, including a sofa, coffee table, and end tables. Lois, Bob, and Ted followed Mark to the kitchen. He was amazed once more when he saw a stove and refrigerator. The house was spotless.

"So far, I really like what I see," Mark said, turning to smile at Bob.

"I'm glad, Mark, because we just put the 'For Rent' sign up a day ago. I didn't think someone would be interested this quick."

"I'm in kind of a hurry to relocate my wife and daughter here from Youngstown, Ohio. So I needed something quick, and so far, this house is great!"

"Mark, go ahead and look upstairs with your uncle. Lois and I will wait down here and give you some time to look around."

Mark and his uncle walked up the steps. Bob and Lois could hear them going into Francis's and Maddie's bedroom.

Lois looked at Bob and said, "I guess I'll have to admit, you were right, and I was wrong. This house isn't evil. It's actually quite comfortable in here today."

"I told you, Lois. You were just stressed out that night from dealing with funerals and working your butt off getting this house ready to rent. You even had me going when you locked me in the closet." Bob smiled at Lois.

"Bob, I told you, I didn't lock you in the closet."

"Yeah, right. I believe you," he said with a smirk. It seemed odd being in the house without being frozen to the bone and hearing noises.

Just then Ted and Mark came down the steps. "I'll take it!" Mark said excitedly. "I won't even need to buy any furniture except for a television."

Lois looked at Bob and laughed. Mark looked at Lois with a questioning expression on his face.

"I laughed because the only thing Bob wanted from this house was the television when we got it ready to rent out," Lois explained, laughing.

Mark began to laugh also. He couldn't wait to call his wife. "How soon can I move in?" Mark asked Lois.

"Tomorrow. If you have the first month's rent, it's all yours."

Mark pulled a wad of cash from his pocket and counted out one hundred and fifty dollars. Handing it to Bob, he shook his hand once again. Bob handed Mark the house keys and said thank you.

"Where should I send the rent money each month?" Mark inquired of Lois.

Lois jotted down her address and said that he could mail it to them at her address, as she handed the paper to Mark.

"Thanks again," Bob said, walking out the door while stuffing the cash into his pocket. Lois was right behind him.

Ted and Mark stayed in the house, looking it over once more as they heard Bob and Lois pulling out from the driveway. "Well, Mark, looks like you're in business!" Ted exclaimed. "All you need to do is get your family moved here."

"I'm going to take care of that today, Uncle Ted."

"What do you mean, Mark?"

"I'm driving to Youngstown today and bringing them back tomorrow. That will give me plenty of time to settle in before work on Monday."

"Sounds like a plan, Mark."

"Well, we better get moving if your going to take me home, call your wife, and drive to Youngstown this afternoon.

"Yeah, we'd better go."

Ted locked the door as they were leaving the house. Mark looked back at the house one last time before he drove away with a gigantic smile on his face. *Life is great,* he thought to himself. It was all working out, and he had Jake to thank for it.

As Lois and Bob were driving home, Bob pulled the cash from his pocket and said, "Finally we have some extra spending money. It's a shame it had to come at Maddie's and Francis's expense, though."

"I know what you mean," Lois said as she grabbed the cash from Bob's hand and pushed it inside her purse.

"What do you think you're doing?"

"We are saving that money. I'm not going to let you waste it on foolishness."

"Well, at least give me twenty dollars to carry in my wallet so I can feel like a big shot!"

Lois laughed and pulled twenty dollars from her purse. "I guess you've earned it," she said, handing it to him and kissing his cheek.

"Thanks, honey," Bob said, excited at his newfound wealth.

Mark pulled into his uncle's driveway and bolted from the car into the house, leaving Ted still sitting in the car. Ted got out of the car slowly and walked to the house. Going through the front door, he could hear Mark on the phone already, talking to his wife.

"Wait until you see the house, Andrea. You and Amber will love it. I'm leaving right now to pick you up. Get our things packed so we can leave early tomorrow morning. I should be there by seven or eight tonight."

Amber was yelling in the background. She wanted to talk to her dad. Andrea put her on the phone. "Daddy, I miss you so much!"

"I miss you too. You know you're daddy's little girl. Honey, I'll be seeing you in seven or eight hours. I love you. Put Mommy on the phone now."

Andrea got back on the phone as Mark said, "Andrea, call my parents and tell them the news. Tell them we will stop over tonight to see them after I get there. I love you."

"I love you too."

He hung up the phone and walked over to his uncle. Thanking Uncle Ted, Mark hugged him.

"You drive safe, Mark, and tell your dad and mom I said hello. I miss seeing them." Ted had not seen Mark's dad in over ten years. They were brothers but not close. It seemed weird to Mark that he was closer to his uncle Ted than Ted's own brother was. Maybe it was because Ted had never married and had kids of his own.

"I will, Uncle Ted. Thanks again." Mark ran out the front door, slamming it behind him, and jumped into the front seat of his car. Starting it, he realized he needed gas. He pulled from the driveway and drove toward the gas station. After filling the tank up, Mark was on his way to Youngstown. It was noon, so he should be seeing his wife and daughter before eight o'clock in the evening. *I can't wait,* he thought as he got on the interstate, driving faster than he should.

By four o'clock he was halfway there and driving in a daze. *I'm glad I won't have to make this drive again,* he thought. His daydreaming was interrupted by a thud. The car almost ran off the road. His heart skipped a beat as he pulled off the road. Getting out of the car, he ran to the front of his old Ford. The tire was flat. "I can't believe this," he said out loud to himself. "It will take me an hour to fix this flat!" He went to the trunk, opened it, and pulled the spare out. Pushing on it, he realized it was low. *I cannot believe my luck,* he thought. Everything was going great until now. He changed the tire anyway. There was enough air in it to make it to the gas station. Putting the spare back into the trunk, he got back in his car and pulled back on to the interstate.

Pulling off the first exit, Mark found a gas station and pulled in next to the pump. "Fill it up," he told the attendant. "I need air in the right front tire also."

"Yes, Sir," the attendant replied.

Mark went to the bathroom. Opening the bathroom door, he was disgusted at the sight and smell as he washed his hands that were filthy after changing the tire. He returned to find the attendant finishing filling the tire with air.

"Sir, do you realize this tire is bald?"

"Yes, I know. I had a flat tire on the interstate and had to put that one on."

"Do you want me to have our mechanic fix your flat?"

"How much time would it take?" asked Mark.

"Maybe a half an hour," the attendant replied.

"Well, considering I have to go several hundred more miles, I better get it fixed." He opened the trunk and handed the flat to the attendant.

"Pull your car over here, and I'll have the mechanic put this tire back on after he fixes the flat."

"Thanks so much," Mark said, relieved that he seemed to have found the perfect garage at which to stop. Mark went in to the station and sat down. Fifteen minutes later, a burly mechanic, wearing a greasy blue uniform that looked as if it hadn't been washed in days, came in and greeted Mark with a grunt. Before he could speak, the mechanic aimed and spit a mouthful of chewing tobacco juice at an old, filthy coffee can sitting in the corner. The spit missed the can, splashing onto the wall and floor. *How disgusting,* Mark thought to himself. *What a pig.*

"Your car is ready." The mechanic choked the words out with brown tobacco juice running down his chin.

"That was quick," Mark replied. "What was wrong with the tire?"

"It had a nail in it, so I plugged it and put it back on. Your spare is lying by your trunk."

"How much do I owe you?" Mark inquired.

"Two bucks ought to do it."

Mark pushed two wrinkled dollar bills into the mechanic's grimy hand. He went to his car and tossed the spare into the trunk. Before getting into the car, he pulled out the rest of the crumpled cash and paid the attendant for the gas, thanking him with a nod.

Driving back to the interstate, he glanced at his watch and realized it was nearly five o'clock, and he was still two hours away from his wife and daughter. Once he was on the interstate, he started speeding again. Driving well over the speed limit, he made good time, and before he knew it, he was pulling into his in-laws' driveway. Their house was immaculate. The beautiful two-story pale yellow house with its perfectly manicured yard and new white picket fence stood out from the others on the block. He was glad his in-laws could not see the house he had just rented. Nothing he ever did was good enough for them. Andrea's father was an engineer who seemed to have more money than he knew what to do with. Funny thing though, he never offered to help Mark out. He often brought gifts home for Andrea and Amber, but never anything for Mark. He did let them move in after Mark lost his job, but he made sure he never let Mark forget that he was freeloading off of him.

Mark opened his car door, thinking he was glad he was finally moving his family out of his in-laws house. As he was going up to the front door, he felt uncomfortable about walking inside. Opening the door, he poked his head inside. The house was spotless and always smelled like cleaning solution. The furnishings looked as if they had been purchased yesterday. Andrea's mother and father always insisted that everyone, even guests, take off their shoes. *What a way to live,* he thought. The walls were painted stark white with not a smudge on them. He hated living that way. Now, finally, he and his family could move out from this sterile, hospital-like environment. Stepping inside and removing his shoes, he yelled, "I'm here!"

Amber ran, squealing, down the stairs into his arms. "Daddy, I missed you so much!" she screamed.

"I missed you too, honey. Where's your mom?"

"She and Grammy went to buy stuff for our new house in Pennsylvania."

Mark smiled, glad that finally he had his own place. "Who's watching you?"

"Pappy is upstairs napping." Mark followed Amber to the living room and sat down on the couch with her.

"Do you like your new job, Daddy?"

"I sure do. Wait till you see our new house, Amber. It has a nice yard you can play in."

"Daddy, do I have to go to a new school? I'm afraid."

"Don't worry; you'll make lots of new friends. It's a great area with lots of mountains and trees." "But I'll miss both of my grammys and pappys."

"We'll come back to visit them. You'll be with Mommy and me, and you will never be lonely, I promise."

"When are we leaving?"

"Tomorrow morning, bright and early, so you'll have to go to bed early tonight. Okay?"

Their talk was interrupted by Andrea's dad coming down the stairs. "Hi, Mark. How was the drive?"

"It was long and tiring, Sam. I got a flat tire on the interstate, and it cost me about a half an hour."

"Well, if you would get yourself a new car, you wouldn't have these problems."

There he goes again, always putting me down, Mark thought to himself as he shrugged his shoulders. "Sam, you can have a flat tire on a new car also, you know," Mark answered sheepishly.

Sam acted as though he didn't hear him. "So, you're finally getting a place of your own. How much are you buying it for, Mark?"

"I'm not buying it, Sam. I'm renting it until I can save enough for a down payment on a house."

"Makes sense, but I hope you're not moving my daughter and granddaughter into a dump."

"It's not a dump, Sam. It's a nice little house in a rural community."

I can't wait to get out of here, Mark was about to say when he caught himself. His face became red and the anger rose within him, but he bit down hard on his lip. He would keep quiet one more time to keep the peace, thinking of his wife and daughter. Andrea and Amber meant the world to him, and he would not make this anymore difficult on them than it already was.

"Andrea and Mabel should soon be home, so let's set the table for supper," Sam suggested.

Mabel, Andrea's mother, was a short woman with gray hair. She had the same nasty disposition as her husband. Mark wasn't exactly in a hurry to see her, but the sooner he did, the sooner he and his family could leave that awful place.

Going to the kitchen, he helped Sam set the table. Neither men spoke as they set the table precisely in the exact order that Mabel always insisted on. Finally Sam broke the silence and asked Mark how he liked his new job.

"I really like it, Sam. It's hard physical work at the brickyard, but I feel good when I come home at night. I get along real well with the other guys, and the supervisors are okay, too. In fact, my supervisor is the one who told me about the house I rented. He's a very down-to-earth man, his name's Jake."

"Well, I'm glad you like your job. Mark, take good care of my daughter and grandchild. I want you to know you are always welcome in my house. If it doesn't work out, you can always move back into my home." This was a side of Sam that Mark had never seen. He seemed almost human for once.

Amber was still in the living room, humming as she colored in her tablets on the coffee table, when Mark walked over to her. "That's a nice picture, honey. Who are you drawing?"

"That's me and you and mommy in our new house," she grinned.

Sam walked up and smiled, "That's beautiful, sweetie. May I keep that for my office wall so I'll always remember you?"

"Sure, Pappy."

Sam looked as if he had a tear in his eye as she handed him the picture. He reached out and pulled her close, hugging her tightly. "Pappy is going to miss you so much."

"I'll miss you too, Pappy, but I'll call you. Can I call Pappy, Daddy?" Amber asked as she looked at her father, eyes shining.

"You sure can, Amber." Mark was a little choked up over the whole scene as the front door opened and Andrea walked in. She looked great. Her beautiful chestnut brown hair was shoulder-length. It appeared as is if she had recently been to the beauty shop because her hair was much shorter than the last time he saw her. He ran to her and hugged her short, slender frame, squeezing her until she squealed.

"Do you like my hair, Mark?"

"You look great, honey." They kissed like they did when they were first married.

"Mom and I got some things for the house. I hope we have room in the car!"

"I'm sure we'll fit it in," Mark replied. "What all did you get?"

"Oh, just some towels and some new bedspreads. I packed up the kitchen things and most of the personal items from the old house. The boxes are in the garage. Amber's and my clothes are also packed up in boxes in the garage."

"Okay, I'll load up the car after supper," Mark replied. "Then we can go see my parents for a little while. I want to be on the road tomorrow by five in the morning, so we can get to the new house and be unpacked by two o'clock. I'd like to relax a little in the evening, since I have to be at work at six o'clock in the morning on Monday."

"Mark, how in the world did you find a completely furnished house for only one hundred and fifty dollars a month?"

"I guess I just got lucky, Andrea. We just got lucky." He proudly smiled. "My boss told me about it. Apparently they only put the 'For Rent' sign up two days ago, so I jumped at it."

Mabel was standing quietly beside Andrea and Mark as they were speaking. "I'm sorry, Mabel," Mark said as he leaned to hug her. "I didn't even say hi! I'm so glad to see you."

Mabel smiled and said, "I think you had a pretty young lady on your mind when we came in, Mark."

"Yeah, I guess you're right. You sure smell good, Andrea," Mark said as he returned his attention to his wife, leaned over, and kissed her passionately.

Andrea whispered in his ear, "I know what you have on your mind."

He looked into her brown eyes and said, "You always could read my mind."

"You kids go into the living room and spend some time together while Sam and I get supper ready," Mabel instructed. Clearly, she was in her usual take-charge mode.

Andrea and Mark gladly did as they were told and sat down beside Amber.

"Amber, you come in here with Grammy and Grandpa and help us cook supper." Without hesitation, Amber ran to the kitchen.

"I thought we'd never be alone," Mark said as he placed his hand on Andrea's breast.

"Mark, cut it out," Andrea whispered. "What if they come in?"

"Come on Andrea, let's cuddle on the couch," he pleaded in response.

"No, you can wait until bedtime tonight."

"No, I can't," he said in an agonizing voice.

"Well, you're going to have to," she said impatiently. She pushed his hand away forcefully.

"If you wouldn't be so beautiful, then maybe I could control myself around you."

"Keep talking that way, and you might get lucky tonight, Mark." They laughed together. Mark grabbed and held her hand tightly; he was so happy. He got up from the couch to turn on the television. Returning to the couch, he sat down beside Andrea once more. They sat there watching television together until they heard Mabel yell in her domineering voice, "Supper's ready!"

Mark and Andrea went into the kitchen and sat down at the table. "Mark, you're not going to leave the television on while we eat, are you?" Mabel asked with raised eyebrows.

"I'm sorry," Mark replied. Getting up, he went back to the living room to turn the set off. He grumbled to himself, "What's the big deal if the set is on while we eat, anyway?" Returning to the table, Mark slumped back into his seat.

"Let us thank God for this food," Sam announced, bowing his head. After the prayer, they enjoyed a feast of steak, potatoes, corn, and homemade apple pie for dessert.

"That was a great meal, Mabel," Sam exclaimed, rubbing his stomach.

"It sure was," Mark added.

"Thank you," Mabel replied, a hint of a smile creeping onto her face.

"Everyone clear your own dish and put it in the sink," Sam bellowed. "Mabel shouldn't have to do all the work."

It was insinuations like that that Mark hated. He intended to do his part without being told. *I would love to tell him off,* Mark thought. Everyone, including Amber, cleaned their plate and put it with their silverware into the sink. "Andrea, help your mom do the dishes while Mark and I clean the table," Sam spit out authoritatively.

"Daddy, you don't have to order us around. We all know what to do without you telling us," Andrea reminded him.

"Okay, little girl. Maybe I am too bossy sometimes."

Mark and Andrea finished cleaning up in the kitchen and announced that they were leaving to visit Mark's parents. Mark took Amber by the hand and walked out the front door without saying good-bye. Once they were in the car, Mark looked at Andrea and said, "I couldn't wait until we got out of that house. Boy, your parents are worse than sergeants in the army."

Andrea looked at Mark sternly and said, "They mean well. We never had to pay for anything while we lived in their house, did we?"

"No, I guess you're right," he supposed, lowering his eyes, "but I will be glad when we are in our own house."

It was dark as Mark drove to his parents' house. Pulling into the driveway, he noticed that the lights were out in the house.

"I hope they aren't asleep, Mark," Andrea said nervously. "I don't want to wake them up. I'll feel bad."

It was nine-thirty and his parents usually stayed up late; Mark knew this. He walked up to the front door and tried to open it. It was locked. *Darn,* he thought to himself. *They are asleep, after all.* He went back to the car and wrote a note saying:

Hi Mom and Dad.

I stopped by to see you, but you were already asleep. I didn't want to wake you. I'll call you next week from the new house. We all miss you both.

Love, Mark, Andrea, and Amber.

He walked back to the house and slipped the note between the screen door and door.

Getting back into the car, Mark exclaimed, "Let's go back to your parents' house so I can pack the car up."

Mark backed the car into Andrea's parents' driveway once more so he could pack the car. Looking into the backseat, he saw that Amber had fallen fast asleep.

Andrea remarked, "I'll open the front door, and you can carry her up to bed, Mark."

"Okay, Andrea. Are you going to help pack the car so we can get to bed?" he winked.

She smiled and said, "All right, fine, fine."

He lifted his daughter from the backseat and carried her to her own bedroom. Sam and Mabel had a three-bedroom home, so Amber had her own big room. Opening the bedroom door, Mark laid her on the bed. They had decorated the room just for Amber. Pretty pink floral wallpaper and polished hardwood floors made the room beautiful. Her bedspread matched the colors in the wallpaper. Amber loved her room, and Mark could see why. "I'll decorate your bedroom back home the same way," Mark whispered to her. He then kissed her cheek and went downstairs.

Going outside, Mark found Sam, Mabel, and Andrea loading the trunk and backseat with boxes.

"It sure is going to be a tight fit," Sam yelled to Mark. "Amber will have to sleep sitting up on the way back to Pennsylvania, I suppose."

"We'll get it all in," Mark said. After several trips to the car by everyone, the car was packed.

"Thanks a lot for helping," Andrea said to her dad and mom.

"Yeah, thanks a ton," Mark chimed in.

"Wow, you two better get to bed if you're going to leave at five," Mabel said.

Andrea went to her mom and hugged her, saying, "I love you, Mom."

"I love you too, Andrea."

She then hugged her dad. "Daddy, I'm going to miss you."

Sam was choked up when he said, "Little girl, it'll be lonely without you around here."

"I love you," Andrea said, choking back tears.

Mark hugged Mabel and shook Sam's hand. Looking at Sam, he said, "I'll make sure they call you once a week."

"You do that," Sam replied. "Go to bed, and be careful driving tomorrow."

"Okay," Mark said, "we'll call you as soon as we make it to Pennsylvania. Goodnight."

Walking up the stairs behind Andrea to their bedroom, Mark wrapped his arms around Andrea's waist and slowly slid his hand down between her thighs. She gasped with excitement as they entered their bedroom. Closing the bedroom door, Mark engulfed Andrea in his arms. Breathing heavily, he slowly undressed his wife, kissing her body as he worked his way down. She smelled of heavenly perfume. Stepping away from her he noticed she was panting as her heart raced. It had been two weeks since they last made love. It felt like it was the first time. She was beautiful. Her body was slender with a tight stomach and perfect ass. Her greatest features, though, were her large, supple breasts, still firm even after having a child.

"Mark, I want you so badly I'm aching," Andrea said. Sliding her hand down over his crotch, she began to gently rub the outside of his pants. Mark became so excited he tore the clothing from his body. Buttons popped as he ripped the garments off, tossing them to the floor. Lifting his beautiful wife into his arms he carried her to the bed. Gently, he placed her onto the bed and slid his body on top of hers. Pulling his face close to hers, she slid her warm tongue into his mouth and wrapped her legs tightly around his waist. He was in sheer ecstasy. They continued to make love until one in the morning and then drifted to sleep in each other's arms.

At four-thirty in the morning, the alarm went off. Andrea shut it off and climbed from her warm bed. "Mark, get out of bed so we can get ready to leave." Mark climbed from the bed and put on his clothes. Andrea went to the bathroom and returned to put on her clothes. "Are you ready to leave, Mark?"

"Yeah, I'm ready. I'll carry Amber to the car." He went to Amber's room. Opening the door, he pulled up the covers and lifted her from the bed. She stirred but did not wake. Andrea already had the front door open. He carried her outside to the car; it was pitch black outside. Mark had to lay her across the backseat because the boxes were covering the entire floor. He looked at Andrea and said, "I'll move the boxes from the floor and put them on the backseat when she wakes up, that way she can sit up and have some leg room." As Andrea and Mark got into the car, Mark looked over at his wife and said, "Finally we can start a new life. I love you, Andrea."

"I love you too, Mark."

Mark pulled from the driveway and headed to the interstate. He had only been on the highway a short time when he pulled off the interstate and drove to a diner. Andrea and Amber were both asleep. When Mark nudged her awake to ask if she was hungry, Andrea did little more than stir in her seat, saying, "No, Mark, I just want sleep."

"Okay," he said, "I'm going to run in and get some coffee to go." Andrea didn't hear him; she had gone back to sleep already.

Mark jogged into the diner and returned with a steaming hot cup of coffee. Starting the car, he was back on the interstate within ten minutes. It was ten in the morning before Andrea woke up. "What time is it, Mark?"

"Ten o'clock, Honey," he replied.

"How far do we have to go?"

"We made good time, so we should be there in less than an hour."

Looking back, Andrea noticed that Amber was still sleeping soundly. "She must have been exhausted from yesterday," Andrea said. "She is usually up and running by seven or eight in the morning."

"Well, I guess the hum of a car motor is just the ticket to slow her down," Mark said. Just then, Amber woke up. She got up and noticed she had no leg room. "I can't sit up, Mommy!"

Reaching back, Andrea pulled her into the front seat between them. "How's that? Better?"

"Good!," Amber squealed.

"Look out the window, Amber," Mark urged his daughter. "We're in Pennsylvania now. Do you like it?"

"Yes, Daddy. The trees are pretty."

The trees were full of color. Deep red and bright yellow colored leaves were everywhere. It was autumn, but you would never have known it by the temperature, which was in the high seventies. It almost felt like early summer.

"Yes, they are, honey." Mark spoke the words mechanically.

"When are we going to be at our new house?" Amber wondered.

"Very soon, Amber. Just sit back and relax." Mark was extremely exhausted, and he just didn't feel like having a long conversation at the moment.

Before they knew it, they were pulling into the old Stone homestead. "What do you think?" Mark asked excitedly.

"Well, Mark, I mean, it looks a little run down," Andrea said in a sullen voice. "There's more paint off the house than on it."

"Andrea, we aren't living on the outside. Just wait until you get to take a look at the inside," Mark tried to explain.

Everyone climbed out of the car quickly; Amber ran to the front yard and danced in circles, throwing colorful leaves into the air as she spun round and round. "I love it Daddy! We have our own yard!"

Andrea smiled at Mark, saying, "I guess it will be all right. Let's go inside."

Mark and Andrea went to the front door of the house. Opening the door, Mark felt a chill coming from the home. "That's awfully strange," Mark said to Andrea. "When we were here yesterday, it was nice and toasty inside." He walked over to the thermostat and looked at it. It was set at seventy degrees. Mark bumped it up to seventy-two degrees and heard the furnace kick on downstairs. "Okay, it should warm up some now."

"I hope so. I sure would hate to have to wear a coat in the house all day," she said laughing.

Just then, Amber ran into the house. "Who's the man upstairs, Daddy?" she asked.

"What man, Amber?" Mark replied.

"I saw him staring out of the upstairs window when I was outside."

No one should be in the house, Mark thought to himself. "I'll check upstairs," he called back to Andrea, running up the steps. "Is anyone here?" he yelled out. No one answered. Mark opened all of the bedroom doors. No one was in any of the rooms. "No one is up here!" he yelled downstairs.

Andrea and Amber ran up the stairs. "Amber, you must be seeing things." Mark laughed as he said it.

"Daddy, I know I saw a man in that window," she said, pointing to the window in Maddie's bedroom.

"Well, honey, as you can see, no one is here."

Amber giggled and ran back down the steps and out the front door to play in the yard once more.

"This will be our bedroom," Mark said to Andrea, pointing to Maddie's old bedroom. It has access to the bathroom here and through the hallway. "Amber can use the door in the hallway if she has to use the bathroom in the middle of the night." They left the bedroom and went in to the hallway.

Walking to Elijah's bedroom, Mark opened the door. "This will be Amber's bedroom after we fix it up. For now, she can sleep in our bedroom with us until she gets used to the house."

"Okay," Andrea said, "it sounds like a plan. Mark can we paint these drab white walls? They are so cold. This place needs some warm colors to make it more homey."

"You can do what ever you want, honey, but first I want to paint and fix up Amber's bedroom. We'll make it look just like her bedroom in Ohio, right down to the pink walls."

"Okay, Mark, can we go look at the rest of the house now?"

"Sure," he replied. They went down the stairs and into the kitchen.

Andrea noticed the black and white checkered pattern in the linoleum immediately. "This linoleum is in good shape, but I don't really like the colors. Everything in the house is black and white." Even the kitchen counters and kitchen table top were an off-white color. The kitchen chairs were metal with white padded seats and vinyl plastic seat covers. "Mark, this place needs some color."

"I agree, Andrea, but can we get moved in first before you start decorating?" he joked. "You'll have plenty of time to make it just the way you want it," he said, as he went to the phone and picked up the receiver. Putting it to his ear, he noticed it had a dial tone. "At least the phone isn't disconnected yet, Andrea. It must still be in the people's name that lived here before us."

"Who lived here anyway?"

"I don't know." Mark had decided it would be best not to tell Andrea the story behind the house. She might feel uneasy living in a house where there was so much death. Handing Andrea the receiver, he said, "You better call your folks and tell them we arrived here safely. Remind me tomorrow to call the phone company and have the bill put in our name."

"Okay, Mark, but you better start hauling boxes in so we can start unpacking."

Mark left the room as Andrea began dialing the number. Going outside, Mark noticed Amber was still playing in the yard. "Amber!" he yelled.

"Yes, Daddy?" she replied.

"Stay out of the garage out back. It's old and dangerous inside there."

"Okay, Daddy, I will." That said, Amber turned and ran to the tree on the side of the house and began climbing it. Mark turned and walked to the car. He unlocked the trunk and began hauling boxes in to the house. Box after box, he carried them into the house. After about the tenth trip, he noticed Andrea had begun to unpack the boxes containing the kitchen items. She was putting the silverware into the drawers when he sneaked up behind her and wrapped his arms around her waist. She turned and kissed him passionately on the lips. "Mom and Dad said to tell you hi."

"I sure am glad we are together in our own home now," Mark said excitedly.

"One big, happy family, or should I say one small, happy family?" Andrea replied, giggling as she said it. "Mark, let's try to get everything unpacked quickly so we can relax before bed."

"Okay, Andrea, but first I'm going to run to the grocery store before it closes and get some food to put in the refrigerator and cupboards. I'm hungry; we haven't eaten anything yet today."

"Mark, take Amber with you, and I'll just keep unpacking."

"Okay, sure thing. I'll see you in a little bit, honey," Mark yelled back to Andrea as he was going out the front door.

She could hear the car pulling out of the driveway as she returned to the living room to get another box. *I wish this house would warm up,* she thought to herself as she returned to the kitchen with another box. As she started unpacking the box, she heard what seemed like a voice upstairs. She poked her head back into the living room and yelled, "Mark, are you back already? What did you forget?" There was no answer. Looking out the front window, she noticed that the car was not in the driveway. *I must be hearing things,* she decided. Returning to the kitchen, Andrea started unpacking again. A chill ran down her spine. She shivered. It was as if someone was watching her unpack. Glancing around, she turned quickly when it seemed as if something brushed her hair to the side. "This is creepy!" she yelled out loud. "Is someone in here?" Then, just as soon as the weird feeling had come, it passed.

After unpacking and placing all the kitchen items into their proper places, Andrea went into the living room. The house now seemed warmer, and she began to sing as she unpacked the items for the living room. Her mother had given her the expensive old lamp that she had adored since she was a child. Placing it on the coffee table and plugging the cord into the wall, she stepped back and began to admire its beauty once more. It was a tall lamp with a statuette of an Indian woman on the base. Cradled in the woman's arms was an infant. The entire lamp was made of hand-carved wood and was actually quite expensive. It was one of her most cherished items. Methodically, she began to unpack the knickknacks she still had from her old home before they had moved in with her parents. They had accumulated all sorts of odd items. There were porcelain buffalos, horses, children, and wigwams. Most everything she had, had something to do with Indians and the Old West. She just loved southwestern items. *I'll theme the entire living room in southwestern*, she thought. *I'll even paint the walls a terra cotta color. It will be beautiful.* Just as she was finishing the last box containing items for the living room, she heard a car pull into the driveway. Looking out the front window, she saw Mark and Amber getting out of the car. Glancing at her watch, she realized they had been gone for two hours. Mark was carrying two arms full of grocery bags.

Amber seemed excited. She was carrying a doll as she rushed into the house screaming, "Mommy, look what Daddy got me!" She was holding the doll like it was a real infant. Very gently, she laid the doll on the sofa and said to it, "Now take a nap while I go play outside in the yard." Amber pushed past her father as he was coming through the door, almost knocking the bags from his arms.

"Slow down," Mark said to her as she passed by. He smiled at Andrea and said, "Do you have everything unpacked?"

"Yeah, thanks for the help," she replied sarcastically. "Did you get eggs and milk?" Andrea asked.

"I knew I forgot something," Mark said laughing. "I'm just kidding. I got everything, including cereal, bread, lunch meat, and cans of soup and vegetables."

"Okay, set them on the kitchen counter, and I'll put them away while you haul boxes upstairs and unpack them, Mark."

"Do I have to?" Mark asked jokingly.

"Get your butt in gear, and I'll fix some sandwiches after I get the groceries put away." Mark didn't hear her he was already ascending the stairs with a box.

Andrea yelled to him as he was coming down the steps for another box. "What?" he asked.

GET OUT!

"Make sure you put sheets and covers on the bed, and put all our toiletries into the medicine cabinet. Also, put all the clothing into the closets."

"I will, I will," he said mockingly as he ran back up the steps with another box. Hauling a large box of Amber's clothing up the steps, he pushed open the bedroom door where Amber would eventually be sleeping. The room was freezing cold, so cold, in fact, that he thought he saw his breath crystallize as it poured forth from his mouth. *Wow, this room shouldn't be colder than the rest of the house,* he thought to himself. Opening the closet door in her room, he felt uneasy. The closet seemed to have an aura all its own. It was full of a man's clothing, as well as his shoes. *This is weird, who would leave their clothing behind?* Lifting all the clothing from their hangers, he piled them onto the bed. Next, grabbing several pairs of shoes as well as a pair of old army boots, he tossed them on top of the clothes. Smiling, Mark carefully pulled each dress from the box and put them on hangers. All of Amber's undergarments, socks, and shoes were perfectly organized in the closet before he closed the door. Next, he took the men's clothing and shoes from the bed and placed them into the empty box. Running down the steps, he ran the box outside to the garage in back of the house. Tossing the box inside the garage, he returned to the house and continued his trips up and down the steps until he finally carried the last box up the steps.

After putting the groceries away, Andrea grabbed a can opener from the drawer and opened a can of chicken noodle soup. Emptying its contents into a pot she had retrieved from her cupboard, she placed it on a burner on the stove. Grabbing an old coffee pot from the same cupboard, she filled it with water and placed it on another burner. It was an old gas stove that could use a good cleaning. The burners had crusted food burnt onto them. *I'll worry about cleaning those tomorrow,* she decided. Opening the oven door and looking in, she thought, what a mess! It also had burnt, black, crusted food everywhere on the grills. *This lady was not a very good housekeeper,* Andrea decided. Shutting the door, she lit a match and turned the gas on. The flames on both burners ignited immediately. Going to a different cupboard, she opened it and pulled a loaf of bread out. Taking lunch meat from the spotless white refrigerator, she made three sandwiches with ham, cheese, and mustard. "Mark!" she yelled as loud as her voice would carry. "Supper is ready!"

He ran down the steps, sweat dripping from his nose, and into the kitchen. "You sure you want to call it supper?" he said, out of breath. "After all, it's only two o'clock in the afternoon."

"Well, call it what you want, but it's ready now, so yell for Amber."

Going out the front door, he returned with Amber on his shoulders. She was laughing as he placed her into a chair and slid it up to the kitchen table. "Daddy, go get Molly. She's hungry too."

"Who is Molly?" he asked his daughter.

"She's my doll. She is sleeping on the couch in the living room."

"Okay, honey, I'll go wake her up and bring her in to supper to join us."

Going to the living room, Mark picked the doll up and cradled it in his arms as he returned to the kitchen. Andrea was laughing as Mark set the doll down on a chair and slid it up to the table. "Let's eat, I'm starved," Mark said, as he sat down. Andrea was already sitting at the table. In front of everyone was a steaming bowl of soup, a sandwich, coffee, and milk for Amber.

"This is our first meal in our new home," Amber squealed.

"Yes it is, and a meal fit for a king, so it is," Mark chided. He grabbed a sandwich and took a bite.

"Daddy, aren't you going to pray like Pappy does before we eat?"

"I'm sorry, honey," Mark said, slightly embarrassed. Bowing their heads, Mark spoke, "God is great, God is good, let us thank Him for this food. Amen."

After lifting their heads, Amber said, "I know that prayer too, Daddy." He smiled as he took a second bite.

After finishing supper, Mark and Amber helped Andrea clear the table and do the dishes. "Well, now we can relax a little? Let's go sit on the front porch and drink some more coffee," Mark suggested to Andrea.

"Not until the bed has sheets and covers on it, Mark."

"Andrea, it's all done! I don't waste time."

"I guess we can relax then," Andrea finally gave in. They all went to the front porch and sat down on the first step.

"This is a nice community, you'll see, Andrea. We'll fit right in."

"I know we will, Mark. You know that we have to enroll Amber in school tomorrow, don't you?"

"I didn't even think about that," Mark said, shaking his head. "I know what. You can drive me to work in the morning and then take Amber to the school to enroll her. Do you have her transcripts from Ohio, honey?"

"Yes, I have everything. What time do you need to get up for work?"

"I have to be there by seven, so I usually get up around quarter till six," he replied.

They sat on the stoop until darkness fell around them. It was chilly outside after the sun went down. It was the first week of November, but the temperature had been in the sixties everyday. It was like an Indian summer. *I hope it stays this way,* Andrea thought to herself. *Even a jacket is unnecessary!*

They got up and went into the house with Amber following closely behind. By now it was six o'clock, so Mark turned the lights on in every room of the house, to which Andrea asked, "Why are you doing that, Mark? Aren't you worried about the light bill?"

"Not yet. It's not in our name yet," he joked.

"Well, I'll take care of getting that and the phone switched tomorrow, after I enroll Amber in school." Sitting on the couch, Andrea asked Mark to get her a magazine to read. "I put them over on the coffee table when I unpacked them today."

He grabbed one for her and then sat on the floor with Amber. Amber had her doll and was playing with it. "Where are my other toys, Mommy?"

"Up in the bedroom," Mark replied for Andrea. "I took them up there by accident earlier today. Just play with that doll, and I'll bring your other toys down tomorrow."

"Okay," she replied without moving her gaze from the doll.

As Amber continued playing with her doll, Mark lay down to the floor, made himself comfortable, and closed his eyes. The house was now nice and warm; the chill that was present earlier had vanished. Drifting to sleep, he woke up two hours later, and Andrea was still reading. Amber had fallen asleep beside her dad. He noticed Andrea yawn. "Let's go to bed, Andrea. We're all tired from the drive."

"Okay, Mark. Carry your daughter up, and I'll lock up and shut the lights off down here." Mark lifted his daughter into his arms and carried her to their bedroom. Placing her into the middle of the bed, he stood back and looked at her. She was beautiful with her long blonde hair and milky white skin. She no longer had the pigtails from yesterday. Andrea was now beside him. "She's beautiful, Andrea," Mark asserted. "That's because she takes after her mom."

"She sure does," Andrea laughed. "I'm glad this is a big king-sized bed like the one from back home in Ohio. It looks like an antique." The bed was solid oak with ornamental lines inscribed into the headboard. The sheets they had brought from Ohio also fit perfectly.

Walking to the bathroom, Andrea opened the medicine cabinet in search of her toothbrush. Her face turned to disgust when she realized that Mark had thrown the items in a pile. "What a mess!" she yelled. She began to organize the entire cabinet when Mark walked into the room. "You have a lot of nerve, Mark. Why didn't you organize this?"

"I was going to earlier, but you yelled that supper was ready, so I figured I'd do it later."

"Well, later is now, so organize it," she ordered as she began to brush her teeth.

"Get out of the way, and I will," Mark barked back at her.

After spitting the toothpaste into the sink, she stepped aside. "I'm going to bed, and it better be organized when I get up in the morning, Mr. Forgetful."

"Yeah, yeah," he said sarcastically as she left the bathroom. Mark was in the bathroom for twenty minutes organizing and brushing his teeth before he returned to the bedroom to find Andrea sound asleep beside their daughter. He turned out the nightlight and crawled into bed. Snuggling close to his daughter, he felt uneasy in the darkness. *Must be because it's the first night in this house,* he thought to himself. It felt like a stranger was in the room watching them. He just couldn't put his finger on it, but something definitely felt awry.

It was eleven o'clock before he finally drifted to sleep. At three in the morning, a knock at their bedroom door woke Mark and Andrea up. "Mark, did you hear that?" Andrea asked.

"Yes, I heard it. I'm up, aren't I?" Mark turned the nightlight on. "Did you lock up before you came to bed?" Mark asked Andrea in a shaken voice.

"Yes, and I made sure to deadbolt the front door too."

Amber was still sound asleep. The knock became louder outside the door. It was not directly on the door this time, but rather, it sounded like someone was knocking on the wall in the hallway. "See what it is, Mark. I'm scared." Andrea was visibly shaking.

Getting out of bed, Mark realized the room was freezing. He could see his breath as he began to search for a club of some sort. Finding nothing, he picked up one of his shoes. "That will really scare a prowler," Andrea whispered sarcastically.

"I can't find anything else," he whispered back. Walking to the bedroom door, he opened it a crack. Peering out through the crack, he strained his eyes to see something. There were no more noises. He opened the door far enough to put his arm outside the door and turn the hallway light on. The hallway instantly became bright. He realized no one was there. Going into the hallway, he looked down the steps to the living room. It was dark downstairs. There were no more noises. Just as he was ready to return to his bedroom, he heard a noise in Amber's soon-to-be bedroom. Rushing to the door, he opened it slowly. "Is anyone in here?" he yelled, shaking from both the cold and his nerves combined. He turned the light on and saw a rat scurrying under the currently vacant bed in the room. Slamming the door shut, he yelled, "Damn!"

He went back to his bedroom and closed the door. "What was it, Mark?"
"You're not going to believe this, Andrea. We have rats in the house."
"I can't live here with rats, Mark."
"Just relax, we can get traps tomorrow."
"Mark, how can a rat knock on the door?"
"Don't ask me, but it was a big rat. I checked everything out, and it's fine."
"Did you check downstairs?" she asked.

Lying, Mark said, "Of course I did. There is no one in this house but us. I need to get to sleep, or I'll be tired all day at work. Goodnight," he whispered as he turned the nightlight out and climbed back into bed beside his daughter. He thought it best not to comment on how cold the house was. There had been enough commotion for one night.

Waking at five forty-five, Mark crawled from bed. The house was freezing cold. He went downstairs to the thermostat. Looking at it, he realized it had been turned down to fifty degrees. Turning it up to seventy, he darted back up the stairs and went to the bathroom. He turned on the tub and felt the water. It was getting nice and hot, just the way he liked it. He went to the medicine cabinet and opened it. Noting that it was now perfectly organized, he reached in and pulled out his toothbrush. While brushing his teeth, he felt someone come up behind him and grab his waist. It was Andrea, and she was laughing out loud. Reaching down, she felt the tub water. "That feels good," she said. Before Mark could rinse his toothbrush off, Andrea had crawled into the tub and was soaking.

"Why did you do that?" Mark asked. "I have to get ready for work; you know that."
"I need a hot bath after last night," she said. "It's freezing in here."
"No kidding. Someone turned the thermostat down to fifty before we went to bed."
"Well it wasn't me, Mark. Maybe Amber was playing with it yesterday."
"Maybe," he replied. "Move over." He winked as he slipped his robe off.
"No way, this tub is too small, Mark!" Andrea insisted.
"There's enough room if I face you on the other end," he pleaded.
"What if Amber comes in?" Mark walked to the door leading to his bedroom, pulled it shut, and latched it. He also latched the door leading to the hallway. Turning around, he smiled at his beautiful wife and said, "Now we

can play." Crawling into the tub with her, he caressed her breast. She leaned forward and kissed him, inserting her tongue into his mouth and swirling it around. There was a knock at the door. Pulling his mouth away, Mark whispered, "Shit." He jumped from the tub and put on his robe.

"Mommy, where are you?" Amber asked.

Quickly opening the door, Mark met his daughter. "Good morning, honey."

"Good morning, Daddy. Where's Mommy?"

"She's taking a bath. Go on in with her and, you can get a bath before school too." Amber went into the bathroom, and Mark closed the door behind her.

He went to his closet door and found his work clothes. Putting them on, he noticed it was a little warmer in the house now. Glancing at the clock, he yelled into the bathroom, "We better get moving if you're going to drop me off at work."

Andrea appeared from the bathroom with Amber behind her. She had a thick white robe draped around her but not tied. Smiling at Mark, she discreetly pulled the robe apart, exposing her naked body without letting Amber see. "Too bad you have to go to work," she teased.

"Yeah, Daddy," Amber squealed. "You could stay home and play with us."

"The only playing you're going to be doing today is at school, young lady."

"You'll make a bunch of new friends today, Amber," added Andrea. Turning to Mark, she instructed, "Run downstairs since you're dressed already, and make Amber a bowl of cereal."

"Yes, Boss," Mark replied jokingly, saluting his wife. "Do you want something too?"

"No, I'm not hungry."

Leaving the bedroom, Mark went downstairs into the kitchen. Andrea could hear him all the way upstairs as he was loudly opening and closing cabinets until he found where she had put the cereal. She quickly helped Amber put on her school clothes. The outfit consisted of a pretty pink dress with white nylon stockings. "You look beautiful, Amber."

"Thank you, Mommy." Amber smiled.

"Now put your black dress shoes on, go downstairs, and your father will get you breakfast." Amber slipped into her shoes and was gone in a flash. *What shall I wear?* Andrea thought to herself. *I don't want to look like a hillbilly when I take Amber to school to enroll her.* She decided on the new blue dress her mother had bought for her weeks ago at a specialty store in Ohio. Drying her hair with a towel, she went back into the bathroom and looked in the mirror. She began combing her soft, beautiful, chestnut brown hair with a brush. Finishing up with bright red lipstick, she opened the door and walked downstairs to the kitchen.

"Wow," Mark whistled as she walked into the kitchen. "You look great."

"Well thank you, honey. If you're real good today, maybe I'll give you a treat tonight."

"That's a deal," Mark replied. "We better get going; it's six thirty, and I'm going to be late for work." Amber ran out the door and was inside the car before Mark turned and locked the door.

Andrea was waiting outside her car door when Mark approached the car. "Mark, how do I find the school?"

"The school is only a few miles from where I work. I'll drive by it on the way to work so you'll know how to get there. After you drop her off, drive around town and check it out. There are a lot of small shops in town, including a hardware store. Get some pink paint for Amber's room, and I'll start painting it after work."

Mark and Andrea got into the car. Starting the car, Mark drove toward the school. "What time does school start?" Andrea interrogated Mark.

"I don't really know, but right there is the school bus." The bus went past their car and continued up the road toward their house. "My guess is that it starts at eight." After driving about ten more miles, Mark was in front of the elementary school. "There is your school, Amber."

"Will you come in with me, Daddy?"

"I can't, honey. I have to go to work, but Mommy will take you in." Looking into the backseat, he noticed tears running down Amber's angelic face. "What's wrong, sweetie?"

"I'm scared. I don't want to go."

"Don't be scared. You'll make lots of new friends today."

She was still sobbing as Mark drove toward the brickyard. He felt a lump in his throat as he pulled into work. "Andrea, make sure you don't leave the school until she is settled in."

"I know!" she said, shaking her head as if he had said something ridiculous.

Kissing Andrea on the lips, Mark got out of his car. Andrea slid over to the driver's seat. Opening the back door, he hugged Amber and said, "Don't worry, you're going to love your new school." He kissed her on the cheek and closed the door. Tapping on the front window, he yelled, "Pick me up at three o'clock sharp."

"I love you," Andrea mouthed to him as she pulled away.

Running into the plant, Mark punched the time clock at seven on the nose. *Wow, that was close,* he thought, as he went to look for Jake to see what was on the agenda for today.

Driving back to the school, Andrea admired the beautiful color of the leaves that were still on the trees. "This seems to be a nice place to live, Amber." Amber didn't answer. Looking into the rearview mirror, Andrea noticed that her daughter had stopped crying but still looked terrified.

It was only a matter of minutes until Andrea parked the car in the school parking lot. They got out of the car and walked to the school, hand in hand. After going through the front entrance, they were met by what appeared to be the janitor. He had on a green uniform with his name sewn into the right corner of his shirt. Apparently his name was Butch. Shaking his hand, Andrea inquired as to where the office was located. "Down that hallway, last room on the right," he responded.

"We are new in the community," she explained to him.

"Is that right?" Butch grunted. "Where you living?" he asked.

"The old Stone house about ten miles down from here. Do you know where I mean?"

"Are you kidding?" Butch shouted. "Everybody knows where the Stones lived."

"Why's that?" Andrea asked with a curious look on her face.

"'Cause it's a shame what happened to that family."

"What do you mean?" she pressed.

"You mean to tell me you moved into that house and don't know?" Butch inquired in disbelief.

"Know what?" Andrea was becoming impatient now.

"The whole family died one after another, all in the past two months. First, the son hung himself out back in the garage. Then the father, Francis, fell down the steps a few weeks later and broke his neck. Finally the mother, Maddie Stone, killed herself about a week and a half ago. Said she was depressed and couldn't take it anymore. I, personally, think the house is jinxed."

"Thanks for everything, Butch. You made my day." Andrea half smiled as she turned and walked toward the office.

"Mommy, what was that man talking about?" Amber asked right before entering the office.

"Nothing, honey, he was just joking around."

Opening the door to the office, Andrea walked to the front desk. There was an older woman who was probably in her sixties behind the counter. "Pardon me, ma'am, is this where I would register my daughter? We just moved into the area," Andrea explained.

"Yes it is, young lady. My name is Miss Hite. Take these papers over to the table and fill them out. Do you have the transcripts from her old school?"

"Yes, I sure do," Andrea replied, handing the packet to the older woman. "By the way, my name is Andrea Jessup, and this here's Amber." Taking the papers from the secretary, Andrea sat down at the table and began filling them out.

After glancing at the transcripts, the secretary turned and picked up the intercom. She paged Mrs. Allen to come to the office. Within minutes, a pleasant-looking young woman walked into the office with a smile on her face. She was wearing a plaid skirt with a pretty white top. "Yes, Miss Hite, what can I do for you?"

"Mrs. Allen, that young lady's name is Amber Jessup. She has just moved to our community and will be joining your class of third graders."

Turning to Amber, Mrs. Allen smiled. "Well, hi, Amber! Do you want to come with me? We are going to have lots of fun today."

Amber clung to her mother as she replied, "Yes, ma'am."

"Let's go meet your classmates." Looking at her mother, Andrea nodded for her to go with the lady. Mrs. Allen took Amber's hand and led her out of the office and down the hall.

After finishing the paperwork, Andrea went back to the counter and handed the papers to Miss Hite. "Well, that's all we need," she said with a smile. "You can either pick her up at three-thirty here at the office or I can see that she gets on the right bus."

"Could you do that for me? I want her to know which bus she needs to ride every day."

"I'll personally put her on the bus and show her the number so she will remember it for tomorrow. I see you live at 322 Haller Road. I'll tell the bus driver to make sure he drops her off at the right address."

"Thank you so much. You're so kind, Miss Hite."

"It's no problem at all. By the way, welcome to our community, Andrea."

Andrea felt good as she was leaving the office. *Everyone is so friendly here*, she thought. Walking down the hall, she decided she would explore the community. While she was walking out of the school building, she noticed some men filling in potholes on the road in front of the school. They began to whistle at her. She looked at them and smiled. "Get back to work, guys," she yelled as she got into her car. They were still staring at her as she drove out of the parking lot and down the road.

Andrea had only driven a few miles when she noticed several storefronts up ahead. Pulling over, she got out of the car and walked down the street to the first shop. It was a clothing shop. Going inside, she browsed until a slender, gray-haired, older woman came up to her and said, "Hi, my name is Joy. Can I help you with something?"

"Well, yes," Andrea replied. "I am looking for some white blouses for myself."

"I think I have just what you are looking for over here." Walking to the back of the store, Joy pointed at a rack of blouses. "All sizes and colors are available. I didn't catch your name," Joy said.

"I'm sorry, my name is Andrea."

"You're new to our community, aren't you?" Joy asked.

"Yes, I am. In fact, I just arrived here yesterday with my husband Mark, and my daughter Amber."

"Well, that's great!" Joy said excitedly. "Let me be one of the first people to welcome you to the area."

"Thank you so much, Joy. Everyone is so kind here." They chatted for almost half an hour before Andrea realized she had to go to the hardware store. Paying for two blouses, Andrea thanked Joy and left. Joy yelled to stop in again as Andrea was walking out the door, and Andrea replied, with a hearty smile, that she would.

Looking down the street, she noticed a small hardware store. Walking up to it, she laughed. The front of the store was in dire need of paint. When the door was opened, a bell jingled. Looking down the narrow aisles, Andrea noticed that they were jammed with items on the shelves and the floor. It was a mess. The owner, a middle-aged, balding gentleman approached her. "How can I help you, ma'am?"

"I need some pink paint, brushes, a roller, a paint tray, and some rat traps."

"What shade of pink?" he asked.

"Do you have color swatches?" Andrea requested.

"Yes, I do. They're right over here," he replied, walking to another aisle.

Andrea had to maneuver around item after item as she followed him to the paint aisle. Upon being handed a swatch board of colors, she noticed there were six shades of pink from which to choose. Immediately she recognized the color of Amber's room in Ohio. "This is the one." "How much do you need?" the owner asked in a pleasant voice.

"One gallon, please," she answered.

After mixing the paint, the man went up and down the aisles getting the other items Andrea had asked for. "Will there be anything else?" he asked.

"Nope, that should do it for now," she replied.

Walking to the front of the store, he rang up the items on a very old register that had to be hit on the side before it would open. "It has a tendency to stick," he said, smiling. "That will be six dollars and twenty-five cents." Andrea handed him the exact amount. After bagging the items, he handed her the bag and said, "Have a great day."

"You too," she replied as she left the store.

Walking back to her car, there was a gentle breeze blowing in Andrea's face. It was warm, and the sun was shining. *What a great day*, she smiled to herself. It was the kind of day that made you glad to be alive. She walked to her car and placed the items in the backseat. Looking farther up the street, she saw a little coffee shop. *How cute and quaint*, she thought. She locked the car and continued on her journey up the street. Standing in front of the coffee shop, she glanced at her watch. It was almost noon. *I could eat a bite of lunch*, she supposed. The minute she stepped into the shop, she fell in love with it. It was small, with only eight tables. Each table had a pretty white linen table cloth with frills adorning the edges. A candle in the center made the setting complete. There were two older couples sitting together at one of the tables, drinking coffee and eating pie. They were so cute, looking to be in their eighties and still in love. *I love this place,* she thought to herself. *We'll have to come here as a family for supper.*

Sitting down at a table in the middle of the room, Andrea noticed a young waitress coming over to her. Handing her a menu, the waitress asked, "Would you like something to drink?"

Handing the menu back, Andrea said, "Do you know what? I think I'll have coffee and pie."

"And what kind of pie would you like, ma'am?" the waitress asked, smiling.

"What are they eating?" she asked, pointing to the older couple. "It looks good."

"That's homemade peach pie right there."

"I'll have a slice of that, with vanilla ice cream if you have it."

"We sure do," the waitress confirmed, leaving to fetch Andrea's order. It was only a matter of minutes until she returned with the ice cream, pie, and coffee. "I didn't know if you wanted it on top of the pie, so I just put it in its own dish."

"It looks delicious." Andrea smiled as she spoke.

"Thank you," the waitress responded as she walked away.

Andrea took a bite of the pie. It was so sweet. She closed her eyes as she swallowed. "I can't remember ever eating a better piece of pie," she said, talking to herself.

After finishing her midday snack, she motioned for the waitress to bring a bill. The waitress walked over and handed her a slip of paper. "I can take that up and get your change when you're ready. The bill came to one dollar and fifty cents."

"Here's two dollars; keep the change," Andrea said as she handed her the money. "It was very good, thank you."

Walking out of the coffee shop back out into the sunlight, Andrea shaded her eyes. It was very bright. Reaching into her purse, she realized she had left her sunglasses in the car. She had to squint her eyes as she walked back to her car. Opening the door, she grabbed a pair of sunglasses from the glove box and said, out loud, "That's better." Andrea started the car and headed toward home. It took only minutes to arrive back at her new house. Pulling into the driveway, she remembered that Mark had locked the door when they left in the morning. *Darn it, I am going to have to get a spare key made,* she thought. When she pulled the keys from the ignition, she realized the house key was on it. She was still smiling she opened up the back door and got the paint supplies out of the car. As she was walking to the front door, she saw a gray squirrel on their front porch that was dancing across the paint-chipped railing. She stopped to watch the agile animal until he spotted her and ran up the closest tree. *Amber would have loved to see that,* she alleged with a grin on her face. Continuing to the front door, she unlocked it and went inside. The house was not cold anymore, but she felt a chill as she closed the door. She thought to herself, *I wish that janitor had not told me about all the people dying in this house. It gives me the creeps.*

She sat the bags on the living room floor and then flopped onto the couch. The chill was still there. As she sat on the couch, she noticed the basement door. *I wonder what's down there,* she thought. Walking toward the door, she suddenly stopped and remembered that she needed to pick up Mark by three o'clock. She looked at her watch and realized that it was almost one. The day was flying by. "I know what, I'll surprise Mark and start painting Amber's room!" Andrea decided out loud. She took the bags and ran up the steps to the bedroom that once belonged to Elijah Stone. Opening the door, she walked in and dropped the bags on the floor. She left and went to her bedroom, putting on a ragged pair of slacks and a worn-out blouse she had in her closet, and then she returned to Amber's room.

She began by pushing all of the furniture to the center of the room. There was a single bed, a chair, and a desk. The walls were painted a faded, dull white. Elijah's dirty handprints could still be seen on the walls. Placing her hand over one print, she couldn't believe the size of the person's hand. They were enormous in comparison to her tiny hands. Her hand still on the wall, she got the same feeling as yesterday. It was as if someone had brushed her hair to the side. Turning quickly, she saw nothing. *I'm getting paranoid,* she concluded.

After the furniture had been pushed to the center, she grabbed the bag containing the paint. *Shoot, I need a screwdriver to open the can,* Andrea realized. As she walked toward the door, she noticed a rather large hole that had been chewed in the baseboard where she had pushed the bed away. "That is where the rat is getting in! Mark had better catch that filthy thing tonight, or I'm not staying here," she said out loud.

She walked back down the steps to the kitchen and pulled a screwdriver from a drawer. *I'm glad I unpacked almost everything. At least I know where to find things,* she thought. Returning to the bedroom, she reached for the can of paint. It wasn't where she had left it. "I know I left it there. I must be going crazy. Look, I'm already talking to myself." Looking around the room, it was nowhere to be found. "This house is playing hide-and-seek with me!" Walking out into the hallway, Andrea glanced down. There was the paint can. She picked it up, went back into the room, opened it, and poured some paint into the paint tray. She pushed the roller over the paint until it became soaked and began spreading it over the walls. The paint went on fast, brightening the room as she finished wall after wall. She stayed away from the edges, rationalizing that Mark could do the trim work tonight. Soon, everything was pink, including the ceiling. She had to stand on the chair to reach it, but finally it was done. Standing back in the doorway, she admired her work. *Looks pretty darn good for an amateur,* she mused.

"Oh, no." She looked at her watch. It was five til three. *He is going to be mad if I'm late picking him up,* she realized. She ran down the steps, slamming the door behind her. Getting in the car, she pushed the key into the ignition. Turning it, nothing happened. "What now, damn it?" she said out loud. Andrea could count the number of times in her life she had sworn. She felt bad already for saying the d-word. "Please start, please start," she kept repeating. Still it would not turn over. Finally, looking down, she noticed the car was in drive. *How is that possible?* she wondered as she slid it back into park. Upon Andrea turning the key once more, it started. As she pulled out of the driveway, she breathed a huge sigh of relief. Glancing at her watch as she raced toward the brickyard, she saw that it was ten after three. *I hope he isn't mad,* she prayed. After all, I painted the entire bedroom.

It was twenty after three when she finally pulled in and saw Mark sitting on a fence by the plant's entrance. She parked the car beside him and slid over into the passenger seat. Getting in the car, he smiled and said, "Did you forget me?"

"I'm sorry, Mark. I forgot about the time. I have a surprise for you when we get home."

"I hope it's what I think it is," he joked.

"Geez, is that all you think about, Mark?"

"I see you changed into something sexy," he laughed. Feeling something under his butt, he leaned to the side and pulled a bag out. "What's this?" he asked, handing it to Andrea.

"Oh, I went shopping after I dropped Amber off at school and got two blouses."

"Speaking of Amber, was she all right when you left her?"

"Yeah, she was a little scared, but she went with her teacher to the classroom. Her teacher's name is Mrs. Allen. She is young and seems very nice. The school secretary told me she would put Amber on the right bus after school."

"That was nice of her," Mark said, relieved. "When does she get home?"

"School lets out at three-thirty," Andrea answered. Before Andrea knew it, Mark was pulling into the driveway. "By the way, Mark," she began as they sat in the parking lot, "do you know what happened to the family that lived in this house before us?"

"I told you yesterday that I don't."

"Well, the janitor at the elementary school filled me in. They all died!"

"I know," Mark confessed. "I didn't want to tell you. I thought you would be uneasy living in the house if I told you."

Andrea punched him in the arm. "You rat, you'd better not lie to me ever again."

Get Out!

"I won't; I promise," Mark said, leaning over for a kiss.

Andrea pecked him on the cheek and said, "You're forgiven. Let's go in so I can show you your surprise." Getting out of the car they ran to the house, arm in arm. Andrea opened the door and told him to close his eyes. Mark closed his eyes, and she led him up the steps to Amber's room. Opening the door, she said, "Now you can open your eyes."

When Mark opened them, he couldn't believe what he saw. "You did all of this by yourself today?"

"Yes, I did. That's why I was late picking you up. There's a brush in that bag there; why don't you finish the trim while I get a bath before Amber gets home?"

"I have a better idea," Mark said. "Let's go to the bedroom and make love before you get a bath, and then I'll finish painting."

"You're so naughty, Mark," she said as she pulled him toward their bedroom. She pulled her clothes off and jumped onto the bed completely naked. "Is this what you want?" Mark's mouth was wide open as he started undressing. He jumped into bed and pulled her close to him. Andrea pushed him to his back and crawled on top.

As they made love, a strange feeling came over Andrea. She sensed someone was in the room watching them. Stopping her thrusts, she looked back and a shadow slid into the bathroom. "Mark, someone is in here!" she yelled, crawling off and pointing toward the bathroom.

"Andrea, don't stop now! You're just imagining things."

"I am not; check the bathroom."

Jumping from bed, Mark dashed to the bathroom. "See, I told you that it's in your head." He dove back into the bed. "That dumbass janitor should have kept his mouth shut. You're going to start seeing things now."

She crawled back on top of Mark and said, "Maybe you're right." They had just finished their lovemaking when they heard a school bus pull up. He ran to the bedroom window and saw Amber getting off the bus.

Andrea ran into the bathroom and locked the door. "Mark, get dressed quick so she doesn't see you naked," she yelled from the bathroom.

Mark pulled his clothes on and heard the water running in the tub as he went to meet his daughter at the front door. "Hi, Amber! How was school?"

"I love it, Daddy. I made three new friends today!"

"Did you learn anything new?"

"Lots of stuff. Where's Mommy?" she questioned him, racing up the steps.

Mark followed her and said, "She's getting a bath because she is dirty from painting your bedroom."

Amber's eyes grew wide as she stared into her bedroom. "It's just like my bedroom in Ohio. It's so beautiful."

"I thought you would like it, honey. Go downstairs and play in the yard while I finish up your room. Mommy will be done soon."

"Okay, Daddy." Amber ran down the steps and out the front door, slamming it behind her.

Walking to his bedroom, Mark noticed that Amber was rolling in the leaves in the front yard. Smiling, he returned to Amber's bedroom and began painting. He was quite good at cutting the paint into the trim. Seldom did he get paint on the white trim. Working his way around the room, he noticed the rat hole. "So that's where you got in last night, you little bastard." He sat his brush down on the paint lid and ran downstairs to his car. Opening the trunk, he retrieved a small toolbox. He jogged behind the house and opened the decaying garage door. It was dark inside as he entered the garage. Looking around, he found some scraps of wood. *This place gives me the creeps,* he thought with a shiver. He backed out of the garage and pushed the door shut. Returning to the house, he ran up the steps and saw his wife dressing in their bedroom. "Hi, honey," he yelled. "I found the rat hole."

"Yeah," she yelled, "I saw it too. I bought mice and rat traps today at the hardware store. You can set them tonight before bed."

"I will, but right now I'm going to fix this hole." Entering the room, a blast of cold air hit Mark in the face. *What the hell was that?* he thought to himself. He went to the rat hole, opened his toolbox, and retrieved a hammer and some nails. Sizing up a small piece of wood he had brought up from the garage, he nailed it to the baseboard, closing the hole. That done, he finished up the last touches of paint in the room. Pushing the bed against the wall, he hid the repaired rat hole. Lastly, he pushed the desk and chair back into place. Opening the closet, he retrieved sheets and blankets. He put the sheets on the bed and finally the covers. Closing the lid on the paint, he yelled for Andrea to come look at the finished product. She was downstairs starting supper but ran back up the steps. "Well, what do you think?" he asked.

"I think I like it better than our room, Mark. Amber will love it."

Mark smiled and said, "You can paint our room next."

"That's a weekend project for both of us," she replied. "I wanted to get her room done so we don't have to sleep three to a bed."

Touching the paint, Mark noticed it was dry already where Andrea had painted earlier that day. "I'll open the window to air it out," he said as he walked to the window. Pushing up on it, he realized that it would not budge.

"Maybe it's locked," Andrea suggested.

"No, it's not locked. Someone nailed it shut," Mark replied looking, down at the base of the window. "Andrea, hand me the hammer on the floor over there." She handed him the hammer and observed as Mark pulled two long nails out. Now, pushing up on the window once again, he watched as it opened right up. Mark turned and smiled at Andrea. "I'm quite the handyman," he teased.

"Why don't you go outside and play with your daughter? I'll finish making supper."

"Sounds good to me!" Mark said as he walked down the steps with Andrea behind him. "What's for supper, anyway?" Mark asked.

"Ham and cheese omelets," Andrea replied. "I didn't get to the grocery store today to get more groceries, so it will have to do."

"Sounds good to me," Mark yelled as he was going out the front door to play with Amber in the yard.

Running to his daughter who was playing around the side of the house, Mark grabbed her and tossed her into the air, catching her as she fell from the sky. The sun was trying to hang in the sky, but it was evident that darkness was just around the corner. "Do you want to race, Daddy?"

"Where to?" Mark asked.

"Twice around the house," Amber replied. "Ready, set, go!" she yelled as she starting running ahead of Mark. Mark raced behind her, realizing that his daughter was growing up as he struggled to keep up with her. Letting Amber cross the finish line first, he bent over, breathing hard.

"What's the matter? Am I too fast for you? Next time I'll let you win, Daddy," she laughed as she danced around Mark, who was still bent over and out of breath.

"You're such a sweetheart," he joked. "Would you really do that for me?"

There was a yell from the house; it was Andrea announcing that supper was ready. "I'll race you to the table!" Amber yelled as she took off running. Mark walked to the front door, still breathing hard as he entered the house and went to the kitchen. Amber and Andrea were already sitting down, smiling as he pulled his chair up to the table.

"So, your eight-year-old daughter beat you in a race?"

"She sure did," he joked as he began to pour himself a glass of milk. Mark said grace, as usual. Devouring the omelet like it was a piece of steak fit for a king, Mark declared, "You are an unbelievable chef, Andrea."

"Stop kidding around, Mark." Andrea's face became red.

"I'm not kidding, Andrea. I love the way you cook. Don't you, Amber?"

"I sure do, Daddy."

After the meal, as was the Jessup family's custom, everybody cleared their own plates and did the dishes together. Darkness had fallen, and it was now pitch black outside.

The family went to the living room and sat down to read. Amber made herself comfortable on the floor, crossing her legs in an Indian-style fashion. Holding a schoolbook, she declared, "I have homework to do."

"Well, you better get on it so you can play a little bit before bed. Your bedroom is finished, so you can sleep there tonight," Mark hinted.

"Can I see it now?"

"After you finish your homework, you can go play in your room until bedtime."

"Oh, all right," she said, grudgingly opening her book.

Suddenly there was a loud noise from Amber's room. "What the heck was that?" Mark said nervously.

"You better go check," ordered Andrea.

Mark ran up the steps, taking two at a time, and bolted through Amber's door. Turning the light on, he noticed the window had slammed shut. Opening and closing it several times, he decided that it appeared to be working fine. Finally, he closed the window and locked it. Walking to a wall, he touched the fresh paint. It was completely dry, and there was no smell. *I guess she can sleep here tonight*, he thought. Leaving the light on, he returned to the living room with mice and rat traps in hand. "Everything is under control. The window just slammed shut. Remember, I had it open to air the room out?"

"Well, Mark, how does a window close on its own?"

"Andrea, did you ever hear of gravity?" he asked, laughing as he walked to the kitchen. Opening the refrigerator, he took out a piece of cheese and returned to the living room.

"Where do you plan on putting those traps, Mark?"

"In the basement, why?"

"Because I don't want them out where people can see we have rats."

"Are you planning on having company over within the next few days? After all, you haven't met anyone yet," Mark needled her.

"Well, I haven't made any new friends yet like Amber has, but I intend to." Andrea smiled as she stuck her tongue out at Mark.

"Don't worry, honey. Your self-esteem will be intact. No one would ever want to go into our basement." Mark walked to the basement door, and opening it, he felt a chill run down his back. The air coming from the basement was eerily cold. "Andrea?"

"Yes, dear?" she answered.

"Do you want to come down here with me?"

"Why?" she asked. "Are you scared?"

"No, just stay where you are. I can handle this." As Mark switched the light on, he realized it was a very low watt bulb in the center of the basement. He could barely see down the steps. The basement had a musty odor to it.

Mark was halfway down the steps when it felt as if someone tripped him, and he began to tumble head over heels. The noise was so loud as he crashed to the basement floor that Andrea screamed and ran to the top of the steps. "Mark, are you all right?"

Bruised and cursing, he jumped to his feet. "I think so," he yelled up the steps.

"What happened?"

"I tripped coming down the steps," he moaned.

"Do you need me to help you walk?"

"No, I said I'm fine. Just go read your magazine."

The traps were scattered around his feet. Picking them up, he reached into his pants pocket and retrieved a piece of crushed cheese. Gazing around the dimly lit basement, he decided to explore it. There was old wooden shelving against the entire back wall with some used and unused canning jars on them. They looked to be canned peaches and tomato juice. *Disgusting,* he thought. *They're probably ten years old and spoiled.* The floor was only partially cement, and the rest of it was packed dirt. The place was filthy. Walking to the far side of the basement, he saw what appeared to be an old oil furnace. *They must have burned coal prior to buying the oil furnace,* he inferred, because there was an old coal chute located about ten feet from the back of the furnace. Bits of coal dust littered the floor, glistening from the dim light being cast from the other side of the room. *No wonder this house is cold all the time,* he thought to himself. *This thing is a piece of shit.* It appeared to have been green when it was new, but now all that was left were blotches of green paint and grease. He knew nothing about furnaces, but still, he started jiggling wires, trying to be manly.

As he was wiping grease from the motor with his hand, the furnace kicked on, scaring the hell out of him. Falling back onto his ass, he felt as if someone was watching him. Scanning the room, he saw a shadow pass by in the farthest corner of the basement. "Is that you, Andrea?" No answer.

A second later, Mark could swear he heard someone whispering. Frozen in fear, he strained to hear what the voice was saying. It was a haunting voice, but he made out the faint words, "Get out."

This is crazy, he thought to himself. *I'm hearing things now. I must have banged my head when I fell down the steps. This damn basement is creepy. I'm getting the hell out of here.*

He set two rat traps using the cheese as bait on the floor near the furnace. After placing the set mice traps on the old wooden shelving, he quickly walked back up the basement steps to the living room. He was covered in grease and dirt when he started to sit down on the sofa. "What do you think you are doing? You're filthy. Get upstairs and bathe before you think about sitting on this sofa," Andrea scolded.

Shaking his head, he went up the steps to the bathroom without speaking. Mark twisted the hot water handle open the whole way. Steaming water gushed forth. Putting his hand under the scolding water, he withdrew it, cursing. Twisting the cold water handle open halfway, he once again felt the water. "Ah, just right," he said quietly. The bathroom was so cold that he yelled down for Andrea to check the thermostat. Yelling back up, she said it was set at fifty degrees. "Who is playing with that thermostat, Andrea?" he yelled back down. "Tell Amber to stay away from it!"

"She said she didn't touch it, Mark."

"Well, someone is touching the damn thing!" he yelled as he crawled into the tub. "Turn it up to seventy and leave it alone!"

The water felt soothing. Mark laid his head back and closed his eyes. He slipped down deep into the water so that only his head was above the water line. *I have to keep warm somehow,* he thought. *This house needs some work.* As he soaked, he drifted into a half-sleep stupor. He felt as if he was in a dream state, and he didn't want to come out of it.

After soaking in the tub for half an hour, he opened his eyes. The water was cherry red, the color of blood. Screaming, Mark jumped from the tub and began gagging. He turned to look away from the water and glimpsed into the mirror. A man in a military uniform appeared in the mirror and then faded away. The hair on the back of his neck stood up. Standing there naked and dripping wet, he watched as Andrea crashed through the bathroom door. "What's wrong, Mark?"

"The tub is full of blood, Andrea!"

GET OUT!

Looking into the tub, Andrea said, "What are you talking about?"

Slowly, he turned around to see that the tub was full of nothing but dirty, black water. "I'm telling you, it was blood red when I opened my eyes while soaking in it."

"Honey, you are so worn-out from working so hard the past few days that you probably fell asleep inside the tub. I bet you were dreaming."

"Maybe you're right." He thought it best not to mention the man in the mirror. Andrea would think he was really going off the deep end.

"Put your underwear on, and go to bed. I'll lock up and tuck Amber into her bed."

Mark went to his bedroom. Examining his body, he noticed numerous black and blue marks on his body from the fall down the steps. Tired and sore, he pulled on a pair of underwear and crawled under the covers. He had felt warm air blowing from the air ducts before crawling under the covers, but the house still felt cold. *I must be getting sick*, he deduced. His mind was in a haze when Andrea finally crawled under the covers beside him. "Hold me close, Andrea, I'm so cold." Sliding her body close to his, he felt her warmth. Reaching out from under the covers, he turned off his lamp. It was pitch black in the room. Now in the dark, Mark asked Andrea how Amber liked her bedroom.

"She loves it. She went right in without complaining. She was hungry before bed, so I made her a snack of milk and cookies to take into her bedroom. She had them eaten before we got to her room."

"That's nice," Mark said. The house was dead silent as he drifted into a sound sleep.

At three in the morning, a bloodcurdling scream woke Mark and Andrea from a sound sleep. It was Amber, crying hysterically. With no hesitation, they sprang from their bed and ran to her bedroom. Amber, in the jet-black room, was sitting up in her bed, crying uncontrollably. Her window was wide open, and cold air was rushing in.

"What's wrong?" Andrea pleaded as she hugged and comforted her.

"There was a man sitting at that desk, and he kept staring at me. He had a glow around his body and wouldn't talk for the longest time. He just sat there and stared at me. I was so afraid that I couldn't move. Then a look of anger came on his face, and he yelled, 'Get out now; this is your last warning!'"

"Amber, honey, the room is dark, and you were asleep. You just had a bad dream."

Mark shut the window without thinking and walked to Amber, lifting her into his arms. "You can spend the rest of the night in our bedroom. Mommy's right; you were probably dreaming because you ate food before you went to sleep. Your mind becomes more active when you eat before going to bed." Carrying her back to his bedroom, he noticed that Amber was shaking as they all crawled under the covers. Their bodies were pressed tight against each other as they drifted back to sleep.

When the alarm went off at six o'clock in the morning, Mark reached over and slammed the button down to turn it off. His head was spinning with a killer headache, so he lay in bed contemplating a sick day.

Andrea slowly crawled from the bed and jostled Amber until she woke up. "Sweetie, get up and brush your teeth for school."

Amber opened her eyes and smiled. "I forgot about school. I get to see my new friends again today!" She happily jumped from the bed and ran to the bathroom, seemingly forgetting about her bad nightmare last night.

Mark still had a pillow over his head when Andrea sat down on the bed beside him. "Mark, aren't you going to work?"

"I don't know," he replied. "My head is killing me."

"Well, if you're going, you had better get up. It's quarter after six."

Pulling the pillow from his head, he asked Andrea to get him some aspirin and water.

"Sure," she replied as she walked to the bathroom and returned with a glass of water and two aspirin. Sitting on the edge of the bed in his underwear, Mark commented on the cold room. *I'm sick of that damn good-for-nothing furnace. If it doesn't start warming up in this house, I'm calling the landlord and tell him we are moving out if he doesn't replace the furnace.*

"Here, take your aspirin, and get dressed."

Mark gulped down the pills and swallowed the entire glass of water. Standing up, he put on a fresh set of work clothes as Andrea returned to the bathroom. He felt so utterly drained and miserable that he didn't bother going to the bathroom to clean up or brush his teeth.

"Mark, are you all right?" Andrea yelled from the bathroom.

"Yes, damn it, I'm fine. Stop asking!" he screamed with utter contempt in his voice. The veins in his neck were protruding as he left the bedroom and walked downstairs. Opening the front door, he was greeted with a blast of crisp, cold morning air. The air was so frigid that he struggled to breathe. He sucked the coldness into his lungs and expelled a breath that he could see billowing out into the air. *I'm so sick and tired of her treating me like a child,* he thought as he walked to his car. Opening the car door, it occurred to him he hadn't said good-bye to Amber or his wife. *The hell with it,* he thought as he backed out of the driveway and drove to work.

Andrea walked back to the bedroom, searching for Mark. "Mark, where are you? You're going to be late, honey." Still no answer, so she ran down the steps and into the kitchen. Not finding him anywhere in the house, she looked out the window into the driveway. The car was gone. *That son of a gun left without saying good-bye,* she thought crossly. "Amber, come down and eat breakfast," she yelled.

"I'll be right down, Mommy."

Returning to the kitchen, Andrea made two bowls of cereal. Amber ran to the kitchen and slid her chair up to the kitchen table. Taking a bite of her cereal, she asked, "Where's Daddy?"

"He was late, so he had to leave right away. You'll see him tonight after school."

"Okay, but I wish he would have kissed me good-bye like he always does."

"Daddy has a lot on his mind, Amber. He has been working so hard, so we need to give him some time to himself."

Finishing her cereal. Amber placed her bowl in the sink and ran to the living room to get her schoolbooks and put on a coat. It was a bright pink jacket her Grammy Mabel bought her. As soon as her grandmother saw it, she knew Amber would love it. Pink was Amber's favorite color. This was evident in almost everything she wore, from her dresses right down to her blouses. Most of her wardrobe had been purchased by her grandmother who loved to spoil her.

It was a quarter after seven when the school bus honked its horn. "Hurry, or the bus will leave without you," Andrea urged her daughter. Kissing Amber and smiling, she stepped out onto the front porch in front of her. She just had to see her daughter get on the bus. The air was bitter, and she wrapped her robe tight around her waist. Amber ran as fast as her skinny toothpick legs would carry her toward the yellow school bus. Before climbing into the bus, she stopped to wave at her mom and blow her a kiss.

"I love you," Andrea yelled as the bus door closed behind her daughter. Closing the door, Andrea went back upstairs to her bedroom. Crawling back under the covers to get warm, she fell asleep.

Mark pulled into the parking lot at twenty till seven. *I'm early for once*, he thought as he punched the time clock. After punching in, he realized he had forgotten his lunch. *Oh well, I'll get a candy bar from the lunch room and a soda,* he decided. *That will tide me over until supper.*

Finding his supervisor, he yelled, "Hey, Jake, what needs done today?"

Jake took one look at him and said, "Mark, you look like shit."

"Well, I feel like shit," he replied. "My head is killing me. That damn house is like an icebox, and my kid was up last night at three in the morning screaming because she had a bad dream."

"Sounds like, all in all, you had the night from hell last night, kid."

"Believe me, I did. That house gives me the creeps. I swear there is more to that house than meets the eye."

"What, kid, now are you telling me it's haunted?" Jake laughed.

"I don't believe in that crap either, Jake, but I swear there is some weird stuff going on in that house. The furnace runs nonstop, but it is still chilly inside. I hear things too."

"You're probably tired from burning the candle at both ends. You've been working a full-time job and trying to move your family into a house from an entire state away. You're just exhausted."

"Yeah, you're probably right, Jake. I'm sure it will get easier after we get settled in." With the aspirin starting to work, Mark's mood improved.

It was nine o'clock when Andrea was startled from a deep sleep by a loud slamming noise. Jumping out of bed, she ran to the hallway. Nothing was out of place, so she went into Amber's room to check to see if something had fallen. Entering the room, she was hit with a blast of cold air. The window was wide open, and the cold morning air was blasting in. The temperature was considerably colder than yesterday, making it evident that winter was just around the corner. She rushed to the window and slammed it shut. Locking it, she became nervous. *How can a window open on its own?* she wondered. *I know Mark locked it last night. At least, I think he did.* Backing up, she sat on Amber's bed and stared at the possessed window. Remembering the window had been nailed shut, she yelled, "What the heck!" Suddenly her hair felt as if someone was brushing it aside. The tiny hairs on her arms and the back of her neck began to tingle. A man's haunting voice which seemed riddled with pain was whispering to her, "Get out. Get out. GET OUT NOW!"

Andrea ran from the room, slamming the door closed behind her. Running into her bedroom, she shut the door and flopped down onto her bed. *Now I'm hearing things,* she thought. *This house must be evil. But spirits don't exist. There is no such thing as haunting. People will think I'm crazy if I say anything to anyone.*

Maybe a hot bath will calm my nerves, she decided. Letting her robe drop to the floor, she exposed her slim, curvy body. Walking past her bedroom window, she glanced out. Startled, she noticed her next-door neighbor spying at her from her living room bay window. All that was exposed was the women's head, as she seemed to be making an effort to hide herself behind he curtains. It was not working, because her dyed blonde hair was making her stand out like a prostitute at a church supper. She had never met the woman before, partly because they had been too busy, and partly because the woman had never made an effort to talk to them. In fact, this was the first time she had ever seen the woman. Standing there naked in front of her bedroom window, she began to wave. Embarrassed, Delores quickly withdrew from the window. The whole scenario caused Andrea to laugh as she walked to the bathroom. *I think I'll pay her a visit this afternoon when I'm done bathing,* she resolved.

After turning the tub water on until steam rose from the cascading water, Andrea went to the medicine cabinet and began brushing her teeth. She was covered in goose bumps from the coldness of the house. She chuckled as she remembered Mark teasing her that the only benefit to living in a cold house was that her nipples were always large and swollen. *That hot bath is going to feel so refreshing*, she thought. The tub water was to the point of overflowing when Andrea finally shut it off. Feeling the water, she shuddered at how hot it was. As she slid her body into the tub, the cold air around her made the water feel all the hotter. Gasping, she could barely take it as her body became acclimated to the hot water. After a few minutes, the water became soothing and relaxing to her aching body. *How can something as simple as a hot bath make a person feel so much better?* she wondered. She lay in the tub with her eyes closed, relaxing for over an hour, occasionally turning on the hot water to keep the tub warm. Finally, she lifted the drain plug and crawled from the tub. Immediately, she noticed how cold the outside air was. Her skin, now shriveled from the extended stay in the water, was once again covered in goose bumps. *Darn, I left my robe in the bedroom,* Andrea realized. Grabbing a towel from the linen closet, she began to dry her wet body as she walked to her bedroom. *Thank God our bedroom connects to this bathroom; a person could freeze to death in this house if they had to walk very far to get their clothes,* she mused to herself. *Funny thing is, I can't remember Amber ever complaining of the cold in this house. Kids must have a fast metabolism or something,* she concluded. Dropping the towel to the floor and once again exposing her naked body, she reached out for her bra lying on the desk. It suddenly felt as though someone's hands were gently caressing her breasts from behind. Feeling violated, Andrea sensed someone or something was there in the room with her. Panicked, she quickly turned around, finding no one. Searching in her closet, under the bed, and back in the bathroom was to no avail. Feeling uneasy, she quickly put her bra on and dressed. *I swear, I must be manifesting all this stuff in my head. I wish that janitor had never told me about the people dying in this house,* she thought.

Warmer now that she had her clothing on, Andrea walked down the steps to the living room. Picking up the romance novel she had begun reading the night before, she sat on the sofa and propped her feet up on the coffee table. *I'm not going to let this house get the best of me,* she thought as she began to read. Hour after hour, she continued to read her book. Before she knew it, she had finished the last page. It was two-thirty in the afternoon when she finally rose from the sofa.

Going to the front door and opening it, she decided to pay her strange neighbor lady a visit. As she walked across the yard to her neighbor's house, she began wishing she had worn a coat. It was freezing out there.

Arriving at Delores's front door, Andrea knocked and knocked, but no one would answer. Delores's home was in much better shape than their house. It had a fresh coat of yellow paint with tan trim. Her yard, however, was overgrown, indicating that she lived alone. *She must have gone somewhere while I was reading,* Andrea assumed. Leaving the front porch, she began walking back to her house; however, before going back into her home she glanced at Delores's house one last time. There, in the bay window, was the same woman's face. No body, just her face peering out from behind those same white curtains. *That woman has a lot of nerve,* Andrea thought to herself as she entered her home. *Well, if she doesn't want to be friendly, the heck with her.*

Lying on the sofa, she heard Mark pull into the driveway. As he came through the door, she yelled, "I hope you got rid of that grouch who left for work this morning without so much as a good-bye."

"Oh, he's gone, and this horny, handsome man has come home to this freezing house in his place," Mark chuckled, spitting the words out. Running to the sofa, he dove on her, forcing her legs apart. Wrapping his arms around her waist and pulling her close, he passionately kissed her lips, sliding his tongue inside her mouth.

"Wow, you are a tiger. What got into you from work until now, Mark?"

"Nothing. My headache is gone, so now I'm the same lovable man you married." He began kissing her breasts and sucking on them through her blouse, making a round, wet mark on each breast. Andrea began to respond to his advances by breathing heavy. *She's mine,* he thought to himself as he unbuttoned her jeans and pulled them off. As he pulled her panties off, she began to rub him through his work pants. He did not bother taking his pants off but rather unzipped the fly on his pants.

"Hurry, Amber will be home from school soon," Andrea said as lust and excitement radiated from her voice. Sitting back on the sofa, Mark became excited as Andrea rose from the sofa, turned toward him, swirling her tongue over her sultry lips, and finally straddling him. They were rougher than usual in their lovemaking. It was as if they were possessed, twisting and writhing until each climaxed.

Withdrawing, Andrea sat up and said, "You're wild today, honey."

"You're not your usual self either," he replied. "I kind of like it that way."

After dressing, they heard the school bus pull up out front. Mark opened the front door and watched as Amber jumped from the bus and ran to the house. Seeing her dad standing there, she jumped into his arms. "Daddy, you forgot to say good-bye and give me a kiss this morning."

"I know, I'm sorry. It will never happen again."

Jumping from Mark's arms, Amber ran to her mother and, kissing her, she said excitedly, "Guess what? I made two more friends today. They are boys, Tommy and Joey. We played together at recess."

"That's awesome, Amber," Andrea replied, winking at Mark. "Do you have homework tonight?"

"Yes, the teacher gave us tons of it, Mommy."

"Well, after supper, you better start on it right away. Are you going to try your own bedroom again tonight?"

"Do I have to?"

"Yes, you have to get used to it, Amber, but no more snacks before bed."

"Okay, Mommy, I will if Molly can sleep with me in my bed."

"She can. Now go wash up because Daddy doesn't know it, but we are going for groceries."

Mark smiled and said, "Don't you need to wash up too, Andrea?" Smiling, Andrea followed Amber up the steps.

Mark was waiting in the car for fifteen minutes before his wife and daughter bounded into the front seat. "We're ready now, Daddy. You drive us to the store."

"What took you so long? I've been waiting here for an hour."

"Nothing like exaggerating, Mark," Andrea chided. "Anyway, it was your fault I had to change my underwear and jeans."

"Why did you change those sexy jeans?"

"I'll tell you why. Because someone got excited and popped the button off today."

Amber cut in, saying, "What are you talking about, Mommy?"

"Oh, nothing, honey. Play with your doll."

Laughing, Mark backed out of the driveway and headed to the market.

Leighty's Market was a small grocery store. It had everything anyone could ever want from a grocery store, including a small deli and meat department, as well as a full line of groceries. Pulling into the store parking lot, Mark parked the car and declared, "I'll wait here while you two ladies shop, if you don't mind."

"That's fine, dear, but you'll have to give me some money."

Pulling out his wallet, Mark handed Andrea forty dollars. "Stock up, Andrea. I don't want to have to come here every day," he laughed.

Mark was asleep in the car for an hour before they returned with a cart-load of groceries. Hearing someone tapping on the window, he groggily opened his eyes. "Mark," Andrea yelled through the window, "put these in the trunk." Getting out of the car, Mark opened the trunk and began lifting heavy bagfuls and placing them neatly into the trunk. Andrea and Amber were already in their seats when he slammed the trunk shut and got back into the car.

Heading home, he yawned and said, "I'm beat. I must have loaded ten ton of block today."

"You didn't seem tired to me. In fact, I could have sworn you had the energy of two men when you first came home," Andrea joked.

"Well, that took a lot out of me too," he kidded back to her.

"Well, guess what we are having for supper tonight?"

"Don't tell me; I want to be surprised. I forgot my lunch today, and I'm so hungry I could eat a horse."

The wind had really picked up in the past hour, blowing leaves and branches all over the road. The temperature was thirty-five degrees, but with the wind blowing, it felt like zero. Struggling to keep the car on the road from the rough winds, Mark finally pulled into their driveway. "Everybody can help haul groceries in," Mark barked as he opened the car door and walked around to the trunk. After opening the trunk, he placed two light bags into Andrea's arms.

"Give me a bag too," Amber whined as she stood in the cold, the heavy, gusting winds blowing hair up over her face.

Placing the lightest bag in her arms, he softly said, "Here you go, sweetie."

She followed her mother into the house while Mark scooped up the remaining three heavy bags and followed them. Dropping the bags on the kitchen counter, Mark declared he was going to get a bath.   Andrea replied, "Go relax, Mark. I'll put these away and make supper." Turning to her daughter, she said, "Amber, start your homework right now so you can play before bed."

It was starting to get dark outside, so Mark turned the lamp on in the living room before heading upstairs. Pausing to look at the thermostat on his way up the steps, he noticed it was set for seventy degrees. Shaking his head, he turned it up to eighty-five. It didn't matter anyway; he could hear that the furnace was already running before he turned it up.

Taking the steps two at a time, Mark was out of breath as he entered the bathroom. After he closed the door, Mark noticed this room seemed to be colder than the rest of the house. His breath was actually visible as he expelled air from his mouth. "Damn, this is ridiculous. How am I going to undress in here and take a bath?" After turning the hot water on as far as the handle would turn, steam began to fill the bathroom, fogging the mirror. Mark went to his bedroom and grabbed his robe. Returning to the bathroom, he undressed and slid into the scalding water. *Ah! That feels so good,* he thought. Shutting the water off, he grabbed the soap and lathered his entire body. By now, his stomach was growling. Rinsing the soap off and pulling out the drain plug, he crawled out of the tub and pulled his robe on. *It's too cold to towel off in here!* he realized. He tied the heavy robe around his waist and allowed it to soak the water from his body. Grabbing a comb from the sink, he began wiping the condensation from the mirror so that he could comb his hair.

He looked into the mirror, but what he saw was unexpected. The image of another man's face was staring straight into his eyes. Startled, he dropped the comb and turned away from the mirror to see if someone was behind him. Of course, no one was there. Mark turned to look in the mirror once more. The image was no longer in the mirror, only his own reflection. *I can't stand this house,* he thought to himself. Combing his hair, he left the bathroom.

Mark bounded down the stairs and returned to the kitchen where Andrea was preparing supper. The smell of steak frying in the skillet drew him to the stove. "That smells great!"

"Mark, you ruined the surprise! I'm making your favorite: steak, potatoes, and corn. Go to the living room and read. I bought the paper and two magazines at the grocery store."

"Okay, okay. I'll go read, but hurry up. I'm starving." Still in his robe, Mark picked the paper up and went to the living room. Sitting on the sofa, he noticed Amber lying on the floor, pondering over her homework. "Do you need help?"

"No, I can figure it out myself, Daddy."

Turning his attention to the paper, he browsed the local section. There was a large article on the brickyard's explosive growth in the past year. Smiling, he yelled to Andrea about the article.

"I'll read it tonight before bed," she assured him.

Finishing the article, Mark heard Andrea yell that supper was ready. Before she finished the sentence, Mark was sitting at the kitchen table, cutting his steak.

"You must be starved! I guess that's what happens when you forget your lunch."

"I guess so," Mark replied with a mouth full of food.

"Amber, come to supper before your dad eats it all," Andrea yelled.

"I'm not hungry," she called back. "I want to finish my homework."

"Do your homework after supper. You have to eat something, because you're not getting a snack before bed."

Disgusted, Amber came to the table and pulled her chair up. "Daddy didn't say grace, Mommy."

"I guess we can skip it one night, honey, since Daddy is so hungry." Andrea set a plate of food with small portions in front of Amber. "Eat it all, and you can go finish your homework." Amber began gulping her food down.

"You must really like doing homework," Mark chimed in, smiling.

"I love school, Daddy, but the teacher gets upset if you forget your homework."

"Well, I guess you better not forget to do it."

"I won't." Amber swallowed her last bite and asked to be excused.

"You're excused, Amber. I'll clear your plate for you so you can finish your homework," Andrea offered.

Amber got up from the table, commenting on how good the food was as she walked back to the living room.

"Well, what did you think of the meal, Mark?"

"I think it was the best steak I've ever eaten. You are one great cook."

"Well, thank you. That's a sweet thing to say."

After they finished eating, Mark helped with the dishes and cleaned the table and stove. "I think we should go to Altoona this weekend and buy a television."

"Mark, we can't afford a television."

"We can if we buy it on time payments."

"Do you really need a television?"

"I don't need a lot of things, but I really would like one."

"Fine, we'll go look." After kissing, they walked to the living room and flopped on the sofa. Andrea tossed Mark a magazine to read.

"I would much rather read a book or magazine than watch television."

"Well, that's the difference between me and you. Reading is too much like working for me; it's a lot easier to let someone else do the work," Mark chuckled.

They quietly sat and read until Amber squealed, "I'm finished!"

"It's about time," Mark teased. "What do you want to do before bed?"

"I'm going to play with my doll Molly."

"I guess that leaves me out." Mark looked dejected.

"You can play dolls with me if you want to, Daddy."

"That's all right, honey, I'll finish reading this magazine."

It was nine o'clock when Andrea declared it time for bed. "Tomorrow's a school day," she reminded Amber.

Yawning, Amber picked up Molly and started walking up the stairs to her bedroom without a fight. Andrea looked at Mark and asked if he wanted to tuck her in.

"You do it, Andrea, while I lock up down here."

Following Amber up the steps, Mark could hear Andrea talking to her. After locking up, Mark went to their bedroom and asked Andrea what she had said to Amber. "I told her if she gets scared in the middle of the night, she can come to our room."

"Andrea, sooner or later, she has to get used to sleeping alone."

"Knock it off. She is used to sleeping alone. When we lived in Ohio, she slept every night in her own room, and you know it. This is only her second night in that room; it will take her a while to get used to it."

"Yeah, you're right. I'm being stupid." Mark removed his robe and put on a pair of underwear, while Andrea went to the bathroom to get ready for bed. Returning to the bedroom in her nightgown, she crawled into bed next to her husband.

"Get close to me," Andrea begged. "I'm freezing." She didn't have to say it twice as Mark pulled her close to his body. "That feels better. Goodnight, Mark."

"Goodnight," Mark replied, turning the lamp off. They fell into a deep, uninterrupted sleep.

It was six in the morning when the alarm went off. Waking up, Mark smiled at Andrea. "Amber made it through the whole night without getting up."

Andrea ran to the bathroom to pee. When she returned to the bedroom, she had a smile on her face. "Guess what, Mark? The house is actually warm for once."

"No way," he said from under the covers.

"It is! Get up and see for yourself."

Mark rolled out from under the covers and landed on his feet like an acrobat. "It's warm," he yelled, smiling from ear to ear.

"You better get ready for work. I'll get Amber up." Opening their bedroom door, Andrea yelled, "Amber, get up and get ready for school!" Andrea removed her nightgown and pulled on her jeans and blouse. "Did you hear me, Amber?" Andrea yelled once more, walking to her daughter's bedroom. Opening the door, she immediately felt a blast of cold air. The window was wide open. "Amber, did you open that window?" Andrea looking at the bed, noticing that Amber had a pillow on top of her head. "Amber, get up," she taunted, shaking the bed. There was still no movement from her daughter. Lifting the pillow from her head, she noticed her daughter's lips were blue, and her skin was pale. Taking Amber into her arms, she knew immediately that her daughter was dead. Her body was cold, stiff, and lifeless.

Mark was startled by a bloodcurdling scream. He ran from the bathroom, tripping and tumbling to his face in the hallway. Blood was pouring from his nose as he regained his footing and stormed into Amber's room. The scene was gruesome; his wife had his daughter's lifeless body cradled in her arms, screaming and crying simultaneously. "She's dead, Mark, she's dead!"

"No! No, she can't be!" Mark screamed. "What happened? There's nothing wrong with her. Wake her up, Andrea! Please wake her up!" he screamed, with tears and blood flowing down his face. Andrea had her daughter held so tightly that Mark could not pry her loose.

Wiping the blood from his face as he ran down the steps, Mark reached for the phone and called the operator, screaming into the phone, "This is an emergency! My daughter is not breathing!"

"Sir, calm down, please. Where are you?"

Mark was going into shock as he mumbled their address. Dropping the phone, he unlocked the front door and ran back up the steps to Amber's bedroom. Andrea was still clinging onto her daughter's body, sobbing.

Crawling into the opposite side of the bed, Mark embraced both of them in a daze.

Within fifteen minutes, a siren could be heard. The ambulance skidded to a stop in their driveway, and paramedics were beating on the door within seconds. Hurrying down the steps, Mark opened the door, crying, and pointed up stairs without speaking. Following two young paramedics upstairs to Amber's room, he pulled Andrea from Amber's body so they could examine her. The paramedic's face told the story they already knew. Amber was dead. Examining her body, they could find no bruises or indications as to how she died. "I'm sorry, ma'am," was all they could say. Mark could tell the two young men were struggling to hold tears back. "We'll transport her body to Spring Cove Hospital in the ambulance," one said, his voice shaking. "One of you can ride with her in the back if you would like." Andrea nodded yes. Returning with a stretcher, they lifted her rigid body and, placing it on the stretcher, covered it with a sheet.

"I'll follow you in the car," Mark sobbed.

"Do you know where the hospital is located, sir?"

"Yes," Mark answered, his voice quivering.

As they were carrying Amber's body downstairs, Mark walked to the window to close it. Sticking his head out the window for some air before closing it, Mark noticed that Amber's doll Molly was lying on the ground below. How was that possible? Hearing the ambulance pull from the driveway, he pulled his head inside and closed the window. The window was fogged over with condensation dripping from it. Written in the condensation were two unmistakable, simple words: GET OUT! Jumping back from the window, Mark screamed, "You killed my daughter, you son-of-a-bitch! Show yourself! Show yourself now!" When this elicited no response, Mark turned and walked from the bedroom. He was no sooner down the steps than he heard Amber's bedroom door slam shut. Running out the front door to his car, Mark got in, but while slamming the car door shut, he realized that Amber's doll was still lying on the ground outside the home. *She loved that doll so much,* he thought to himself ruefully. Opening the door, he ran from the car to the side of the house and retrieved the doll. Mark returned to his car, got inside, started the vehicle, and sped from the driveway, the tires spitting shale everywhere as he raced toward the hospital.

The ambulance drove toward Spring Cove Hospital slowly with only its lights flashing. There was no need to run the sirens, as the child was dead. Spring Cove Hospital was located in the small town of Roaring Spring, fifteen miles from Claysburg. It was a small hospital, serving the town of Roaring Spring as well as the surrounding communities.

Andrea sat in the back of the ambulance with the paramedic. Pulling the sheet back from Amber's face, she continued to sob as she looked at her daughter's innocent face. Amber's eyes were wide open; however, they had rolled upward, revealing only the whites of her eyes. That, along with a look of horror still embedded in her facial features, caused the paramedic to look away. "Ma'am, are you sure you would not be more comfortable covering the child's face?" he asked.

"She has a name," Andrea screamed, sobbing uncontrollably. "Her name was Amber, and no, I don't want her face covered."

"I am so sorry for your loss, ma'am. I just don't know what to say."

Andrea said nothing the rest of the way to the hospital.

The paramedic drove the ambulance to the back of the hospital where the emergency room was located. Backing up to the door, two orderlies ran out to greet the paramedics. Opening the back door of the ambulance, the orderlies were greeted with a ghastly sight, a mother cradling her dead child in her arms with the paramedic trying to pull her away from the child. "Please, ma'am, we need to remove her body from the ambulance."

Within minutes, Mark had pulled up beside the ambulance and ran to the back. Seeing his hysterical wife, he lost all control. "Get your damn hands off my wife," he screamed at the paramedic as he crawled into the ambulance. Once inside, Mark pulled Andrea from Amber's body and wrapped his arms around her. "Come with me, honey. These gentlemen need to take her body into the hospital." As they crawled from the ambulance, Mark had to steady his wife. Andrea was in shock and could not walk. Carrying her inside with the orderlies in tow, Mark placed his wife on a bed in the emergency room.

Within minutes, a doctor was there examining her. Pulling Mark to the side, the doctor informed him that Andrea was in shock and he was going to sedate her. Andrea began thrashing about on the bed, trying to get up to see her daughter. "Hold her down," the doctor yelled to the orderlies.

As they grabbed her arms and legs, she began screaming, "I want to see my daughter. Please! I'm begging you, please let me see her."

The doctor pulled a needle from a tray provided by a heavy set older nurse and injected it into Andrea's arm. Within minutes, she stopped thrashing and began to relax. "She'll be asleep in a few minutes," he announced to everyone.

Looking at Mark, he sympathetically said, "What about you? Do you need something to calm your nerves? You've been through a lot today."

"I'm fine," Mark replied sharply. "Just take care of my wife." Looking down at his wife, he noticed she was asleep. "I'm sorry," Mark said, his voice shaking.

"Don't worry about it," replied the doctor, obviously moved by the whole scene that had transpired before him.

Mark walked to the waiting room and sat down in a chair. Holding his head in his hands he began to cry. *How could this have happened? We were the perfect family.* "That house be damned!" he screamed out loud, causing everyone in the waiting room to jump.

He was sitting there in the chair for a half a hour when a short, slender police officer sat down beside him. "Hi, Mark. My name is John Robinson. I know we have never formally met, but I'm the police chief in Claysburg, and I need to ask you a few questions."

"Can't this wait?" Mark screamed. "I just lost my daughter."

"Well, son, when would be a good time?"

"Let's just get it over with," Mark barked. "What do you need to know?"

"Start from the beginning, Mark. When did you notice the child had died?"

"This morning when my wife and I got up, she went to Amber's bedroom and found her dead. There wasn't a mark on her precious body. She was just lying there, unresponsive. The bedroom window was open, which I thought was strange, and when I closed it, I saw that there were words written on it. It said 'Get out!' on the window."

"What do you mean by written on it?" Chief Robinson asked.

"What I mean is there were words written on the glass, not in paint or anything, in the condensation on the window."

Just then, the medical examiner, Bob Simmons, sat down beside the police chief. "John, I take it you're here concerning the child that just came in."

"Yes, I am, Bob. This is the child's father, Mark Jessup."

Shaking Mark's hand, he said, "I guess you're going to want to hear this too. The child died of asphyxiation. In layman's terms, she was smothered to death, most likely by her own pillow or something soft. There were no marks on her face or neck that would indicate that she was choked by someone's hands. I'm ruling the death as a homicide, John."

"Were there any signs of struggle?" John asked.

"No, John, it's the damnedest thing, Usually someone who is being smothered claws and fights for their life, but this child did not have so much as a scrape of skin under her nails. There were no signs of sexual abuse, and other than her physical death, there was not a bruise on her body. It is a very unusual case. I don't know what else to tell you." Shaking both their hands, Bob rose and left.

"Mark, do you mind if I go to your house now and check it out? I want to see if someone could have used a ladder to gain access to your daughter's bedroom."

Shaking his head in disbelief, Mark said to go ahead.

"One last thing, Mark, before I go, was the front door locked this morning when you got up?"

"Yes, I'm positive it was because I had to open it for the paramedics. It was locked and dead bolted. I could also have sworn that Amber's bedroom window was also locked," Marked mumbled as Chief Robinson was leaving.

Mark got up from his seat and went to Andrea's bedside. She was in a deep, peaceful sleep, her face no longer riddled with grief. Crawling into her small bed beside her, he closed his eyes and drifted to sleep.

Chief Robinson pulled into the Jessup's driveway. Getting out of his car, he walked to the side of the house where he knew Elijah's bedroom used to be. Looking up at the window, he could have sworn he saw a man's face peering out of the window. Shaking his head, he again looked up. There was nothing there. *That is weird,* he thought to himself. Glancing down at the ground, Chief Robinson searched for indentations suggesting a ladder had been placed there. There was nothing indicative of the idea that anything had been placed there to enter the home. Turning around, he glanced at Delores's house. There she was, looking out her living room window. The chief motioned for her to come out. She shook her head strongly, refusing.

Walking to her front door, Chief Robinson began to knock. Delores would only open it a crack. "Delores, may I come in?" he asked.

"You can talk just fine from where you are standing," she replied with anger in her voice.

Shaking his head at her mean disposition, he asked, "Delores, did you notice anything or anybody at that window last night?"

"No. Why do you want to know?" she barked.

"I'll tell you why; a child was murdered there last night."

"I didn't see anything," she said in an unemotional tone. "That house is evil. If you were smart, you would tear it down. There's been too much death in that house."

"Delores, you're just superstitious. You need to get out more." Disgusted, Delores slammed the door in his face.

The chief walked away from Delores's house and returned to the front door of the Jessup home. Trying the doorknob, he noticed it was unlocked. Going inside, he entered the living room. The temperature in the house was freezing. *Why the hell don't these people turn the heat up?* The thermostat was located on the wall in the living room by the steps that led upstairs. Walking to it, he noticed it was set at seventy-two degrees. *There is no way it is seventy-two in this house. Someone needs to look at that furnace,* he thought. After finishing his thought, he heard something slam upstairs. "Anyone in here?" he yelled, spooked by the noise. Rushing up the stairs, he opened the door leading to Elijah's bedroom. "Anyone here?" he bellowed once again. There was no answer, but he did notice that the window was wide open. "I am positive that the window was closed," he said, talking out loud to himself as he walked to the window and closed it. The condensation was no longer present on the window. Looking around the room, he searched for signs of a forced entry. Nothing in the room suggested it. The room was painted a pretty pink. *A typical child's room,* he thought to himself. Examining the windowsill, he searched for scratches that would indicate someone had entered through the window. There was nothing that suggested that either. Either someone was extremely careful coming through the window, or he would have to include each parent as a prime suspect, he decided. Writing some notes into a notepad he always carried with him, Chief Robinson left the room. *I have every thing I need from here,* he thought to himself. Walking down the steps, he remembered he had left the door to Amber's room open. Turning around to go back up the steps, he heard the door slam shut. "What the hell is with this house? I'm getting the hell out of here." The chief ran down the steps and out the front door, slamming it behind him. No one would believe this. *They would call me crazy if I tried to tell someone about this house,* he concluded.

Pulling from the driveway, Chief Robinson decided he would write the death up as a pending homicide investigation. *I need to go back to the hospital and get more details from the wife. Hopefully she is awake by now,* he thought.

Andrea stirred; she had been asleep for two hours and was just starting to wake. Everything was blurry as she came to. *Where am I?* she thought to herself. Jerking, she noticed someone was lying beside her. It was Mark. *Why is he in bed with me? Where am I?* The morning's events seemed to be blocked from her memory.

Andrea shook Mark, and he groggily woke up. "Mark, where are we?" she asked. "Why are we in a hospital bed?"

"Andrea, don't you remember what happened?"

"What are you talking about?" she asked.

"Andrea, Amber is dead!"

Slowly the day's events returned to her. Andrea began shaking and crying. "What happened to her?"

"The medical examiner said she was smothered to death in her sleep."

"Who would have done that to our precious daughter?"

"I don't know, but remember how the window was open this morning? There's something else, Andrea. When I closed the window, 'Get out!' was written in the condensation. Remember what Amber said the night before, about the man who was sitting at her desk? She said he told her to get out. There's something else I never told you; I've also been hearing a voice in the house. Over and over, the voice kept saying to get out when I was in the basement the other night. I didn't tell you because I thought you would think I was nuts. The police were talking to me earlier today. They are investigating Amber's death as a homicide. Apparently, because the window was open, they feel someone entered her room in the middle of the night and murdered her." Andrea began to sob once again. Mark pulled her close and hugged her. "Honey, you need to call your parents and tell them what has happened."

"I can't, Mark. They loved her so much."

"You still need to call them. They deserve to know."

Climbing from the bed, Andrea walked to the emergency room hallway and picked up a phone. Mark stood back and watched the scene unfold from a distance. It seemed as if everything was in slow motion. Andrea was fine talking on the phone, and then, without warning, she collapsed to the ground. Rushing to her, Mark lifted her into his arms and carried her back to her bed. She had fainted, and her breath was shallow. A nurse rushed in with a doctor, and giving her another injection, the doctor suggested Mark give her some time to rest. Mark returned to the hallway, noticing the receiver was still off the hook. He walked to the phone and picked it up, placing the receiver to his ear so he could hear Mabel's hysterical voice screaming, "Hello? Hello? Hello?! Please, someone answer me."

Mark paused for a second and answered, "Mabel, this is Mark."

"Mark, where is Andrea? She was talking, and then the phone went dead."

"She fainted, Mabel. The stress is unbearable for her."

"The stress from what?" she asked.

Realizing Andrea had not told her, Mark asked Mabel to sit down.

"I am sitting down. Now what is going on?"

"Mabel, is Sam there?"

"Yes, he's standing beside me. Please tell me what happened."

"Mabel, Amber is dead."

There was dead silence on the phone, followed by screaming as Mabel told Sam what had happened. Sam picked up the receiver and, in a calm voice, asked, "What the hell happened?" It was the only time Mark had ever heard Sam swear.

"Sam, she was murdered in her sleep. Someone came into her bedroom in the middle of the night and smothered her to death."

A long pause was followed by a bellowing voice, saying, "You mean to tell me you allowed someone to break into your home in the middle of the night and murder my granddaughter, you son-of-a-bitch? What kind of a father are you?"

Mark could not take it any longer. He hung up the phone on Sam with his shaking hands.

Returning to Andrea's hospital room, Mark was happy to see that she was sitting up in her bed, talking to Chief Robinson. "Are you alright, honey?" he asked in a concerned voice.

"I feel better now, Mark. Whatever the doctor gave me has calmed my nerves."

"Did you need something else, Mr. Robinson?" Mark asked.

"Well, Mark, I just wanted to hear Andrea's side of the story."

"I told you how we found her; isn't that good enough?"

"Mark, calm down. I'm just doing my job. Her story matches yours. I just thought you might have missed something."

"Did you find anything at the house?" Mark inquired.

"Not a thing, Mark. If someone broke into your house last night, they didn't leave a single clue. Where are you folks going to be tonight in case I need to call you?"

"Well, I can tell you one thing," Mark yelled, "we are not going to spend one more night in that damn house. We are taking our daughter's body back to Youngstown, Ohio tomorrow to bury her, and we're never coming back to this God-forsaken area ever again."

"Well, I need to inform you that you and your wife are suspects in the murder of your daughter; therefore, I need to know where I can locate you in the event that more evidence presents itself."

"You filthy son-of-a-bitch! You have the gall to tell us that on the day our daughter is killed?"

"Mark, I didn't mean it that way. At this time, everyone is a suspect, including your next-door neighbor. We just need to be able to find you and your wife, you have to understand that. I can see you both loved her dearly. I'm not an idiot. Either you two are the best actors in the world, or there is a murderer out there running around. I just have to do my job. You want to see justice served, don't you?" The chief handed Mark his notepad.

Mark wrote his parents' address and phone number down, as well as Andrea's parents'. "You can reach us at either of these addresses or phone numbers," he replied, handing the pad back to Chief Robinson. "Don't call us until you find the bastard that killed our daughter." Mark thought it best not to elaborate on his theory of the house being haunted and evil. *They would commit me and throw away the key,* he thought to himself.

Chief Robinson stood up and said, "I wish the best for you both, under the circumstances."

Shaking his hand, Mark said, "Thank you."

"I'll be in touch," Chief Robinson replied, leaving the room.

"Andrea, go back to sleep, I'm going to make arrangements to have Amber's body sent back to Youngstown tomorrow for burial. By the way, I told your parents what had happened. As usual, your dad blamed everything on me."

"What did he say, Mark?"

"I didn't give him much of a chance to say anything because I hung up on him."

"Mark, why can't you two communicate?"

"It's not me, Andrea. You talk some sense into his thick head, and I'll communicate." That said, Mark left the room and went to find the hospital administrator.

Walking down the long white corridors of the hospital, Mark had never felt more alone. He had not even bothered to call his parents and tell them of the tragedy. He had to muster up the courage; they did, after all, have the right to know that their only grandchild was murdered.

Walking into the hospital administration office, he asked to speak to the supervisor. A tall, slender, friendly gentleman, looking to be in his fifties and dressed in a blue suit, came out of his office. He walked to Mark and shook his hand. "Hi, my name is William Thompson. What can I do for you, sir?"

Gazing down to the floor, avoiding eye contact, Mark spoke in a low sullen voice. "Hi, my name is Mark Jessup. I guess you're the person I need to talk to about having my daughter's body delivered to Youngstown, Ohio for burial. She was brought here this morning."

"I'm sorry for your loss, Mark. I heard about it this morning when I came to work. Yes, I can take care of it for you. Would you like me to contact a local mortician to provide a driver and a hearse, or would you prefer to handle the matter yourself?"

"Could you please handle it? I don't think I can take much more stress today."

Writing down the address of Makin's Funeral Home in Youngstown, Mark handed it to Mr. Thompson. "This is the address where I would like Amber's body delivered. The owner is William Makin; he has been a friend of our family for many years. Whomever you find to transport her body may bill the Makin Funeral Home for their costs. I'll call Bill and tell him to expect her body tomorrow evening. I really appreciate all you are doing for me, Mr. Thompson. Could I trouble you for one last thing? Here is my address in Youngstown," jotting it down on a piece of paper, Mark handed it to him. "I would like the bill for your hospital's services sent to me here. My wife and I are not coming back to this area."

"I'm sorry to hear that. I'd be glad to do that for you."

Shaking the man's hand, Mark left his office and began searching for a telephone. Finding a phone at the end of the corridor, he called the operator and asked to make a collect call. His father, Arthur, picked up the phone. Accepting the charges, he immediately asked what was wrong.

"Dad, is Mom there?"

"Yes, she's right here beside me, Mark," his father said with a questioning tone in his shaky voice.

Mark could not control his emotions any longer, and he began sobbing into the phone, to which his dad said, "Calm down, son. What's wrong?"

"Dad, Amber is dead. Someone killed my baby."

There was silence as Mark heard his dad telling his mother what had happened. He heard his mom screaming and crying in the background. "Mark, how did it happen?"

Mark was surprised by how calmly his father was taking the news. His dad never did seem to show his emotions very well. "We don't know, Dad. We found her in her room this morning, and she wasn't breathing. Her bedroom window was open, so police think someone came in the bedroom in the middle of the night and smothered her with her pillow." Mark's sobs turned into uncontrollable crying.

"Listen, Mark, you are going to have to settle down. You need to be strong for Andrea. She is going to need you now more than ever. Do you understand me?" he said in a stern voice.

Calming down, Mark replied, "Yes, sir. Dad, I need you to take care of some things for me out there. I'm having Amber's body taken to Bill Makin's funeral home. Could you call him and tell him to expect her body sometime tomorrow? I'm going to have them bury her in our family plot beside Grandma. I told them to bill him for the transportation costs, and I will pay him."

Mark's father and Bill Makin had grown up together and been friends since they were kids. "Listen, Mark, don't worry about a thing. I'll call Bill right away, and he and I will take care of everything. You just be strong for Andrea."

"Dad, is Mom all right?"

"She'll be fine. She ran to her bedroom and is in there crying. I'll keep an eye on her. When are you driving home?"

"I would like to leave later tonight if they release Andrea."

"What the hell is wrong with Andrea, son?"

"She went into shock this morning, and they admitted her into the hospital. She is fine now that they have her on nerve medicine. I'm going to ask the attending physician if he will release her so that we can head back home to Youngstown right now. Dad," Mark paused before speaking, "I'm not coming back here to my job. Would it be all right if we stayed with you and Mom for a few weeks until I find a job out there?"

"Son, we'd love to have you, but what about Andrea's parents? Didn't they insist you live with them the last time you were looking for a job?"

"I don't want to get into it on the phone right now, Dad. I'll tell you about it when we get to your house tonight."

"Okay, Mark, I'll see you tonight. Drive carefully. I love you, son."

"I love you too, Dad."

Hanging up the phone, Mark breathed a sigh of relief that his father was so understanding. Walking down the hall to the emergency room, Mark saw the doctor that had treated Andrea that morning. "Excuse me, sir, you were treating my wife this morning in the emergency room."

"Yes, I remember you quite well," he half-joked. "By the way my name is Dr. Robert Scott. I never did get a chance to formally introduce myself to you this morning under the circumstances."

"Thank you, Dr. Scott, for all you did for me and my wife this morning. I believe you know that my name is Mark Jessup."

"Yes, I think everyone in the hospital knows your name, Mark," he said, smiling.

"Anyway, I have a favor to ask you, Doctor Scott. Would it be possible for you to sign the release papers on my wife so we can head to Youngstown, Ohio tonight? I need to handle funeral arrangements for my daughter."

Pausing to think for a second, the doctor nodded his head yes. "Come with me, and I'll take care of it now, Mark. I'll even give you some nerve pills to calm her until you see your family doctor in Youngstown."

He followed the doctor to the admissions office and waited outside while the doctor went in. Returning minutes later, he told Mark to take the paper to the nurse's station in the emergency room, and they would get a wheelchair for his wife and deliver her to his car. Handing Mark the paper and a packet of pills, he instructed, "Give her one of these pills every four hours, and they will keep her calm. I'm sorry for your loss."

Shaking his hand, Mark walked briskly to the emergency room. Going to the office window, he handed the nurse the paper and explained what Dr. Scott had said. The nurse smiled and told Mark to pull his car up outside, and she would personally bring his wife to him.

"Thank you so much, ma'am. Everyone has been so kind here."

Mark was waiting at his car when the nurse pushed Andrea out into the parking lot in a wheelchair. Andrea's face was a pasty white, and it looked as if she had aged ten years in a day. Sensing some wobbling as she rose to her feet from the wheelchair, Mark had to immediately grab her arm to steady her. As he helped her into the car, Andrea lay across the seat, since she was unable to sit up. Still feeling good from the injection, Andrea smiled at Mark as he climbed into the car. "Lay there and sleep, Andrea. We are going home now." Laying her back down, Mark pulled out from the parking lot of the hospital and headed back to Claysburg.

The beautiful scenery was a blur to him as he drove, consumed in thought. *I'll go into that place from hell one last time and get only our clothing and the lamp Andrea loves so much,* he decided right away. *They can keep everything else.* Continuing to drive, anger started raging within him. *I ought to burn the damn house to the ground. That evil son-of-a-bitch murdered my daughter. I don't care what happened to him while he was alive. All I know is that he's messing with the wrong man,* Mark stewed furiously.

Pulling into the driveway for what he decided would be the last time, Mark glanced up to his bedroom window. A young man was staring out, smiling. It did not appear to be a shadow but a physical person. Jumping from the car, he stormed into the house and ran to his bedroom, bursting through the door. No one was there. *He's playing with me, that filthy son-of-a-bitch,* Mark thought in a frenzy. "Where the hell are you?!" Mark screamed so loud it could heard from the outside of the house.

Running into the bathroom, he looked into the mirror. "Where is your face now? You don't scare me!" Upon smashing his hand into the mirror, it shattered and splintered in thousands of small, web-like pieces. "I hate you!" Screaming, Mark ran to Elijah's room and kicked the door open. A blast of icy cold air rushed to his face. The window was open once again. "Show yourself to me, you dirty bastard!" Suddenly, the window slammed shut right before his eyes. A fog spread across the glass, forming condensation, as Mark watched. Anger was now replaced with fear. He began shaking from a combination of the cold air and the fear now consuming him. Frozen in his tracks, he stood and watched as the following letters began to form on the window pane:

Y O U W E R E W A R N E D. G E T O U T N O W.

With the hair on the back of his neck standing up, Mark backed out of the bedroom. He was no sooner out of the room than the door slammed in his face. Racing to his bedroom and quickly opening the closet door, he grabbed Andrea's entire wardrobe with the speed of lightning. Mark ran a leg race to his car and threw the clothes into the backseat. Returning to the house, he repeated the same process, grabbing his clothes this time. Pausing a moment at the vehicle, Mark bent over, holding his side to catch his breath. He contemplated leaving behind the lamp that Andrea loved so much. *I know I'm pushing my luck going back in there,* he realized.

Shaking the thought off, he raced toward the house one last time, bursting through the front door he grabbed the lamp, unplugged it and ran back out side. Looking into the car, he noticed Andrea was now sitting up, staring at him with a pained look that unnerved him. Throwing the lamp into his backseat, he slammed the car door shut. Opening the driver's side door, Mark looked at the house one last time with his heart pounding a mile a minute. "Shit, I left the front door open, Andrea." As he stood there beside his car, he watched in amazement as the front door slammed.

Andrea, watching too, screamed, "Let's get out of here, Mark. Please!" Mark did not need to be told twice.

Within seconds, he was in his car and speeding away from the house. "You saw the door slam shut by itself, didn't you, Andrea?"

"Yes, I saw it, Mark."

"Andrea, there is an evil force in that house. I know it wasn't a prowler that killed Amber. I will never set foot in that house again. I can't talk about it

GET OUT!

now, honey, but someday I will tell you what just happened to me in there. We can never tell anyone that we suspect the house is haunted, especially our parents. They would think we are nuts."

"Where are we going now, Mark?"

"We are heading back to Youngstown. I am having Amber's body sent there for burial. My dad asked us to live with him until we get on our feet."

"What about my parents?"

"I don't want to talk about it now. For now, we'll stay at my parents' until we get on our feet."

Snow flurries were swirling around Andy Wyandt's head as he walked to the mailbox. Wearing his bulky, blue, winter coat, he pulled up the zipper up. The wind had really kicked up, and even though the house was only fifty yards away, he couldn't take the stinging feeling from the bitter cold. The sky was overcast, making it appear that darkness was close by, even though it was only three o'clock. Andy had just gotten home from school and was doing his daily chore of bringing the mail to his mother. Opening the mailbox, he took out a single letter. Glancing at it, he noticed that it was postmarked from Youngstown, Ohio. Shoving it into his coat pocket, he ran toward the house. Upon reaching the front porch, his mother, Lois, opened the door to greet him. "How was school, Andy?"

"Fine," he said, reaching into his pocket and shoving the letter into her hand as he ran past her up the steps to his bedroom.

Lois took the crumpled letter into her hand. *Who do I know in Youngstown?* she wondered to herself. Walking to the kitchen table, she sat down and tore the letter open. It was written in perfect penmanship. The letter was from Mark and Andrea Jessup and read as follows:

> Bob and Lois,
>
> As, no doubt, you have already heard, our daughter was murdered in the home we rented from you. Let this letter serve as notice that we have moved from your rental property. We have returned to Youngstown to live. You may keep the remainder of this month's rent as we have no intention of returning to that house ever again. I have also called the electric company and phone company to terminate service. The electric company informed me that you need to call them to continue uninterrupted service since winter is approaching. They said that your pipes would freeze if they shut the power off. We have left behind some of our

belongings, including our child's clothing. Do with these items as you wish.

Sincerely,
Mark Jessup

Just as she finished the letter, Bob walked into the kitchen. "Why the glum look on your face, Lois?" Handing Bob the letter, she walked to the stove and put on a pot of fresh coffee.

After reading the letter, Bob said in a sullen voice, "I didn't realize it was their child who was murdered. That's a damn shame."

"I told you, Bob, there is something weird about that house. That makes it four deaths in that house in the last two and a half months."

"I'm putting a 'For Sale' sign on the property tomorrow, and that's all there is to it," Bob said angrily.

"How much do you think we should ask for it, Bob?"

"There you go, Lois, always thinking about the almighty dollar."

"You have a lot of nerve, Bob, like you won't be spending the money too."

Shaking his head, Bob went to the living room and turned on the television. Following Bob to the living room, Lois became angry. "Don't shake your head at me, Bob Wyandt."

"Lois, do we really need to get into this now?"

"All I asked you was what price we should ask for the house!"

Sitting down on the sofa, Bob smiled at Lois and said, "All right, sit down here, and we'll figure it out." It was only four in the afternoon and already it was dark outside. Strong, gusty winds could be heard outside as they pounded against the house.

"I think we should get a real estate agent to handle the sale. They will have to do all the leg work of showing the house and telling us what it is worth. Don't you think that makes sense, Lois?"

"No, I don't think it does, Bob. They will also get a nice big fat commission off the sale of the house. I would rather do it myself and save that money."

"All right then, if you're dead-set on doing it yourself, let's start out at $10,000. We can always drop the price if it doesn't sell."

"Do you really think it is worth that much, Bob?"

"No, I don't, but if it gets you off my back so I can watch television, I'll say it is."

"Stop it. If you agree to get a 'For Sale' sign on the front yard tomorrow with our phone number, I'll leave you alone."

"Fine, your sign will be up by four o'clock tomorrow."

Months and months passed, and no one called about looking at the house. It was now the month of June, and the days were becoming somewhat hot and humid. It didn't get dark now until after eight in the evening. Andy was out of school for summer vacation and running the neighborhood with his friends till dark every day. For a while, it had seemed like all the town could talk about was the curse on the Stone home. Lately, though, it seemed as if everyone had forgotten about it, which was fine with Bob and Lois. They never did solve the murder of that poor child who had lived in the home last year. Lois was getting discouraged that no one had inquired about the house and was considering listing it with an agent. They had to continue paying an electric bill on the place every month, and even though it was small, it still irked her. She would have listed it sooner, had Bob not suggested it to begin with. She just could not let him think he was right. *I'll give it till the end of the month, and then I'll give in and list it with someone*, she thought to herself.

Don and Leslie Knisley rented a small ranch home in Albany, New York. They had rented and lived in the same home for the past sixteen years, never bothering to buy a home because Don had aspirations of returning to the area were he was raised. Being of average height, Don was a good-looking man with short brown hair. He and his wife were the same age, forty-eight. She was a petite, blonde woman with drop-dead good looks, even for her age. They had one child, Mike, who was fifteen years old. He was Don's pride and joy, an all-around spectacular athlete who lettered in football, track, and wrestling. Mike was as tall as his dad already, and at five feet eleven inches, he outweighed his dad by twenty pounds. His muscular frame intimidated most grown men.

Don had been the personnel director for a pre-manufactured home company in Albany for the past sixteen years since graduating from New York University. Originally from the Claysburg area, he had always hoped to return but could never find a job that would pay as much as his present position. He had a large extended family still living there, including his parents.

After coming home from work on Tuesday, he received a call from his father, Patrick. "Don, you're not going to believe this. I was talking to my friend, Bill Myers, at work today, and he said the brickyard in Claysburg was advertising a need for a personnel director." Don's dad had worked at the local paper mill in Roaring Springs for the past thirty years. The mill was the area's largest employer with the Claysburg Brickyard coming in at a close second. "Son, there are up to four hundred employees now. If you are serious about moving back here, you should send your resumé out there tomorrow."

The company Don was presently working for had only one hundred employees, and Don was hesitant before he answered. "I don't know, Dad, that sounds like a ton of responsibility."

"Listen, Don, I brought you up not to be intimidated by challenges. Besides, I bet they would pay you a hell of a lot more money than you're making now."

"I'll tell you what, Dad, I'll call them tomorrow and see what they have to say."

"Now that's the boy I raised," Pat laughed on the phone. "Call me tomorrow night and let me know how you make out."

"Sure thing, Dad," Don replied hanging up the phone.

Leslie and her entire family were from New York. She was born and raised there, so she was not thrilled about leaving. His son, on the other hand, could care less; he was an adventurer and was always up for new challenges in life.

Sitting at the dinner table that night, Don broke the news to both of them that he was considering applying for the job. Leslie became teary-eyed while Mike joked and said, "How soon do we leave, Pop?"

"It's not definite yet. I'm going to call them tomorrow to check them out. If the pay is not at least two thousand more than I'm making now, I won't even consider it."

"How much do you make a year now?" Mike asked.

"None of your business," Don joked.

"No, really, Dad, how much do you make?"

"Well son, I guess I can tell you, just under fifteen thousand dollars a year."

"Wow, I didn't realize you made so much."

Puffing out his chest, Don smiled and said, "That's what a college degree will do for you, Mike."

Before leaving for work the next morning, Don called the operator and got the phone number for the Claysburg brickyard. Arriving at work, he walked into his office at seven sharp. It was a small, ten-foot-by-twelve-foot office with no frills. There was even a window for him to look out. Glancing around, Don thought to himself, *You would think after sixteen years they would give me a little recognition and provide a better office for me.* Looking on his desk, he noticed a stack of papers that needed attention immediately. *The hell with them,* he thought, picking up the phone and dialing the brickyard's number. A secretary answered the phone, saying, "Claysburg Brickyard, how may I direct your call?"

"Yes," he replied, "I'm calling about the personnel director's job opportunity. Who would I talk to?"

"Hold one second, please," she replied.

Minutes later, the plant safety director picked up the phone and said, "This is Pete Miller, what can I do for you?"

Immediately, Don recognized the voice and the person. He had graduated from high school with Pete. "Hi, Pete, how are you doing? This is Don Knisley."

"Don, I haven't heard from you since high school. How are you, Buddy?"

"I'm doing great, Pete. I've lived in Albany, New York for the past sixteen years. I went to college up here and got a job as a personnel director with a pre-manufactured home outfit straight out of college."

"Well, what can I do for you?"

"I'm calling because my dad said the brickyard is advertising for a personnel director. I've been wanting to come back to the area for years, but I could never find anything that paid what I'm making up here."

"Well, your dad is right, we've been growing in leaps and bounds here. There's four hundred and twenty employees here now. Tom Mahoney, our current personnel director, is retiring at the end of the month, and we need someone within the next two weeks. I've been interviewing people for the last two weeks. How soon can you get down here to meet with me?" he laughed.

"Well, before I make a commitment to come down, can you give me a ballpark figure of what it pays?"

"I can do better than that," Pete replied. "I can tell you that the starting salary is twenty thousand dollars per year with full company benefits for you and your family. You do have a family, don't you, Don?"

"Yeah, I have a wife and son."

"Well, I'd love to meet them sometime. So, do you think you'd be interested?"

"I sure am, Pete. I can be there on Friday, or I can mail you a resumé today if you would like.

"I don't need a resumé from you, Don. Just get your ass down here on Friday, and I'll show you what the job entails. We'll go from there, okay, buddy?"

"Sounds good, Pete. How about Friday at nine in the morning?"

"I'll see you then, Don."

Hanging up the phone, Don raised his arm and pumped his fist in the air. "Yes!" he yelled out loud.

Arriving home that night, Don burst through the front door and yelled, "Leslie, guess what?"

"What?" she called from the kitchen.

"I have an interview in Claysburg on Friday. I told them I was taking two personal days — tomorrow and Friday — to visit my parents in Roaring Spring.

"What made you decide to do it, Don?"

"I'll tell you why, the starting salary is twenty thousand dollars a year, and I have an in. I graduated from high school with the person who will make the final decision on who gets hired." Smiling as he said it, he continued, "His name is Pete Miller."

"Well, I guess we'll be visiting your parents tomorrow, won't we?"

"You're not upset, are you, Leslie?"

"How can I be upset when you will be making so much more money? It just means I can spend more," she smiled.

"I called my mother from work and told her to expect us tomorrow. As usual, she was excited that we would be visiting. We'll stay till Sunday and leave in the morning to come back home, okay?"

Mike, who was listening in the living room, yelled, "All right, Dad! You're going to be making the big bucks."

"Mike, it's not a sure thing, but it looks promising."

Pulling from his driveway the next morning, Don was whistling as he started the long drive to his parents. The four-hour drive was always a hassle for him in the past, but today he was looking forward to it. It was seven in the morning when they started, so he happily stated, "We should be there by eleven if we don't stop anywhere. Mom said she would have lunch ready for us."

"Don, we'll have to stop to go to the bathroom," Leslie insisted.

"Aw, come on, Leslie. I think you can hold it for four hours."

"Yeah, Mom," Mike chimed in, "suck it up."

Smiling, Leslie said, "Just drive."

It was a gorgeous day. The sun was shining, the birds were chirping, and the scenery was spectacular as they drove. Don was driving a band new Ford he had just purchased a month ago, and it still smelled like a new car. It had a shiny black finish with chrome hubcaps that stood out, making everyone who saw the car comment on its beauty. It also had great acceleration compared to the Ford he had just traded in. *I might be able make it in three and a half hours the way this baby moves*, he thought to himself. Daydreaming, he mused at how good life had been to him. He had a great family, a new car, and an excellent job prospect.

Pulling into his parents' driveway, Leslie and Mike were asleep as Don looked at his watch. *I made great time,* he thought. *It's only ten forty-five.*

His parents' house was a two-story with white wood siding and green trim. His dad kept the outside of the house and yard in perfect shape. Nothing was allowed to be out of place outside as well as inside the home.

"Time to get up, you two sleepyheads!" he yelled, startling Mike and Leslie.

"Did you have to scare the crap out of me, Dad?" Mike laughed.

"Well, we're here." Looking up, Don noticed that his mom was at the front door, waving.

Waving back, Don opened the car door and yelled, "Hi, Mom!"

"Don, I'm so glad to see you and your family."

Mike ran from the car and hugged his grandmother, saying, "I missed you, Gram."

"I missed you too, honey."

"Hi, Leslie," she yelled. "Come on in, and sit down."

Walking into the house and entering the living room, it was evident that as meticulous as the outside was kept, the inside was no different. The living room was a brilliant yellow in color, with matching drapes and plush green carpeting. Even the light green sofa and chairs were carefully matched to coordinate the color scheme in the living room. *Sadie is an excellent interior decorator,* Leslie thought to herself.

After everyone was in the house, Don's mother, Sadie, declared, "I'm fixing a turkey with all the trimmings for lunch."

"Mom, you didn't need to go to all that trouble."

"I know I didn't, Don. I did it because I love you all, and I only get to see you twice a year if I'm lucky."

"Well, it smells great, Gram," Mike chimed in. "You can make turkey for me anytime you want," he said, smiling.

Kissing Mike on the cheek, she said, "Why don't you go wake your grandfather up? He worked third trick last night at the mill and has only been sleeping since seven this morning."

"Let him sleep a little longer, Mom," Don whispered.

"Don, he said I was to get him up when you got here, and you know how he is. If I don't wake him, he'll be mad at me."

Nodding his head okay, Mike ran up the steps and woke his grandfather. Minutes later, Pat was walking down the steps with a big smile on his face. "It's great to have you all here." Ruffling Mike's hair, Pat declared, "Don, what are you feeding this boy? He's as big as a house!"

"I know what you mean, Dad. I think he can lick his old man already, and he's only fifteen."

Mike smiled and said, "Stop kidding, you guys."

"Aren't you tired from working all night, Dad?" Don asked.

"Boy, when you work somewhere thirty years, you get used to trick work. Sadie, when are we going to eat? I'm hungry."

"It's almost ready, Pat. Go to the kitchen table, and sit down." Everyone went to kitchen and sat down at a large pine table that had been stained a light brown. Sadie, smiling, began hauling the turkey and all the fixings to the table.

The kitchen, just like the living room, was perfectly decorated, with large grapevine wreaths interwoven with silk flowers hung on bright white walls. The countertops were light blue, setting off the birch-colored cabinets surrounding them.

As Pat was carving the turkey, he asked Don how the job prospect looked.

"It looks good, Dad. I graduated with the guy doing the hiring."

"Well, that's a plus, Don! When do you meet with him?"

"Tomorrow at nine in the morning in his office at the plant."

"Pat, let them enjoy their meal. You can talk shop after they eat," Sadie chided. Smiling, Pat handed Mike the plate of turkey.

After the meal, they went to the living room, feeling so stuffed they could hardly move. Don said, "That was great, Mom, I love your cooking."

"Yes it was, Sadie," Leslie added.

"Thank you," Sadie smiled and went back to the kitchen to clean up with Leslie. "So, Leslie, what do you think about possibly moving here?"

"I'll go wherever Don's work takes him."

"That's the spirit!" Pat yelled from the living room.

"I'm going to drive around Claysburg this afternoon to check out the housing situation," Don told his father. "Do you want to tag along?"

"No, you and your family can do that, Don. I need to get some more sleep. I sure hope you get the job so I can see you more often. Your mom and I really miss you guys."

GET OUT!

"I hope so too, Dad. I'd really like to be back in the area."

Going out to the car, Don smelled the familiar old smell of the paper mill. "What is that smell, Pop?" Mike asked, holding his breath.

"That's the mill where your pap works."

"I don't think I could stand that smell every day," Leslie gagged.

"You get used to the smell," Don chuckled. "Anyway, if we move here, we'll look for a place in Claysburg close to the brickyard. Do you want to go see it?"

"Sure," Mike and Leslie answered together.

Getting in the car, they began driving to the brickyard in Claysburg. It only took ten minutes before Don was pulling into the parking lot of an enormous plant. "Wow, Dad, this place is unbelievable."

Don could not believe how much the place had expanded since the last time he was here years ago. There were six separate buildings spanning across what seemed to be acres of ground. Three of the buildings were quite old, while the other three looked as if they had been built within the last several years. Chain-link fence surrounded the entire complex. "It looks more like a prison than a brickyard," Mike noted.

"It is quite an operation, isn't it?" Looking at Leslie, Don said, "While we're here in Claysburg, let's drive around and see if any homes are for sale."

"Sounds good to me," she replied.

Don began driving through the small town of Claysburg. Noticing all the small, quaint shops, Leslie became excited. "Let's stop and shop a little," she pleaded.

"I thought we were just looking around," Don scolded.

"Oh, all right, just keep driving."

"Good. There's the high school, Mike. Do you think you will kick some butt there if we move here?" Don asked his son.

"You know it, Dad."

Turning left, Don drove up a winding country road. "What is the name of this road?"

Finding a street sign, Leslie replied, "It's called Haller Road." Continuing up the road, they noticed that the homes looked older, but the scenery was unbelievably beautiful. The distance between the homes allowed for yards that were much larger than the homes in Roaring Spring. "I really like this area," Leslie smiled as she took in the country atmosphere.

They had driven on that road for only a few minutes when Mike yelled, "Look, Dad, there's a house for sale by owner!"

Pulling into the driveway, they got out of the car and began walking around the home. "It's in dire need of a paint job, that's for sure," Don laughed. Looking at Leslie, he could tell instantly she was in love with the old home. "What do you think, Leslie?"

"I love it, Don. We could paint the siding a pretty light green with dark green trim. The yard and the trees are beautiful. It is the country home I always dreamed of, not like back home where every house is side by side with hardly any yard in between."

"Dad," Mike yelled from out back, "check this out." Walking around the house, Don and Leslie saw Mike looking inside a garage that looked like it could collapse at any moment. The siding was falling from the sides, and the roof looked as if it would give way if a good, strong wind blew against it. "This garage must be a hundred years old," Mike joked.

"Stay out of it, Mike. It doesn't look safe," Leslie scolded.

"I'm just looking, Mom. Don't throw a hissy-fit."

Shaking her head, she turned to Don and said, "We could tear that down and build a nice two-car garage out front."

Smiling, he said, "You already have the house bought, and I don't even have the job yet."

"Don, just write down the number on the sign. I don't care what it looks like inside," she pleaded. "We could remodel the entire house and make it like new. The most important thing to me is the location, and I love this one."

"Okay," he consented, "but I think we should call them from Dad's house and at least see the inside today or tomorrow."

"All right, but do it as soon as we get back to your parents' house. I don't want to lose it to someone else if you do get the job."

Jotting the number down, they walked back to the car and got inside. "They better not want much for that place, Dad," Mike remarked. "It's going to cost a ton to fix it up."

"Don't you worry about that, young man. That will be my job," Leslie said excitedly. Don couldn't remember the last time he had seen Leslie so excited about anything. "Your father can make the money, and I'll spend it all," she said to Mike, laughing. "It's such a gorgeous day, Don. Let's go back to town and park. Then we can walk around for a few hours."

"I have a better idea, Leslie. Sit back and relax, and I'll drive you to Blue Knob State Park, about fifteen miles from here. It has some great hiking trails."

"That sounds like fun!" Mike yelled from the backseat.

"Okay, Don, I'm up for that," Leslie said excitedly.

Backing out of the driveway, Don drove back down Haller Road and turned right onto Dunn Highway. "I think you're going to like this place," he said. "I came here as a child with my parents." After several miles on Dunn Highway, Don turned onto a rural road that was barely wide enough for one car.

"What'll we do if a car's coming the other way," Mike joked, "play chicken with them?"

Laughing, Don replied, "No, we stop and pull over to the edge of the road as far as we can go, and then we close our eyes and pray."

The road finally widened somewhat after several miles, and everyone rolled down their windows to take in the picturesque scenery. Even though it was a hot day in the eighties, the cool breeze from the shade provided by the trees along the road blew in. "This is spectacular, Don," Leslie replied, in a trance from her newfound love of the area. "Why in the world didn't we ever come and see these places in all the years we have been coming down here?"

"I don't really know," Don said, dumbfounded. "I guess we just never made the time. I had no idea you would like it so much." Finally, Don arrived at a small parking area. There were only two other cars, so Don pulled beside them and grinned. "Let's go for a hike!"

As they stepped out of the car, the sun glimmered through the multitude of trees, casting shadows that seemed to dance among them. The shade provided by the abundance of trees was invigorating and refreshing as they walked to the closest trail.

"Don, are you sure you know your way around these trails? If we get lost, we might never be found," Leslie worried. "Your parents have no idea where we are."

"Stop being a baby, Mom, and get moving," Mike yelled, running down the trail.

"Slow down, Michael Knisley. I came here to enjoy a family outing together, and you're going to ruin it."

"The boy can't help it, Leslie; he's an athlete and likes to run." Mike was out of sight when Don and Leslie rounded the first bend in the trail.

"Don, he's going to get lost. Make him come back."

"He's fine, Leslie. Just enjoy the beauty of nature, and relax."

"It's wonderful Don. If we do move here, just you and I can come up here and have a little picnic together. Know what I mean?" she said, winking.

"I know exactly what you mean," Don replied, pinching her rear.

They had walked for over a mile without seeing a glimpse of Mike when they came upon a split in the trail. The trail was wide enough now that it allowed the sun to beat down upon them and make it uncomfortably hot.

"I told you to make him stay with us," Leslie griped. "Now which trail do we take?"

Don began yelling, "Mike, where are you?" There was no answer after repeated attempts. "You would think that a full grown boy, almost a man, would have the common sense to know to wait at a fork in the trail. I've half a mind to kick him in the ass when we find him. Tell you what, Leslie, you walk that trail and I'll walk this trail until we find him. We'll meet here at this split in the trail at three o'clock."

"Do you think that is the smart thing to do, Don, letting a woman walk these trails alone?" Leslie asked nervously.

"Well, Leslie, we don't have much of a choice, do we? The little son-of-a-bitch won't answer me."

Don had been walking his separate trail for what seemed like miles but, in reality, was only several hundred yards, when he heard what sounded like footsteps behind him. "Leslie, is that you? Mike, are you back there?" There was no answer, so he continued on. Walking about another five hundred yards, he heard footsteps running behind him. Every time he would stop, the footsteps behind him would stop. Don was now in a stretch of woods where the trees were packed tightly together, making the path so dark that it appeared as if it were night. He became apprehensive. "Who's back there?" he screamed, to no avail. Contemplating turning back and finding his wife, Don shook off the fear and continued walking and yelling for Mike every fifty yards or so. Entering an area of the woods that looked extremely secluded and pitch black, he became nervous once again. Hearing tree branches cracking several hundred yards behind him, Don had had about enough. *Leslie has probably found him by now anyway,* he thought to himself. *The problem is, if I turn back and she didn't find him, she'll rip into me for sure.* Screaming at the top of his lungs, "Mike, where are you?" Don began to sweat profusely. He continued to hear what he thought were footsteps behind him and in the woods all around him. Walking slowly down the dark, scary trail, all of the sudden, someone jumped down from the trees above him and scared the living hell out of him. It was Mike. "You little bastard," he screamed. Mike began laughing so hard he fell to the ground and began rolling around. "I ought to kick your ass," Don said, now smiling. "Your poor mother is wandering these woods alone, looking for you. She is going to be so mad at you that you'll be in the doghouse for the next year."

"No, she isn't," he said, pointing behind his father. There was Leslie, laughing so hard she had to hold her sides.

Squealing with laughter, Leslie could barely spit out the words, "Don, I thought you were the big man that wasn't afraid of anything? You were so scared I thought you were going to pee your pants!"

"You mean to tell me that both of you were in on this?" Don asked.

Nodding her head yes, Leslie pointed to Mike and said, "It was his idea, so don't be mad at me."

"When did you plan this, Mike?"

"When you were back at the fork in the trail, I was up in a tree listening to everything you and Mom were saying. After you left and started down the trail, I caught up with Mom and told her to follow me. You were hearing us run up behind you, you big baby. Then I went out around you and climbed this tree while Mom continued to walk behind you. I wish I had a picture to show Pap just how much of a sis his son is," Mike said, teasing.

"I'll get even with you, Mike. Maybe not today, but someday, you're going to get what's coming to you. Let's head back to the car; I've had enough hiking for one day." Turning around, all three started walking out of the dark forest in single file.

Arriving at the car, they were greeted by a blast of sunshine peeking through the trees once again. The car was filthy, covered in dust from their drive to the park. Don had an idea. "Guess what you get to do when we get back to Mom's and Dad's house, Mike? This car is going to be washed and dried until it looks like a brand new car."

"That's not fair, Dad. You're just punishing me for scaring the crap out of you."

Smiling, Don replied, "Payback's a bitch."

Pulling into his parents' driveway, Don looked at his watch and noticed it was almost five. Getting out of the car, Don looked at Mike and said, "Tell you what, you can come in and eat supper before tearing into the car."

"Great," Mike replied, "I get to work on a full stomach."

Sadie was about to put supper on the table just as they were walking into the house. "It's about time you came home. What were you doing?"

"We found a house in Claysburg that Leslie really likes if I get the job."

"It's a fixer-upper, but the location is wonderful!" Leslie squealed with delight. "It will be the first house we have ever owned if we get it, so we plan on doing some major renovations to it over the next few years."

Pat had been listening on the stair steps when he chimed in, "So you really sound like you want to move here, Leslie."

Smiling and nodding her head yes, she declared, "We also went for a drive and hiked in Blue Knob State Park. The country atmosphere of the Claysburg area is great, and we'd be so close to you. The only thing keeping us in New York is Don's job. I'll really miss my parents and friends, but we can drive back to visit them a couple of times a year."

"Pap, wait till I tell you what I did to Dad while we were hiking today."

Smiling, Pat said, "Well, let's go to the dinner table, and you can tell me all about it while we eat."

Everyone sat down while Sadie began bringing charcoal-grilled steak and potatoes to the table. The succulent smell wafted throughout the kitchen. "Wow, that smells great, Mom."

"I know how much you like steak, Don, so I thought I would surprise you." Sadie was in all her glory as everyone complimented her on the great meal.

"Well, Mike, are you going to tell me what you did to your dad?" Pat asked.

Mike went through the entire story with Pat laughing so hard he almost fell from his chair.

"Your dad always was afraid of his own shadow, especially as a child. He had to sleep with a nightlight on until he was sixteen."

"Hey," Don yelled, "don't tell him everything you know about me, Dad. I want the boy to respect his old man."

Laughing, Pat finished the last bite of his steak.

After the meal, Leslie helped Sadie with the dishes while Mike, Pat, and Don went outside to the porch. Don and Pat sat down on the porch swing while Mike grabbed the hose and started washing the car. "It sure is good to have you home, son," Pat remarked.

"I missed you too, Dad. Hopefully this interview tomorrow will work out. They said they would need someone before the end of the month, so it all could happen very quickly. I doubt I would have time to work out a two-week notice at the plant back home."

"Well, Don, when opportunity knocks you have to jump on it."

"I guess so. Dad, can you do me a favor tomorrow?"

"Sure, what do you need?

"Leslie is so stuck on this house we looked at today that she wanted me to call before I even found out if I got the job. She said she didn't even care what it looks like inside, but I know better. Could you call in the morning when you come home from work and make an appointment for us to see the house at one in the afternoon tomorrow? If I don't get the job, I'll just break the appointment. The way Pete talks though, I think I have a good shot at getting it."

"No problem, Don. I'll call as soon as I get home from work at seven-thirty. Didn't you say your interview isn't till nine though?"

"It wasn't supposed to be, but since I got here today, I'm going to drop over at six-thirty and surprise Pete."

"I don't know, son. He might get pissed if you drop in unannounced," Pat said, shaking his head.

"Trust me, Dad, we were very good fiends in high school. He won't be mad."

Looking up, Don noticed that the car was shining once again as Mike was putting the finishing touches on drying the vehicle. "Shines like a baby's bottom, don't it, Pap?" Mike exclaimed.

"You did a good job, that's for sure, Mike."

Putting the hose away, Mike returned to the front porch and said, "Mind if I watch some television, Pap?"

"Go right ahead, Mike. In fact, your dad and I will join you."

Going inside, the entire family sat around the television and watched it until Pat had to leave for work at ten-thirty. Saying his good-byes, Pat left the house with his black lunch bucket in hand.

"Well, Mom," Don said, "I'm ready for bed."

"Go on up, son. I have the covers turned down in the spare bedrooms."

"I love you, Mom."

"I love you too. Night."

Leslie and Don walked to their bedroom, while Mike and Sadie stayed in the living room, chatting and watching television.

They were sleeping in the very same bedroom Don had used growing up as a child. It was a fairly large room, completely done over since his childhood. It was now decorated with a woman's touch. There was a double bed with a thick red and white checkered quilt. Plush tan carpeting was set off with light-red curtains. The room had a lot of character to it, and Leslie loved it.

Don woke up at six o'clock on Friday morning and quietly crawled out from under the covers. Leslie was softly snoring as he went to the bathroom to shower and shave. Returning to the bedroom, Don put on his blue suit and black dress shoes. Bending down and pecking Leslie on her forehead, he watched as she stirred and opened her eyes. "Good luck, tiger," Leslie whispered, rolling to her side and closing her eyes once again.

Don walked down the green carpeted steps, feeling a little nervous as he went to the kitchen. His mother was already up and had a pot of coffee brewing. "Morning, son. Do you want some breakfast?"

"No, Mom. Coffee's fine, thank you."

"Are you nervous, Don?"

"A little," he replied.

"You'll do fine. If it's meant to be, it will happen."

Kissing his mother on the forehead, Don left the kitchen and walked out the front door. It was a sunny morning, but it was still rather chilly as he got into his car.

Driving to the plant, he began second-guessing himself about arriving earlier than his appointed time. *I hope Pete doesn't mind*, he prayed.

Don parked his car in the visitors' section and briskly walked to the building that had "Office" painted in bright white lettering on its side. Going inside, the secretary immediately smiled at him and said, "How can I help you?" She was young and very pretty, with a mesmerizing smile. The name plate on her desk read Bobbi Graham. "Yes, I think you can," he replied. "I'm here to see Pete Miller. My name is Don Knisley."

"Have a seat over there, Don, and I'll call him." Picking up the phone, she dialed an extension and began talking to someone. Hanging up the phone, she smiled once again and said, "He'll be here in a few minutes."

Sitting in a chair with his legs crossed and his hands folded, minutes seemed like hours until Pete finally walked into the office. "Don, how are you?" he asked, shaking his hand. "I thought our appointment was for nine o'clock."

"It was, Pete, but since I got to town yesterday, I just stopped by early to see if you wanted to talk now so I could visit with my folks a little longer today."

"How are your folks?"

"They're doing great. Thanks for asking."

"Well, since you're here, follow me to my office."

They walked out of the main office and down a well-lit corridor to Pete's office. Going inside, Don could not believe the size of his office. It had a large window, allowing the outside sunshine to filter through sheer, white drapes. The desk was twice the size of Don's desk back in New York, and the office was completed with a full-size sofa. Sitting behind his desk, Pete told Don to pull up a chair. "So how have you been, buddy? It's great to see you."

"Pete, I'm doing great. I can't believe you've done so well for yourself. This office is unbelievable."

"Yeah, it is nice compared to the one I was in when I started here. They just built this building a year ago to update the offices. The plant is really growing, but we are still not modernized enough. We still do a lot of labor by hand. The plant's owner plans on making some major capital investments the next couple of years to bring us up to speed, though. We're shipping bricks into ten states now and plan to expand our territory into five more this year."

"Sounds great, Pete. I would love to take a tour of the plant."

"We'll do that a little later, but first, how many employees do you manage up in New York?"

"It's nothing of this magnitude, but we still have over one hundred employees. I take care of the hiring and firing, as well as all employee records. I even handle company benefits for all the employees."

"Where, up there, do you sit as far as the chain of command goes?"

"I report directly to the plant manager, why?"

"Well, it's a three tier chain of command here." Pete explained further, drawing a diagram.

Owner (Philip Stash)
Plant manager (Jesse Becker)
Safety director (Pete Miller) Personnel director (Bob Medley)
Plant supervisors, Office Manager
Employees

"As you can see, there is quite a bit of responsibility that falls on the personnel director. The owner is seldom here and only meets with the plant manager once a month, concerning long-term growth of the plant. The day-to-day operations are handled by the plant manager, as well as me and Bob. With Bob retiring this month, we need a real go-getter to fill his shoes."

"Why isn't Bob interviewing his replacement, Pete?"

"Because Phil thought it wouldn't make sense to have Bob involved in the process since he would never be working with the guy. Jesse didn't want to mess around with interviewing people, so it fell onto my shoulders," Pete said, smiling. "I've interviewed twenty people already, from all over the state. Some were qualified, but I didn't think their personalities were a fit with our company. Phil gave us until the end of this week to make a decision, and then you called. I've known you since we were kids, buddy, but I still have to make it look official," he said, smiling.

"Does that mean I have the job, Pete?"

"Hell yes, Don. You're qualified. You have a college degree and sixteen years experience. What else could Phil and Jesse ask for? Bob will work with you for the next two weeks, bringing you up to speed before you have to fly solo. The thing is, Don, because we put off the decision for so long, you have to be able to start Monday morning. Is that a problem?"

"Well, kind of," Don said, rubbing his head. "That means I will have to leave the company I work for now without notice."

"It can't be helped, Don. Do you want the job? I'll tell you what, if it helps with the decision, I've been authorized to go all the way up to twenty-five thousand dollars per year base salary and profit sharing, plus benefits. We will also pay for a moving truck to pack and bring your belongings down here."

Smiling, Don said, "I'll be here first thing Monday morning."

"Well, all right," Pete said, jumping up and shaking his hand. "Let's go meet the rest of the team. By the way, Don, if you like this office, wait till you see yours," he said, grinning.

The rest of the morning and afternoon was a blur consisting of Don meeting with the owner, the plant manager, and finally, the personnel director. The tour of the plant was so impressive that Don could not believe he was now part of the team. At noon, Pete said, "You better go now. You have a lot to do before Monday."

Turning, Don shook Pete's hand one last time and said, "Thanks, Pete. I really appreciate your confidence in me."

"Don't mention it, Don. It will be great working with you. After you get settled in, my wife and I will have your family over for dinner."

"Sounds good, Pete, take care."

"See you Monday, Don."

Driving back to his parent's house, Don's head was spinning. *How am I going to do this in two days?* he wondered. *I have to call my plant and tell them I won't be coming back to work as soon as I get to Dad's. Then we need to find a place to live.*

He could not remember driving to his parents' as he pulled into their driveway. He ran from the car and burst through the front door. His dad had not gone to bed yet and was sitting on the sofa beside Mike. His mom and Leslie ran from the kitchen into the living room when they heard him come through the front door. Smiling, Don screamed, "I got the job!" Leslie ran to him and hugged him. "The problem is, I have to start Monday." Don spit the words out as his mom and dad ran to embrace him.

"How are we going to get our things from New York before Monday?" Mike asked in a puzzled voice.

"Sit down, and I'll explain. Here is what they agreed to do. They will pay to have a moving company pack and bring our belongings here. They also bumped my base salary to twenty-five thousand dollars per year, plus benefits."

"Are you serious?" Leslie asked, wide-eyed.

"Yes, I'm serious."

"Don, do you realize I've worked over thirty years in the same job and I only make fifteen thousand dollars a year?" Pat said. "You will have it made now, son."

"I'll be fourth man down on the totem pole, as far as chain of command goes. It will be a lot of responsibility."

"So what, Dad? They are paying you a fortune!" Mike chimed in.

After the shock wore off, everyone gathered around in the living room and sat down. "I guess you're going to want to go see that house you looked at yesterday," Pat said, grinning. "The owners are going to meet you there at three-thirty this afternoon."

"Thanks, Dad. I'm sorry you didn't get a chance to go to sleep yet."

"That's what dads are for," he said, winking at Sadie.

"I forgot all about the house," Leslie cried. "Thanks for calling, Pat."

"You're welcome," Pat replied as he rose from the sofa slowly, tired from working all night and not going to sleep yet. "I'm going to bed now. I hope you like the house, but you're welcome to stay here as long as you like if you don't."

"Night, Pap," Mike said as he walked to the television and turned it on.

Sadie rose and said, "Come to the kitchen, and I'll fix you a sandwich before you go house-hunting, Don."

"Okay, Mom. I'm starving," he replied, following her to the kitchen with Leslie right behind him.

Once in the kitchen with his mother, Don went to the phone. "I'm dreading making this call, Mom," Don said nervously. "They've been so good to me at the plant in New York, and now I have to call and tell them I won't be coming back to work. It's not so bad taking a new job, but not giving them any notice is wrong."

"Don, you have to do what is best for your family. They'll understand. If they don't, then that's their problem, not yours."

Dialing the number, Don's hands were actually shaking as the secretary answered the phone. "Doris, this is Don Knisley. Can you put Keith on the phone?" Keith had been the plant manager for the past twelve years. He was a no-nonsense type of manager. Don had become good friends with him over the years and hated letting him down.

Keith answered the phone and Don said, "Hi, Keith. How is everything going?"

"Real good, Don. What's up?"

"I have some bad news, and there's no easy way to say it."

"Well, then just spit it out," Keith said curiously.

"I've taken an executive position with a company here in Pennsylvania, and they are requiring that I start first thing Monday morning." There was dead silence on the phone. Breaking the silence, Don continued, "I hate to leave you hanging, Keith, but I can't pass this up. It's the best thing I can do for me and my family. They're giving me the sky, buddy. I don't know what else to say."

Finally Keith spoke, his voice angry. "I don't blame you for taking a better position, but don't you think you could have given me a little notice and worked out at least two weeks for us to train a replacement?"

"I had every intention of doing that, but at the interview today, they said they were working too close as far as a time schedule and said it was basically take it or leave it. I can't pass up this opportunity, so I agreed to start Monday."

"Well, you made your decision," Keith replied, hanging up the phone without so much as a good-bye.

Hanging the phone up, Don looked at his mother and sarcastically said, "Well, that went well."

Sadie put her arm around his shoulder. "You did the right thing, Don. I'm sure of it."

"Thanks, Mom," he said, picking up the sandwich his mother had made for him and taking a bite.

It was two-thirty, and Don and Mike had dozed off on the sofa while watching television. Leslie came into the living room and yelled, "Let's get moving, Don, or we'll be late for our appointment to see the house!"

Wiping his eyes, Don rose from the sofa and stretched. "Boy, am I whooped. I don't know why I am so tired. Get up, Mike, if you're going with us." Don kicked his leg, waking Mike from his afternoon nap.

"What?" he moaned.

"Are you going with us to look at the house?"

"Yeah, yeah," he said, rising from the sofa.

Walking outside, they found Sadie weeding in the garden. "Do you want to ride along, Mom, to see the house?"

"Okay, but wait till I wash my hands."

Everyone got into the car. Several minutes later, Sadie came from the house and got into the backseat with Mike. As they pulled from the driveway, Mike asked his grandmother how she could stand that smell from the paper mill every day.

"Oh, it's not so bad after you get used to it. Some days are worse than others. It's the lifeblood of this town, so everyone just accepts it."

"Well, I don't think I could ever get used to the smell," he replied.

"You would if you lived in this town, Mike."

The drive to Claysburg was pleasant. It was sunny and warm, so everyone rolled down their windows and reveled in the beauty of the day. The air blowing through the window was cool and refreshing. It was just a great day to be alive. Driving down Haller Road, Sadie remarked at how peaceful and beautiful the rural area was. "This would be a nice area to live in, Don."

"Yeah," Mike laughed, "notice, Gram, that the air smells fresh here."

Nudging him, Sadie said, "Mike, you missed your calling. You should have been a clown."

Pulling into the driveway of the old Stone homestead, there was an old, beat-up pickup sitting in the driveway. "Look, Dad, the house matches the owner's truck," Mike said.

"Knock it off, Mike," he said.

"You had better be on your best behavior, young man," Leslie chimed in.

Getting out of the car, they were greeted by a tall, husky gentleman. "Hi, my name is Bob Wyandt, and this is my wife Lois."

"Pleased to meet you," Don said. "My name is Don Knisley, and this is my wife Leslie, my son Mike, and his grandmother Sadie."

"Hello. So your father said you're moving to the area and wanted to see the inside of the house. It's a two-bedroom home with a basement and a crawl space in the attic. The garage is in bad shape, as you can see, but the house is in decent shape inside." Walking to the front door, Bob unlocked it and walked inside with everyone following behind. There was a chill in the house, the kind of chill that seems to seep into your bones and settles there. The house smelled musty from sitting empty for months.

"Well, at least the house is cool compared to outside," Mike elbowed his dad.

Leslie looked around the completely furnished living room. "It's a nice-sized living room, don't you think, Sadie?"

"Yes, it is Leslie. It has a lot of potential."

"All the furniture is included with the sale of the house, including the stove and refrigerator," added Lois.

"We have most of our own furniture," Leslie replied.

"Whatever you don't want you can throw out."

Walking to the kitchen, Leslie smiled. There was a window above the sink, looking out into the backyard. "It's a glorious view, don't you think, Don?" Appeasing her, Don nodded. "Of course, it will need new linoleum and countertops eventually. I can live with the cupboards, but they will need refinished."

Lois looked at Bob and rolled her eyes.

Looking around, everyone realized that Mike was nowhere to be found. "Where did Mike go, Don?" Leslie asked.

"How would I know, Leslie?"

"Mike!" she yelled.

"I'm upstairs," he answered. Leaving the living room, they walked upstairs. Mike was in Elijah's old bedroom. "I guess this will be my bedroom," he laughed, pointing to the pink walls.

"Don't worry, Mike. We'll remodel it the way you want it."

Walking to the closet, Mike tried to open the door, but it appeared to be locked. "That's strange," Bob remarked, tugging at the door. "There isn't a lock on this closet." Finally giving up, they were about to walk out of the room when the closet door seemed to open by itself. There, in the closet, was the complete wardrobe of a small child. It was cluttered with dresses and shoes, as well as toys. "The people who rented this house last year left a lot of their things when they returned to Youngstown, Ohio," Bob explained.

"Why in the world would they do that?" Leslie inquired.

"I don't know," Bob said, lying. "Probably because they skipped out on paying the rent." Lois elbowed him before he could finish his explanation.

"I don't know, Mike, you could probably fit into some of those dresses," Don joked.

"Real funny, Dad. Do I need to remind you about yesterday?"

Giving him a dirty look, Don walked out into the hallway and went into the master bedroom. "Leslie, look here," he called. "You're going to love this."

Leslie came into the room and immediately whispered to Don, "I want this house." The room was spacious, with its own access door to the bathroom. It had two windows, allowing for lots of natural light, one facing the front yard, the other facing the neighbor's house. Bob and Lois waited in the hallway, making small talk with Sadie, as Don, Leslie, and Mike checked out the rest of the house.

GET OUT!

A half an hour had passed when Don called upstairs to them, asking them to come to the living room. "Well, we like the house if the price is right. It's going to need a lot of work. I went to the basement, and it looks like the furnace is in sad shape. How much are you asking for it?"

Bob thought for a second and said, "We're firm at ten thousand dollars."

"Tell you what," Don said, "if you take all the furniture out except for the stove and refrigerator, we'll take it. I'm having my furniture brought down by a moving company next week, and we need a place to live as soon as possible."

"How fast could you close on it?" Bob asked.

"I don't know," Don replied, "unless you would consider doing the financing."

"We never considered that. How much could you put down on it?"

"I can write you a check today for two thousand dollars and pay you five hundred a month until the balance is paid off."

Bob looked at Lois who shook her head yes. "Tell you what," Bob said, "since you're paying such a large chunk of money per month, we won't charge you any interest."

"That sounds great," Don replied, shaking Bob's hand. Just as Don pulled his checkbook from his back pocket, they heard a loud slamming noise upstairs. "What the heck was that noise?" Don asked.

Looking at Lois, Bob nonchalantly said, "What noise?"

Looking around, Don noticed that Mike wasn't around. "My son's probably upstairs knocking stuff around."

"Let's go outside into the fresh air, and you can finish writing the check out there," Lois said hesitantly.

"Fine," Don said, walking out the front door to his car. Placing the checkbook on the hood of the car, he began writing the check out to Bob Wyandt. "Downpayment on home. Balance to be paid in sixteen equal payments of five hundred dollars per month for property located at 322 Haller Road," he wrote under the memo section. Handing Bob the check, Don took out a piece of paper and wrote up a bill of sale, having Bob and Lois sign it. He included in the bill of sale that they would present the deed to him upon his last payment, free and clear of all encumbrances.

"Thank you," Bob replied, handing Don the keys to the house. "I'll have a moving company empty the house on Monday, as we agreed," he added, getting into his pickup truck with Lois.

Once inside the pickup and pulling from the driveway, Bob looked at Lois and said, handing her the check, "Can you believe it? We're finally rid of that God-forsaken house."

"Bob, I can't believe you lied about the clothing in that child's bedroom."

"Lois, I didn't want to get into the history of the house with them. You wanted to sell the damn thing, didn't you? Who the hell would want to buy a house with a reputation for death? It's better this way. As soon as we get home, call the Salvation Army, and see if they want the furnishings in the house. Tell them they can have everything but the stove and refrigerator with the stipulation that they have everything out by Monday at noon."

"How did you think of that, Bob? That's a great idea, and it won't cost us a penny. They have their own trucks."

Smiling, Bob said, "I guess I'm good for something."

Don and Leslie walked to the front of the house. Wrapping her arms around his waist, Leslie passionately kissed him on the lips. "Thank you, honey," she said, squeezing him tightly.

"Whatever my wife wants, she gets," he replied jokingly.

Sadie walked over to them and announced, "Congratulations, you two. It's your first home, and you can do with it as you please."

Leslie said, "I want to take measurements for drapes and curtains before we leave, Don. Sadie, will you go in town with me tomorrow to buy some things for the house?" Leslie asked.

Smiling, Sadie said, "That sounds like fun, Leslie."

Don opened the trunk of his car and pulled out a tool box. Opening it, he tossed Leslie a tape measure and said, "Enjoy yourself."

Sadie followed Leslie into the house with a piece of paper and a pen in hand. Putting the toolbox away and closing the trunk, Don noticed that Mike was jogging to the car from back behind the house with an old pair of boots. "Hey, Dad, look what I found back in that garage. It's an old pair of army boots. There's a box of men's clothes back there and a ton of old tools. Can I keep the boots, Pop?"

"I guess so, yeah," Don said. "We just bought the house, and they said everything goes with the sale. Why do you want old, worn-out army boots anyway?"

"Because they're neat," Mike said. Sitting down on the gravel driveway, he slipped them onto his feet. "Wow, whoever owned these sure had big feet." The tattered, scuffed boots were at least two sizes too big for his feet. "I'll grow into them," Mike said, laughing.

"You're nuts," Don said, cuffing him on top of the head. "They look like elf shoes with the toes turned up."

"So, you want to rumble with a combat veteran?" Mike laughed, jumping to his feet and circling his father. The oversized boots caused him to trip as he continued to circle him with his arms held high, ready for combat. Don, turning to face him, lunged at Mike when he noticed he was off-balance. Knocking him to the grass, Mike's athletic prowess allowed him to twist and land on top of his father, knocking the wind from him. Stunned, Don tried to roll his son off him. Mike immediately interlocked his arms, trapping them to his back and forcing more air from him.

Turning red, Don could barely breathe, let alone speak, as he hissed, "Get the hell off me, boy."

Mike jumped from his dad to his feet and once again stood in a combat stance. "Want some more of this?" he said to his dad.

Slowly getting to his feet, Don smiled and said, "You're lucky you caught me off guard, or I would have kicked your ass."

"Yeah, right, old man," Mike taunted. "Wait till I tell Pap I kicked your butt."

"Keep it up, Mike, and you'll be washing my car into the next century."

"Sore loser," Mike sneered, walking back toward the garage. "Come on, Dad, check out this garage. It's creepy."

Don turned and followed him to the garage. Mike had disappeared inside the garage when Don finally walked inside. It was so dark he had to strain his eyes to adjust. The floor appeared to be made of dirt and shale. There were several benches to the rear of the garage loaded with all types of tools. "What do you think, Dad?" Mike asked.

"I think this death trap needs to be torn down and a new garage built."

"You have to admit it is creepy in here," Mike said, moaning like a ghost.

"Let me put it this way, Mike, you couldn't pay me to spend the night out here." Suddenly the door slammed shut, trapping them in the garage.

"What the heck?" Mike yelled, running to the door with his father and pushing on it. It was being held shut from the outside. Don backed up and slammed into the door with his shoulder, causing it to creak but not give.

"I don't like this, Mike. How the hell did that door slam shut? The wind wasn't blowing today."

Mike appeared from the back of the garage with a sledgehammer in his hands. "Do you mind if I do a little demolition work, Dad?"

"Be my guest," he laughed.

Raising the hammer high above his head, Mike slammed it down at the door's hinge. The force of the blow knocked the entire door from the frame.

Mike walked outside with the hammer in his hands and looked at his dad saying, "You don't mess with the Knisley crew."

Don laughed, saying, "You were so scared in there I thought you were about to cry."

"Yeah, right, who got us out?" Mike snarled, flexing his muscles.

"Come on, blowhard, I'm hungry. I hope your mom and gram are ready to go."

Leslie and Sadie were sitting in the car when they rounded the corner of the house. Opening the car door, Don said, "How long have you been in the car?"

"A couple of minutes, I suppose. Where were you? We called and called for you two. Why didn't you answer?"

"Because we accidentally got locked in the garage out back, and he-man there had to bust the door down with a sledgehammer."

"That garage looks dangerous, Don. You better be careful going in there."

"Trust me Leslie, I don't plan on making a habit of it."

"Hey, Gram, check out my boots," Mike said raising them into the air so his mom could see them also. "I found them in the garage and Dad said I could have them."

Sadie smiled and shook her head, saying, "Do you realize that they're way too big for your feet?"

"I know, but I still like them."

Glancing at his watch, Don exclaimed, "Wow! It's six-thirty; no wonder I'm starved. Do you think Dad is up yet?"

"No, he just went to bed at one-thirty. I won't get him up until ten to get ready for work."

"In that case, I'm treating everyone to supper at Poke's Diner in Claysburg!" The diner was packed as they pulled into the parking lot. "Is it always this busy on a Friday night, Mom?"

"How do I know, Don? We usually eat at the restaurant in Roaring Spring."

Mike jumped from the car and ran inside, sitting down in a booth.

"I guess he's hungry," Leslie said, smiling.

By the time everyone joined Mike at the booth, a waitress had appeared and was taking his order. She looked to be a young high-school girl who was very attractive. Smiling at Mike, she asked, "Will that be all?"

"Well, no, they need to order their meals also, and I need your phone number," he joked. It was obvious that she was flustered waiting on Mike. He seemed to have that effect on girls.

Don elbowed him as he sat down beside him. "We'll all have cheeseburgers and fries with a Coke, Miss. Thanks."

"Sure," she said, once again smiling at Mike before she left.

"Michael, do you think you will ever stop clowning around?" Leslie scolded.

"Who's clowning, Mom? I do want her phone number," he said, grinning from ear to ear.

"He's a chip off the old block, isn't he, Mom?" Don smiled.

"I'm afraid so," Sadie replied. "Your dad was always courting girls when he was your age," she laughed to Mike. "I guess the apple doesn't fall far from the tree, as the saying goes."

After twenty minutes, the food finally arrived. As the waitress handed Mike his plate of food first, he winked at her.

"Thank you, Miss," Don laughed as he received his plate last.

Lifting his burger from the plate, Mike noticed a piece of paper lying under it. Opening the note, it revealed her phone number. "Score!" Mike yelled to his dad, shoving the note in his pocket.

"Eat your food, clown," Don snickered. The jumbo-sized burgers were tremendous, dripping with grease and cheese. Starving, Mike and Don polished off their meals in a matter of minutes.

"Hurry up, Mom, I want to watch television," Mike whined.

"I'm eating as fast as I can," Leslie replied with a mouth full of food.

"Will that be everything, sir?" the young waitress asked, handing Don the bill.

"That will do it," Don replied, handing her ten dollars and telling her to keep the change.

"Thank you very much," she smiled, mouthing the words "call me" to Mike as he was leaving the diner.

The drive home was quiet. Everyone was tired from a long, full day. Arriving at his parents' house and pulling into the driveway, Don yawned. "I'm going to bed now; I can barely keep my eyes open. When dad gets up, tell him we bought the house, Mom. I'll talk to him about it tomorrow when he gets home from work."

Entering the house, Sadie went to the kitchen to make Pat's lunch bucket for work. Mike went directly to the television and turned it on. Don climbed the steps slowly, aching from his encounter with his son earlier in the day. "Night, Mike."

"Good night, Dad." Sitting down on the sofa beside his mother, he propped his feet up on the coffee table.

"Get those boots off if you're going to prop your feet up there, young man," she scolded.

Saturday morning was overcast as they climbed from bed. Don could barely move because he was so sore from the day before. Complaining to Leslie about his discomfort prompted her to ask what it was from. He explained that he had wrestled with Mike the day before in the yard.

"You're too old to be doing that. That boy is going to hurt you one of these days, the way you two horse around," Leslie insisted.

"That will be the day," Don grumbled. "I'm going to the bathroom to take a hot shower."

"Be quiet so you don't wake your dad. It's nine, so he's home and in bed by now."

"Okay, I'll be quiet," he whispered. Leslie followed him out into the hallway and into the bathroom. While he was showering, she brushed her teeth and changed into a fresh pair of jeans and blouse. Grabbing the shower curtain, she flung it open. "What," Don said, "do you want to join me?"

Shaking her head and grinning, she said, "No, I just wanted to tell you I'm taking the car and leaving to go in town with your mom after I eat breakfast."

"Okay. I'll see you in a few hours, sweetie."

After showering and changing into his clothes, Don walked down the steps to find Mike lying on the sofa in his usual position, watching television. "Hi, Dad, are we going to the house today? I want to clear that garage out and see if there is any more neat stuff in it."

"Your mom took the car in town with your grandmother, so we're stranded here."

"We can take Pap's car. He won't care, he's out like a light."

"Let me eat some cereal and write your mom a note." Going to the kitchen, Don fixed himself a bowl of cereal and wrote a note telling his dad he was borrowing his car. He wrote a second note telling his mom and Leslie to come to the house when they got home. Finishing the bowl of cereal, he posted the notes in plain sight on the kitchen table, grabbed his dad's car keys, and went to the living room. "Are you ready to go, Mike?"

Lifting his feet into the air, displaying his army boots, he replied, "The combat veteran is ready, sir."

"Come on, you nut," he yelled, walking out the front door. "Go to Pap's garage and get a couple flashlights and his tool box," Don barked, getting into the car. Mike returned with the items and threw them into the backseat.

Climbing into the front seat with his dad, he smiled and said, "We could go cruising for chicks if you want to."

GET OUT!

"Mike, do you ever think you could be serious for an entire day?"

"Nope," he answered, rolling down his window. The overcast skies were starting to clear and it was warming up as they drove to their new house.

"The first thing we're going to do when we get to that house is toss out the old curtains and drapes," Don decided. "Your mom is getting new ones today."

Within fifteen minutes, they were pulling into the driveway. There was a large truck in the driveway already. Written on the side of it was Salvation Army. Getting out of the car, Don noticed it was half full of items from the house.

Two men appeared on the front door carrying a mattress. "Hi!" they called out.

"Hi," Don yelled back, walking over to them.

The two fellows looked like the odd couple. One was no taller than five feet three inches, with a fat pot belly. He was at least fifty years old with a long, gray beard, and a dumbfounded look was ingrained on his face. The taller of the two men, standing at about six foot three inches, and weighing no more than a hundred and fifty pounds, looked to be in his forties and was definitely in charge. He was soaking wet with sweat and was barking orders to the short guy like he was a moron. "They said everything goes," he called to Don.

"Everything but the stove and refrigerator," Don replied.

"You can take the drapes and curtains too," Mike added, smiling at his dad.

"What about out back in the garage, does anything go from back there?"

"No," Mike yelled before his dad could put a word in edgewise.

"Okay, wise guy, let's help them carry stuff out."

"They seem to be doing a great job without our help, Dad. Let's go explore the garage!"

"Do what I told you, and get your ass moving, Mike." Dejectedly, Mike followed his dad inside the house.

The men, returning to the house once again for another load, walked over to Don with a questioning look on their faces. He immediately noticed that their names, Byron and Steve, were sewn on their greasy ragged shirts. Byron, the one in charge, was the first to speak. "What's with this house? It's cold as a bitch in here."

Before Don could speak, Mike chimed in, "I bet you wouldn't be complaining if it was ninety degrees outside, right now, would you?"

"You got a point, kid," he said, picking up a coffee table.

"Mike, run upstairs and get the kid's clothing and toys out of your room," Don yelled, trying to avoid a confrontation. "They can take all those items with them." Mike flew up the steps, tripping halfway on his oversized boots. "Be careful, you're going to kill yourself in those damn boots." Sheepishly, he slowed down and walked the rest of the way up.

Opening his bedroom door, he noticed the window was open and there was a strange, pungent odor in the room. *That smells like shit,* he thought to himself. *If Dad thinks I'm sleeping in here with that smell, he's got another think coming.* Walking to the closet, Mike tugged on the handle, but the door would not open. *Not again,* he thought to himself, pulling harder. Finally, kicking the door, it seemed to open by itself, displaying toys and clothing neatly organized on clothing hangers and shelves. Grabbing an armful, he ran it downstairs and out to the truck. "Where do you want this stuff, Steve?" he asked.

"Throw it anywhere. They'll unpack it today when we get back."

Throwing the items in the truck, he ran back up to the room for another load. The smell was gone, and the window was closed. It didn't appear as if anyone had been in the room. *Dad must have closed it,* Mike decided. Grabbing another arm-full, he repeated the process until the entire closet was bare. Walking to his dad's bedroom, he found him sitting on the floor in a now empty room. "What's up, Pop, you tired?"

"No, I was just daydreaming. Is your room empty?"

"Yep, down to the bare walls. Let's go check that garage out again."

"Do a room check up here first to make sure they have all the curtains and stuff out of every room."

Mike walked through every room upstairs, including the bathroom. Walking down the steps, he informed his dad that the rooms were totally bare from wall to wall. The house seemed much larger now that all the rooms were empty.

Don went outside and thanked Steve and Byron just as they were ready to pull from the driveway. "No problem," Steve yelled. "Thank you."

Looking at his watch, Don noticed that it was two-thirty. "Your mom will be surprised when she sees the house now." Mike did not answer back. As Don looked around, he was nowhere to be found. Walking back to the garage, Don heard a loud clanging inside. "Mike, are you inside there?"

"Yeah, Dad, come on in."

The garage was now lit quite well with the two flashlights and the garage door knocked down. "Find anything worthwhile, Mike?"

"Not yet, just a bunch of tools and old magazines and newspapers." Shining the light on the bench, Don noticed the name Elijah Stone carved very neatly into the bench. "I wonder who that is," Mike said upon seeing the carving.

"He must have been the last person who lived here. You're probably wearing his army boots right now."

"Look here, Dad," Mike yelled, pulling out a small cardboard box containing old black-and-white photographs. Sorting through the pictures with his dad looking over his shoulder, Mike pulled out one of a handsome young man in a military uniform. "Elijah's first year in the military, 1958" was written on the back.

"Well, that explains the army boots," Don said.

"Yeah, I wonder what happened to him. The picture is only two years old." There was only one picture of him in his army clothes; the other photographs were of what appeared to be the man's mother and father and him as a child. "I'm keeping them, Dad."

"Go right ahead. I don't want them." Voices could be heard yelling from the driveway. "Your mom is here. Come on, and bring the flashlights."

Scooping up the box, they jogged to the front yard and were greeted by Leslie, Sadie, and Pat. Smiling, Don said, "Hi! Wait til you see inside, Leslie. Aren't you tired, Dad?"

"A little, Don, but I wanted to see your new house."

"Well, come on inside."

Leslie yelled for Mike to bring the stuff in from the car, and after entering the house, she began grinning from ear to ear. "Wow, how did you get rid of all that furniture already?"

"When Mike and I got here this morning, there was a truck here from the Salvation Army. I guess Bob called them yesterday."

"This is great, Don. I can get painters in here this week and have our furniture brought down by the middle of the week."

"Leslie, be realistic. Painters are not going to be able to come in here right away. They have other jobs; they can't drop everything for you because you tell them to."

Pat was smiling as Leslie said, "Do you want to bet?"

"Yeah, I'll bet you."

"Don't, son, you're going to lose," Pat laughed. "I called some of my buddies from work who paint on the side. Two of them are on vacation this week, so they said they would jump right on it for me. Your wife is a real go-getter. Or should I say, your mother and your wife. When they got back from town, Sadie made me get my butt out of bed and call them. Then, to top it off, they forced me to go to the department store in town and help them pick colors."

"I'm sorry, Dad. I know you're tired from working third trick all week."

"I'm just kidding, Don. I'd paint the rooms myself this week if they weren't available. But trust me, these guys do a professional job. They said they could start on the outside of the house in two weeks."

"That's great! It's all coming together perfectly."

Mike walked into the house with a gigantic load of items. "Here's the curtains I picked out, hon," Leslie said, sheepishly grinning as she pointed at Mike's arms, which were overflowing. "I hope you're not going to be mad when you see how much I spent."

"Don't worry about it, Mom," Mike yelled. "Dad's making the big bucks now."

"You can fix this house up anyway you want, Leslie," Don smiled. "After all, I'm uprooting you from your home."

"Thanks, honey" she replied, lifting the drapes up in the living room and saying, "That's the look I was trying to achieve."

"Come on, Pap! I'll show you my room," Mike yelled. Mike ran up the steps with Pat on his heels. Going into his bedroom, Mike noticed that the window was once again open.

"Mike, you should keep the window closed. This house is already fifteen degrees cooler than mine."

"Pap, I'm positive it was closed the last time I was here." Closing the window, Mike declared that the darn thing must have a mind all its own.

"I really like the color of your room," Pat laughed, admiring the pink walls. "This room was recently painted. I think you should leave it this way."

"Yeah right, Pap. The girls would love me for sure then. I think I will stick with dark blue like in my bedroom back home."

"I like the patch job someone did on that rat hole too. It adds a nice personal touch," Pat declared, smirking. "I'll get my buddies to fix that the right way when they come to paint Monday."

"Thanks, Pap. Let's go downstairs and see if we can talk Dad into leaving. I'm hungry."

Walking down the steps, Mike pulled his dad to the side. "Pap wants to go and get something to eat. Are you ready?"

"Dad, are you hungry?" Don asked his father.

"I could eat a burger if you're ready to go. Your mom has hamburgers thawing at home. I'll drive home now with Mike and throw them on the grill. By the time you bring the women home in your car, supper will be ready."

"Sounds good to me," Don said, throwing his father his car keys.

Mike and Pat left while the others were discussing color schemes in the living room. Walking to the car, Mike looked at his pap. "Do you want me to drive, Pap? You look tired."

"Mike, you can't drive yet."

"Well, my dad lets me drive around the block back home sometimes," he said, lying.

"Tell you what, Mike, you can drive to the end of Haller Road. Then I'm taking over from there, okay?"

Smiling, Mike jumped into the driver's seat of Pat's car. Starting the car, Mike put the vehicle into drive and gave it gas. The car lunged forward. Pat hollered, "What the heck are you doing, boy? Put the car in reverse, not drive. You never drove before, did you?"

"No, I lied, Pap. Please let me try it."

"Your dad will shoot me if you wreck this car."

"Come on, Pap. Please. I'll be careful."

Shaking his head, Pat said, "Put your foot on the brake, and slip the car into reverse." Tensely, Mike did as he was told. "Now take your foot off the brake, and back up slowly to the end of the driveway." As Mike backed up, he accelerated too quickly, causing the car to jerk. Slamming the brake down too hard, he skidded to a stop.

"Well, that's enough lessons for one day," Pat declared. "Put it in park, or we'll never get home in one piece. I'll take you to a back road someday and teach you. How's that sound?"

"Okay," Mike said, disheartened that he had failed miserably at his first try at driving. Switching seats, they headed toward Roaring Spring with Pat driving.

Leslie was going from room to room with Sadie, taking notes on what each room needed, as far as paint color and décor. Don was following along, trying to act as if he were actually interested in what they were saying. Entering the kitchen, Leslie caught him yawning and said, "Why didn't you just ride home with the boys if you're tired?"

"Because I didn't want to leave you two ladies here alone," he said.

"I'm a big girl, Don. I don't need you to hold my hand every minute of every day. We're almost done anyway. Go upstairs and make sure all the windows are locked up before we leave."

Don sprinted out of the kitchen and up the steps. Walking to his bedroom first, he checked each window, making sure it was locked. Leaving his bedroom and walking into the hallway, he thought he heard voices in Mike's bedroom. Assuming the women had come upstairs, he burst into the room. No one was there, and the voices had stopped. The window was wide open in Mike's room. "Is anyone here?" he whispered. There was dead silence in the room. Slamming the window shut, he locked it and left the room, closing the door behind him. Hearing whispers once again, he opened the door quickly to find nothing. *That's freaky,* he thought, closing the door once again and walking down the steps. "Are you ready?" he called to Leslie.

"Yeah, we'll meet you at the car in a second."

Don walked to the car and got into the backseat. Lying down, he closed his eyes and drifted to sleep. Waking, he sat up and found himself in his father's driveway, alone in the car. *How did I get here?* he wondered. Getting out of the car, he went inside his parents' house to find everyone eating burgers at the kitchen table.

"Finally up, sleepyhead?" Mike teased, taking a bite from his burger.

"I must be tired, because I don't remember you driving here, Leslie."

"You were out like a light, and your mom and I didn't have the heart to wake you."

"Sit down, and eat some supper," Sadie added, handing him a plate full of food as he thanked her.

After supper, everyone retired to the living room to relax and watch television. "Two more nights of third trick, then I'll have two days off to help you with the house, Don."

"You don't have to, Dad. You've already done enough for us."

"Donald, you know by now you're not going to be able to keep your father from that house until it's finished," Sadie laughed.

Smiling, Don said, "Well, I appreciate everything both of you are doing for us."

"I think Pap has ulterior motives, Dad. He knows the quicker our house is finished, the quicker he gets his television back from me," Mike laughed.

"He does take control of the television," Pat said with a smirk on his face. "Well, I'm going to take a nap before work. Get me up at ten, Sadie."

"Pat, how many years have I been waking you up? I don't think in all the years we've been married, that I ever let you oversleep, and I don't intend to start tonight."

"Night, Pap," Mike yelled, walking to the television and changing the channel.

"Night," Pat yelled back as he walked up the steps.

When the grandfather clock located in the living room struck nine, Don yawned and said, "Are you ready for bed, Leslie? I'm bushed."

"Yes, I'm tired too."

"You have to be kidding me," Mike snorted from the sofa. "You two act like you're eighty years old. I guess Gram and I will have to watch television without you old timers."

"Goodnight," Leslie called out, walking up the steps in front of Don.

At the top of the stairway, he slid his hand around her waist and kissed her neck. "I know what you want," she said, turning to kiss him.

"Make sure you're quiet," Don whispered. "I don't want anyone to hear your screams of passion." Laughing, Leslie grabbed his hand and led him to their bedroom.

Sunday morning dawned bright and sunny. It was nine-thirty when Don and Leslie woke up. Lying in bed, she leaned over to kiss him, saying, "You were an animal last night!"

Smiling, he replied, "You were pretty wild yourself. What do you want to do today?"

"Let's get Mike and walk around Roaring Spring. We've never really walked around the town."

"Sounds good to me," Don said, crawling from bed. "We'll shower and eat breakfast first."

Don and Leslie had never really been too religious. Don was brought up going to church regularly on Sundays, but since moving away from home, he rarely attended church with his family except on Easter and Christmas. Sadie had admonished him many times and said that he should be taking Mike to church, but he always enjoyed sleeping in on Sundays.

After showering, they went to the kitchen to eat breakfast. Lying on the kitchen table was a note from his mother saying, "Mike and I went to church. We'll be home around twelve-thirty. Love, Mom."

Picking up the pen lying beside the paper, Don wrote his own note. 'Leslie and I went for a walk in town. We'll be back sometime this afternoon. Love, Don."

"Well, so much for taking Mike on our walk," Leslie said, smiling. "You better get used to going to church again now that we're living here, Don. Your mother will see to that," she said, smiling. "Yeah, I guess I better. Mom won't take no for an answer when it comes to church."

After a hot breakfast of eggs and toast, they did the dishes and walked outside into the warm, sunny air. It was a perfect day for a walk except for the stench emanating from the paper mill. "I know where I can take you, Leslie," Don said, excitedly grabbing her hand.

"Where?" she asked as he tugged her arm, forcing her to follow him.

"It's a surprise. Just come on."

They had walked about ten blocks when they came to a large spring that was dammed up to form quite a large pond. In the center of the pond was a fountain spraying cool, refreshing water into the air. It was surrounded by lush green grass and flowering dogwood trees. "This is like something out of a picture!" Leslie squealed excitedly. "I love it. Why do they have this in the middle of a town?"

"Because the mill needs a ton of fresh water to produce paper, and this spring supplies it," he replied. "It's called the Spring Dam. I figured you would like it," he said, sitting down at the water's edge. As they sat admiring the beauty of nature, ducks paddled up to them making the scene even more perfect.

"I love you, Don. This is so wonderful."

Kicking their shoes off, they dipped their feet into the cool water and relaxed, lying back on the soft, carpet-like grass. They spent the entire morning and part of the afternoon holding hands and enjoying each other's company. Looking at his watch, Don saw that it was three in the afternoon. "We better head back; they're probably wondering where we are." Pulling Leslie to her feet, he kissed her lovingly on the lips.

"Honey, we haven't spent this much quality time together since we were first married," she said.

"Follow me. I want to show you one more thing before we leave." They walked to the back of the pond, and he pointed at a black pipe protruding from the side of the bank. It had water gushing from it. Leaning down, he put his mouth close to the gushing water and took a long, deep drink of its refreshing water. "That is so good." Standing, he said, "Try it, Leslie."

She bent over and drank for what seemed like forever. Standing up, she looked at Don and said, "That water is so cold and tastes better than any I've ever drank."

"People come from miles around to bottle that water and take it home," Don said proudly. "After we get settled into our new house, we'll come over and get some to keep in our refrigerator."

"Okay," she said, grabbing his hand and running through the grass, holding her shoes in one hand. They walked the ten blocks back to his parents' house in their bare feet, holding hands the entire way.

It was four in the afternoon when they walked through the front door, giggling like school kids. "Well, it must be nice," Mike said as they walked through the front door. "I hope you two had a wonderful time while I sat here all afternoon."

"We did, thank you," Leslie replied sarcastically.

"Where's Mom and Dad?" Don asked.

"They're upstairs taking a nap. Pap said this is his last night of third trick, so he wants to get caught up on his sleep. He said he won't go to bed on Monday after he gets home from work until the evening. That man is a machine, Dad. I don't know how he does it."

"He's used to it after thirty years, Mike. Your body builds up a tolerance."

"Well, I still don't think I could do it."

"I have an idea. Let's go get some ice cream," Leslie said, looking at Don.

"Sounds good to me, honey," he replied. "Mike, tell Mom and Dad where we went when they get up," Don kidded.

"Yeah, right," Mike bellowed. "You're not going anywhere without me."

"I was kidding. Come on, get in the car."

After piling into the car, Mike grimaced and said, "Guess where I have to go tonight at seven?"

"Where?" Leslie inquired, looking rather puzzled.

"With Gram to church again. She informed me that I am her new church buddy, and I better get used to it because she's picking me up every Sunday, even if you two don't go. Dad, do I have to go every week?"

"Listen, Mike, I'm not taking my mother on concerning your spiritual well-being. It won't hurt you one bit spending some time with your grandmother," he said, laughing.

"Easy for you to say! You don't have to sit between a bunch of old ladies and listen to a monotone preacher for two hours straight."

"Well, I guess Gram figures you need to make up for the last fifteen years you haven't been attending regularly."

"Well, what about you and Mom? You two haven't exactly been setting a record for attendance the past fifteen years either."

"Trust me, Mike, we'll be going too after we get settled into our new house. Your gram will see to that."

Don drove to Martinsburg, a small town about twelve miles from Roaring Spring, nestled in amongst a farming community whose main agricultural yield was milk from the dairy cows. On the outskirts of the town was a milk processor called Richman's Dairy. They had a small store which sold milk and ice cream made right on the premises. Don had grown up eating this rich, full-flavored homemade ice cream. It had been a trip that, as a boy, he had looked forward to after church every Sunday with his parents.

After driving on long, winding, dusty, rural roads, he finally pulled into a parking lot jam-packed with cars. Smiling at Mike and Leslie, he said, "You are about to eat the best ice cream ever made." Going into the store, they stood behind a long line of people waiting to buy this favorite hometown treat. Finally making it to the counter, they viewed twenty flavors of colorful ice cream. After ordering two cones of butter pecan and one cone of white house cherry, all three stood salivating, waiting for the young female clerk to dip the ice cream.

The girl handed Mike his cone of ice cream first. Looking at his dad, he whispered, "See what good looks get you? I always seem to get my food before you and Mom." Laughing, he walked outside.

Minutes later, Don and Leslie were outside enjoying their cones with Mike. "Well, what do you think, Mike?"

"I think she was pretty good-looking," he said, beaming.

"I meant the ice cream, you idiot."

"Oh, it's pretty good too," he laughed.

Leslie leaned over to Don and said, "We do have a good-looking son, don't we?"

Don laughed and said, "I hadn't noticed. What I did notice is that he's a pain in my ass most of the time."

The gooey ice cream dripped down over their hands as they finished it in the hot June heat. It was just the ticket for a scorching afternoon. Finishing their cones, they got back into the car and headed back home.

When they arrived at his parent's house, Mike declared half-heartedly, "Well, I better get ready for church. Aren't you and Mom going too?"

"Next week, we'll go," Don promised. "Your mother and I need to talk about what all needs done to the house," he said, winking at Leslie.

Sadie was sitting in the living room in her church clothes with Pat when they walked through the door. "Where did you go?" she asked inquisitively.

"I took them to Richman's Dairy for ice cream," Don replied.

" I'll bet they enjoyed that! It's the best ice cream in the state," Pat said, smiling.

"I have to say it ranks up there with the best I've ever eaten," Leslie added.

"Are you two going to church with us tonight?" Sadie asked, looking stern.

"We'll go next week, Mom, I promise. We just want to relax before I start my new job tomorrow. Besides, Mike is really looking forward to going with you tonight."

"You mean to tell me that your father, who is working third trick, is going, but you can't muster up the energy to go, Donald?"

"I promise we will all go with you next week."

"Well, okay, but I'm holding you to that promise, young man. Mike, you and Pat run up and change now. I don't want to be late for the service."

"Yes, ma'am," Mike said, looking to his dad for support. Receiving none, he followed his pap upstairs to change.

Minutes late, they returned wearing their dress clothes. "You two look so handsome," Sadie remarked as she stood to leave. Mike was wearing his dark blue suit with a light paisley blue tie that Leslie had bought for him last year. Pat was wearing his one and only light blue leisure suit that he had worn since Don was a child.

As they were walking out the front door, Pat looked back laughing and said, "Hold the fort down till we get home, and don't do anything I wouldn't do."

The front door closed behind his parents and Don swept Leslie into his arms. "We are finally all alone, honey. You can make all the noise you want."

"Don, I feel weird doing this in your parents' living room."

"Trust me, this sofa isn't about to talk and tell anyone what is about to go on here in a few minutes," he said, stripping down to his underwear. Don walked to the front of the living room to turn off the lights.

Turning around, Leslie had nothing on but her bra and panties and was wearing a grin from ear to ear. "Well, what are you waiting for?" Don rushed to her, pulling her to the sofa and kissing her passionately.

They were only on the sofa for a few minutes when the door sprang open, and Mike rushed in. Leslie screamed, searching for her clothing. "Well, what do we have here?" Mike asked, laughing. "I thought you two were going to talk about fixing up our new house. Maybe you had better come to church with us after all."

Leslie was beet-red, trying to cover her exposed body parts from her son. "What the hell are you doing back here?" Don asked angrily.

"Gram forgot her purse and told me to run in and get it."

"Well, get the damn thing and get out of here."

"Easy, big guy," Mike teased, grabbing the purse. "You wouldn't want me to tell Pap what's happening on his sofa."

"You so much as breathe a word of this to anyone, and I'll give you the ass-whooping of your life."

"Keep it up, Dad, and I'll run upstairs and put my combat boots on, and then we'll see who gets the ass-whooping," he continued to tease. Before closing the door behind him, he stuck his head back inside and yelled, "Carry on."

After they heard the car pull from the driveway, Leslie looked at Don almost in tears and asked, "Why didn't you lock the door?"

"I'm sorry, honey. Don't worry about it. The boy is not naive. He knows his parents have sex."

"Well, let me tell you one thing, Don. This is one parent who has no intention of having sex tonight."

Leslie scooped her clothing into her arms and ran upstairs to their bedroom, visibly upset. *That damn boy has it in for me,* Don thought to himself, dressing. Walking to the television, he turned it on and went to the sofa to lay down. *Some night this is going to be,* he thought irately.

Don drifted to sleep within fifteen minutes as he watched the television. Suddenly, he was awaken by warm, wet lips being pressed against his. It was Leslie, wearing only a see-through nightgown with no undergarments on underneath it. The silhouette of her milky white body under the nightgown aroused Don. She was beautiful, with her flowing blonde hair and red lipstick. "You could be a model, Leslie," he said excitedly.

She lay her petite frame on top of him and continued kissing him. "We've had such a wonderful romantic day today, Don. I'm sorry for storming up the steps. Do you forgive me?"

"Honey, the way you look now, how could I ever be mad at you?" he replied.

"Don, you've been such a sweetheart today, I don't think I've wanted you this badly since when we first met."

Breathing heavily, he rolled Leslie off the sofa and down to the carpeted living room rug. "Wait one second," Don pleaded, running to the front door and locking it. "I'm not making the same mistake twice," he said, smiling and turning the lights off.

Next, he ran to the kitchen and returned with a large, round white candle. Lighting it, shadows danced around the room as he placed it on the coffee table. Still lying on the soft carpeting where he had left her, Leslie seductively rose to her feet and began swirling her moist tongue over her luscious red lips. Slowly, she began to undress him, pulling each article of clothing from his body and tossing them across the room. Don was ready to explode by the time she removed the last piece of clothing from his body. Jumping into his arms, she wrapped her arms around his neck and circled his waist with her legs. Lifting her petite body into the air, Don lovingly laid her once again on the soft carpeting. They made passionate love for over an hour, enjoying each other's body. After finishing their lovemaking, they lay in each others arms. Leslie gazed into his eyes, drinking in his loving stare. "I love you so much, Leslie. This is the start of a new chapter in our lives."

"I just know we are going to be so happy here," she replied. Don rose from the floor, picked up his clothing, and unlocked the door.

"Come on, Leslie, let's go upstairs and take a shower together." Smiling, she rose from the floor, blew out the candle, and followed Don upstairs.

It was almost nine o'clock, and realizing his parents would be home from church soon, they showered quickly. Returning to their bedroom, Leslie, flushed from the hot shower, said, "I'm starving. Do you realize we haven't eaten anything since breakfast?"

"You're forgetting about the ice cream we had just a few hours ago," he teased.

"Tell you what, Don, you crawl under the covers, and I'll go to the kitchen and fix us some sandwiches to eat up here in bed."

"That sounds great," Don answered, pulling his underwear on and crawling into bed. "I have to get up at five-thirty tomorrow for work. I want to get there an hour early to get a feel for everything."

Smiling, she left the room clad in her flannel nightgown, replying, "You'll be fine."

Don could hear his parents and Mike coming through the door as Leslie went down the steps. Lying there in his bed, Don could not make out what they were saying as he picked up a magazine and began to read.

Ten minutes later, the door opened to his bedroom, and Leslie walked in, grinning, with a tray of sandwiches and drinks.

Sitting up in bed, Don asked, "Did Mike blow our cover and tell Mom and Dad what we were doing while they were at church?"

Laughing Leslie said, "I don't think so. At least, they didn't let on that they knew. Your mom fixed these sandwiches for us and said to tell you good luck for tomorrow."

"What are they doing now?"

"Mike and your dad are watching television while your mom is in the kitchen fixing them a snack."

"That's good," Don smirked. "I don't want to deal with Dad teasing me for the next year about Mike busting in on us." He took a bite of his food and sighed. Enjoying their sandwiches in bed, they finished the food and went straight to sleep.

The alarm went off at five-thirty, startling Don from a deep sleep. Sleepy-eyed, he slammed the button down and crawled out of bed. Tripping over his feet from still being tired, Don put his brown suit on, kissed Leslie on the cheek, and went downstairs.

He jumped when he heard a noise in the kitchen. Glancing back the hallway toward the kitchen, he noticed his mom brewing fresh coffee and cooking something on the stove. Quietly, he walked up behind her and kissed the back of her head. "Why are you up so early, Mom?"

"Because I wanted to make sure you had a hot breakfast before your first day on the job," she said, smiling at him.

"You didn't have to do that, but I sure do appreciate it."

He pulled a chair up to the kitchen table where she had already placed a steaming cup of coffee. Taking a sip, he said, "That is just the ticket." Walking from the stove, Sadie slid a plate of pancakes and eggs in front of him. "That looks great, Mom."

"Enjoy your breakfast, and have a great day at work. I'm going back to bed," she said. "Leslie, Mike, and I are going to the house with the painters, so stop over after work, okay?"

"I'll be there around three-thirty or four," he replied. "Thanks again, Mom," he whispered, as she left the kitchen to go back to bed.

Don pulled into the brickyard parking lot at six. The lot was still almost empty except for a few cars parked in the management section. Smiling, he noticed a parking space with his name on it, so he pulled the car into it. The sun was just high enough now to shower its warmth upon the ground as Don hopped from his car and walked to the office. Once inside the office he was greeted by Pete Miller.

"Hi, Don. Are you ready to tear into your new job?"

"I sure am, Pete," Don replied, following him back a corridor.

"Well, you'll be spending most of the day with Bob Medley. He'll fill you in on what is expected of you as far as day-to-day activities here at the plant, and then at one o'clock this afternoon, we'll all meet in the conference room for a two-hour meeting. We have this meeting once a month to plan and set short- and long-term goals for the company. The meeting is attended by the owner, Philip Stash; the plant manager, Jesse Becker; the personnel director, yourself; Bob Medley; myself; and all the mid-level plant supervisors. If you have any questions or concerns, you can bring them up at this meeting. By the way, Don, make sure you intercom the secretary and give her directions for the moving crew to pick your belongings up in New York. If you need to rent a storage trailer down here until you find housing, the plant will pick up the expense for that also."

"That won't be necessary, Pete. I closed on a house already just a few miles from the plant. It's located on Haller Road, and we should be able to get moved in by the end of the week."

"That's great, Don. Remember, after you get settled in, I would like for our families to get together."

"That sounds good," Don replied.

Pete opened the door to Don's office, exposing a huge room with a desk at least three times larger than his desk in New York. The office was painted white with three paintings that looked to be expensive hanging on the walls. A plush brown leather sofa completed the office décor.

"Make yourself at home, Don. Bob Medley will be in around seven. He has already emptied the desk of all of his personal items and will be available to you in an advisory capacity for the next two weeks. I'll see you at the meeting," Pete said, closing the door behind him.

Don walked behind his desk and sat down in a thickly padded brown chair that swivelled in circles. Pivoting the chair to the left, Don looked out an enormous window which was now splashing sunlight throughout the entire office. *I can't believe this,* he thought to himself, swiveling the chair back to the desk. He intercommed the secretary at the front office. Answering the intercom, she replied, "What can I do for you, Mr. Knisley?"

"First of all you, can call me Don," he said in an upbeat voice.

"Okay, Don. What can I do for you?"

He explained to her the directions for his home in New York and instructed her to have the movers pick his belongings up on Wednesday morning. "Tell the movers I'll have my father-in-law meet them there with the key to the house. He'll show them all the items they are to remove and deliver to my new residence. They can bring the items to 322 Haller Road on Thursday morning around nine in the morning. My wife will meet them there and show them where to place the items in our new home."

"I'll do that right away, Don. Is there anything else you need?"

"No, that will be all, Bobbi. Thank you."

It was seven in the morning now, and Pat walked through the door, coming home from work. He could hear Sadie cooking breakfast in the kitchen with Leslie. Walking to the kitchen, he found Mike sitting at the table eating eggs.

"Well, good morning, everyone," he said in a pleasant voice. As he sat down at the table, Leslie brought him a plate of eggs and toast. "We have to eat fast," Pat said, already gulping down his food. "I told the guys we would meet them at the house at seven-thirty to let them in to start painting the living room."

Leslie smiled. "I can't wait to see what it looks like," she said excitedly.

"You'll be surprised at how fast these guys are," Pat added.

Mike rose from the table. "I'm ready," he said.

"Good," Pat said. "Go to the shed, and get my toolbox, saws, and that small pile of lumber, and put them in the trunk of my car. There's also a wooden box on my workbench that has all sizes of nails and screws in it. Put it on the backseat."

"Sure thing, Pap," Mike yelled, running from the kitchen to the front door.

Mike had just finished putting the last box into the car when everyone came from the house. "Nice of everyone to show up after I have everything packed into the car," Mike teased.

"Well, if you haven't figured out yet that you're the low man on the totem pole, you soon will," his pap laughed, ruffling the hair on his head. "Come on, you can ride with me in the front seat, and we'll let the women folk ride in the back."

"Can I drive, Pap?" Mike asked, laughing. Pat put his finger to his lips, signaling for Mike to be quiet.

When they pulled into their driveway, the painters were already sitting on the front porch drinking coffee out of paper cups. They were wearing white jumpsuits that had a kaleidoscope of colors splashed on them from previous jobs they had done. Jumping from the car first, Pat walked to his friends and asked if they had been waiting long.

"Hell no, Pat. We got here about five minutes before you pulled in."

Sadie and Leslie walked over to the men. "Leslie, this is Jim Ackner and Denny Cowmen. They've worked with me at the mill for over twenty years now. Guys, this is my daughter-in-law, Leslie, and her son, Mike. You know my wife, Sadie."

"Nice to meet you all. Well, Pat, let's knock this thing out. Which room do you want us to start first?"

Unlocking the front door, Pat looked at Leslie and said, "Well, you're the boss, where do you want them to start?"

Smiling, Leslie walked into the living room and said, "Right here will be fine."

Pat looked at Mike and instructed him to bring the paint in from the car. "I know, I know," Mike yelled going to the car. "I'm low man on the totem pole." Mike made three trips to the car, carrying everything back into the house and placing it on a pile in the center of the living room. When he looked up, he saw that Jim was already scraping loose paint from the walls while Denny was following behind him and putting spackling compound on the areas that needed it. "Wow, Pap, these guys don't waste any time, do they?"

Smiling, Pat said, "Carry my tools up to your bedroom. You and I are going to fix up that rat hole in your room the proper way."

"What do you want us to do?" Sadie asked, looking at Jim.

"You can start wiping down the walls with a mild soap and water compound in all the rooms you want painted."

"That'll be every room, Jim!" Sadie laughed.

"Well, there you have it, don't you?" Jim replied. "You better get cracking."

Leslie and Sadie walked to the kitchen, while Pat and Mike went upstairs. Pat held the bedroom door open for Mike to carry the tools inside. Both immediately noticed that the window was open again and that awful stench was back in the room. Pat looked at Mike, laughing, and said, "Did you go to the bathroom in your pants, boy?"

"Yeah right, Pap, I think it was you!"

"It smells like someone died in here," he kidded back.

"Well, I'll tell you one thing," Mike yelled angrily, "if Dad thinks he is sticking me in this bedroom with that smell, he's in for a rude awakening. He and Mom can stay in this room, and I'll sleep in theirs."

Starting to laugh uncontrollably, Pat snorted, "I'll bet you that doesn't happen."

Mike walked to the window. "What's up with this darn thing? I close it, and every time I come back into the room, it's open."

"I don't know," Pat teased with a glimmer in his eye. "You know, they say a lot of these old houses are haunted."

"I hope so," Mike laughed. "I'm getting tired of kicking Dad's butt. Maybe it's time for me to kick some ghost butt, too." Closing the window, Mike stated matter-of-factly, "I know one thing for sure! If I find out whomever or whatever is opening this window, we will be going for a round or two."

Pat walked to the board covering the rat hole, and with his claw hammer, he pulled it off, exposing a large hole with chew marks on the edges. "I can't understand why anyone would do a patch job like that in their home." The baseboard looked to be a six-inch pine board with the edge slightly rounded. Taking his claw hammer once again, he pulled the chewed board from the wall. It was six inches high by eight feet long.

"Hey, guess what, Pap. I saw a couple of those trim boards in the garage out back. They're probably only about four feet long though."

"Go get one," he instructed. "I'll miter them together, and you won't be able to see the seam with a coat of white paint on them."

Mike left and returned, minutes later, with an old, dirty piece of wood trim. "That's what we need," Pat declared, taking the trim from him. Pat cut the first board he had pulled from the wall at a forty-five degree angle, just in front of the rat hole. Nailing it back onto the wall, he measured for his next cut using the same angle. Sliding the board in, they both saw that it was clearly a perfect fit.

"Pap, you are quite the carpenter."

Smiling, he explained, "You pick a few things up over the years, I suppose."

Joking, Mike replied, "Well, Dad must need a few more years then, because I doubt if he knows which end of the hammer to hold."

Laughing once again, Pat said, "Well, we're done here, Mike. Get some rags, soap, and water, and we'll wipe down the walls upstairs."

Just as Mike turned to leave the room, the window flew open, and the bedroom door slammed shut. "What the hell was that?!" Pat screamed, startled by the slamming noises. The room suddenly chilled, and both were visibly nervous.

Mike grabbed the door handle and tried to pull the door open. The knob would not turn, no matter how hard he tried. Looking at his pap, he replied, nervously, "You were kidding about the ghosts, weren't you, Pap?"

Pat, looking at Mike, said, "There has to be an explanation."

Mike released the door knob and stepped back, saying, "We're locked in here!" Yelling at the top of his lungs, Mike screamed for his mother to let them out.

Pat was still dumbfounded as Leslie pulled the door open from the outside. "What do you want, Mike?" she asked, irritated that she'd had to run up the steps.

"The door slammed shut by itself and locked us in here, honest, Mom. Ask Pap. He'll tell you I'm not lying."

Pat, trying to act as if he wasn't nervous about the scene that had unfolded around him, replied, "I don't know, Leslie. I was over here when Mike said the door was jammed. I didn't bother trying to open it because he had already yelled for you to come up."

"Well, it opened right up for me," she said, still annoyed.

"Okay, fine," Mike replied, starting to get angry. "I imagined the window opening by itself too, I guess."

Shaking her head, Leslie looked at Mike and said, "You better stop clowning around. We have a lot of work to get done to this house, and I want to be moved in by the end of the week."

Mike said nothing as he pushed past his mother and went downstairs to get the rags his pap had ask for. When he entered the living room, he could not believe his eyes. The painters had already started painting the room, and two walls were completed. Leslie came up from behind him and said, "Well, what do you think?"

"I think it looks awesome, Mom. I really like the color," Mike answered, his initial resentment wearing off.

She had picked a light green color for the walls. "The trim is going to be this color," she added, placing a dark forest green swatch beside the completed wall. "It's a perfect contrast, don't you think?"

"Yeah. It's going to look great, Mom."

Mike went to the kitchen, grabbed a handful of rags and a bucket of water, and ran back up the steps to his bedroom. His pap was examining the window when he walked into the room. "Thanks for backing me up, Pap," Mike said sarcastically.

"I didn't want your mother to think we're both nuts," he said laughing. "This window is the damnedest thing. Let's try closing and locking it shut," he said, slamming it down. "Now we both saw that it's locked. We'll check later to see if it opens by itself again. Grab a rag, and let's start wiping off the walls and baseboard in your room. After that, we'll finish the other rooms."

Sadie was in the kitchen wiping down the counters and cabinets, while Leslie concentrated on cleaning the walls. "I don't know about this floor," Leslie commented to Sadie. "A black and white checkered pattern seems so bland."

"I agree, Leslie, but it's in such good shape that it seems crazy to replace it. After they paint in here, you'll have a better idea of what the whole scheme will look like. I think you're going to be glad you have neutral colors on the floor, countertops, and cabinets so it doesn't contrast negatively with the light blue paint they're going to be putting on the walls."

"You're probably right," Leslie replied, deep in thought. "We'll know soon enough. They said they'll be done in the living room in half an hour, and I'll have them start here next."

Don had just finished his meeting with the other executives in the conference room and was returning to his office to lock up. The meeting, which was only supposed to last two hours, had somehow turned into four. Looking at his watch, he was stunned that it was a quarter after four, and moreover, he was dog tired. *I can't believe they are expecting so much from me already,* he thought to himself, locking his door. *I bet everyone is mad at me for not being home early to help with the house,* he worried. *They'll just have to understand I'll be putting long days in until I get up to speed with everything that is going on here at the plant,* he rationalized.

Walking to his car, Don sighed, thinking, *I can't believe I have to go paint now. I'm whooped.* The parking lot was half-empty as he got into his car. Second trick, which started at three and ended at eleven, had only half the manpower working as first trick did. In fact, that had been one of the items they had discussed at the meeting. Plans were being put in place to double the second trick work force. That meant a lot more work for Don since he was now in charge of all hiring, among other things.

Don cranked down his window and pulled from the parking lot, waving good-bye to Pete, who was now also in his car. The sun was blinding him as he drove toward their new home. Reaching into the glove box, he pulled out a thick pair of black sunglasses and put them on. The drive home took only a matter of minutes. As he pulled into the driveway, he had to park out in the yard because the driveway already had two cars parked in it. One he recognized as his father's white Ford. *The other must be the painters' truck,* he thought to himself.

Walking into the living room, he could not believe his eyes. It was beautiful. The entire room was finished with a light green color, and the trim was finished off in a dark forest green. The ceiling was painted a bright white. They had done a beautiful job, filling in and sealing all the cracks with spackle. It looked as if the whole room had been rebuilt that very day. Walking through the living room to the kitchen, his mouth dropped wide open. It, too, was completely done. A light sky blue paint had been applied to the walls, with dark blue trim complementing it. The kitchen shined. The floor had been waxed, and new, white curtains hung above the windows. Even the stove and refrigerator looked as if they were new, having been cleaned so thoroughly.

GET OUT!

Don could hear voices upstairs as he jogged up the steps to Mike's bedroom. Mike and his pap were in his room, finishing up the final touches on the trim. Mike's room was now a dark Mediterranean blue with bright white trim.

"What do you think?" Pat asked Don as he entered the room.

"I can't believe you got this much done in one day. It looks great," Don said, completely astonished.

Mike was covered in white paint as he snuck up on his dad and touched his cheek with the white paint-coated paintbrush. Jumping back, Don yelled, "Damn it, Mike! I have a suit on!"

"I didn't get any on the suit," Mike chuckled.

By now, Leslie was in the room with Sadie behind her. "Do you like it, Don?" Leslie asked.

"I love it, honey," he replied. "You guys must have worked your butts off."

"We did, but Jim and Denny are the real speed demons. Those guys can paint so fast. They don't even need to tape anything off when they do the trim. I've never seen anyone who can paint as good as those two. They didn't get a drop of paint on any of the floors or carpeting either."

"Hey," Mike yelled, "what about me and Pap? We did the trim in here and in the hallway."

Don looked at Mike and said, "You did a good job, too, but I think you have as much paint on your clothes as you do on the trim!"

"He's a good worker," Pat added, closing the lid on a paint can.

"Look, Dad! Pap fixed the rat hole in my room. You can't even tell it was there."

"Yeah, Mike found some matching trim in the garage out back, so it didn't take long at all," Pat said, showing Don where the hole used to be.

"The room looks like new, Dad," Don grinned.

"Come here, Don," Leslie called from their bedroom.

Stepping into the hallway, Don noticed that the paint had been redone there also. It was still white but now had a bright glossy look to it. "Don," he heard Leslie yell, once again, from their bedroom.

"Keep your pants on," he joked, coming into the room. "Wow," he exclaimed, walking to the center of the room and turning in a circle. It was a dark peach color with satin white trim. New, frilly, white curtains now hung around the windows, accentuating the peach color of the walls. "Leslie, I'm not just saying this to humor you, but the house looks awesome."

Jim and Denny were in the bathroom finishing up painting the last room when Don poked his head into the room. "Hi, guys," Don yelled.

"Well, look," Jim laughed, "it's little Donnie all grown up."

"How have you been, Don?" Denny chimed in.

"I didn't know you two clowns were doing the painting. If I did, maybe I wouldn't have been so quick to let you do the job!" Don teased. Don had known both men for years. In fact, as a boy in high school, Don and his father had accompanied them on many fishing trips. "When did you two start painting on the side?" he asked.

Jim smiled and said, "About ten years ago, and it appears that you're lucky we did."

"Glad to have you back in the area," Denny said, reaching out to shake his hand. "Your dad said you're a big shot at the brickyard now. I hope you're not so big that you can't fish with us and your old man again."

"Hell no," Don laughed. "You just name the time and place, and I'm there. I'll even spring for the beer," he whispered. "Mike and I did a lot of fishing up in New York, but it wasn't near as good as back here."

"Your son is one big son-of-a-bitch," Jim joked. "I'd be afraid to piss that muscle-bound behemoth off, that's for sure."

"He still can't take his old man yet," Don whispered, making sure Mike could not hear him. "He's quite an athlete," Don bragged. "I suspect you'll be hearing about him in the next school year. Football, wrestling, and track, the boy does it all."

"Well, I still don't plan on ever pissing him off," Denny laughed.

"Well, anyway, are you satisfied with the job we did, Donnie?" Jim asked.

"You guys are aces," he replied. "You have no idea how much we appreciate you guys doing this so quickly."

"Don, your dad was so tickled about you moving back here, if we would have said we couldn't do it today, he would have kicked our asses. So, here we are. I'm glad it was nice and hot today; the paint dried almost as quickly as we applied it," Denny said.

"It's a good thing, too," Jim laughed. "Your wife was hanging the curtains before we were even done in the rooms."

"Yeah, she's pretty anxious to move in," Don added.

All three men walked downstairs to the living room where Pat was standing in the front doorway. "We're all done, Pat."

"Thanks a lot, guys," he replied. "How much do we owe you?"

"Not a damn thing," Jim yelled. "You've done enough for us."

"You have to let me pay you something," Don pleaded.

"Tell you what Donnie, buy us a couple of cases of beer, and we're square."

Pat was smiling from ear to ear when Don replied, "Done. I made Mike clean out your brushes and rollers with water and put them in your truck," Pat said to the two men as they walked outside.

Don was still in the living room when his father returned. "That was nice of them, wasn't it?" Pat said to Don.

"It sure was. Thanks a lot for all you've done for us, too."

"No problem, son."

"Looks to me like you can call the movers to get your things right away now. Jim and Denny said that they'll start on the outside within the next three or four weeks, but they are going to have to charge you for that job."

"How much do you think they are going to want to do the outside, Dad?"

"They ballparked it around three hundred dollars."

"That's reasonable," Don said, smiling at his dad.

"You're damn right it is! If it were anyone else, they would charge five hundred bucks. They have a ton of scraping to do on the outside of this house. It will take longer to prep the house than to paint it. Make sure you and Leslie pick the colors and have the paint bought so that when they show up, they can rip right into it."

"Okay, Dad. I'll make sure I get it next week."

Going back into the living room, they were joined by the rest of the family. "It's been a long day," Pat yawned. "Let's go to Poke's and get some food."

"Sounds good to me," Mike chimed in. "I could eat a horse."

"By the way, Don, we forgot to ask how your first day of work was," Sadie asked curiously.

"It was grueling," he replied. "I knew I would have a lot more responsibilities, but I wasn't prepared for this. We had a four-hour meeting today outlining what is expected of me, as well as short- and long-term goals. They plan on hiring at least fifty to one hundred people within the next two months, and guess who has to do all the screening and hiring, as well as keep up with his normal day-to-day responsibilities. It's expected of me to meet with over five hundred employees, maintain personnel files on each one, and hear their grievances when there is a problem. My last job was small potatoes compared to this one," he said smiling.

"You'll do fine," Sadie said, patting him on his back. "Let's go get something to eat."

As they pulled into Poke's Diner at five-thirty, the parking lot was nearly empty. "Yes! At least we'll get to eat quick," Mike squealed happily.

Walking to the diner, Don nudged Leslie and said, "Before I forget, call your dad tonight and ask him to meet the movers on Wednesday to let them in and show them what all they need to load and bring down here."

Leslie replied, "I just called him early this morning to make sure he has been checking in on our house. He said everything is fine, and he will tell our landlord that we are moving out. I really miss him and Mom."

Hugging her, Don said, "After we get settled in, we'll drive back up to visit them for a weekend."

"You guys coming?" Mike called from the diner entrance.

"Yeah, we'll be right there," Don yelled back.

Wednesday morning arrived bright and sunny as Don drove to work. The past two days had gone smoothly, and he was really starting to enjoy his job. Thursday was sure to be a trying day, though; he had scheduled fifteen appointments for potential employees seeking a job. This screening process was sure to take up his entire day, and he still had to deal with the movers coming in from New York. Leslie was to meet them at the house first thing this morning with his mother and Mike. Hopefully the movers would have most of the work done until he got home. They planned on spending their first night in the house tonight.

Don pulled into his parking space and went to the main office. It was a quarter till seven, and Bobbi was behind her desk and on the phone, as usual. Flashing Don a smile, she placed her hand over the receiver and whispered, "Good morning, Don."

"Morning," Don whispered back. "How are you today?"

Taking her hand away from the receiver, she said, "May I call you right back?" Hanging up the phone, Bobbi replied, "Why, I'm just fine, Don."

Don leaned on her desk, flirting. "Bobbi, I'm having about fifteen people coming in today for interviews in thirty-minute intervals. Could you have them each fill out an employment application and then send them, one at a time, to my office?"

Flashing a smile at him, she replied, "Sure. I'll intercom you before I send each one down."

"That would be great," he said, hesitating before leaving her office. "I want you to know what a great job you're doing, Bobbi. I really, truly appreciate it."

"Thanks, Don! No one has ever told me that before."

"Well, I just wanted you to know that I'm grateful for how good you are at your job."

Don turned and walked from Bobbi's office, grinning. In a matter of minutes, he was sitting at his desk, going through a large stack of papers containing personal files on every person who worked at the plant. He had made it a point to learn something about each and every person working there before he had to meet each one in the coming weeks.

Leslie, Sadie, and Mike pulled into the new house's driveway at seven-thirty to wait for the movers. Pat had to work first trick, so he wouldn't be able to help until after three that afternoon. They piled out of the car and were opening the front door when a large blue and white moving van backed into the driveway and beeped the horn. "They're here already!" Mike yelled to his mother.

"That's great," Leslie yelled. "I'm ready to decorate."

Two tall, heavyset men jumped from the truck and walked toward the front door. They looked as if they were twins, sporting identical black hair and beards, making them look somewhat threatening. Sadie whispered to Leslie, "I wouldn't want to meet those two in a dark alley at night."

Both were wearing a navy blue shirt and brown work pants as they walked up to Leslie and Sadie and asked, "How are you ladies doing today?"

"Fine, thank you," both said, in unison.

Mike appeared in the doorway. "Wow, are you two brothers? You look like twins," he said with a grin on his face.

"That's because we are," the one with a name tag that read Brent laughed. "As you can see, I'm Brent, and this is my twin brother, Joe."

"That's awesome!" Mike said, smiling. "You get to work with your brother every day?"

"Yeah, we've owned and operated this truck for about five years now. It's nice being your own boss. By the way, I assume you are Leslie," he said, looking at her. "Your dad said to tell you he misses and loves you. You're also to make sure you call your mom at least once a week."

Smiling, Leslie replied, "Thank you for the message, Joe."

"Tell you what," Brent said, "we'll start hauling your furniture in and you show us where you want it. We're even supposed to put your beds together and hang the pictures and shelving for you. The brickyard is picking up the tab for everything," Joe added. "We won't leave until you're satisfied and everything is the way you want it."

"That's great, gentlemen. You can get started whenever you like," Leslie smiled, swinging open the front door.

Joe and Brent went to the truck with Mike following closely behind, and Brent swung open the back door. Pulling out a large ramp from under the truck, they put it in place and walked up it, grabbing a light green sofa. Lifting it as if it were a toy, they walked down the truck and carried it toward the house. Mike grabbed a box with what seemed to be clothing in it and carried it behind them. Entering the living room, Leslie said, "You can put that right here." Dropping the sofa into the exact spot she had chosen, they walked back outside. "Look, Sadie, it matches the walls perfectly. You couldn't have done a better job picking the color if you would have had the sofa here when they painted on Monday," she exclaimed.

Mike opened the box that he had carried inside. It was full of his clothes. "You might as well take it straight up to your bedroom and put it in your closet," Leslie barked.

"Yes, ma'am!" Mike yelled as if his mother was a drill sergeant. Jogging up the steps to his bedroom, he opened the door and carried the box inside to his closet. Glancing to his right, he noticed that the window was once again open. *Oh, no, not again,* he thought to himself, walking to the window. Staring out the window, he caught a glimpse of his neighbor who was staring out her living room window. It was hard to see her because only her head was poking around the side of her drapes. Mike waved to her, and she immediately withdrew her head from the window without waving back. "That's rude," he said out loud. Slamming the window shut and locking it, he walked back to the closet. He tugged on the door, but it was sticking and wouldn't open. "Dang it," he said talking to himself, "Pap must have painted the darn thing shut." Placing a foot against the baseboard, he pulled with all his might. The door sprung open like it had not been sticking to begin with. *This room is becoming a pain in my ass,* he thought. He reached inside the closet to pull the hangers from their rod and felt a blast of cold air that made the hair stand up on the back of his neck. *Where the heck did that come from?* he wondered as he shivered, looking inside the closet. The closet was completely empty, and there were no trap doors leading to the attic. It seemed as if there was a presence with him as he backed away from the closet and shook the thought off. *If I mention this to Mom or Dad, they'll just call me a baby,* he realized scornfully. Quickly, he placed each item of clothing on the hangers and hung them. Finished, Mike ran down the steps and out to the truck to grab another box.

"Mike!" Leslie yelled from the house.

Carrying another large box inside, he yelled, "What do you want, Mom?"

"These four boxes contain the rest of your clothes. Take them up to your room and put them away."

Saying nothing, he stacked two boxes on top of each other and hoisted them into the air. The weight of the boxes caused Mike to stumble and trip every couple of steps he walked. "You should carry one at a time, Michael," Sadie scolded.

"I can make it, Gram," he yelled from halfway up the steps.

Walking into his room, he dropped the boxes to the floor beside the closet. The door was closed again, and the window was wide open. "The hell with it," Mike yelled. "I know I left the closet door open and that window was locked. I hope you're a friendly ghost," he yelled into the closed closet. Pulling the door open once again, he reached into the box and pulled out five pairs of shoes. Lining each pair up uniformly on the closet floor, he reached back into the box and removed underwear, socks, shirts, and more pants. Picking up the empty boxes and walking out the door, he turned and whispered, "I'll leave the window open for you."

Walking down the steps, he could not believe his eyes. The living room now looked like something out of a catalog. The sofa and matching armchair were in place, as well as the coffee tables and end tables. The television, RCA's latest model, was placed in front of the sofa against the back wall. There were paintings hanging on two walls, as well as white shelves which housed pictures of family members from both his mother's and father's side of the family. A large, beautiful grapevine wreath decorated with colorful silk flowers now hung on the far wall of the living room. He did not recall having such a wreath in New York. "Do you like the wreath, Mike?" Leslie asked, smiling. "I bought it yesterday at the Roaring Spring Variety Store."

"Mom, the living room almost looks too good to live in," he praised. "Dad is not going to believe it when he gets home."

Joe and Brent were like machines, never stopping for more than five minutes to take a break. By lunch, they had two-thirds of the truck empty. They were carrying a mattress in at noon when Sadie yelled out and asked them to come to the kitchen to eat something. Walking to the kitchen, Joe said, "You don't have to feed us, ma'am."

"Yes, I do," Sadie said, smiling. "You two boys are doing a wonderful job."

Smiling, Brent walked to the dark cherry-colored table and chairs they had hauled in earlier and sat down. "We sure do appreciate this," he said.

Mike ran into the kitchen asking, "What's for lunch?"

Sadie came to the table and set a large plate of ham, cheese, and tomato sandwiches in the center. "Dig in," she said. Going to the stove, she lifted an enormous round pot of homemade chicken soup and carried it to the table.

"That smells tremendous," Joe said, choking the words out with a mouthful of sandwich.

Sadie went to a large brown box and pulled a stack of white glass bowls out. Carrying the food to the table, she said, "Serve yourself."

"What are we supposed to eat it with, Gram, our fingers?" Cuffing Mike on the back of the head, she dropped a handful of spoons on the table.

After they each ate three sandwiches and two bowls of soup, the men rose from the table, holding their stomachs. "That was the best homemade soup I've ever eaten," Brent said, rubbing his stomach.

"It sure was good, ma'am," Joe added. "Thank you."

Walking from the kitchen and back to living room, they lifted the queen-sized mattress, looked at Leslie, and Brent asked, "Which room do you want this in?"

"Go up the steps, and turn right. It's the bedroom at the back."
Nodding in reply, they dragged the mattress up the steps and dropped it in Leslie's bedroom.

Don was sitting in his office, having just finished the last interview. Stretching, he glanced down at his watch. It was four thirty. *Leslie is going to kill me; I told her I would try to be home early tonight to help unpack.* Jumping from his chair, he ran to the door, turned off his light, and locked the office door.

Pete, walking down the corridor, yelled, "Hey, Don, I thought you were leaving early today to unpack."

"I was supposed to," he called to Pete. "I ran late interviewing people."

"Leslie is going to kill you," Pete laughed.

"I know," Don yelled, running past Pete and out the door to his car. He jumped into his car and sped from the parking lot. Within minutes, he was sitting in his empty driveway. *The movers must have gotten lost,* he thought to himself, walking to the house. Turning the doorknob, he noticed that it wasn't locked as he walked into the house.   Before he could get through the door, Leslie wrapped her hands around his eyes and screamed, "Keep them closed!" She walked him to the center of the living room, kissed his lips, and said, "Okay, open them."

"Wow," Don said excitedly as his eyes wandered around the room. "This is more than I had ever hoped for. This is beautiful, Leslie. How did you get it done so quickly?"

"This is only the living room, Don. The whole house is unpacked and ready to live in."

"How is that possible?" he said, looking dumbfounded.

"The two men who unloaded the truck said they were told to unpack everything and not leave before everything was in its place. Your company is paying for everything," Leslie said, grinning.

"Where are Mom and Mike?"

"We had to drop your dad off at work this morning so we could have his car. He said he would catch a ride home. Your mom and Mike went to get him to show him the house."

Don walked through every room in the house, amazed at what had been accomplished in such a short time. "It's like a brand new home, Leslie, don't you think?"

"It sure is," she replied. "Except for the outside. I'm going to pick colors tomorrow morning with your mom. Is it okay if I run you to work and then pick you up later so I can have the car all day tomorrow?"

"That's fine," Don said, wrapping his arms around her and kissing her once again.

Hearing a car pull into the driveway, Leslie pushed him away and ran to the front door. "It's your parents, honey. By the way, the phone is finally working, so I called Mom and Dad to thank them for helping the movers empty our house. I told them they won't believe how nice our new home looks, but I don't want them to see it until we have the outside finished."

"Looks great!" Pat yelled as he walked through the door. "You should be proud, Leslie. You really have a wonderful home now."

"I am," Leslie squealed with delight as she pointed to the large wreath hanging from the wall. "We could never have done this without you and Sadie, though. I don't know how we can ever repay you for all you've done for us."

"Just saying that makes it paid in full," Sadie said with a hug.

Pat walked through every room with Mike at his heels, while everyone else sat in the living room, chatting. Walking down the steps, he shook his head and said, "I can't believe how much was accomplished today. You all must be dog tired. Come on, Sadie, let's go home and give them some peace for their first night in the house."

Smiling, Don hugged his mom and dad and said, "Thanks for everything."

"Pick me up tomorrow morning, Leslie, and we'll go pick the colors out for the outside of the house," Sadie reminded her.

"I'll be there bright and early," she replied as Sadie and Pat got into the car. Waving, they pulled from the driveway and headed home.

Sitting on the sofa, Don asked Mike to turn on the television. "Okay, Dad," Mike said, pulling the knob and then joining him on the sofa.

Leslie, sitting in the arm chair, yawned, saying, "I wonder why our neighbor hasn't come over to say hi."

"I'll tell you why," Mike laughed, "she's a freak. I saw her staring at our house today through my bedroom window so I waved to her. Do you think she would wave back? No way, she just jerked her head from the window without so much as a wave. Anyway, she looks like a haggard old witch," Mike stated matter-of-factly. "I don't care if we ever talk to her."

"Michael Knisley, you should be ashamed of yourself. You will not treat another human being that way. Tomorrow, I'm going to bake some cookies, and you're going to run them over to her."

"No way, Mom. I'm not going near that old witch."

"Don, tell him," Leslie said, getting angry.

"Mike, you're going to do whatever your mother says. Is that understood?"

"Oh, all right, but if I don't come back, you better send out the dogs," he said, laughing.

"That's not funny, Mike," Leslie rebuked, still mad.

"What's for supper, honey?" Don asked.

"Well, your mother and I have the refrigerator completely stocked up. What would you like?"

"I could eat spaghetti and meatballs," he said, rubbing his stomach.

"What about me, don't I have a say?" Mike whined.

"Tell you what, Mike, when you start buying the food, then you can have a say," Don growled. "You are walking a fine line anyway, so I suggest you eat the spaghetti and like it."

"Fine!" Mike yelled, slouching back into the sofa.

Leslie walked to the kitchen to cook supper while Mike and Don were glued to the television. "Hey, Dad, I didn't want to say anything because I thought you would think I was a baby, but there is some weird stuff going on in my bedroom."

Don, annoyed that Mike had interrupted his concentration on the television program, replied, "What are you talking about, Mike?" Facing his father on the sofa, Mike whispered, "For instance, the window opens by itself, doors slam shut, and there is an ungodly cold air that radiates from the closet. Not to mention that half the time the room has the odor of death to it."

Don, laughing uncontrollably, replied, "You're right, you are a big baby." He slapped his knee, still chuckling. "Here, Mike," Don said, taking a handkerchief from his back pocket and handing it to him. "Since you're such a baby, you better carry this with you so you have something to cry into."

"Bite me. I'm serious. Pap even saw it! You can ask him."

"Well, he was just here. Why didn't he mention it?"

"Just drop it," Mike said angrily.

"Supper's ready," Leslie yelled from the kitchen.

Both Don and Mike jumped from the sofa at the same time to race to the kitchen, but before Don could take a step, Mike shoved him back into the sofa and beat him to the kitchen table. "You ass," Don yelled, "or should I say, baby," finally pulling a chair up to the kitchen table.

"You snooze, you lose," Mike laughed.

"Get a load of this, Leslie. Mike says there is a ghost in his bedroom."

"Shut up, Dad. I can't tell you anything without you trying to make a fool out of me."

"Don, stop picking on him," Leslie scolded.

"Thanks, Mom. He's being a real butthead tonight."

"Okay, that's enough out of both of you. Sit there and eat and don't say another word.

Mike looked at Don and sneered. "He's sneering at me, Leslie," Don complained.

"Stop it. I'm not going to say it again," Leslie smiled.

Everyone ate their meal without another word said. Mike rose from the table first. Walking to his mother, he kissed her on the cheek and said, "The meatballs were great, Mom."

"Thank you, Mike. You can go watch television. Don, you need to stop being so hard on him."

"Leslie, I'm not hard on the boy. Hell, he's harder on me than I am on him. The boy is like an ox, and he can damn near kick my ass. I tease him a little, but he knows he can always count on me."

"I guess I'm just tired from working so hard today," Leslie replied, yawning. Don helped her clear the table and do the dishes.

"I'm going upstairs to read a book in bed," Leslie declared, walking into the living room.

"It's only seven o'clock, Mom. Why don't you watch television with me and Dad?"

"Because I'm tired, Mike."

"Okay. Night, Mom," Mike yelled as she walked up the steps.

Don sat down beside Mike on the sofa. "What do you want to do tonight, Mike?"

"Dad, we're watching television."

"Do you want to sit here and watch television all night, or do you want to go outside and throw the baseball around?"

"I don't feel like baseball. I know what we can do. Let's go check the basement out. Maybe there is some stuff down there I can add to my Elijah Stone collection."

"Where did you put those pictures anyway?" Don asked.

"I stuck them under my bed. Why?"

"I was just wondering. I'd like to know more about the people who lived here before us. I wonder if they are still alive. Why don't you ask the woman next door when you take her the cookies tomorrow?"

"Thanks for reminding me I have to see the wicked old witch tomorrow. Okay, I'll ask her. Come on, let's check the basement out," Mike said, pulling his father from the sofa.

"Haven't you been down there yet?" Don asked.

"No, have you?" Mike replied.

"Yeah, I went down the day we bought the house. It's like a dungeon down there. If there is a ghost in this house, that's where he's going to hang out," Don laughed.

Mike opened the basement door and looked at his dad. "You first, Mr. I Don't Believe In Ghosts," Mike teased.

Don looked down the steps into total darkness. Feeling along the wall, he found a light switch and turned it on. A light turned on in the basement, barely casting enough glow onto the steps to make them safe enough to walk down. "I'll tell you one thing, Mike, I'm going to get an electrician in here to light this basement up like Christmas. This is ridiculous only having one light in this whole basement."

Mike pushed his dad, saying, "Come on, big shot, let's check this place out."

Don walked down the steps, making ghostly sounds as he descended the steps. "Oh, it's so scary down here, Mike," he teased.

When they reached the bottom of the steps, they noticed a horrendous odor in the room. "See what I mean, Dad? Do you smell that?"

"Yes, I smell it, you moron. Who wouldn't smell that?" Don walked across the room and, looking down at the floor near the furnace, yelled, "Here is your smell, Mike."

Mike walked over and saw a decaying rat caught in a trap. "That is disgusting," he yelled, holding his nose.

"That is probably the smell in your bedroom too, Mike. I bet it was getting in your room through the duct work. Take it out of the trap and throw it outside," Don barked.

"No way," Mike yelled. "I'm not touching that filthy thing. I bet it has all kinds of diseases."

Laughing, Don said, "Well, I'm not picking it up. If you want that smell in your room, just leave it there."

Looking at Don, Mike complained, "Why do I have to do all the shit work?"

"Watch your language, young man. If your mother heard you talk like that, she'd wash your mouth out with soap."

Shaking his head, Mike picked up the trap, the decaying rat barely staying in one piece, and walked up the basement steps. Getting to the top of the steps, he turned the light off and walked toward the front door. "Turn the light on, you little shit!" Don yelled from the pitch black basement. Mike did not hear him; he was already out the front door and hauling the decaying carcass to the backyard.

I'm going to kick his ass when he comes back down here, Don decided. Don was afraid to move for fear that he would trip over something. Standing alone in the dark basement, he felt a chill come over his entire body. In the far corner of the darkened room, he thought he could make out a silhouette of someone standing there, whispering. Chills ran down his spine as he strained to hear what the apparition was saying. It sounded as if the words which were barely audible were, "Get out. Get out!"

"Who's there?" Don yelled. "Answer me, damn it." Visibly shaken, Don started feeling his way backward toward what he thought were the basement steps. Suddenly, he ran into something soft; it felt like another human. As Don began screaming, a flashlight switched on, revealing a man's face. Mike had snuck down the steps and turned the flashlight on, shining it only on his face to scare his dad. "You little bastard!" he yelled. "You scared the crap out of me."

Mike was laughing uncontrollably as he jogged up the steps and turned on the light. Returning down the steps laughing, he said, "I got you good, didn't I, Dad?"

"You sure did, Mike, but remember what I told you before, paybacks are hell. How did you get over in that corner without me noticing?"

"What corner?" Mike asked.

"Right there." Don pointed to the far corner where he saw the apparition.

"I wasn't there," Mike replied, perplexed. "I wasn't behind you for more than a minute before I turned the light on."

"Bullshit," Don said. "I saw you in that corner, whispering something. It sounded like you were telling me to get out."

"Honest, Dad, I was nowhere near that corner."

"You little liar," Don yelled, cuffing him on the head. "You better stop trying to scare me. One of these days, you're going to give me a heart attack."

"You're too young to have a heart attack," Mike teased. With the flashlight still in his hand, Mike walked around the basement, shining the light on some old wooden shelving. "Look, Dad, here's some old canned vegetables. Do you want to take them upstairs for Mom to cook tomorrow?" he joked.

"No," Don replied seriously, "but I am going to make you clean all this garbage out as soon as I get this basement lit properly."

Walking to the side of the wood shelving, Mike shined his light along the wall. There, trapped between the wall and the shelving, was what looked to be a thin, black book. Sliding his hand between the wall and shelving, Mike pulled the book out. Don was now standing beside Mike as he flashed the light on the cover. Written in bold letters was the title, *The Art of Witchcraft*. "What the hell is that doing in this basement?" Don yelled. "Why in the world would anyone want a book on witchcraft, let alone hiding it in your basement? Mike, if your mom knew that was down here, she would throw a fit. Let's get the heck out of this basement and throw that thing out before your mom finds out it was down here."

Mike followed his dad up the stairs, turning the light off before closing the door. Walking to the sofa, they both sat down. Don focused his attention on the television, while Mike opened the book and began reading. The book was signed at the bottom in barely legible writing. It read, "This book is the property of Elijah Stone." He nudged his dad to look at the writing. Don yelled, "I told you to get rid of that thing!"

"I want to see what this guy was doing with a book like this."

"Remember, Mike, curiosity killed the cat. Just hide the darn thing so your mom never finds it, okay."

"I will, Dad," Mike replied, getting up from the sofa and walking upstairs to his room. Opening the bedroom door, Mike was greeted with the usual open window. It was a warm night, so he did not mind as he jumped onto his bed and opened the book. From what he could tell, Elijah had purchased the book in 1955. The book was worn and tattered, giving it the appearance that it had been read many times over. Hand-written notes were scribbled in pencil on various pages, particularly in sections involving talking to the dead. It was obvious that the owner of this book was deeply curious about the black arts and witchcraft. Mike began to feel anxious about holding the evil book. He was brought up to steer clear of something so evil. Guilt began to overwhelm him as the closet flung open and a blast of cold air surrounded him. Jumping from bed, he ran downstairs to the living room. Explaining to his dad what had happened, Don screamed, "Enough is enough!" Taking the book from his hands, he walked to the trash bin and tossed in the book. "Mike, if you read garbage like this, you're going to start imagining things. Now get back to bed, and grow up, for Pete's sake."

Mike did not say a word as he climbed the steps back to his bedroom. Entering the room, he saw that the closet door was now closed, and the window was shut. *I'm going to go crazy living in this house*, he thought to himself as he crawled back into bed. Mike picked up a fishing magazine laying next to his bed and began to read. It was ten o'clock when his dad poked his head into Mike's bedroom and said good night. "Night, Dad," Mike called back to him. "Turn out the light for me. I'm ready to go to sleep." Don turned off his light and closed the bedroom door.

The room was pitch black except for a glimpse of the moon shining through his window as Mike lay in his bed, staring at the ceiling. What little light the moon provided caused shadows to dance across the room, making it appear as though someone were in the room with him. Chills ran down Mike's back as he closed his eyes and drifted to sleep.

Don opened the door to his bedroom only to find Leslie lying sound asleep on top of the covers, completely nude. Lying next to her was a cookbook titled *Fine Italian Cuisine* by Anthony Castellucci.

I guess I should have come to bed a little earlier, he thought to himself. *Maybe I would have gotten lucky.* Stripping down to his underwear, he turned off the light and crawled into bed. Pulling Leslie's warm body close to his, he drifted to sleep.

It was three in the morning when Mike was awakened from a sound sleep by whispering in his room. Opening his eyes, he saw what appeared to be a glowing, translucent soldier standing beside the closet, staring at him. The soldier appeared to be extremely angry, based on his facial expression. Turning, the soldier walked to Mike's solid oak desk and sat down, continuing to stare at him. Mike felt as if he was in a dream state. His body could not seem to move as he lay in his bed, trying to stir himself from the hellish dream he was having. Or was it not a dream? He could not seem to tell, as his head was spinning. Suddenly, the soldier spoke to him in what seemed to be clear, audible words. "Get out!" Mike sat straight up in bed, screaming at the top of his lungs. No longer in what seemed to be a dream state, his eyes focused on his desk as his dad rushed through door. The apparition was no longer there. "Mike, are you all right?" his dad yelled, out of breath.

"I'm fine, Dad. I think I was dreaming. It was a dream I hope I never have again," Mike replied, sweat dripping down his forehead. "For some reason this house gives me the creeps."

"Go back to sleep. You'll get used to the house." Don went back to his bedroom and closed the door.

Mike went downstairs to the living room, turned on the light, and plopped down on the sofa. Closing his eyes, he drifted to sleep.

It was six in the morning when Mike felt someone shaking him. It was his dad; he had come down the steps to get ready to go to work. "Did you sleep here all night, Mike?" he asked.

"I guess so. To be honest with you, I don't remember coming down here last night, Dad."

"Well, go back up to your bed or you're going to get a stiff neck from sleeping on that sofa." Mike rose without saying another word and climbed the steps back to his bedroom.

Don ate a bowl of cereal and was out the front door and on his way to work by six-thirty. Today was Friday, and he was looking forward to having the weekend off; not to mention, today was payday. Whistling as he drove to work, he suddenly realized Leslie wanted the car today. *She is going to kill me,* he thought, turning the car around. Within minutes, he was back in his driveway and running through the front door. "Leslie!" he yelled. "Are you up?" Running up the steps to his bedroom, he saw that Leslie was now sitting on their bed in a nightgown. "I thought you wanted the car today."

"I do. Why didn't you get me up earlier?"

"I forgot all about it. Run me to work quick and you can keep the car. Come on, I'm going to be late."

"I can't take you in my nightgown," she replied.

"Why not? You're not getting out of the car."

"Oh, all right," she consented, following him down the steps and out the front door.

GET OUT!

As Leslie drove him to work, Don asked teasingly, "Don't you think you could have at least put a bra on under that see-through nightgown?"

"If you say one more word, I'm turning this car around, and you can walk to work."

Leslie pulled into the brickyard parking lot and drove Don to the office entrance. Leaning over, he kissed her and said, "Pick me up at four o'clock sharp, okay?"

"I'll be here on time," she yelled as she pulled away from him.

Arriving home, Leslie went to the phone and called Sadie, informing her that she was running late and would not be able to pick her up until eleven to go look at paint swatches.

"That's fine," Sadie replied, "It will give me some time to get housework done. See you at eleven," she replied, hanging up the phone.

Leslie reached into her cupboards and began taking out the ingredients to bake cookies. She had just finished placing the dough on a cookie sheet to put in the oven when Mike came into the kitchen. It was nine-thirty, and it looked as if he hadn't slept the entire night. "What's wrong, Mike? You look tired."

"I don't know, Mom. I'm still beat," he said, rubbing his eyes. "It must be because I'm not used to the house yet. I didn't sleep real well last night." The sun was shining through the kitchen window, causing him to squint as he wiped the sleepers from his eyes.

"Make yourself a bowl of cereal. I'm going up to take a bath, hon." Nodding, Mike went to the refrigerator as she left the room.

Leslie went into her bedroom, closing the door behind her. Slipping out of her nightgown, she walked into the bathroom and noticed a chill as she turned the hot water handle on. The water gushed from the faucet, causing steam to rise in the chilled room. Goosebumps appeared on her skin as she stood beside the tub, waiting for the water to fill up. Walking to the medicine cabinet, she took her toothbrush and toothpaste from the cabinet and began brushing her teeth. The mirror was completely fogged over, so she brushed her hand across it to clear the steam. Startled, she jumped back from the mirror and took a second look. There was nothing in the mirror but her own image. Whispering to herself, she said, "I could have sworn I saw a man's face in the mirror." Spitting the toothpaste into the sink, Leslie walked to the now full tub. Shutting the water off and slipping her fingers in, she softly said out loud, "Ahh, that feels so good." Slowly, she slid her body into the hot water until nothing was exposed but her head. Closing her eyes, she soaked in the tub for almost half an hour before she was once again startled by what felt like someone brushing her hair to the side. It was as if someone was watching her in the tub. The feeling bothered her so much that she pulled the plug on the drain, and rose from the tub. Looking all around the room, Leslie could not shake the eerie feeling as she stepped from the tub and grabbed a towel. The steam had cleared from the mirror, but she could not bring herself to look into it. Walking from the bathroom back to her bedroom, Leslie dressed quickly into tight-fitting jeans and a low-cut blue blouse without a bra. *Don will love this outfit when I pick him up tonight,* she mused. *I'll have to beat him off with a stick.* Walking down the steps, Mike caught a glimpse of his mother. "You get right back upstairs and put on some decent clothes," he teased.

"So what do you think? Do I still have it after all these years?"

"Mom, that's sick, asking your son that," he laughed.

Leslie giggled and walked over to the kitchen and took the fresh baked cookies from the oven. The wonderful smell began to immediately drift through the entire house and, like a magnet, drew Mike out to the kitchen. "Give me a couple of them, Mom," he pleaded.

"Mike, I told you yesterday I was making these for the neighbor."

"Aw, I thought you would forget about that conversation. You're not going to make me go over there, are you?"

"I most certainly am. I'm leaving now to go to your grandmother's, and when I return, those cookies had better not be here. Understood?"

"Yes, I understand," he said, walking upstairs to change his clothes. As Mike was returning down the steps, he heard Leslie pulling from the driveway. It was ten o'clock as he lifted the plate of freshly baked cookies from the counter and walked out the front door. Even though the walk to the neighbors was only a hundred feet or so, it felt like an eternity until he arrived on her front porch. Mike noticed that her yard was in dire need of a cutting, and the shrubs were overgrown. The entire time he had been at the new house, he had not seen her step foot outside her house. *I wonder how she goes shopping*, he laughed to himself as he began knocking on the door. After several knocks, no one answered the door, so Mike, in his usual stubborn manner, continued knocking louder and much harder. She must be hard of hearing, he thought after about the twentieth knock. Finally, the door opened slowly, only a crack, and an older woman's face appeared in the crack. "What do you want?" she hissed.

"Hi, ma'am. My name is Mike Knisley. I live next door, and my mom asked me to bring you these cookies.

GET OUT!

Seeing the cookies, Delores opened the door and snatched them from his hand. "Thank you. My name is Delores," she replied and started to close the door.

"Ma'am," he yelled before she closed it completely, "could I come in and talk to you for a few minutes?"

Opening the door and scowling, Delores replied, "If you must."

Walking into her home, Mike could not believe how dark and dusty the place was. It was not dissimilar to the way she kept her yard. Mike sat down on her sofa, which appeared to be over twenty years old. Delores sat in an armchair that was directly adjacent to the sofa and stared into Mike's eyes. "Now, what do you want to ask me?"

"Well, I was wondering about the house we just bought. Who lived there before us?"

"Son, I'll tell you this once and once only. That house is evil. There has been nothing but death in that house for the past year. I lived beside the original owners, Francis and Maddie Stone, for many years. They had a son named Elijah who hung himself in that old garage out back last year while he was on leave from the military. He was a handsome young man, and no one, including his parents, had a clue as to why he did it. He left no note and was only home for one day before he did it. After his death, it couldn't have been more than two weeks before his dad fell down the steps and broke his neck. They said he died instantly. Maddie was a dear friend of mine, but she became so distraught over their deaths that she withdrew from everyone, including her sister-in-law, Lois, the lady you bought the house from. She told me she felt a presence in the house right before she died."

"How did she die?" Mike asked nervously.

"She took her own life. I was the one who found her, but I don't want to get into that," Delores said, tears welling up in her eyes. Wiping the tears away, she continued, "Then there was the young couple who rented the house right after their deaths. They had a young child; I believe the paper said her name was Amber. They found her dead in the bedroom I saw you looking out of the other day. She was smothered to death, the paper said. I think the police suspected her parents, but I believe there is an evil in that house. They never did solve the murder. I haven't gone near the place ever since I found Maddie, and if I were you, I would leave that house as soon as I could pack my belongings."

Mike felt uneasy as the old woman continued staring into his eyes. "The room you saw me in, was that Elijah's bedroom?" he asked.

"Yes, it was. Why do you ask?" she answered.

"Because weird things have been happening in the room. My dad thinks I'm nuts, but I feel a presence in the room with me when I'm in there. The window opens and closes by itself, and doors slam."

Delores, with a solemn look on her face, replied, "I've never believed in ghosts, but I do believe there are evil forces at work in this world. And Mike, you and your parents can believe it or not, but there is an evil in that house."

"Would you happen to have any newspaper clippings of their deaths so I can show my dad?"

Delores got up without saying a word and walked to an old, weathered desk with deep scratches dug into the top and sides of it. Opening the middle drawer of the desk, she withdrew several neatly folded scraps of newspaper clippings and handed them to Mike. "That's all I have to say. You better go now, and remember what I told you. I don't expect you or your parents will ever need to see me again," she said, closing the door behind him.

Mike, walking slowly back to his home, glanced toward his bedroom window. There, in plain sight, was the figure of a man staring at him from the now closed window. Mike did not take his eyes from the window as he continued walking to the house. Then, as suddenly as he had seen the figure, it was gone. Chills ran down his spine as he walked to the front door. Try as he might, he could not bring himself to go in the house alone.

After sitting on the front porch for several minutes, he rose and started walking down the road to clear his head. It had turned into a blistering, hot day, and the sun was beating down on him as he strolled down the road. He must have walked for several miles when he saw an old man sporting a long grey beard walking toward him. "Hi, young man," he called as Mike got closer to him. He appeared to be an old farmer, wearing faded, torn, blue bib overalls. "Out for a walk?" he asked as Mike walked up to him.

"Yes, sir, I am. How are you?" Mike asked.

"Well if I was any better, I'd be twenty years old again," he replied laughing. "You're new to the area, aren't you? I know most everyone around here."

"Yeah, my parents and I moved into the old house up the road there," Mike replied, pointing.

"Whereabouts up the road?" the old-timer asked.

"The old Stone house," Mike replied, wiping the sweat from his brow.

"Oh, that house has had a run of bad luck the past year, but I guess you already know that, don't you?"

"Unfortunately, I do," he said, looking down to the ground.

"Well, you know what they say, don't you?"

"No, what?" Mike replied.

"Bad luck can always be changed. It's a matter of perspective."

"I hope you're right. I don't care to have any of the bad luck that house has been dishing out the past year. By the way, my name is Mike Knisley. I didn't catch your name."

"That's because I didn't throw it," the old man laughed once again. "My name is Rupert Long, and I live in that farmhouse over there with my wife, Ann," he said pointing. "I guess that makes us neighbors, and you're welcome to visit me any time, Mike."

"Thanks, Rupert," Mike said, shaking his hand and continuing his walk.

Walking an additional six or seven miles, sweat was dripping from all of his pores when he noticed a car approaching. It was his mother with a confused look on her face as she pulled to the side of the road. "How did you get all the way down here, Mike?"

"How do you think?" he replied sarcastically, getting in the car. "I walked." Irritated, he continued, "I just felt like taking a walk." He did not have the nerve to tell his mother what he had learned about the house. It would only make her uneasy staying there.

"Did you take the cookies to the neighbor next door, Mike?"

"Yes, Mom," he replied, making every effort to avoid this conversation.

"And what did she say?" Leslie asked on the drive home.

"Her name is Delores, and she seems to be a private person. She, in no uncertain terms, told me thanks for the cookies, but don't bother her again."

"Well, that is rude," Leslie said, puzzled.

"Believe me, Mom, I'm glad she doesn't want to socialize; the woman gives me the creeps."

Pulling into their driveway, Leslie exited the car and walked to the house. Looking back, she noticed that Mike was still in the car. "Aren't you coming, Mike?"

"I'll be in in a few minutes," he yelled, still sitting in the vehicle. Leslie opened the door and walked inside.

Mike stepped from the car and walked to the front porch, sat down on the cool, shaded concrete, and he sighed. It was the sigh of a person who had the weight of the world on their shoulders. *How is it possible, with all the homes Dad could have bought, that he had to buy this one?* Mike wondered to himself. Reaching in this pocket, Mike pulled out the neatly folded newspaper clippings and began to read each article detailing the deaths of each family member. The articles seemed to be typical obituaries, stating their ages and some of their accomplishments in life. However, they failed to mention that both Elijah and his mother Maddie had committed suicide. It did mention that Elijah was given a military funeral. No twenty-one gun salute or anything, just a burial in his full military uniform with several members of the local VFW (Veterans of Foreign Wars) attending. The last article contained the unsolved murder of Amber Jessup, an eight-year-old child who attended school at the local elementary school. Apparently she had only lived at 322 Haller Road for about a week before she was murdered in her sleep. The words from Delores, "The house is evil," kept hounding Mike as he rose from the porch and went inside the house. He shoved the clippings back into his pocket and sat down on the sofa. His mother was in the kitchen cooking something when he finally mustered up enough nerve to climb the steps to his bedroom. Leaving the door open, he hopped into his bed and sat up. The window was closed, and everything seemed normal. "The old hag is probably crazy," he said out loud, lying back down. He was so tired from not sleeping well the night before that he drifted right to sleep.

It was quarter till four when his mother climbed the steps to check on him. Looking into his bedroom, she saw that Mike was sound asleep. Not wanting to disturb him, Leslie walked softly down the steps and out the front door. It was time to pick Don up from work. And she was not about to be late and hear him complain the whole way home. Backing out of the driveway, she glanced up to her bedroom window. The sun was shining in her eyes, but she could still see someone looking out the window, smiling. *It did not appear to be Mike, but it had to be,* she thought to herself. Putting the car into drive and starting toward the brickyard, she laughed. "That little rat was acting like he was asleep so he didn't have to ride along."

When Leslie pulled into the parking lot at the brickyard, Don was already outside waiting for his ride. It was five after four when he hopped into the passenger seat.

"You're late," he growled, tapping his watch.

"Really, Don, if you call five minutes late, you need your head examined."

"Five minutes can seem like an hour when you're waiting for someone, Leslie," he laughed. "Did you and Mom pick the paint for the outside of the house today?"

"We sure did. I even had them mix it today. I have ten gallons of it in the trunk. Do you think that will be enough?"

"I have no idea, but if they start running out, you can run to Roaring Spring and get more, can't you?"

"Yes, I made sure they wrote the color code down and put it into a file with my name on it. Sadie and I decided to go with a slate blue color for the house and a dark grey for the trim. The two colors look great together. Do you think you will like it?"

"Leslie, I told you before you can do whatever you want to that house. I don't care if you paint it orange with purple polka dots," he laughed.

Mike was sound asleep when he was jarred awake by his door slamming shut. Sitting up in bed, he watched as the closet door flung open and icy cold air spewed forth. "What do you want from me?" Mike yelled hysterically. "Leave me alone, you dirty bastard." Jumping from his bed, he slammed the closet door shut. The veins were popping from the side of his neck as he screamed, "You are not going to drive me from this house, Elijah! Yeah, Elijah, I know it's you. You better get used to it, because this is my room now!" he yelled defiantly. Mike walked to the bedroom door and tugged on it. It seemed to be locked from the outside as he pulled harder. The window slammed open, causing Mike to spin around. There was a barely perceptible voice coming from the closet. Straining to hear, Mike frantically pulled at the door once again.

A voice from downstairs yelled, "Mike, are you up yet?" It was his dad, finally home from work. Mike was ready to yell for him to open the door when, all of a sudden, the door slowly opened by itself.

Mike ran from the room and down the steps to the living room. His dad was sitting on the sofa laughing as he ran into the room. "You look like you've seen a ghost."

"Listen, Dad. We need to talk right away."

"About what? Mike, I'm tired."

Leslie was in the kitchen starting to prepare supper as Mike grabbed his father's arm and pulled him off the sofa. "Follow me upstairs, please, Dad." Don walked behind Mike to his bedroom. Going inside, Mike shut the door and sat down on the edge of the bed. "Dad, you can call me whatever you want, but there is something going on in this house. That window opens and closes by itself. This room seems to be possessed. Doors slam shut by themselves, and there are voices whispering in the closet. I can't take it. I tried telling myself it was in my head, but now after talking to the old hag next door, I know something is going on."

"For God's sake, Mike, slow down, and tell me what she said."

Mike explained everything Delores had said to him, including her bit about the house being possessed by evil. Taking the newspaper clippings from his pocket, he tossed them to his father. "She's not lying, Dad. Read these."

Don read each clipping and, finally lifting his head, he said in a very concerned tone, "Mike, this doesn't mean anything. You know there's no such thing as ghosts or evil spirits lurking around. The only thing that is evil is that old woman telling you these stories to scare you."

"Dad, you're in for a rude awakening."

"Listen, let's keep this nonsense between you and me. I don't want your mother thinking she is living in a haunted house. There is no need to scare her because you have issues, all right."

"Ok, Dad, if that's the way you want it."

"That's the way I want it, Mike."

Leslie yelled up the steps that supper was ready. Pushing Mike back into the bed, Don yelled, "Race you to the table!" Mike jumped from the bed and double-leg tackled Don before he could take one step. Rolling across the top of him, Mike traversed the steps four at a time and was sitting at the table before Don had even gotten back to his feet.

Walking down the steps, Don was rubbing his elbow where it had smacked the floor when Mike pummeled him. Walking into the kitchen, he said, "I hope you pound people like that this year during football season."

"You can count on it," Mike smiled, taking a bite of his food.

"This looks and smells great, Leslie. Pot roast, potatoes, and corn."

Mike's plate was overflowing with food as Don looked at it and laughed, "I see you still have your appetite."

"He's a growing boy, Don. Leave him alone."

"He's also a Momma's boy too," Don teased.

"Looks like you want to wrestle a little after supper," Mike barked, giving his dad the look that said, "I'm going to kick your butt."

"Okay, tough guy, you're on. After supper we'll wrestle in the front yard."

Don and Mike ate quickly and walked to the living room. "I have to change out of my suit first, and then I'll meet you in the front yard," Don said.

Leslie yelled from the kitchen, "Mike, you better not hurt him."

"I'll take it easy on him," Mike teased.

"Leslie, what in the world is wrong with you?" Don yelled angrily. "Don't you mean I should take it easy on him?"

"You heard me right the first time, Don."

Shaking his head in disgust, Don jogged up the steps to change. He returned and opened the front door, wearing an old pair of work pants and a tattered t-shirt. Walking to the front yard, he noticed Mike had on his combat boots and was standing there with his hands on his knees, ready to do battle.

"Should I put one hand behind my back to make it fair?" Mike teased.

"Keep it up, Mike, and I'll give you an old fashion ass-whooping." Don slowly circled his son, tapping his forehead every so often to agitate him. Mike lunged at his legs, attempting a double-leg takedown, but before he was in deep enough, Don sprawled, causing Mike to fall flat onto the ground while Don spun behind him. Forcing Mike to carry all his weight as he rode him, Mike began breathing heavy. "What's the matter, tough guy, can't keep up with the old man?" Don chopped his arm and forced Mike's entire body to collapse flat on the ground. Applying a half nelson, Don rolled Mike to his back. Mike was kicking and flailing furiously to get off his back, but, by now, Don had him so tight he was forcing the air from his body.

Leslie ran to the front yard and cuffed Don on top of the head. "That's enough! Can't you see you have him? He can't breathe with all your weight on him, you big ox. Get off of him this instant, Donald."

When Leslie called him Donald, he knew he was in for it, so he withdrew from Mike, teasing, "Do you have to have your mom fight your battles?"

"Aw, Mom, I was just about to get out. Why did you have to come out?" Mike wheezed, out of breath.

"What are you talking about?" Don laughed. "I had you pinned. Your back was so flat on the ground that I thought we would need a pancake flipper to get you up. You were like a fish flopping out of water," he continued to tease.

"Don, I said that's enough," Leslie barked.

Mike and Don were covered in sweat and grass stains as they stood up and walked toward the house. Don's elbow was slightly bleeding from ramming it into the ground when he had sprawled. Wiping the blood on Mike's shirt, he teased him, saying, "Here's a souvenir of getting your butt kicked, tough guy."

"Wait till next time," Mike sneered. "Mom won't be around to save you."

As they entered the house, Leslie shook her finger at both and yelled, "Straight upstairs and get a bath."

"You first," Mike said, turning the television on and plopping down on the couch.

Don walked up the steps, aching from head to toe. *I'm getting too old for that crap,* he thought to himself as he walked into the bathroom and drew a bath. Taking his clothes off, he threw them into a pile on the floor and jumped into the warm water. The water soothed his aching muscles as he lay back, closed his eyes, and daydreamed. He had only been soaking for several minutes when he felt a chill in the bathroom. It had come on suddenly but did not make any sense since it was eighty-five degrees outside. The chill seemed to engulf his body, even penetrating the warm water. Opening his eyes, he saw the silhouette of a young man standing beside the closed bathroom door. His face was wearing an evil smirk, which caused the hair to stand up on the back of Don's neck. Shaking his head and closing his eyes, Don opened them once again. The apparition had vanished. "Now Mike has me seeing things," he laughed out loud. The chill which had been in the room was now gone, so he finished his bath and dressed for bed. Yelling down the steps, he told Mike he was done. Don was in his bedroom relaxing his aching muscles on the bed when he heard Mike in the bathroom. "Hurry up, loser," he yelled, just loud enough so that Mike could hear, but not loud enough to bring the wrath of Leslie down on his head.

Mike was in and out of the tub in less than five minutes before poking his head into his dad's bedroom. Mike was not wearing a shirt as he stood in the doorway, revealing how muscular and toned his body had become. Flexing his arm muscles, he growled and said, "Tomorrow we play football, so you better rest up that tired, old body of yours. Are you going downstairs to watch television?"

"How in the world can you take a bath that quick and be clean?"

"I'll tell you how, I have bathing down to an art," Mike laughed. "Speed is all it takes, old-timer."

Shaking his head in amazement at how silly Mike was acting, he replied, "Anyway, Mike, I'm not watching television tonight. I'm going to stay in bed and read."

"I get it," he teased. "You and mom need to discuss something in the bedroom, and that's why you're going to bed so early."

Laughing, Don said, "You better not let her hear you say that, or you'll be in hot water."

Saying goodnight, Mike closed the door. After walking down the steps, he assumed his usual position on the sofa. The television was broadcasting the news, so he lifted himself from the sofa and walked to the television, adjusting the tuner to bring in a radio station. Soon, soft, melodic music was playing through the speaker on the television. Out of the corner of his eye, he caught his mother sneaking up the steps. Not wanting to embarrass her, he acted as if he had not seen her. Returning to the sofa, he lay down on the soft cushions and closed his eyes. The music, a waltz, was soothing and seemed to erase all the uneasiness he had been feeling throughout the day. The house was quiet except for the soft music drifting throughout the rooms. Slowly, he drifted to sleep as the tension left his body.

Leslie walked into the bedroom, smiling. "I guess it's about time we break this bedroom in," she said, removing her blouse and exposing her breasts. "I'm glad you like what I wore for you today." Standing topless in her tight-fitting jeans, Don could not believe this beautiful woman was all his. He lay in the bed, reveling in her beauty. Slowly, she unbuttoned her jeans, pulling them down in a teasing manner. Soon, she stood before him with nothing on but her silky panties. Jumping from the bed, Don lifted her into his arms and carried her to the bed.

Mike had been asleep on the sofa for several hours before waking in the dark living room. The music was no longer playing, suggesting his parents had shut it off. Straining to focus his eyes on the clock, he barely could make out the time. It was ten o'clock, and he had been asleep for almost three hours. Shadows danced around the room as the moon attempted to force its light through the windows. The setting made him nervous, being downstairs all alone. Lifting his body from the soft sofa, he made a break for the stairway, running up the steps as fast as his legs could carry him. His bedroom door was open, so he ran through the door and dove into his single bed, closing his eyes. Wrapping the covers around his body, he lay perfectly still; the only sound he could hear was his racing heartbeat. Afraid to open his eyes, he drifted to sleep once again, not noticing that his window was once again open.

At three in the morning, a loud, crashing sound could be heard in the hallway. Mike jumped from his bed, meeting his father in the dark hallway. "What the hell was that?" Don whispered, out of breath.

"I don't know," Mike replied, straining to see what had made the noise. Don felt around the wall until he found the light switch and turned it on. There, lying on the floor at their feet, was every picture that had been hanging on the walls, six in all. The weird thing was that none had broken, not even the ones that had glass frames.

"I told you, Dad," Mike whispered. "There is something going on in this house." Don examined the walls where the pictures had been hanging, and every single hook was still in its place. It was if someone had lifted each picture off the wall and dropped it to the floor.

Mike looked up and noticed a hatch in the ceiling had been lifted off. "Dad, did you know that was up there?" he asked in a soft voice.

"You don't need to talk so low, Mike; your mom has her ear plugs in. She's dead to the world."

Leslie had always slept with ear plugs in, ever since she was a small child. It was next to impossible for her to get a good night's sleep without them. Every little noise used to wake her, but now with the ear plugs, she slept so soundly that she had trouble hearing the alarm go off in the morning.

"And no, I didn't know that was there. It must be the access to the attic. Check it out in the morning, and see if there is anything up there," Don grinned, "like a dead body."

"Go ahead and make jokes, Dad. You know there is something weird about this house, and you're just afraid to admit it."

"Go back to bed, Mike, and stop talking silly. Night," Don whispered, closing his bedroom door behind him.

Mike turned the hallway light off and ran back into his bedroom. Jumping under the covers, he closed his eyes tightly as if keeping them closed would protect him from what was in the room with him. As he lay there, eyes closed tightly, trying to force himself back to sleep, he heard a whispering sound from the corner of his bedroom. There was a chill in the room as he heard his bedroom door slowly close. *If that's Dad playing a practical joke, I swear I'll get even with him,* he thought angrily. The whispering continued with Mike refusing to open his eyes. The voice became louder, and finally Mike could understand what was being said. "Get out. Get out. Get out," the voice kept repeating, in an angry tone, over and over. The voice coupled with the chill was so haunting that Mike began shaking uncontrollably. Slowly, he squinted his eyes open, revealing the glowing silhouette of a young man sitting at his desk and staring at him with an angry expression on his face. The man was clad in what appeared to be a uniform. Mike quickly closed his eyes as if this offered him some protection from the intruder. He lay there going into a dream state, drifting in and out of consciousness. Finally, after being sound asleep for no more than half an hour, Mike woke gasping for his breath. A pillow was being forced over his face with someone applying steady pressure, trying to smother the life from him. Adrenaline raced through his body as he ripped the pillow from his face and sucked in fresh air. Jumping from the bed furiously, he looked around the room to see if it was his dad playing a practical joke. Still angry, Mike walked to his parents' bedroom to tell his dad off. *The practical jokes are going to stop. This is the last straw,* he thought to himself as he opened his parents' bedroom door. Looking inside the pitch black room, he could hear his father snoring loudly. Walking to the bed side, Mike tapped his dad on the shoulder. Startled, Don woke from a deep sleep and whispered, "Who's there?"

"It's me, Mike. Come to my bedroom, please."

Following Mike to his bedroom, Don said, "What is wrong with you, Mike? It's four in the morning." Mike explained what had just happened, on the verge of tears.

Don, for the first time, believed him, or at least he believed that he was truly petrified of the room. Patting him on the back, Don said, "Tell you what, Mike, I'll sleep here the rest of the night, and you go sleep in my bedroom. Wake me up in the morning when the alarm goes off so I'm not late for work.

Visibly shaken, Mike could barely mouth the words, "Okay," as he left the room, leaving the door open.

Mike crawled into bed with his mother, physically worn-out from being up half the night. The steady breathing of his mother beside him made him feel secure, and within minutes, he fell into a deep sleep.

Don lay in Mike's bed, upset that his son was so distraught. *That damn woman next door caused this. She has the boy afraid of his own shadow,* he thought to himself, lying in bed, staring at the ceiling. He had been in the room for no more than fifteen minutes when he heard whispering coming from the closet. The bedroom door slowly closed by itself as he felt a chill engulf the room. It was just as Mike had described it. The window slammed shut, and a terrible odor filled the room, causing him to gasp for air. The odor was not that of a dead animal, but rather, it was a sulfurous smell. Don began to shake, as much from the cold as the happenings around him. He pulled the covers over his head and cupped his ears, trying to block out the terrifying sounds. Finally, he could take it no more. Jumping from the bed, he raced to the door and pulled the handle. It would not budge, no matter how hard he pulled. Turning the light on in the room shocked his eyes as his pupils struggled to adjust to the sudden burst of light. Grabbing the knob once again, he pulled, and the door finally opened. Don raced from the room and down the steps to the sofa. Curling up on the sofa, shaking, he tried to make sense of what had just happened. His nerves were on edge as he drifted to sleep, exhausted.

The alarm went off at six o'clock, waking Mike from a sound sleep. Reaching over instinctively, he slammed the off button. Crawling slowly from the bed so as to not wake his mother, he walked to his bedroom to wake his father. Noticing his bedroom door was closed, his anxiety level rose as he turned the knob. Poking his head into the room, Mike jumped back when he realized his dad wasn't in the room. Slamming the door shut, he ran down the steps, now wide awake. There was his father, sound asleep on the sofa. Walking to the sofa, he began to shake his father. Startled, Don jumped from the sofa in a stupor and began cursing. Realizing it was only Mike, he asked, "What time is it?"

"It's six o'clock, Dad. You better get ready for work."

Sitting down on the sofa, Don motioned for Mike to join him. "Mike, there is something going on in that room. I couldn't sleep in there last night. It scared the hell out of me. There is some sort of demon or spirit inhabiting your room who is definitely pissed about something. I'm calling off work today, and you and I are going to figure this out." Rising from the sofa, Don went to the phone. Mike could hear him talking to the secretary.

Returning to the living room, he told Mike to get a flashlight. They quietly climbed the steps to the hallway. Turning the flashlight on, Don shined it at the trap door on the ceiling which had opened last night when the pictures had fallen from the wall. The hatch had somehow closed itself during the night. "Dad, what do you think is up there?" Mike asked nervously.

"I don't know, Mike, but we are going to find out." Placing his hands together, he instructed Mike to put his foot in his hands while he hoisted Mike up to the hatch. Pushing the hatch door aside, Mike poked his head into the attic and shined the flashlight around the room. He couldn't see anything but some old cardboard boxes stored to the far side of the attic. Using his arms, he pulled his entire body into the dusty attic. It smelled of mildew and appeared to be used only for storage. The room was dark, sending a chill down his back. The boxes contained old clothing apparently put into storage decades ago. Shining the light to the far back wall of the attic, Mike noticed some floor boards sticking up. Crawling on all fours, he worked his way back to see if anything else was hidden from his limited view. The floorboard was so loose that it was easy to lift out of place. Shining his light down revealed a small wooden box hidden under the floor boards. "I wonder why anyone would hide something up here." His hands shaking, Mike lifted the box from its hiding place and opened it. Taking a quick inventory revealed all sorts of trinkets, a small book, and a note. Closing the box, he shined the light around the rest of the attic. There was nothing else of interest. It was just an old dirty attic that gave him the creeps. He crawled back to the hatch and poked his head out.

His dad, who had been patiently waiting, whispered, "Well, did you find anything?"

Mike handed the wooden box down and said, "It was hidden under some floorboards, Dad."

"Okay, jump down from there." Mike leapt from the ceiling, landing on his feet in the hallway. "Be quiet," his dad hissed, "you'll wake your mom up."

"Shouldn't we close the hatch?"

"Don't worry about it, Mike. The way strange things are happening in this house, it will close by itself," he laughed.

They took the box downstairs and examined its contents. Lifting a gold chain from the box, Don set it to the side. He also withdrew several black and white pictures of a small child playing in the front yard. The child seemed to be happy, throwing leaves in the air. Next, taking out a small black book that fit perfectly into his palm, Don read the title, *Book of Practical Applications of Witchcraft*. As he held the small book in his hand, it seemed to crawl up his arm. Don grasped the book tightly and instructed Mike to bring the metal trash can from the kitchen along with some matches. "We are burning this evil book right here and now," he yelled.

Mike ran to the kitchen returning with the can and matches. Don held the book out while Mike lit it. The book burst into flames as if it had been soaked in gasoline, burning Don's hand. Cursing, he threw the book into the can and watched it burn itself out. "Mike, this guy was into some unnatural things. His soul must be in torment, and if you ask me, he deserves everything his spirit is going through right now. He deserves to burn in hell for messing with that garbage while he was alive."

Mike reached into the box and withdrew a picture similar to the one he had found in the garage. It was a soldier in full uniform wearing a smile from ear to ear. "He seems happy here, Dad." Turning the picture over, Mike noticed the words 'Elijah Bootcamp' written in sloppy penmanship. "I think Elijah was into some evil demonic things he hid from his parents and friends. He looks so innocent in the pictures though, doesn't he?" Mike asked.

"There is a lot more to this young man than the pictures are telling, Mike. We need to know more about him."

Mike pulled the last item from the box, a note which he opened and handed to his dad. Reading it out loud, Don's face reddened as he realized it was a suicide note. "Mike, do you have the newspaper clipping you showed me yesterday?" Pulling it from his pocket, he handed the obituary on Elijah to his father. "I can't believe this, Mike. Do you realize his parents gave him a military funeral against his wishes? I bet they didn't want the community to know he had received a dishonorable discharge. That is why the old woman next door said no suicide note was ever found. His father made sure of that by hiding it in the attic. He probably didn't have the courage to destroy the last thing his son had ever written while he was alive, so he hid it where he thought no one would ever find it."

"Dad, let's just pack up our stuff and move from this cursed house," Mike pleaded.

"No way, Mike. I gave them a two-thousand-dollar down payment on this house. I'm not going to lose that money. They never did bring an article of agreement for me to sign like they said they would."

"Well, then tell them you want your money back. Maybe you can sell the house to someone else," Mike said with a terrified look on his face.

"First of all, Mike, do you want to sell this house to someone else, knowing what is going on in here? A small child was murdered here, and we don't know how she really died. I won't do that to someone. The people who sold this house to us just wanted rid of it for a reason, and I'll bet they won't even consider refunding my deposit. Second of all, your mother loves this house. She has no idea what is going on here, and you and I are going to keep it that way for now, okay?" Looking at his watch, Don said, "Let's go pay these people a visit. You don't know where they live, do you? I'll go up and change my clothes while you call the operator and ask for an address."

Minutes later, Don walked down the stairs and met Mike at the front door. "Did you get it?" Mike handed his dad a slip of paper with the address written on it. "Let's go," he said, walking out the door to his car.

"Dad, do you think it's okay to leave Mom here alone?"

"You have a point, Mike. You better stay here just in case she gets up and wonders where you are. You'll be all right; just stay out of that bedroom. Don't say a word to her. Do you understand me?"

"I already told you I wouldn't," Mike replied angrily.

"I'll be back in an hour or so after I have a friendly chat with Bob and Lois Wyandt."

Mike watched as his father pulled from the driveway and drove toward town.

It was seven-thirty when Don pulled into Bob and Lois's driveway. Knocking, he was surprised when a young boy answered the door. "Can I help you?" Andy asked.

"Yes, is your dad or mom home?"

"Mom is," he said. Turning, he yelled, "Mom, it's for you."

Lois came to the door with a puzzled look on her face. "Is something wrong, Mr. Knisley? If it's about the article of agreement, the lawyer said we have a binding contract with your down payment. He said we could write up a hand-written piece of paper detailing the terms, and it would save us attorney fees." Lois was talking so fast Don could not get a word in edgewise.

"Lois, can I come in and sit down?"

"I'm sorry. Yes, please, come in. Have a seat on the sofa. Andy, go upstairs while we talk," Lois ordered.

"Is your husband home?" Don inquired.

"No, he's at work, but you can talk to me. After all, the house was in my name. It was my late brother's."

"That is what I want to talk about. There are strange evil things going on in the house, and I believe I know why." Don continued to tell her what had been happening in Elijah's bedroom, along with showing her what had been found in the attic.

Tears were flowing down her cheeks as she read the note Elijah had written. "There is no way that Elijah was involved in black magic," she said angrily. "Don't even try to insinuate that."

Don's face became red as the anger flared within him, "Well, the way I see it, you can give me my deposit back, or you can let me exhume the body of Elijah Stone and remove his military uniform."

"I'm going to say this just once," Lois screamed hysterically, "you are not getting your deposit back, nor are you going near my nephew's grave. Is that understood?"

Don did not say another word as he rose from the sofa and walked to the front door. Turning, he looked at Lois and said, "You knew damn well what was going on in that house when you sold it to me. You'll be hearing from me again," he yelled as he slammed her door shut.

Driving home, he did not notice it was a beautiful, warm summer day with birds chirping. He thought of driving to his dad's house and explaining the whole scenario to him, just to see what he would do. On second thought, he knew how his dad would react. *He would say I'm acting ridiculous,* Don decided. *No, I have to handle this on my own. Somehow I have to get that body exhumed and stripped of its uniform. Leslie will not want to leave her dream home under any circumstances.*

As he pulled into his driveway, he saw Mike was in the living room, sitting on the sofa. Before he parked the car, Mike was out of the house, yelling, "What did she say?"

Shaking his head, he explained what had happened at Lois's house.

"Well, where do we go from here, Dad?"

"Follow me," he said, walking into the house and to the telephone. Pulling the newspaper clipping from his pocket, he read that the funeral director was Latchkey's Funeral home. Picking up the phone, he called the operator and ask to be connected to the funeral home. "Latchkey's," a woman's voice answered as the connection was made.

"Could I talk to the owner, please?" Don asked.

Minutes later, a man picked up the phone and said, "Tom Latchkey speaking."

"Sir, I have a quick question for you that will sound strange, but I really need to know the answer."

"Go ahead," Tom said inquisitively.

"If a person wanted to have a body exhumed from its grave, how would you go about it?"

There was a pause as Tom gained his composure. "Two things would be necessary to do such a thing. First, you would have to have permission from the deceased's family, and secondly, an undertaker would have to consent to digging up the deceased. Could I ask your name and why you want to know this?"

Acting as if he had not heard the question, Don continued, "Could you give me directions to Upper Claar cemetery?"

Tom, not thinking, replied, "You take Dunn Highway south, turn right onto Haller Road for about ten miles, and then you turn left onto Claar Road. Stay on Claar Road for ten to twelve miles, and you'll see the cemetery." Tom had barely finished his sentence when the phone went dead. Don had hung up without saying good-bye. He knew what had to be done, and he was taking it into his own hands.   Leslie, dressed in blue jeans and a black blouse, was on her way down the steps when he had hung the phone up. "Why are you home, Don?" she asked.

"I took a day off to spend some time with you and Mike," he said, smiling.

"Do you think that is a good idea? You've only been there for a week? Won't they be mad?" Leslie inquired.

"Leslie, you're forgetting, I'm the boss," he joked. "Come on, let's go for a drive in the country, and then I'll take us all out to breakfast."

Smiling, she said, "That sounds like fun. Let's go, Mike."

Don pulled from the driveway and turned right, driving up Haller Road. "Why are you going this way, Don?" Leslie asked.

"I feel like exploring the area, honey," he replied. He had only driven several miles when, on the left side of the road, he saw a sign that read Claar Road. Turning onto Claar Road, he wound his window down, allowing the fresh summer air to fill the car.

"It's a gorgeous day," Leslie said, taking a deep breath. "I love this area. The scenery is wonderful."

They drove past pastures filled with lush green grass and milk cows grazing. The road steadily climbed uphill until, finally, Don saw what he had been looking for. On the right side of the road was a small church, and behind it was a small cemetery sitting up on a hill. "Look," Don said as if surprised. "There's an old cemetery. Let's stop and look to see if any of the graves are interesting."

"Don, why in the world would you want to look in a cemetery?" Leslie asked, surprised at his request.

"It's history, Leslie. I like looking at old cemeteries."

"Yeah, Mom," Mike added. "I want to see it too."

Don pulled into the church parking lot and stopped the car behind the church. The area was extremely remote, with no houses in sight for miles. "I guess you would call this a country church," Leslie laughed, looking around at the remote location.

Mike jumped from the car and ran up the hillside, looking from tombstone to tombstone.

"He acts as if he knows which tombstone he is looking for," Leslie said, watching him go from gravesite to gravesite.

Don and Leslie had not walked for more than fifty yards when they heard Mike yell, "Hey, Dad, check out this grave!" Mike was almost at the top of the cemetery, and by the time they reached him, they were out of breath.

"That's a steep climb," Don wheezed. Mike pointed to a gravesite with a small wooden marker that read "Elijah Stone." Because the grass covering it was brown and dead, the solitary grave stood out from all the other graves in the cemetery which were covered with lush green grass.

"That is very strange," Leslie said, looking at the grave. "Why is it the only one without grass? Look, even his parents who are buried beside him have green grass on their graves. He just died last year, Don. He was only twenty-one years old. I wonder how the poor fella died." Leslie's eyes drifted to his parents' markers. "Wow, they all died last year. Now that's odd, isn't it?"

"It sure is," Mike chimed in. "Let's get out of here; this place is creepy, even in broad daylight."

"Yeah, I'm hungry," Don said, yawning from not sleeping well the night before. The climb down the hill was much easier than the walk up. They arrived at the car, barely breathing hard from the hike, and climbed inside.

They arrived at Poke's Diner by nine-thirty and went in to have breakfast. Ordering their food, Leslie rose from the table and said, "I have to go to the ladies' room."

As soon as she was out of earshot, Mike whispered excitedly, "Did you see that grave?"

"Yeah, I saw it," Don whispered back.

"Now what do we do?"

"I'll tell you what you and I are going to do tonight. We are going to that cemetery with a lantern, a pick, and a shovel, and we're digging him up tonight and removing that uniform."

"No way, Dad, I'm not going near that place in the dark."

"Okay, Mike, you can stay at home and spend another night in your bedroom, and we'll see what happens from there."

There was silence for a minute, then, "Okay, I'm in. Do you really think that will stop what's going on in the house?"

"You read the suicide note; he specifically asked not to be buried in that uniform. That uniform is the key to him resting in peace, and we are removing it tonight."

Leslie walked up to the table and asked, "What are you two whispering about?"

"Guy things," Mike replied grinning.

The pancakes arrived, dripping with fresh strawberries and whipped cream. "It looks too good to eat," Leslie stated, admiring the dish.

"Speak for yourself," Mike laughed, gulping down a mouthful.

After breakfast, they spent the rest of the morning and part of the afternoon shopping in Claysburg. Leslie bought three outfits for herself at a small clothing shop, while Mike and Don shopped at the hardware store. Meeting them at the car at one-thirty, Leslie noticed shovels, a pick, and a gas lantern in the backseat. "Why in the world are you buying that stuff?"

"Were going to dig a garden and use the lantern for some night fishing this summer," Don lied.

Getting in the car, they drove to the brickyard parking lot and pulled beside the office. "Why are we stopping here?" Mike asked.

"Today is payday, and I have to get my check."

"Dad, if you go inside, they're going to know you're not sick."

"Mike, I didn't tell them I was sick. I'm a salaried employee. I get ten personal days a year and two weeks of vacation. I can use my personal days any time I want to."

Amazed, Mike stated, "I hope I get a job like that someday."

"That is what a college education can do for you," Don reminded him, getting out of the car and walking into the office. Minutes later, he returned, carrying a white envelope which he tossed to Leslie as he got into the car. Pulling from the parking lot, he drove toward their house while Leslie opened the envelope. "Wow," she exclaimed, looking at his paycheck.

"What are you yelling about?" Don asked, smiling.

"Don, your take-home pay is four hundred and seventy-two dollars! That's a third more than you made in New York."

"Not bad, huh?" he teased.

Pulling into their driveway, they got out of the car and went into the living room. Leslie went to the kitchen to start supper, while Mike and Don walked to the sofa and noticed they had left the wooden box beside the sofa with some of the items still strewn around the floor. Don shoved the items back into the box, including the suicide note he had been carrying in his pocket, and he told Mike to take it to his bedroom before Leslie saw it. Hesitating, Mike grabbed the box and sprinted up the steps. Crashing through his bedroom door, he threw the box on his desk and ran from the room, slamming the door behind him. Going back down the steps, he was out of breath as he plopped down on the sofa beside his dad. "I hope after tonight I won't have to be afraid of going into my own bedroom."

"Trust me Mike, after we take care of this tonight, there won't be any more problems in this house."

It seemed as if the day would never end. They spent the entire afternoon and evening watching television. Leslie rose from the sofa, declaring, "It's time for bed. Don, are you coming? Tomorrow is Saturday, and I want to go visit your parents after breakfast." Following Leslie up the steps, Don turned and winked at Mike.

Mike stayed on the sofa, glued to the television, as they went to bed. An hour had passed, and his dad still had not returned. He walked up the steps quietly to see what was keeping him. Stepping into the hallway, he was startled by a voice coming from his room. Turning around, he sprinted back down the steps and jumped onto the sofa.

Mike lay on the sofa for another hour before drifting to sleep. He woke to find his dad standing over him, whispering, and "Are you ready?"

"Yeah, what took you so long?"

"I wanted to make sure your mom was sound asleep. Come on, let's get this over with."

They walked outside into the darkness. There was heavy cloud cover preventing the moon and stars from casting any light. It looked and felt as if it was going to rain at any minute. The wind was kicking up, causing the night air to have a chill to it. Closing the car door, Mike whispered, "This is just great, a perfect night to dig up a body. We are going to get soaked; you do realize that, don't you?"

"Stop complaining," Don hissed, pulling out a white sheet from under his shirt.

"What, may I ask, is that for?"

"To wrap his body in, you idiot, after we strip him of his uniform."

"That's disgusting, Dad. I'm not taking his clothes off. You'll have to do it."

"Would you shut up?" Don yelled as he backed out of the driveway without his headlights on. He drove past their house for about half a mile before he finally turned the headlights on. There was not another car in sight as they drove up the steep road to the cemetery. Arriving at the church, Don turned the headlights off and pulled around back.

"I don't think I can do this, Dad. I'm scared. I've never been in a graveyard at night," Mike said worriedly.

Don opened the car door and grabbed the shovels and pick without talking. "Get the lantern and follow me," he whispered, heading up the hill to the gravesite. Don strained his eyes to see the path leading up the hill, but it was to no avail. Tripping over tombstone after tombstone, he finally relented and pulled a flashlight from his pocket. Turning the light on, he hurried up the hill with Mike at his heels.

Raindrops were starting to fall as they reached the site where Elijah was buried. Tossing a shovel to Mike, he whispered, "Start digging." The rain began to soak them as they shoveled a heaping pile of mud and dirt beside the grave. They had dug about four feet down when they started hitting stone. Mike grabbed the pick and continued, while Don took a rest. It was three in the morning when Mike finally hit the casket with the tip of his shovel. The grave was about six feet deep as he started using his hands to scrape the last of the dirt from the lid of the coffin. He was tired and covered in mud as the darkness enveloped him in the tomb. Terrified at what lay beneath his feet, he held his hand in the air. Don pulled him from the grave, whispering, "Did you open the lid?"

"No way. I did most of the digging. You're opening the lid."

"Get the lantern," he said, jumping down into the hole. Mike handed the lantern and a sheet down to his father.

The rain had stopped, and the cloud cover was starting to disappear, allowing the moon to shine its light once again. Mike stood above the grave and watched as his dad lit the lantern. The muddy casket was wood and still seemed to be in good shape as Don reached around the side of it and unlatched the lid. There was barely enough room to open the lid as Don tugged and pulled it open, exposing a gruesome sight. The smell caused him to vomit on the decaying body. As the odor rose from the deep grave, Mike had to look away. "Mike," Don whispered, "take the lantern." He coughed the words out, gasping for fresh air. Mike reached down and snatched the lantern from his father's hands, giving him a perfect view of the rotted, decaying body. The eyes were wide open, a sight which would haunt him forever. "Hurry, Dad. I'm going to vomit. I can't stand the smell."

With all the courage he could muster, Don pulled a pair of scissors from his pocket and began cutting the uniform from the corpse. "You thought of everything," Mike said, watching him cut and pull the uniform and pants from Elijah's body. The flesh fell from his body as he tugged away the last article of clothing. The clothing reeked of death as Don tossed it out of the grave and threw the sheet over the body. Slamming the lid shut, he yelled, "Get me out of here!" Mike grabbed his hand and, with all the strength he could gather, lifted Don from the grave. "It's almost four. Get this thing covered, and I'll burn the clothes," Don instructed.

Mike began shoveling furiously as he looked up every so often and watched his dad pour lantern fuel over the clothes and set them on fire. The fire was so bright that it illuminated half the cemetery. As the fire burned, both shoveled the last of the dirt into the grave and packed it tight by walking back and forth across the grave.

By the time they had finished filling in the grave, the fire had burned itself out, and they were carrying the shovel and lantern to the car. After loading the tools into the backseat, Don and Mike pulled from the church parking lot, leaving their headlights off. They drove toward their home, using only the light of the moon to guide their way.

Pulling into their driveway, Don looked at Mike and said, "It's finally over. Never, and I mean never, mention a word of this to anyone. Swear to me, Mike," Don said looking into his eyes.

"I swear, Dad. This is between you and me."

"Good. Let's go inside and get cleaned up." Mike felt relieved that it was over as he walked to the house beside his father. Before entering the house, they kicked their muddy shoes into a pile on the front porch and went inside. It was five in the morning, and both were physically and mentally exhausted. Don walked to the kitchen to wash his hands which still reeked of a deathly smell as Mike walked to his bedroom. Don heard Mike calling him from upstairs as he finished washing his hands. Rushing up the steps, he whispered, "Keep your voice down; you'll wake your mother." Mike was standing in the doorway to his bedroom, and he was now shaking uncontrollably.

"What's wrong, Mike?" Walking to the desk where he had placed the wooden box earlier that day, he pointed to a piece of paper lying on top of the desk.

It was the suicide note now containing additional wording at the bottom of the page in the same penmanship. It read, "YOU WERE WARNED. GET OUT!"